THE Magical Christmas Cat

THE Magical Christmas Cat

Lora Leigh · Erin McCarthy

Nalini Singh · Linda Winstead Jones

BERKLEY SENSATION, NEW YORK

THE BERKLEY PUBLISHING GROUP
Published by the Penguin Group
Penguin Group (USA) Inc.
375 Hudson Street, New York, New York 10014, USA
Penguin Group (Canada), 90 Eglinton Avenue East, Suite 700, Toronto, Ontario M4P 2Y3, Canada
(a division of Pearson Penguin Canada Inc.)
Penguin Books Ltd., 80 Strand, London WC2R 0RL, England
Penguin Group Ireland, 25 St. Stephen's Green, Dublin 2, Ireland (a division of Penguin Books Ltd.)
Penguin Group (Australia), 250 Camberwell Road, Camberwell, Victoria 3124, Australia
(a division of Pearson Australia Group Pty. Ltd.)
Penguin Books India Pvt. Ltd., 11 Community Centre, Panchsheel Park, New Delhi—110 017, India
Penguin Group (NZ), 67 Apollo Drive, Rosedale, North Shore 0632, New Zealand
(a division of Pearson New Zealand Ltd.)
Penguin Books (South Africa) (Pty.) Ltd., 24 Sturdee Avenue, Rosebank, Johannesburg 2196, South Africa

Penguin Books Ltd., Registered Offices: 80 Strand, London WC2R 0RL, England

THE MAGICAL CHRISTMAS CAT

These stories are works of fiction. Names, characters, places, and incidents either are the product of the authors' imaginations or are used fictitiously, and any resemblance to actual persons, living or dead, business establishments, events, or locales is entirely coincidental. The publisher does not have any control over and does not assume any responsibility for author or third-party websites or their content.

Book design by Kristin del Rosario

PRINTING HISTORY
Berkley trade paperback edition / October 2008

ISBN: 978-0-425-22355-0

An application to register this book for cataloging has been submitted to the Library of Congress.

PRINTED IN THE UNITED STATES OF AMERICA

10 9 8 7 6 5 4

CONTENTS

THE Magical Christmas Cat

Stroke of Enticement

NALINI SINGH

Wishes

December 8, 2060

Dear Santa Claus,

I'm not sure I believe in you anymore, but I don't know who else to ask, so I hope you're not just imajinary like daddy says. I'm in the hospital, but don't worry, I don't want you to use up your majick to make me better. The M-Psy came and looked at my leg and said I'd walk again. You know the Psy don't have feelings. I think that means they can't tell lies. And the nice changeling nurse—the one that can shapeshift into a deer—she told me with ~~rebalit~~ rehab, I'd be o.k.

The reason I'm writing to you is because I'm lonely. Don't tell my mom, o.k.? She comes to see me but she's always so sad. She looks at me like I'm broken, like I'm not her strong little girl anymore. And my daddy doesn't visit me. He never paid any ~~atent~~ attention to me anyways, but it still makes my heart hurt.

I know you can't make my daddy come see me, but I was wondering, since you're majick, do you think you could send me a friend? Someone fun who wanted to be with me and who didn't care that my leg was all mangled up. The kids here are nice, but they all go home after a little while. It would be wonderful to have someone who was mine, someone who didn't have to leave.

My friend can be human or Psy or changeling. I won't mind. Maybe you could find someone who was lonely, too, and then we could be unlonely together? I promise I'll share all my things, and I'll let her (or even a boy) choose the games we play.

I think that's all. Thanks for lisening.

Annie

p.s. I don't mind if you don't give me any other presents at all.

p.p.s. I'm sorry about the speling mistakes. I had to miss a lot of school but now I'm trying really hard to catch up with the hospital's computer tutor.

Chapter 1

Annie looked up and met the angry eyes of the seven-year-old sitting at the child-sized desk in front of her own, arms crossed and lip jutting out. Bryan glared at her, the fury of his leopard apparent in every line of his body. Annie was used to teaching changeling children—a lot of DarkRiver kids came to this school, close as it was to their territory. She was used to their affectionate natures, their occasional accidental shifts into leopard form, and even their shorter tempers when compared with those of human children. What she was not used to was such blatant disobedience.

"Bryan," she began, intending, once again, to try to get to the bottom of this.

He shook his head, stuck out his chin. "I'm not talking to anyone but Uncle Zach."

Annie glanced at her watch. She'd called Bryan's uncle twenty minutes ago, not long after last bell. "I left a message. But he might not check it straightaway."

"Then we wait."

She almost smiled at the stubbornness of him, but knew that that would only make matters worse. "Are you sure you don't want to tell me why you hit Morgan?"

"No."

Annie tucked back a strand of hair that had escaped the bun she'd anchored with a pair of lacquered chopsticks in a vain attempt at style. "Perhaps we could talk to your mom together—would you feel more comfortable discussing things with her?"

She'd already called Mrs. Nicholson to tell her that Bryan would be late getting home. The woman had taken it in her stride—she had three boys. "And one of them's always in detention," she'd said with a laugh, love in every syllable. "Since you're waiting on Zach, he can drive this misbehaving baby home."

"Bryan?" she prompted, when her little mischief-maker remained silent.

"No. You promised I could wait for Uncle Zach." He scowled. "Promises are for keeping, that's what Uncle Zach always says."

"That's true." Giving in, she smiled. "Let's hope your uncle makes it here soon."

"Hot date?" The voice was rich, dark, and completely out of place in her classroom.

Startled, she stood to face the man leaning in the doorway. "Uncle Zach?"

A smile that cut her off at the knees. "Just Zach's fine." Vivid aqua-colored eyes, straight black hair cut in a careless way, copper-gold skin and bones that spoke of an ancestor from one of the native tribes. "You called."

And he'd come.

She felt her cheeks blaze as the thought passed through her head. "I'm Annie Kildaire, Bryan's teacher."

When Zach accepted the hand she'd extended in a gesture of automatic politeness, the heat of him seared through her skin to burn her on the inside. She felt her breath catch and knew she was going even redder. Dear God, she was useless around beautiful men. And "Uncle" Zach was the most beautiful man she'd ever seen.

He was also staring at her. Probably at her always messy knot of hair, her bright red cheeks, her mortified brown eyes. Tugging at her hand, she tried to extract it. He held on as he glanced at Bryan. His nephew continued to sit there with a mutinous expression on his face. Seeing their clasped hands, he favored his uncle with a look that shouted "traitor."

Zach returned his attention to Annie. "Tell me what happened."

"Could you—" She tugged at her hand again.

He looked down, seemed to consider it, then finally let go. Fingers tingling in sensory memory, she quickly moved to busy herself tidying the stack of book reports on her desk. "If you'd like to take a seat?" He towered over her. That wasn't particularly difficult, but he was big in a very intimidating way. Solid shoulders, pure hard muscle and lean strength. A soldier, she thought, aware of some of the ranks within the DarkRiver pack, Zach had to carry the rank of soldier.

"I'd rather stand."

"All right." She didn't sit either. It didn't give her much of an advantage—or any advantage if she was being honest—but if she sat down with him looming all big and intense over her, she'd probably lose the power of speech. "Bryan punched a classmate during last period. He refuses to tell me what caused the incident."

"I see." Zach frowned. "Why isn't the other boy here?"

She wondered if he thought she was playing favorites. "Morgan is in the sick bay. He's rather . . . delicate."

Zach raised an eyebrow. "Delicate?"

She wanted to glare at him herself. He knew perfectly well what she was talking about. "Morgan gets sick very easily." And had a mother who treated him as if he was made of spun glass. Given that the same thing had driven Annie insane as a child, she might've tried to talk to Mrs. Ainslow about it, except that it was obvious Morgan *liked* the fussing. "He was too upset to stay near Bryan, though I would've preferred to talk to them together."

"Human?" Zach asked.

"No," she said, trying not to feel *too* satisfied by his look of surprise. "Swan."

"Swans aren't predators"—which, Annie knew, was why Morgan's family had been allowed to stay in DarkRiver territory—"but they're not exactly weak."

"While all humans are?" she was irritated enough to say.

He raised an eyebrow. "Did I say that, sweetheart?"

Her face heated from the inside out. "I am Bryan's teacher."

"Not mine." A grin. "You could be though. Wanna play classroom, Teach?"

She dealt with DarkRiver cats throughout the year, but for the most part, they were mated pairs, or couples in long-term relationships. She had no clue how to handle a teasing male who was clearly not only aware of the effect he had on her but confident enough to take advantage. Focus on the facts, she told herself, just focus. "Bryan is normally very good." He was, in truth, one of her best students. "He's kind, intelligent, and before today, he's never once hurt a classmate."

Zach's expression turned serious. "Strength is for protecting, not hurting. Bryan knows that as well as anybody in the pack."

Annie's heart clutched at the absolute way he said that, as if it was simply a fact of life. That core of unflinching honor was one of the things she most admired about the DarkRiver males she'd met. The other was the way they didn't make even the slightest attempt to hide the adoration they felt for their mates. It was . . . nice.

It was also yet another point of contention between her and her mother. Professor Kimberly Kildaire had very determined views on what men should be like. The word "civilized" appeared often in the description, along with generous helpings of "rational"—a man who teased with sensual ease was far too wild to ever make the professor's cut.

However, Annie knew her own mind, and her reaction to Zach was anything but rational. "That's why," she said, forcing herself to think past the nerves that threatened to turn her mute, "I was so surprised by what he did. Frankly, I have no idea what could've caused it. Morgan and Bryan don't even tend to play together."

"Give me a couple of minutes with him." With a nod, he walked to his nephew. "Come on, Jumping Bean, let's talk."

"Over there." Bryan got up and led his uncle to the back of the classroom. Annie looked away out of politeness, knowing she wouldn't have been able to hear the conversation even if they hadn't moved—changeling hearing was generally far more acute than a human's. But, and though she tried to keep her eyes on the book reports, her curiosity got the better of her.

She looked up to see Zach crouched in front of Bryan, his arms braced loosely on his knees. The position had raised the sleeve of his T-shirt to expose part of a tattoo on his right biceps. She squinted. It was something exotic and curved, something that beckoned her to stroke. Thankfully, before she could surrender to the urge to get closer, Bryan began to gesture so earnestly, she wondered what on earth he was saying.

"I didn't even hit him that hard, Uncle Zach." Bryan blew out a breath that made his dark brown bangs dance. "He's a sissy."

"Bryan."

"I mean he's 'delicate,' " Bryan said, proving he had very big ears. "He's always crying, even when nobody does anything on purpose. He cried yesterday when Holly elbowed him by accident."

"Oh?"

"Yeah—Holly's a *girl*. And she's human."

Zach knew exactly what Bryan meant. No matter their animal, changelings were physically tougher than humans. Their bones were stronger, their bodies healed faster, and, in the case of predatory changelings, they could do a hell of a lot more damage. "Which doesn't explain why you hit him." He knew and liked his nephew. The boy had been born with a solid code of honor, a code that had been strengthened by the rules DarkRiver men lived by. "You know we don't bully weaker people."

A shamefaced expression. "I know."

"Did the cat get angry?" The leopard was part of who they were. But for the younger ones, the wilder side of their nature was sometimes difficult to control.

Right then, Bryan's curvy temptation of a teacher shifted up front. Her delectable scent whispered over on disturbed air currents, ruffling the leopard's fur in the most enticing way. He barely bit back a responsive groan. Sometimes, adults had trouble with the cat, too. "Come on, JB. You know I'm not going to get mad at you if you lost control."

"Yeah, I guess I kinda got mad." Bryan shuffled his feet. "I wanted to growl and bite, but I hit him instead."

"That's good." A leopard's jaws could do a lot of damage.

"And it wasn't just the cat," his nephew elaborated. "It was all of me."

Zach understood. They weren't human, and they weren't animal. They were both. "What made you angry?"

"Morgan said something mean."

Zach knew that sometimes it was those who appeared weakest who bore the nastiest of streaks. At least Ms. Kildaire seemed well aware of that—he hadn't missed the fact that she hadn't automatically blamed Bryan. "Tell me what it was."

Bryan darted a glance toward his teacher, then leaned closer. "I didn't want to say anything to Miss Kildaire, 'cause she's nice, and I like her."

"I like her, too." A truer statement had never been said. There was something about the little teacher with her jet-black hair and dark brown eyes that had the cat purring in interest. He wondered if she realized she had one hell of a sexy mouth, then wondered if she'd let him do all sorts of wicked things to that mouth. *Later,* he promised himself. Right now, Bryan needed him. "What does this have to do with Ms. Kildaire?"

"Morgan said that his mother said that Miss Kildaire is sitting on a shelf."

Zach had to think about that one for a few seconds. "He said she's on the shelf?"

"Uh-huh." An emphatic nod. "I don't know why Miss Kildaire would sit on a shelf, but that's what Morgan said."

"I'm guessing there's more."

"And *then* Morgan said that his mother said that Miss Kildaire was too fat to get a man."

What a load of horseshit, Zach thought. Morgan's mother was probably some shriveled-up jealous twit. "I see."

"And then Morgan said she was a cripple."

Zach had a sudden urge to punch out the little rat himself. "Go on."

"I told him to take it back. Miss Kildaire is the nicest teacher at the school, and she's not a cripple just 'cause she has a sore leg sometimes and has to use a cane." Temper flared in Bryan's eyes, the irises shifting to the jagged green of the leopard.

"Hold the cat, Bryan," Zach said, forcing a choke hold on his own anger. Cubs had to be taught control. Once, a long time ago, the animal fury of changelings had run unchecked, and it had led to the carnage of the Territorial Wars.

The other races might've forgotten those tormented years, but changelings never would. And they'd never allow it to happen again. "Hold it." He put his hand on Bryan's arm and allowed a low growl to rise from his throat. It was a gesture of dominance, and it worked to bring Bryan's leopard back under control.

"Sorry."

Zach felt his own cat pacing inside him before it became distracted by the exquisite scent of the luscious Ms. Kildaire. "It's okay. We all had to learn."

"Yeah." Bryan blew out a breath. "Anyway, Morgan kept saying she was a cripple, and I got mad and hit him."

Zach found himself in a quandary. He really couldn't disagree with his nephew's actions, but punching out another kid was against the rules. He looked into Bryan's intelligent face and made the only decision he could. "JB, you know we don't condone this kind of violence."

Bryan nodded.

"But I understand the provocation." Lying wasn't how the pack worked. And Bryan was old enough to know that understanding didn't mean approval.

His nephew's face melted into a smile. "I knew you would." He threw his arms around Zach's neck.

Zach hugged that small, sturdy body and waited until Bryan drew back before asking, "Why didn't you call your dad? He would've understood, too." Joe ran a bar that was a favorite gathering place for the pack, but he was also a fellow soldier.

"He's watching Liam's soccer game today. I didn't want to mess that up—Liam's been practicing his kicks for like a month."

Zach ruffled his nephew's hair. "You're a good kid, JB." Standing, he nodded at the cubbyholes that lined the back of the classroom. "Grab your stuff while I go sort this out with Ms. Kildaire."

Bryan grabbed his hand. "You won't—"

"I won't say anything. Promise."

Relaxing, Bryan went to a cubby to their right and began to gather his things.

Zach watched Annie rise from her chair as he walked over and had to fight the urge to growl that she sit back down. He'd noticed her shakiness earlier—her left leg was bothering her. But if he said what he wanted to, he'd be as bad as that runt, Morgan. Annie Kildaire had to be perfectly capable if she was running a classroom of seven-year-olds.

"Did he tell you?" she asked in that husky voice that brushed like black velvet over his skin. The cat stretched out, asking for more. Being stroked by Ms. Kildaire, he thought, both sides of him in agreement, might just be the best Christmas present ever.

"Yes, he gave up the goods."

She waited. "And?"

"And I can't tell you." He watched her brow furrow, her lips purse. He couldn't decide if he wanted to bite down on that full lower lip or lick the upper one.

"Mr. . . . Zach."

"Quinn," he supplied. "Zach Quinn."

Her cheeks flared with little red spots of temper. "Mr. Quinn, Bryan is a child. I expect you to act like an adult."

Oh, he had plenty of plans to act like an adult around Ms. Kildaire. "I promised JB."

She stared at him, then blew out a breath. "And promises are to be kept."

"Yes."

"What do you suggest I do?" She folded her arms. "I have to punish him, and I can't do that without knowing why he did what he did."

"I'll take care of it." Bryan had hit someone, and his nephew knew he'd be disciplined for it, provocation or not. But some things, Zach knew, were worth fighting over. "I'll make sure the punishment fits the crime."

"It's a school matter."

"It's a leopard matter."

Chapter 2

Understanding filtered into those pretty melted-chocolate eyes. "He's usually so well controlled, I forget he's only seven."

"Boy'll grow up to be one of the dominants, probably a soldier." He glanced behind him. "Ready?"

Bryan nodded, backpack slung over his shoulder. "Yep."

Zach watched as his nephew walked up to the desk and said, "I'm sorry I dis—"—a frown of concentration—"disrupted the classroom. But I'm not sorry I hit Morgan."

Zach was looking at Annie and saw her struggle to hide a smile. "That's not a very good attitude, Bryan."

"I know. And I'm ready for the punishment. But I'm still not sorry."

Brown eyes flicked to him. "Is stubbornness a family trait?" Her lips curved just a little, just enough to make everything in him sit up in attention.

"Now that, sweetheart," he said, a stunning realization taking form in his chest, "is something you'll have to decide for yourself."

Well, hell.

She colored again. "Thank you for coming in, Mr. Quinn. I'll look forward to seeing Bryan in class on Monday."

He didn't move, tasting the realization that had him by the throat. It was hot, wild, *right*. Utterly, absolutely right. The knowledge made his smile slow and seductive. "Why don't you walk out with us?" The corridors had been close to empty when he arrived, and he couldn't hear any movement now. No way was he leaving sweet Annie Kildaire alone in a building with winter darkness only an hour away at most.

"I'll be out in a moment." She began to gather the papers on her desk.

"We'll wait." He glanced at Bryan. "Can you wait?"

"Yep." A sunny smile. "But I'm hungry."

Reaching into the back pocket of his jeans, he pulled out a muesli bar he'd grabbed on his way here. "I got you this for the ride home."

Bryan caught it with cat-quick reflexes and happily went off to scramble into a seat, backpack at his feet. Meanwhile, Ms. Kildaire was giving him a guarded kind of look. "Really Mr. Quinn—"

"Zach. You can only call me Mr. Quinn when you're angry."

"Mr.—"

"Zach."

Her hand fisted. "Fine. Zach."

He smiled, liking that she was already comfortable enough to argue with him. Some women found him a little too dangerous to play with. And he very much wanted to play with Annie. "Yes, Teach?"

He could hear her gritting her teeth. "I'll be perfectly fine walking out alone. I do it every day of the week."

He shrugged, enjoying the verbal sparring. "I'm here today."

"And what you says goes?" Looking down, she shoved her papers into an untidy pile.

"Unless you can talk me out of it." He saw her jaw set and knew she was gritting those human teeth again. All that beautiful passion, he thought in pleasure, hidden behind the shyness that had first stained her cheeks.

"And why should I be talking you out of anything?" She grabbed what looked like a black leather-synth satchel and put the papers inside. "You're nobody to me."

The cat didn't like that. The man didn't either. "That wasn't very nice."

She turned to shoot him a glare, then recommenced packing her satchel. He could almost see her trying to figure out if he was being serious or if he was teasing her. That it took her that much focus, told him she hadn't been teased much. That was a shame. Because when Annie got mad, she forgot to be shy.

Now, she slapped her satchel closed and swung it over her shoulder. Or tried to. Zach slid it out of her hand and brought the strap over his head, settling it diagonally across his body.

"Mr. Quinn!" She looked like she wanted to bite him.

His cat purred in interest, even as Bryan giggled. "Nobody calls Uncle Zach that."

"Yeah, nobody does," Zach added. "Come on, Jumping Bean. We're moving out." He nodded at the coat thrown carelessly over the back of Annie's chair. "Don't forget that. It's cold out." He began to walk to the door, knowing she'd have no choice but to follow.

After a taut second, she did. He heard her clothing rustle as she put the coat on over her stern gray pants and tailored white shirt, his mind obliging him with a fantasy slide show of the feminine softness he knew lurked underneath. Pity it was all covered up now.

"After you, Teach." Letting Bryan scamper a few feet ahead, he held the door open and watched Annie Kildaire walk toward him.

Her limp was very slight, but even that meant the injury had to have been horrendous. Either that, or the impairment was a natural one surgeons hadn't been able to repair fully. And there wasn't much surgeons couldn't repair these days. "What happened to your leg?" he asked once they were out in the hallway.

She faltered for a second before her shoulders squared. "There was a freak bullet-train derailment when I was seven. My leg was crushed so badly, it was pretty much unrecognizable as anything other than meat with a few fragments of bone."

He heard the simmering pride in her, had the sense that she was bracing herself for a blow. "They did a good job of reconstructing it. Titanium?"

He could tell from her expression that that wasn't the response she'd expected. "No. Some kind of new plassteel. Very high-tech. It 'grew' as I grew, so I only needed a couple of extra surgeries over the years."

"And now?"

"I shouldn't need any work done on it unless I injure the leg in some way."

Zach knew that couldn't be all of it. "Still hurt?"

She hesitated. "Sometimes." She indicated a corridor to their left. "I want to make sure Morgan's been picked up."

"JB, hold up." Knowing he could trust the boy not to dart outside, he followed Annie the short distance to the sick bay. Looking over her shoulder, he saw the darkened interior. "He's gone."

She jumped. "You walk like a cat!"

"I am a cat, sweetheart." He wanted to tease her again, so he let a low growl rumble up from his chest. "See?"

Streaks of vibrant color stained her cheeks once more. But she didn't back down. "Are you planning to move?"

"No." He drew in a deep breath, fighting the urge to nuzzle at her throat. "You smell good. Can I taste you?" It was a half-serious question. "Just a little?"

"Mr. Quinn!" She took a step around him and headed off.

But he'd already caught the tart bite of arousal in her scent. Satisfied, he followed, on his best behavior now. It wouldn't do to scare Annie away. *Not when he planned to keep her.*

A moment later, they reached the front door, where Bryan was waiting. Zach pulled it open. "Stay with me," he told his nephew. The boy was leopard-fast, but he was still a boy. Sometimes, he didn't look where he was going, and cars could hurt him as easily as they could a human or Psy child.

The outside air was cold, but it made Zach sigh in exhilaration. Being outdoors was in his blood, the reason why he loved his day job as a ranger in Yosemite. The work fitted naturally into his duties as a DarkRiver soldier—he could run patrols and check up on his wild charges at the same time.

"Where's your car?" he asked Annie, noticing that her face had brightened, too. Sexy, kissable Annie Kildaire liked being outside as much as he did. It pleased the cat, soothed the man.

"Over there." Giving him a look still colored with the tart kiss of temper, she pointed to a little compact that would cut his legs in half if he was ever insane enough to try to fold himself inside. But she was on the small side, he thought, wondering if she'd mind tussling with a taller man. The idea of the games he wanted to play with Annie made him grin. "JB and I will walk you over."

She didn't argue with him this time, simply asked about his vehicle. He jerked a thumb in the direction of the rugged all-wheel-drive parked a few spaces away.

"I suppose you need that in the forest?" Her voice held a touch of wistfulness.

"Yeah." DarkRiver's territory covered a lot of beautiful but harsh land. And now that they had allied with the SnowDancer wolves, that territory included the Sierra Nevada mountains. "Have you ever been out in Yosemite?" The nearest edge of the massive forest was only about an hour from here, the reason why this school was so popular with the pack. Many of them lived on the fringes of Yosemite.

"Just the public areas." She pressed her thumb to the door of her car, deactivating the security lock. "I guess those sections only make up a tiny fraction of your territory?"

Zach nodded. In the past, DarkRiver had been relaxed about offering access to other parts of the forest—so long as people obeyed the rules that protected the land and its wild inhabitants. However, right now, with the Psy Council looking for any weakness in their defenses, they'd become more stringent. Nobody but Pack went in past what DarkRiver considered the public boundary. Of course, members of the pack could bring guests in. "Want to see more?"

Her expression was startled. "I—" She snapped her mouth shut, and he saw her gaze dip to her leg. The movement was so quick, he would've missed it if he hadn't been watching her so closely.

Someone, he thought, a growl building inside him, had done a number on her confidence. "I can drive you up tomorrow," he said, clamping down on the anger, "show you some of the sights most people never get to see."

"I shouldn't." But temptation whispered through her eyes. "I have to prepare for the class's contribution to the Christmas pageant." A fond look directed at Bryan.

His nephew jumped up and down. "We're going to do the story of how the Psy once tried to cancel Christmas. It's gonna be so funny!"

"Make sure you get me a ticket," Zach said, but his mind was on how to secure Annie's company for tomorrow. Challenge might work. Or perhaps . . . "Once-in-a-lifetime offer," he said with a smile that he tried to keep from being ravenous. If she caught even a hint of what he truly wanted from her, she'd never get into a car with him, much less let him drive her into the lush privacy of the forest. "Pack's getting strict about who we allow in."

She bit down on that full lower lip of hers, arousing his jealousy. He wanted to do the biting.

"Well," she said, clearly torn.

Then Bryan clinched the deal for him. "You should come, Miss Kildaire! Then after, you can come to the picnic."

"Picnic?" She looked at Zach. "It's winter."

"Winter picnic," he said, as if that was normal. It was, for DarkRiver. "It's informal, just a chance for people to get together before the Christmas madness."

"Please come, Miss Kildaire," Bryan pleaded. "*Please.*"

He saw Annie melt at that childish plea and knew he had her.

"All right," she said, and looked up. Her smile faded . . . because he'd let the cat seep into his eyes, let her see the dark hunger pumping through his blood.

"I'll pick you up at nine." He leaned closer, drawing in the scent of her. "Be ready for me, sweetheart."

Annie closed the door to her apartment and asked herself if she'd lost her mind. Not half an hour ago, she'd agreed to spend an entire day with a man so dangerous, a sane woman would've run in the opposite direction . . . instead of fantasizing about kissing him on those should-be-illegal lips. Her entire body went hot as she remembered the look in his eyes as he'd asked her to be ready for him. Dear God, the man was lethal.

"Calm down, Annie," she told herself. "It's not like he's really going to do anything." Because while Zach Quinn might've flirted with her, might even have looked at her as a man looks at a woman he wants, she was pragmatic enough to know that it had probably been nothing more than a momentary diversion on his part. A man that good-looking had to have women begging to crawl into his bed.

The idea of Zach sprawled in bed, all gleaming skin and liquid muscle, made her stomach flutter. Then she imagined him crooking a finger, that teasing smile playing over his lips. "If he ever looks at me like that," she whispered, pulling the chopsticks out of her hair as she walked into the bedroom, "I'm a goner." Her black hair tumbled around her face in a mass of soft curls.

Zach's hair had looked heavier than hers, sleeker.

Her thoughts went from his hair to what he might look like in leopard form. A predator, all muscle and power covered with a gold-and-black coat. Would he allow a woman to stroke him? Her fingers tingled in awareness, and standing as she was in front of the vanity mirror, she saw her lips part, her eyes widen. The ache between her thighs turned into an erotic pulse.

Her cell phone beeped.

She ignored it, shocked by the raw intensity of the hunger surging through her. She'd never before reacted this passionately to a man, until her entire body trembled with the force of it. "Lord have mercy." Because if this was what simply thinking about him did to her, how in the world was she going to survive being alone with him for an entire day?

Beep. Beep. Beep.

She answered the cell just to shut off the sound. "Yes?"

Chapter 3

"Angelica, what's the matter? You're snapping."

She took a deep breath. "Nothing, Mom. I just got home."

"Well, it's Friday, so you can relax a little. Drink that chamomile tea I got you."

Annie hated chamomile tea. "You know I don't like it."

"It's good for you."

She'd heard that so many times it no longer made any impact. "I think I want to be bad, today." And it wasn't herbal tea on her mind. "Very, very bad."

"Honestly, Angelica!" Kimberly blew out a frustrated breath. "Forget the tea. I wanted to tell you to dress nicely for dinner tomorrow night."

Dinner? Annie's stomach sunk to the bottom of her toes as she realized she'd blanked the event from her mind. "Mom, you said you wouldn't—"

"He's a nice young professor from London. Over here on a sabbatical."

"When you say young . . ."

"He's only forty-three, dear."

Annie was twenty-eight. "Oh." She rubbed her forehead. "The thing is—"

"No arguments. Your father and I want you settled. We won't be around to look after you forever."

"I can look after myself." She felt her hand fist, released it with effort. There was no point in getting angry, not when this was a conversation they'd been having for more years than she could remember. "I'm not a child."

"Well you can't spend the rest of your life alone." Her mother's tone was harsh, but it held an edge of desperation—Kimberly really was worried by the thought of her daughter living a solitary life. She'd never bothered to wonder if Annie was single by choice. "Professor Markson is a lovely man. You could do a lot worse."

What her mother actually meant, Annie thought with a stab of old resentment, was that it wasn't as if she had any other options. To Kimberly, Annie was a damaged and fragile creature most men would bypass. "Is Caro coming?"

"Of course not." Her mother made a sound of annoyance. "We want the professor's attention on you. Much as I like her, your cousin tends to steal the limelight, even now that she's married."

Annie's headache intensified—Caro was usually the only point of sanity at these ritual humiliations. "Right."

"I'll expect you at seven for cocktails."

"I might be a little late."

"Work?"

"No." How did she say this? "I, er, arranged an in-depth tour of Yosemite." Though she didn't live far from the forest, her parents were closer to San Francisco. Even in a high-speed vehicle, it would take her over an hour to make the trip.

"Really, Annie. You knew we were having this dinner."

"I said I didn't want to be set up on any more dates." Especially when she had no intention of marrying or entering into a long-term relationship. *Ever.* And most certainly not when the men came in expecting someone like Caro and got Annie instead. "I'll try to be there as soon as I can, but I can't promise anything."

Her mother hung up after a few more sharp words. Rubbing her forehead, Annie walked out of the bedroom and to the bathroom, cell phone still in hand. After that call, she definitely needed the soothing properties of a bath liberally laced with mineral salts. Stripping off, she sat on the edge of the tub while it filled, taking the chance to massage some of the stiffness out of her thigh.

Does it hurt?

Such a simple question, without judgment or pity. It had undone her just a little. Not only that, but Zach had continued to flirt with her even after discovering that she was less than perfect. It might not have meant much to him, but it had meant something to her.

No, Angelica, you can't do that. Your leg's too weak.

Too often, it felt as if her mother had been born into the wrong race. She would've made a good Psy, with her analytical mind and need for perfection in all things.

The only place Kimberly had failed was with Annie.

Her mood might've dimmed again, but she was too busy daydreaming about kissing Zach on those beautiful lips of his. The man was too sinful to be real. And the way he flirted . . . wow. It would've been nice to be confident enough to flirt back. "Instead of blushing and going tongue-tied," she muttered.

She'd seen enough DarkRiver couples to identify the kind of

women dominant changeling men found attractive—and Zach was definitely a dominant. Those women were all striking in some way, but it was their self-assurance that really shone through. Vividly intelligent, they didn't hesitate to speak their minds, or give back as good as they got. Feminine strength didn't scare men of Zach Quinn's ilk, it enticed them.

And that was exactly what attracted her to him. She knew after having met him only once that he'd never tell her she couldn't do something. Zach would simply expect her to match him. And that was a seduction all on its own.

The bath pinged to alert her it was full. She was about to step in when her eye fell on the cell phone she'd left on top of her discarded clothes. She grabbed it, deciding to give Caro a call. Her cousin was an expert on men, and it was advice on that subject that Annie needed right now.

Putting it within reach, she sank into the hot water with a moan. After ten minutes of just lying there soaking in the heat, she reached out to get the phone. It beeped an incoming call as her fingers brushed the case. Rolling her eyes because it was probably her mother again, she flipped it open without checking the display and answered audio only.

"It's me," she said, dropping her head back against the wall and pressing her feet flat against the end of the bath.

"Hello, me."

Her breath stuck in her throat at the sound of that sensually amused voice. "Zach . . . Mr. Quinn—" She'd have jerked upright except that she was frozen in place.

"Zach," he corrected. "I hope I'm not disturbing you."

"No, I"—water dripped as she raised a hand to push streamers of hair off her face—"I was just relaxing."

"In the bath?"

She blinked, mortified that she'd left the visual feed on by accident. But no, it was switched off.

"Leopards have good ears."

Her cheeks colored. "Of course." She stayed very still, not wanting him to hear her splashing about.

"I didn't mean to intrude into your relaxation time." An apology made in a voice that was close to a purr.

Annie told herself to breathe. "That's okay." Realizing he couldn't see her, she stopped fighting herself and allowed her face to suffuse with the pleasure she got from simply listening to him. She'd never before met a man with a voice like Zach's—so masculine, but with that delectable hint of play. As if while he might be a honed blade of a soldier, he knew how to laugh, too. "Was there a problem with Bryan?"

"No, JB's fine. No runs with the other kids for a week for him."

Annie frowned. "I thought he'd have entertainment privileges suspended."

Zach chuckled, and it rippled through her like living fire. "That *is* his favorite form of entertainment. Leopard changelings, especially boys his age, hate being trapped inside."

"Of course." She remembered one of the other parents saying something along those lines during a parent-teacher conference. "Was that what you called to tell me?"

"That, and I wanted to warn you about the cold up in the higher elevations. We might even hit some snow. Dress in layers."

"Okay." She bit down on her lower lip, wanting to keep him on the phone but not knowing what to say to achieve that goal. "So, 9:00 a.m. tomorrow?"

"Hmm." He sounded distracted to her ears.

"I should let you go," she began.

"Tired of me already?"

She really didn't know how to deal with him. "No."

Another male chuckle. "Tell me something about you, Annie."

"What do you want to know?" *Why* did he want to know?

"How long have you been a teacher?"

"Five years," she said with a smile. "I started teaching new entrants, but for the past couple of years, it's been kids Bryan's age."

"You like it."

"I love it." She found she'd relaxed again, soothed by the timbre of his voice, so easy, so deliciously male. "What do you do?"

"I'm a forest ranger, specializing in the predatory species that call Yosemite home."

The work fitted him better than anything she could've imagined. "Do you like what you do?"

"It's in my blood." He paused. "Someone's at the door. I'll pick you up at nine on the dot. Sweet dreams." The last was a husky murmur laced with temptation.

"Bye." She ended the call and just sat there, flushing alternately hot and cold. Surely she was reading too much into the conversation. He'd called to make sure she dressed right. The way his voice had felt like a caress over her most sensitive skin . . . that was the result of her pulse-pounding susceptibility to him. It didn't mean he wanted her, too.

But she couldn't quite stop herself from hoping.

Zach pulled open the door to his small home, already aware of his visitor's identity. He'd picked up the scent the instant the other changeling stepped out of his vehicle.

"Luc." He welcomed his alpha inside. "What's up?"

Lucas walked in, dressed in a dark gray suit that said he'd come straight from DarkRiver's business HQ. "Nice place."

"Nice suit." Opening the cooler, he threw Lucas a sleek glass bottle before taking one for himself.

"What the hell is this?" Lucas scowled at the pale blue liquid inside. "And the suit's camouflage."

"It's some new energy drink Joe's come up with." He twisted off the top. "We're supposed to give him feedback."

Lucas took a pull. "Not bad—for something that looks like it glows in the dark."

Zach grinned. "So, why the camouflage?"

"I had a meeting with a Psy group today."

"New deal?" DarkRiver had recently completed its second major construction project for Psy Councilor Nikita Duncan. The success of the venture had been so dramatic, they'd attracted considerable interest from other Psy businesses.

"Signed and sealed." Lucas's grin was very feline in its satisfaction. "I wanted to talk to you about some of the land you cover during your duties as ranger."

Zach nodded. "Is there a problem?"

"Shouldn't be, but I want you to keep an extra sharp eye out. Psy don't usually venture anywhere near our territory, but they've been changing the rules recently."

"You think they might be trying to use the land to familiarize themselves with the forest," Zach guessed. Psy weren't, as a rule, comfortable in wide-open spaces. They preferred the cities, with their towers of glass and steel. But as Lucas's mate, Sascha, showed, the psychic race was supremely adaptable.

"I don't think it's happened yet, but there's a possibility it might—we'd be fools if we didn't prepare for the unexpected."

"I'll keep you updated." He put down his empty bottle beside the one Lucas had just finished. "You didn't really come here for that." Lucas's caution was something Zach was a senior-enough soldier to figure out for himself.

Lucas shrugged, the clawlike markings on the right side of his face standing out in vivid relief. "I was passing through to talk to

Tammy about the Christmas celebrations, decided to drop in, touch base."

Since Tammy and Nate were Zach's closest neighbors, that made sense. "Tell Nate I saw his cubs chasing a dog yesterday."

Lucas grinned. "Sounds about right."

"Can I ask you a question?"

Lucas raised an eyebrow and waited.

"How fragile are humans?" He'd had human lovers before, but he'd never wanted any woman, human or changeling, with the raw fury that colored his hunger for Annie. It worried him that he might hurt her in passion. "How much do I have to hold back?"

"They're not as breakable as we tend to think," Lucas said, and Zach knew he was speaking from experience. Physically, Psy were even weaker than humans, yet Lucas was very happily mated to Sascha. "Just don't use the same force on her that you'd use on me or one of the other males and you'll be fine."

"Who said there's a 'her'?"

"There's always a her."

"Her name is Annie, and I'm bringing her to the picnic tomorrow."

Lucas's eyes gleamed cat green. "You're introducing her to the pack? When did you meet her?"

"Today."

"Well, hell." Lucas rocked back on his heels. "She have any idea what that means?"

"She's a little wary, but she likes me," he said, thinking of how her eyes had drunk him up. A man could get used to being looked at that way. Especially when the woman doing the looking was someone he'd like to eat up in small, delicious bites. "I'm going to court her first." But he already considered her his—because not only did Annie Kildaire arouse his most primal instincts, she was his mate . . . and he was a possessive kind of cat.

Chapter 4

Annie was ready by eight the next morning. Feeling jumpy and overexcited, she checked her clothing in the mirror one more time. She'd taken Zach's advice and layered it up, beginning with a plain white tee and a thin V-necked cashmere-blend sweater that felt divine on her skin . On the bottom, she'd worn her favorite jeans, along with a pair of hiking boots, in case the drive turned into a walk. Completing her outfit was an insulated puffy jacket.

"I look like an egg." Caroline had made her buy the cheerful yellow garment, insisting it brightened her face. Annie had agreed because it looked sunny. But it wasn't exactly flattering. Oh well, she thought, peeling it off and putting it on the little backpack that held her camera and water, it wasn't as if this was a date.

Sweet dreams.

The memory of Zach's voice sent desire skittering through her veins. All she could think about was what it would be like to have that voice whisper in her ear while those strong hands touched her with bold confidence. "Oh, man." She pressed a hand flat to her stomach. "Calm, Annie. Calm." It was difficult to listen to her own advice when she'd spent the whole night dreaming about him. The tattoo she'd glimpsed on his biceps fascinated her—in her dreams, she'd stroked her fingers over the exotic lines of it, pressed her lips to that muscled flesh . . . and then touched another, harder part of his body.

"A whole *day*," she almost moaned, and went to shove a hand through her hair before realizing she'd pulled it back into a ponytail. Now she glanced into the mirror and made a face. She'd eschewed makeup—who went to a forest with makeup on?—but had given in to the urge to slick on some gloss. It plumped up her lips . . . except that her lips were already plump. "Argh." Too late, she remembered why she never used gloss. She was searching for a tissue to wipe it off when the doorbell rang. "Who on earth?" Running to the door, she pulled it open.

A leopard in human skin stood on the other side. "I was hoping to wake you," he drawled, leaning against the doorjamb. "But you're all dressed." He tried to look sad, but the wicked lights dancing in his eyes made that impossible.

"You're early," she said, unable to stop staring at him. He was wearing a pair of faded blue jeans, hiking boots and a soft gray sweatshirt stamped with the San Francisco Giants emblem. Casual clothes, but his hair was still damp from the shower and his jaw freshly shaven.

It was all she could do not to run her fingertips over that smooth skin and nuzzle the masculine scent of him into her lungs.

"I woke up early—had somewhere I wanted to be." He smiled at her, slow and persuasive. "Are you going to invite me in?" Raising a hand, he showed her a brown paper bag bearing the logo of a nearby bakery. "I brought breakfast."

She knew she shouldn't let him get his own way so very easily, but stepped aside in welcome. "What did you bring?"

"Come and see." He waited for her to close the door, then followed as she led the way into the kitchen through the living room of her apartment. "You like to read."

She saw him glance at the paperbacks on the shelves, stacked on the coffee table, placed face down on the arm of her sofa. "Yes."

"Me, too." He put the bag on the counter and slid onto a stool. "Why are you standing over there?"

She looked at him from the other side of the counter. "I thought I'd make coffee."

"Okay." He kept the bag closed. "But you're not seeing what's in here until you come around to this side."

He was definitely flirting. And she was definitely playing with fire by allowing it to go on. Because if there was one thing she knew about predatory changeling men, it was that they were quite ferally possessive—and belonging to anyone was simply not on her agenda. Of course, she was also getting *way* ahead of herself. He was only flirting. It wasn't as if he planned to drag her off to the chapel. "What do you read?" she asked, telling herself it was okay to try to flirt back, that this pull she felt toward him was nothing more than sexual attraction.

"Thrillers, some nonfiction." He looked around her open-plan kitchen and living room. "It's a small place."

"For you, maybe." He was so big, so unashamedly male, he took over the space . . . threatened to take her over, too.

He glanced at her, expression shifting to something darker and infinitely more dangerous. "Hmm, you're right. You're a bit smaller than me."

She tried to control her erratic breathing as she finished putting on the coffee. He just sat there and watched her with a feline patience that had her nerves sparking in reaction.

"How long have you lived here?"

"Last five years. I moved in after I got the teaching job."

"Did you live at home before that?"

She laughed through the thudding beat of her pulse. "Lord, no. I was outta there at eighteen."

"You ever get lonely, Annie?" he asked, his tone liquid heat over her skin.

"I like living alone. I intend to keep it that way." She thought she'd surprised him with that, but instead of replying, he lifted up the bag and raised an eyebrow. It was a dare. Annie had never considered herself particularly courageous, but she walked around the counter. He nodded at her to take the stool beside his.

Knowing it would be silly to refuse, she got up, rubbing her thigh with one hand. He noticed. "It hurt today?"

"What?" She looked down. "Oh, no, not really. It's habit." It was always a little achy in the mornings. "So, breakfast?"

His eyes went cat on her between one instant and the next. She sucked in a breath at the intensity of that green-gold gaze. "Wow."

He smiled. "Let's play a game."

She had a feeling that playing with this big kitty cat was a very bad idea, but since she'd already given in to her insanity, she said, "What're the rules?"

"Close your eyes. Eat what I give you, and tell me what it is."

The notion of having him feed her had her heart racing at the speed of light. "What do I get if I guess correctly?"

"Mystery prize." His lashes lowered, and she thought she caught a glimpse of something edgy, something that blazed with raw male heat, but when he looked back up, there was nothing but amusement in those leopard eyes. "Yes?"

"Yes." She watched mesmerized as he opened the paper bag with those hands she wanted to have all over her.

"Close your eyes, sweetheart."

She swallowed hunger of a far different sort and let her lashes flutter down. It made her even more aware of the scent of him, the warmth of him, the sheer presence of him. When he shifted position to put one of his feet on the outside of her stool, effectively trapping her, she opened her mouth to tell him . . . something.

But his finger brushed over her lips. "Taste."

He was all around her, in her blood, in her breath. Losing her train of thought, she closed her teeth over the pastry he put to her lips. The flaky stuff just about melted in her mouth, and she licked her lips without thinking about it.

Zach seemed to go very still, but when he spoke, his words were light. "Guess?"

"Danish."

"Wrong." She went to open her eyes, but he said, "No, keep them shut."

"Why?"

"I'm going to give you another shot. Right now, you owe a single forfeit. Let's see if we can even the decks."

"Forfeit?" She wondered why the thought sent excitement arcing through her. "You never said anything about a forfeit."

"You never asked."

As she'd thought—playing with this cat was an invitation to trouble. "Now I am."

"Later. First, taste this." He put something else to her mouth, and she bit down, determined to get it this time—he sounded far too delighted by the idea of having her owe him a forfeit.

She smiled. "Blueberry muffin."

A finger brushed over her lips, making her eyes snap open. "A crumb," he said.

"Oh."

He didn't smile this time, watching her with an intensity that reminded her that for all his playfulness, he was a DarkRiver soldier. And DarkRiver controlled the greater San Francisco area. More than that, they were allied with the bloodthirsty SnowDancer wolves.

"What're you thinking?" he asked her.

"That you're dangerous."

"Not to you," he said. "I wouldn't bite unless you asked very nicely."

Heat flooded her cheeks at the teasing promise, and she was more than glad to hear the coffeemaker ping. "Coffee's done, I'll grab it."

He let her go, but she had a feeling the game had only just begun. And that she was the prey.

Zach wanted to groan in frustration as he watched Annie move about the kitchen. He'd come within an inch of kissing the life out of her when she'd licked her lips. Perfect, luscious, bitable lips. He'd resisted the temptation for two reasons. One, the cat liked the chase. And two, the man liked the idea of having Annie melt at his touch. He planned to seduce her until she purred for him.

"Coffee." She put a cup in front of him, and he took a sip, attempting to behave when what he really wanted to do was haul her close and just *take*. Patience, he told himself. The last thing he wanted to do was scare Annie with the wild fury of his hunger.

"It's good." Sighing in appreciation, he passed her the muffin and a flaky croissant with a chocolate center. "The reason for your forfeit."

She scowled at the pain au chocolat. "So do the win and loss cancel each other out?"

"No. I'll collect my forfeit." His eyes drifted to her lips and lingered there. "A kiss, Annie. You owe me a kiss."

Her lips parted, her breath whispering out in a soft gasp. "And"—she coughed—"my winnings?"

"I'll give them to you later today." He wanted to drink up the scent of her, spiced as it was by the seduction of her growing arousal. However that arousal was nowhere near enough to satiate the savagery of his own need. But the cat was a patient hunter. By the time this day was through, he planned to have coaxed and tempted Annie Kildaire until she was as desperate for him as he was for her. "Now eat, or we'll be late."

She nibbled at her croissant, shooting him quick glances as he finished off the bagel he'd bought for himself. "When are you going to . . . collect?" she asked afterward, clearing away the cups with feminine efficiency that failed to mask her responsive awareness.

"I've got all day." He slid off the stool and smiled. "Ready?"

"You look very much the cat when you smile that way," she said. "You're enjoying teasing me."

He walked over and took the basket she'd picked up from the small table in one corner. "What's this?"

"I packed a couple of things for the picnic, and some snacks for the ride."

He peeked in. "Chocolate cake?"

"Chocolate *mud* cake," she said, with an adorable note of pride that made him want to claim his forfeit then and there. "I made it last night, gave it time to settle."

"You'll be Sascha's new best friend." Leaning in, he brushed his lips over her ear. "And yes, Teach, I like teasing you."

Annie still hadn't gotten over the sensation of his lips on her skin as Zach pulled away from her ground-floor apartment and out into the street. Open sexual heat laced his teasing, but she wasn't sure quite how far he'd take it. If he pushed, would she surrender?

The temptation was blindingly strong. Not only was he beautiful in the most masculine way, she flat out liked him. Being with Zach, if only for a night, would be, she already knew, a delight. He wouldn't be the least bit selfish, she thought. His partner's pleasure would matter to him. And, given his nature, he wasn't likely to want any kind of a commitment.

It was perfect.

Yet Annie found herself hesitating. Already, she reacted to him more deeply than she had to any other man her entire life. What would it do to her to sleep with him, to know him that intimately . . . then watch him walk away? Her mind flicked to a slide show of images. They were all of one woman. A woman with years of disappointment in her eyes.

"Look."

She jerked up at the sound of his voice. "What?"

"There." He pointed out the windshield.

Her eyes widened at the parade of old-fashioned automobiles on the other side of the road, all huge bodies and gleaming paint. They were so old they had no hover capacity, but there was something very sexy about them. "They look amazing. I wonder where they're going?"

"I read something about a vintage-car show about a twenty-minute drive from here. We could swing by after the picnic today."

Despite her fear at how quickly he'd gotten under her skin, she couldn't help but be delighted that he wanted to spend more time with her. Hard on its heels came disappointment. "I have to be back by six," she said. "Family dinner."

Zach shot her a quick glance. "You don't sound too enthusiastic."

She understood the surprise in his voice. All the DarkRiver cats she knew had one thing in common—family was the bedrock of their world. And Pack was one big extended family as far as they were concerned—she'd had senior pack members turn up to parent-teacher conferences more than once when the parent was ill or unavoidably delayed. "My mom keeps trying to set me up with men."

Zach's expression changed and, for the first time, she saw the ruthless soldier in him. "What kind of men?"

"Academics." She shrugged. "Mom and Dad are both professors at Berkeley—math and physics respectively."

"Are academics your type?"

"No."

He glanced at her again, and those eyes had gone leopard on her. "Are you sure?"

"Quite." She found herself refusing to be intimidated by the sense of incipient danger in the air. If she gave an inch, Zach would take a mile. And while she might not be a dominant female, it was important that he respect her. She frowned. Of course it was important, but that thought, it had been so vivid, so strong, so *visceral*—as if her mind knew something it wasn't yet ready to share.

Then Zach spoke again, breaking her train of thought. "So you'll be skipping the dinner." It was an order plain and simple.

Annie opened her mouth. What came out was, "No, I'll take you."

Chapter 5

Zach's grin was openly pleased. "What's the blind date going to say?"

She couldn't believe she'd just done that, ordered him to do something. More, she couldn't believe he'd agreed. "Probably, 'Thank God.' "

"Huh?"

"My cousin Caroline works at the university, too. The men come in expecting a statuesque, intellectual, blond beauty and get me."

"So?"

She scowled, wondering if he was teasing her again. "So, I'm about as opposite Caro as you can get."

"If they ignored you, that's their loss. Too damn bad for them." He shrugged. "Do you want to put on some music?"

She blinked at the way he'd swept aside the disappointments of the past with that simple statement. If she hadn't already liked him, that would've done it. "No, I need to tell you something about my mom." She swallowed, realizing she'd made a mess of things. If she hadn't mentioned the dinner, she could've avoided this altogether.

Zach groaned. "Don't tell me, she's a vegetarian?" he said, as if that was the worst thing possible.

She supposed for a leopard changeling, it was. "No." For once, he couldn't make her smile despite herself. "My mum is a little"—she tried to find an easy way to say this and failed—"biased against changelings."

"Ah. Let me guess—she thinks we're only one step up from animals?"

She felt very, very awkward discussing this, but she had to warn him about what he might face if he went to dinner with her. "It's not so blunt. She has no problem with other humans, and she admires the Psy, but she's never wanted me dating, or getting friendly with"—she raised her fingers in quotation marks—" 'the rough changeling element.' "

"What about you?" A deceptively soft question.

"That's an insult, Zach," she said as softly. "If that's what you really think of me—"

He swore. "Sorry, Annie, you're right, I'm being an ass. My only excuse is that you hit a hot button."

"I know." She couldn't blame him for his reaction. "It makes me really uncomfortable, but I've tried to change her mind, and it's never worked."

"What does she think of you teaching in a school with such a big changeling population?"

"That it's my version of acting out." She laughed at his expression, awkwardness dissipating. "No, she doesn't seem to realize I'm a grown-up, as the kids would say."

"Why do you let her get away with it?"

She was beginning to expect the straight-up questions from him. "My mom was on that train with me. She tried and tried and *tried* to get me out even though I was pinned under so much wreckage, she didn't have a hope of shifting anything." Her throat choked with the force of memory. "Her arm was broken at the time, but she didn't cry a single tear. She just kept trying to get me out."

Zach reached out to run his knuckles over her cheek. "She loves you."

She found comfort in the touch, and when he returned his hand to the steering wheel, she realized he'd somehow given her strength. "Yes. That's why I let her get away with so much." She leaned her head against the seat. "This thing she has for the Psy, the way she almost deifies them, it has its roots in the accident, too."

"How?"

"There was this boy—I don't know where he came from, but he was small, my age or younger. Cardinal eyes." She shivered at the memory of the chill in those extraordinary white-stars-on-black-velvet eyes. Psy lived lives devoid of emotion, but she'd never seen a child that utterly cold. "He lifted the wreckage off me."

"Telekinetic." Zach whistled. "You got lucky."

"Yeah." The Council didn't release its telekinetics for mundane rescue work—especially not when an incident affected mainly humans and changelings. "The medics told me he'd saved my life. My internal organs were close to collapse—a few more minutes, and I wouldn't have made it."

"Did you ever find out who he was?"

She shook her head. "He disappeared in the chaos. I've always thought that he teleported in from another location, after somehow seeing me in the live coverage. I remember there was a remote media chopper flying overhead, and if he was strong enough to lift the amount of wreckage that he did, he was strong enough to teleport." She couldn't imagine the strength of will it took to harness that much power. "He can't have been on the train—his clothes were spotless, and he didn't have so much as a smudge on his face."

"Psy aren't born lacking emotions," Zach told her, "they're conditioned to it. So it could be that he was still human enough to feel the need to help when he saw what had happened."

"How do you know about the conditioning?" She answered her own question a second later. "Your alpha's mated to a cardinal Psy." The news of that mating had sent shockwaves throughout the country.

"Sascha," he said, nodding. "Vaughn, one of the sentinels, is also mated to a Psy."

She couldn't imagine a member of the cold Psy race embracing emotion. But changeling leopards mated for life, and the bond between mates was a dazzling beacon apparent even to a human observer. If these women had mated with DarkRiver cats, they were undoubtedly as radiant and as strong as the other women she'd seen. "Will I meet them today?"

"I know Luc and Sascha are coming. Likely Faith and Vaughn will, too." He turned down a quiet road lined with trees. "I'll try to get you back by six so you can get ready for dinner, but we might cut it fine."

She bit the inside of her cheek. "I think I should cancel. I really don't want my mom to . . . I would hate for you to feel that—"

"Hey," he said, shooting her a glance that spoke of the soldier within, "I'm a big boy. I can handle it. Promise."

Promises are for keeping.

Deciding to trust him, she dug out her phone from the pocket of her jeans. "I'll tell Mom I'm bringing someone and that we'll be late."

"Yeah. It'll give your date time to find another partner." That lethal edge was back in his voice.

Her stomach muscles tightened. "Zach?"

"Might as well get this out in the open." He pulled the car into a small layby and turned to brace his hand against the top edge of her seat. "I'm not real good at sharing."

She swallowed. "Oh."

Zach could've kicked himself. He'd gone to all this trouble to lull her into a relaxed mood, then the cat had struck out in a burst of primitive jealousy. "Scared?"

Wary caution crept into her eyes, but she shook her head. "You said you wouldn't bite unless I asked . . . very nicely."

Surprise had the cat freezing. He'd forgotten that beneath the blushes and big brown eyes was a woman quite capable of calling him on his behavior. "That's true," he drawled, letting the cat out to play. "Come closer and ask me."

She shook her head again.

"Please."

Her cheeks colored, but he knew the heat wasn't because of embarrassment. Her arousal was a decadent whisper in the confines of the car, a drug his cat could lap at for hours. But what he really wanted to do was lap at her. He moved a little closer.

She held up the phone. "I need to make this call." Her voice was breathless, her tone jagged.

Instinct urged him to keep pushing, but he didn't want to make her feel cornered. No, he thought, shifting back into his seat, he'd do his teasing out in the open arms of the forest. "Go on, sweetheart." He smiled. "I've got all day to play with you."

She sucked in a breath. "Is that what this is? Play?"

"Sure." He drove them back onto the road, knowing she was talking about more than his teasing promise—pretty, sexy Annie Kildaire thought they were heading for a quick, hot fling. He grinned inwardly. Poor baby was going to get one hell of a surprise when he told her the truth, but she wasn't ready for that yet. "The best kind of play."

She was silent for a few minutes, then he heard her coding in the call. With her being so close, he could hear both sides of the conversation. Most humans who lived with changelings tended to get earpieces, so they could have private conversations. He'd have to get Annie one, he thought absently.

"Mom, it's Annie. About tonight," she began.

"Don't you dare cancel, Angelica Kildaire."

Angelica?

"I'm not," Annie said, obviously attempting to keep her temper in the face of the sharp response. "I'll be late, and—"

"We're doing this for you," her mother interrupted. "The least you can do is turn up on time."

Annie pressed her fingers to her forehead and seemed to mentally count to five. "I'm bringing a guest," she said without any lead-in. "His name is Zach."

Complete silence from the other end. Then, "Well good grief, Annie. Now you tell me. I'll have to find another woman to balance out the table. Who is he?"

"A DarkRiver soldier."

The silence was longer and deeper this time. Zach could feel Annie's distress at the reaction, but he was proud of her for sticking to her guns.

"Mom?"

"Aren't you a little too old for childish games?" her mother asked. "I know some women find those rough types attractive, but you have a brain. How long do you think he'll be able to keep that engaged?"

Zach's cat smiled in feral amusement. He was used to the preconceptions some humans, and most Psy, had about changelings. The majority of the time, it rolled off his back. But this time, it mattered. Because this was Annie's mother.

"I am not having this discussion with you," Annie said, tone final. "We'll be there for dinner. If you'd rather we didn't come, just say so."

"No, bring him," was the immediate response. "I want to meet this Zach who's got you ordering your own mother around." She hung up.

Annie stared at the phone for several seconds before thrusting it back into her pocket. "How much did you hear?"

"All of it."

She shifted uncomfortably. "Sorry—"

"Annie, sweetheart, leave your mom to me." He shot her a grin brimming with deliberate wickedness. "Today, I want to lead you astray."

Her returning smile was a little shy but full of a quiet mischief he figured most people never saw. "Are you sure I'm not already beyond redemption?"

He chuckled. "How could you be with a name like Angelica?"

She made a face. "I'm an Annie, not an Angelica."

"I prefer Angel."

"Do you like your women angelic?"

He chuckled. "No, baby, I like my woman exactly as she is." He knew he'd surprised her, waited to see what she'd do.

"So, this thing . . . you want more than just a day?"

He wasn't going to lie to her. "Are you going to run if I say yes?" He pulled into the forest proper, taking a narrow track that would lead them to one of the smaller waterfalls. It was only a trickle right now because of the cold, but it was still a sight to be seen.

"I'm here today, aren't I?" A question with a slight acerbic bite.

Tasting the piquancy of it on his tongue, he decided he liked it. "All alone with a big, bad cat who's rethinking his policy on biting."

Arousal colored the air again, and he sucked in a breath to contain his most primal instincts. "Look ahead," he said, voice husky.

"Oh!" Her eyes went huge. "It's a buck," she whispered, as if afraid the animal would hear her. "His antlers are huge."

Zach slowed the vehicle to a crawl, but the buck caught his

scent and shot off into the trees. "Sorry. They tend to scatter the instant they smell leopard. It's why I look after the predators—it's hard for me to check data on the nonpredatories."

"They know they're prey." She looked at him. "Do you hunt them?"

"When the cat needs it, yes." He glanced at her. "Can you handle knowing that?"

"I teach a lot of little cats," she reminded him in a prim, schoolteacher voice. "I might not be an expert on changeling behavior, but I've picked up enough to know that when in animal form, you behave according to the needs of the animal."

He couldn't help himself. He turned and snapped his teeth at her, making her jump. When he began to chuckle, her eyes narrowed. "You're as bad as Bryan. He does that to Katie all the time."

"Odds on, he has a crush on her."

Her lips twitched. "That's what I think, too. Was the fight about Katie?"

"Sneaky, Ms. Kildaire, but I'm sworn to secrecy." Laughing at the face she made, he reached over to tug at her ponytail. "You up to a small hike?"

Shadows swept across her face. "You don't think I can do it?"

He parked the vehicle off to the side of the track and turned. "I don't know your limits yet," he told her honestly. "That's why I'm asking."

She colored. "Sorry. I'm a bit touchy on the whole subject."

He shrugged. "If I think you can't do something, I'll make sure you're not doing it." Protecting the vulnerable was instinct. Protecting Annie would probably become an obsession.

"You'll *make* sure I'm not doing it?" The arch sound of a human female metaphorically flexing her claws.

"Definitely." He held her gaze. "I'm flexible, little cat, but I'm not a pushover."

Her arousal spiked at his words, but so did her anger. "As if I ever believed that."

"Annie, you're used to academic types who probably let you walk all over them."

"Hold on," she began, eyes snapping with temper.

God, she was pretty. He reached forward while she was distracted, gripped her chin. And kissed her.

Chapter 6

She was softer than he'd imagined, more luscious than anything he'd ever experienced. Cat and man both purred inwardly, and when her lips parted on a gasp, he swept inside to taste her. Sweet and tart, innocent and woman, she was his own personal brand of intoxication.

He bit her lower lip, sucked on it, let her gasp in another breath before kissing her again. "Mmm." It was a sound of sheer pleasure as he indulged his need to touch this woman. Leopard changelings were tactile as a rule—something that translated into sensual affection in a relationship. It didn't always have to lead to sex. Sometimes it was just about the pleasure of skin-to-skin contact.

When he drew back, her lips were a little swollen, her pupils dilated. He rubbed his thumb over her lower lip and tried to temper his escalating need. She wasn't ready, not yet. As he'd learned this morning, her soft exterior hid a fierce core of independence—

the instant she learned what he really wanted, she'd stop playing with him.

And that was simply not acceptable. "You know how to kiss a man, Angel." He dropped his gaze to the rise and fall of her generous breasts. The temptation to caress them was so wrenching, he took his hand off her chin and thrust it through his hair. "About that hike . . . ?"

She gave a jerky nod. "I can walk."

"Tell me if it hurts."

"It won't."

Frowning, he grabbed her chin again and this time, he wasn't playing. "I mean it, Annie. I need to be able to trust you. I'm giving you that. You give me honesty. That's fair."

Her expression shifted again, a true smile curving over her lips. "I will, I promise. It'll probably ache some, but that's normal. If it gets any worse, I'll tell you."

He wanted to kiss her again but knew full well that if he didn't get them out of the car quick smart, he'd end up taking her right there—like some randy juvenile in his parents' car. "Let's go." Grabbing her little pack, he thrust his own bottle of water inside and opened the door.

She met him a few feet from the vehicle, her fluffy yellow jacket a dash of pure summer. "I know," she said, when his eyes landed on her, "I look like a baby duck."

Not bothering with a coat himself, he took her hand. "No. I like it." Her hand was small, but not weak in his. "It suits you." Pretty and bright and sunny, that was his Annie.

They walked in silence for a while, and he felt his beast sigh in pleasure. The forest was home, and it called to both parts of his soul. But today, he had a new reason for happiness—Annie. "You're in shape," he said after a while.

"Nowhere close to you." She made a rueful face. "I know you're keeping your stride shorter for me."

He hadn't even noticed, the act had been so natural. "Of course," he said matter-of-factly. "How would I have my wicked way with you if I left you in my dust?"

Her smile was startled, but it grew until the leopard batted at its warmth, utterly captivated. "I exercise," she said. "I have to, or the leg will freeze up."

"Every day?"

She nodded. "It's a habit now." Looking up at the trail as it wound its way into the forest she took a deep breath. "It's so beautiful here."

"Yeah." He watched her face suffuse with joy and felt the razor-sharp bite of envy. The cat really wasn't good at sharing. Neither was the man—he wanted to be the one to put that look of delight on her face. Soon, he promised himself.

She glanced at him, smile changing into a very feminine look of realization. "Zach." Her lips parted.

It was all the invitation he needed. Dipping his head, he claimed another bold kiss, curving his hand around the silken warmth of her neck. When her hands came to rest on his chest, the cat stretched out in pleasure within him. He wanted those hands on his bare skin, his hunger for her so extreme it would make her bolt if she knew about it.

That thought in mind, he pulled on the reins. Even so, he couldn't keep from nipping at her lip.

Her eyes widened even as her hands clenched on his chest. "You only had one forfeit."

He felt his mouth curve. "Put it on my account," he said without an ounce of repentance.

She laughed, and he knew that today was going to be one of the best days of his life.

* * *

Several hours later, Annie sighed and rested her head back against the seat as Zach drove them to the Pack Circle. "That was wonderful. Thank you."

"You fit here," he said quietly, his voice lacking its usual playfulness. "The age of the trees, the immensity of the forest, it doesn't scare you."

"It makes me feel free," she admitted. "Out here, no one's watching, waiting for me to stumble." She wondered how she'd come to trust him so quickly—quickly enough to reveal a vulnerability she kept hidden from even her closest friends.

It scared her a little, the intensity of the emotions growing in her heart. She tried to tell herself it was nothing but a silly crush, but all she could think of was the way his kisses had tugged at her soul. All day long he'd stolen them, until her lips remembered the shape of his, and her breasts ached for his touch. Swallowing, she attempted to redirect her thoughts. "The Pack Circle's usually kept secret."

"We don't take strangers there," he acknowledged. "Only those we trust to honor our faith."

Her heart warmed from the inside out. "Thank you."

"Don't thank me just yet. Wait till you meet the pack—they're a nosy bunch."

Nerves snapped to full wakefulness as Zach parked his vehicle behind several others and turned to run his knuckles over her cheek. "Don't be nervous."

"How do you know—"

"I can smell the change in your scent."

She was still sitting there, mind awash with the implications of what he'd said, when he walked around and opened her door. "Come on, Angel. Let's go face the masses."

She got out but didn't take his hand. "You can smell the changes in my body?" She watched him reach in back for the picnic basket.

"Yes." Basket in hand, he tugged her hand from where she'd wrapped her arms around herself. "Does that bother you?" A direct gaze.

She saw no flirtation in those eyes for the first time in hours. "A little," she admitted.

"You'll get used to it." He said that as if it was inevitable.

She wasn't sure. Privacy was a big deal for her—she'd spent almost a year in the hospital, only to go home to her mother's constant hovering. Those experiences had combined to make her zealous about guarding her personal space, and what was more personal, more private, than her body itself?

Zach glanced at her as they walked past the other cars. "It's natural to us," he said. "We don't tend to notice a particular scent unless it's something that matters."

"But other people will know," she said, her stomach in knots. She could accept her hunger for Zach, accept that he knew, but to have everyone else be aware of it, too?

Zach raised her hand to his lips and kissed her knuckles, the tenderness undoing her. He was, she realized, far more a threat to her than she'd initially thought. If she wasn't careful, Zach Quinn would steal her heart and leave her with nothing, her worst nightmare come to life. But even knowing that, she couldn't help moving closer when he tugged at her.

"Your arousal is a vibrant thread to me," he whispered, voice husky, "but for the others, it'll simply be background noise. They'll be focused on their mates, lovers, children—different threads. There are millions of them in any one instant."

His explanation made sense, enough to release some of the tension in her stomach. However, she couldn't help but be a little wary as they entered the Circle. Then several people cried out hellos, and, to her shock, she realized that though they weren't all parents, she knew a good number of them from various school events. The friendliness washed over her in an effervescent wave.

"Miss Kildaire, you came!" Bryan skidded to a stop by her feet. "Did Uncle Zach show you the forest?"

Conscious of several interested adult gazes, she nodded. "What have you been up to?"

"I'm playing hide-and-seek with Priyanka." With that, he ran off. She was still smiling after him when she felt Zach's hand on her lower back.

"Come on, I want to introduce you to someone."

She walked with him, cognizant of the possessiveness implied by his touch. A warning bell rang in her head, but she silenced it. His dominant nature wasn't going to be a problem—it wasn't as if she was his mate. He'd be gone as soon as he'd satisfied his curiosity about her. "Where's the picnic basket?" she asked, trying to ignore the stab of pain provoked by that last thought. After all, she had no desire to tie herself to a man—even a man as enticing as Zach.

"I gave it to one of the juveniles," Zach answered with a smile so bright, she couldn't help but smile in return. "Cory will stick it with the other food so everyone can grab what they want." He stopped beside an older woman with snow-white hair and a face that echoed his own so strongly, Annie knew they were related. Not only that, it was clear where Zach had inherited his sun-kissed skin and bones.

As he leaned forward to kiss the woman's cheek, she said, "Zach, my dear." Her eyes went to Annie, and they were as sharp as her body was toned. Given the way she stood, her supple strength, Annie guessed her to be a soldier, too. It wasn't surprising—changelings didn't really slow down until well into their eighth or ninth decade. "And who have you brought me?"

"Grandma, this is Annie," Zach said, his love for his grandmother a shining light in his eyes. It hit her right in the gut, making her wonder what it would be like to have that open and powerful love directed at her. "My grandmother, Cerise."

Cerise held out both hands, her smile so welcoming that Annie accepted the touch without hesitation. "Don't let this boy talk you into anything wicked," Cerise said. "He's been getting his own way since the day he first looked at his mother and batted those pretty eyelashes."

Annie felt her lips curve, but before she could answer, Zach was set upon by a pair of identical teenage girls. "Zach!" they screamed, wrapping their arms around him from either side. "We haven't seen you in ages!"

"You saw me three days ago." Laughing, he hugged them to his sides.

Sparkling eyes landed on Annie. "Ooooooh," one of them said, "you brought a giiiiiirrrrrrrrrrrl."

"Who is she?" her twin whispered, brushing aside a waterfall of sleek black hair. "Where did you meet? How long have you been dating?"

Cerise frowned. "Girls, manners!"

The girls dimpled. "Sorry, Grandma."

Zach looked at her. "Annie, meet my baby sisters, Silly and Giggly."

"Hey!" They both slapped his chest. "I'm Lissa, and that's Noelle," the one on the left said.

Annie was beginning to be able to tell them apart. They were both confident and cheerful, but Lissa had more mischief in her eyes, while Noelle's smile was wide enough to light up any room she entered. "Nice to meet you."

Cerise squeezed her hands before letting go. "Where are your sisters?" she asked the twins.

Annie felt her eyes widen. More sisters? Zach saw her look and began to laugh. "Four of them," he said. "*Four*. Jess—she's Bryan's mom—and Poppy, are older than these two brats."

"Aw, you know you love us, big brother." Lissa reached up to press a kiss to his jaw. "I'll go look for them. They'll want to meet your girl."

"Talk to you later, Annie." Wiggling her fingers, Noelle ran off with her twin.

Annie didn't know whether to laugh or shake her head in amazement. "Four younger sisters?"

He wrapped an arm around her shoulders and cuddled her to his side. "They're the reason for my gray hairs. See?" He dipped his head.

The dark silk of his hair made her want to stroke it. "You big liar. You don't have a single gray hair." Held against him, she'd never felt safer or more protected. Fear ignited. Okay, she thought, quashing the emotion, this relationship was becoming more important than she'd originally believed it would, but it wasn't as if she was going to do something stupid—like begin to rely on Zach.

Cerise laughed. "She's on to you, boyo. I bet she gets along with Jess like a house on fire."

"Speaking of Jess"—Annie frowned—"doesn't Bryan have an older brother? When did Jess get married? Mated," she corrected herself.

Cerise was the one who answered. "At twenty. She's thirty now, only a year younger than Zachary here. Her oldest is nine."

"Twenty's so young," she murmured.

"She found her mate early," Zach said, a shimmering joy in his tone, the love of a brother for his sister. "And that was that. She always wanted a big family, so the kids came soon afterward. She's happy." A simple statement, and yet it spoke of such love, such trust. Annie couldn't imagine taking that big a leap of faith, putting that much of herself into a man's hands.

"Yes, she's very happy," Cerise agreed. "But enough of family talk—why don't you two grab some food before the juveniles inhale it all. I swear, I don't know where it goes."

"Into the hollow leg every teenage boy possesses, of course." The voice was male and familiar.

"Lucas." Cerise hugged the tall man with green eyes, as Annie pegged him for the DarkRiver alpha. "Oh dear." Zach's grandmother drew back, her attention on something over Lucas's shoulder. "I think I need to go rescue a cub that's climbed a bit too high. And if that's not one of Tammy's boys, I'll eat my boot." She headed off in the direction of an ancient fir, from where Annie could hear the pleading strains of an adorable growl.

"Hello, Annie, isn't it?" Lucas held out a hand.

As she took it, she had the strangest sensation that everyone was watching her. "Good memory. You only met me once, at last year's Christmas pageant."

He grinned. "Let's just say I had some advance intel. So, how was the tour?"

"Perfect," Zach said, arm tightening around her. "But for some unfathomable reason, Annie's still deciding if she wants to date me."

"Zach!" She glared up at him.

He grinned and dropped a fast kiss on her lips. Blushing, she wondered if such public affection was normal within the pack. She got her answer a few seconds later as an exotically beautiful woman wrapped her arms around Lucas's neck from behind and pressed a kiss to his jaw. Her eyes, when they met Annie's, were the night sky of a cardinal Psy. White stars on black velvet.

"Hello, you must be Annie." Her voice was summer breezes and open fires, welcoming and gentle. "Lissa and Noelle," she explained, at Annie's surprised look. "They've been telling everyone they covet your jacket. They're planning to charm it off you before you leave. Be careful."

Annie couldn't do anything but smile in response to the warmth in that voice. "Thanks for the warning."

"Sascha," Zach said, "Annie made chocolate mud cake."

Sascha's face lit up like a child's. "Really?" She moved to grab Lucas's hand. "Come on, or the juveniles will eat it all. Talk to you later, Annie!"

Annie watched the pair leave and breathed out a sigh. "Your pack's . . . overwhelming."

"You'll get used to them." He rubbed the back of her neck. "They're just curious about you."

She felt another warning flicker in her mind, but then someone else was calling out Zach's name, and she was being introduced to more people, and then Zach was feeding her with the teasing smile of the cat flirting on his lips, and she forgot what it was that she'd worried about.

Chapter 7

They arrived at her apartment a few minutes after six. "I'll shower and change quickly," she told him as she unlocked the door and entered.

"Can I use your shower after?" He lifted up the suit bag he'd carried inside. "I got a packmate to drop by my house and bring this to the picnic. Want to make a good first impression on your folks."

Her stomach sank. "It probably won't make any difference."

"I told you, don't worry." Draping the suit bag over the back of her sofa, he prowled over. "Go, shower." It was a whisper that implied all sorts of sinful things. "I'll just sit out here and imagine the droplets racing over your skin, touching you . . . stroking you."

She felt her legs tremble. "Come in with me." It was the boldest invitation she'd ever made.

He smiled. "I plan to. But not today." He brushed his lips over hers. "When I shower with you, I don't want a time limit."

"Oh." Her mind bombarded her with images of the undoubtedly delicious things he'd do to her in the shower. "I should go . . ."

He rubbed a thumb over her bottom lip before shaking his head and pulling back. "Go, before I forget my good intentions. We'd never make it to the dinner then."

She hesitated.

He tapped her lightly on the bottom. "Don't even try it. I'm meeting your parents." So he could look them in the eye and let them know that regardless of what they thought of him, he was now in their daughter's life, and they had to deal with it. No more blind dates.

"Bossy." Annie shot him a scowl but went into the bedroom to grab her stuff.

She was going to be all hot and wet and naked soon.

"Christ." Shoving his hands through his hair, he tried to get the hard thrust of his cock to settle down. It refused. Especially since he could hear the rustle of cloth sliding over skin, of boots hitting tile, of lace being peeled off . . . or maybe that was his imagination.

But he definitely heard the shower come on. Groaning, he began to pace around the room, distracting himself by looking at Annie's things. Aside from books, she had several holoframes on the walls. Family photos, he guessed, noting her resemblance to the older woman in the central portrait. The man in the photo—her father, he assumed—was smiling genially, but there was something about him that struck the cat as distant.

The shower shut off.

"Shower's free!" came the call a few minutes later.

He gave her another couple of minutes to close herself in the bedroom, not sure he'd be able to resist if he saw her swathed in the tempting impermanence of an easily removable towel. When he entered the small, tiled enclosure at last, it was to find it steamy with the lavish scent of some feminine lotion. But the soap, he was glad to see, was nothing too girly. A man had to have standards, he thought, and programmed the shower to freezing.

It finally succeeded in cooling down his body.

Annie sat in Zach's car in her parents' drive and twisted her fingers in her lap. "I've never brought a man home," she blurted out. "It didn't seem worth the fuss."

"I'm flattered."

She frowned at him. "Don't tease me now." But she felt her nerves loosen a fraction. "Come on, we might as well get this over with." Opening the door, she stepped out.

They met at the front of the vehicle. "At least it's a nice night," she said.

Zach put an arm around her with the lazy grace of the leopard he was. "I like your dress," he murmured, playing his fingertips over her hip.

"Oh." Her nerves frayed again, for a different reason. She'd chosen the black crossover dress because it would give her mother nothing to complain about. But Zach's words made her realize it might actually qualify as sexy. "You don't think I'm not thin enough for it?"

"I'll tell you tonight . . . after I unwrap you." He made her sound like a present.

She felt her eyes widen, her pulse jump. "Behave."

"Do I still get to unwrap you?"

A moment of silence, the night sky cut with shards of glittering diamond.

"Yes." She wanted to dance with the wildness in him, wanted to feel what it was to be treated like a beautiful, sensual woman. But more, she wanted to lie with this man who'd already made a place for himself in her heart.

She knew she was about to break one of her most fundamental rules in deepening this relationship, in putting her heart on the line, but she also knew that if she didn't love Zach, she'd regret it for the rest of her life. Perhaps, she thought for the first time, perhaps her mother's choices hadn't been as simple as the child in Annie had always believed. Perhaps with that one man who mattered, there *was* no choice, no protecting yourself against the inevitable end of the dream. "Yes," she said again. "You get to unwrap me."

"Then I'll be on my best behavior." He pressed a kiss to her temple. "Let's go, Angel."

She was already used to the nickname. Strange as it was, it felt as if he'd been calling her that forever . . . as if it was *right*. Walking up to the door, she held that sense of rightness to her like a talisman. "Here we go." She pressed the doorbell.

Her mother opened it a couple of seconds later. Dressed in a severe black dress accented with a discreet string of pearls, her dark hair twisted into a sleek knot, Kimberly Kildaire looked what she was—a successful, sophisticated, professional. No one could've guessed at the deep vulnerability that Annie knew lay beneath the polished surface.

"Angelica." Her mother leaned forward to allow Annie to peck her on the cheek.

After drawing back, she said, "Mom, this is Zach Quinn."

Her mother's expression didn't change, but Annie knew that Kimberly would have noted everything about the man by her side, from his black suit, to his sleek silver belt buckle, to his crisp white shirt. Open at the collar, it looked both formal and relaxed. She'd about swallowed her tongue when she'd walked out of the bedroom and seen him waiting for her by the door. Zach wild was enough to blow her mind, but Zach playing at being tame . . . wow.

"Mr. Quinn," her mother now said, holding out her hand—

Professor Kildaire might not think particularly highly of changelings, but no one would ever criticize her manners.

"Mrs. Kildaire."

Releasing his hand, Kimberly stepped back. "Do come in." She led them through the hallway and into the sunken living room off to the right.

There were far more people mingling below than Annie had expected. "I thought this was supposed to be a small dinner?"

Her mother's smile did nothing to warm the cool disapproval in her eyes. "I invited some university people. I thought your . . . friend would feel more comfortable if it wasn't just family."

It was a very subtle insult. Professor Markson was worthy of a family dinner. Zach wasn't. Temper spiked, not so much at the slight against Zach—he was tough enough to take care of himself—but because Annie couldn't believe her mother would try to sabotage her and Zach's relationship with such calculated rudeness.

But before she could say something she might not have been able to take back, Zach squeezed her hip lightly, and said, "I'm honored you went to so much trouble to put me at ease." His voice was smooth whiskey and effortless warmth. "I know how close Annie is to you, so I'm delighted by the welcome."

Annie saw her mother's expression falter for a second, but Kimberly Kildaire was nothing if not quick on her feet. "Of course. Come, I'll introduce you." She led them into the knot of curious people below.

Caroline was the first to come over. Though she told herself not to, Annie found herself tensing up as she waited to see Zach's reaction to her cousin. Caro was one of her favorite people in the world. She was also quite impossibly stunning. Annie had never before been jealous of the way her cousin drew men to her like moths to a flame—no man had ever mattered enough. But Zach did.

She saw him smile at Caroline's exuberant welcome . . . but it was the same kind of smile as he'd shared with his sisters. "Congratulations on your baby," he said, his voice gentle.

Caroline beamed. "Can you tell? I'm not showing yet. I can't wait to get big and Madonna-like! Oh, and I want the glow everyone talks about—I so want the glow!"

Zach's lips quirked. "I don't think you need to worry. You already glow."

Caroline laughed. "You're a charmer, aren't you?" She looked to Annie. "I like him, Annie. He'll give you beautiful babies."

"Caro!" Annie didn't know whether to blush or thank her cousin for breaking the ice so completely. Several people laughed, and Zach sent her a teasing smile, his eyes heating in a way they hadn't for Caro.

"How did you know?" her mother asked pointedly. "Caroline is right—she's barely showing. Even most women don't notice."

"Her scent, Mrs. Kildaire," Zach replied with open candor. "Changelings always know when a woman has a life within her."

"A breach of privacy, wouldn't you say?" Kimberly raised an eyebrow.

Zach shrugged. "It's simply another sense. Ours just happens to be keener in that area—no different from an M-Psy being able to see inside the body, or you yourself being able to tell her condition because you know the subtle physical signs."

Annie bit the inside of her cheek to keep from interfering. Caro took the chance to whisper, "Oh, he's good. Wherever did you find Mr. Scrumptious?"

Annie threw her a quelling look. "Where's Aman?"

"My darling husband is driving back from a meeting in Tahoe. He'll probably make it in time for dessert." She smiled. "I know what *you're* having for dessert."

Annie felt Zach's hand move on her waist. It was obvious he'd heard Caro's outrageous prediction, and that he liked the idea. However, when she looked up, it was to find his attention not on her, but on someone else—a stranger her mother had just waved over.

"This is Professor Jeremy Markson," she was saying. "This is Annie's . . . friend, Zach Quinn."

Given that her own temper was close to igniting, Annie figured Zach would blow this time—he'd been blunt in saying he didn't share. But, to her surprise, he remained completely relaxed.

"Markson." Zach inclined his head in masculine acknowledgment. "What's your field, professor?"

"Molecular physics," Markson said. "It's a fascinating subject. Do you know anything about it?"

Arrogant twerp, Annie thought. "No, I don't, Professor," she said before Zach could respond. "Perhaps you'd care to enlighten me."

The professor blinked, as if he hadn't expected her to speak. "Well, I—"

"Tell them about your latest project," her mother encouraged, shooting daggers at Annie.

Markson nodded, and off he went. Annie's eyes began to glaze over after the first few minutes. "That's so interesting," she said, when he paused for breath. "Do you work with my father?"

"Yes." He beamed.

"Where *is* Dad?" Annie asked, deliberately changing the focus of the conversation.

Her mother waved a hand. "You know your father. He's probably lost in research." The words were light, but Annie heard the hurt Kimberly had never quite stopped feeling. "He promised he'd try to be here by the time dinner was served."

Which meant, Annie knew, that they'd be lucky if they saw him tonight. "What's on the menu?" she asked with a smile, hating that bruised pain in her mother's eyes.

Kimberly brightened. "I made your favorite vegetable dish for an entrée." Her words were sincere, her love open. "Don't start, Caro," she said, when Caroline opened her mouth. "I made your favorite pie, too."

"That's why you're my bestest aunt."

Thankfully, the conversation stayed light and easy from then on. They were about to move into the dining room when wonder of wonders, her father walked in. Erik Kildaire was dressed in the rumpled clothing of a man for whom looks mattered little, but he seemed to be with them today, rather than in his head.

Her mother's face lit up from within, and Annie smiled. "It's good to see you, Dad," she said, accepting her father's enthusiastic kiss on the cheek. Love swelled in her heart, but it was a love that had learned to be cautious. She'd never had the tangled relationship with her father that she had with her mother, but that was probably because he'd never been around to argue with her. A different kind of hurt altogether.

"And who's this?" he asked, looking Zach up and down while sliding one arm around her mother's waist.

Annie made the introductions, but her father's reaction was not what she'd expected.

"Zach Quinn," he muttered. "That's familiar. Zach Quinn. Zach—" The fog cleared. "The same Zachary Quinn who published a study on the wildcat population of Yosemite last year?"

Beside her, Zach nodded. "I'm surprised you recognized my name."

"Not my department," her father acknowledged, "but my good friend Ted—Professor Ingram, was very excited by it. Said it was the best doctoral thesis he'd seen his entire tenure."

Zach had a *Ph.D.*?

Annie could've kicked him for keeping that from her, especially when her mother shot her a look of accusation. Thankfully, her dad said something at that moment and drew her mom away, leaving

Zach and Annie alone for the first time since their arrival. She raised an eyebrow. "Keeping secrets?"

He had the grace to look a little sheepish. "To be honest, I didn't think anyone would realize or even care. You told me they were math and physics people."

"My father knows everything about everyone. And a Ph.D. is a Ph.D.." She rapped a fist gently against his chest. "If you'd told me you had one, I wouldn't have worried so much about my mother's reaction—even she can't argue against a doctorate."

"Your mother's not the one whose opinion I care about. Does the Ph.D. matter to you, Annie?" The look in his eyes was guarded.

The hint of unfamiliar vulnerability caught her unawares. "Zach, if degrees mattered to me," she said honestly, "I'd have married the triple-Ph.D.'d physicist my mother picked out for me when I was twenty-two. Or the MD with more letters after his name than the alphabet. Or the multipublished grand pooh-bah who stared at nothing but my breasts for the entire meal."

His smile creased his cheeks. "The man had excellent taste."

"Stop making me blush." But she wasn't, not any longer—somehow, Zach Quinn had earned the trust of her vulnerable feminine heart.

It startled her, made her afraid.

But before the dark emotion could grow, Zach bent to brush his lips gently over hers, acting in the way of changelings, not caring that they had an audience. When he drew away, she leaned into him, fear—if not forgotten—then at least temporarily caged.

Chapter 8

Two and a half hours later, Zach found himself on the balcony sipping coffee while Annie stood inside, chatting with her cousin. God, but she was beautiful to him—all he wanted was to take her home, hold her safe, and keep her just for himself.

It was an unalterable part of him, this possessiveness, coming from the cat and man both. But no matter his primitive instincts, he wouldn't do that to Annie, wouldn't contain her that way. Still, he needed to mark her—to take her until his scent was embedded so deep into her skin, no one would dare question his right to her. An animal desire. Yet often, the animal's heart was far more pure, far more honest, than the thinking man's.

"Mr. Quinn."

He glanced at Kimberly Kildaire. "Please call me Zach."

"Zach." A regal nod. "Let me get straight to the point—from the instant Angelica told me about you, I was prepared to dislike you."

"I guessed."

"I've changed my mind."

Zach raised an eyebrow. "The Ph.D.?"

"No. In certain departments, any monkey can get a Ph.D." It was a gauntlet.

He picked it up. "Good thing I'm a leopard, then."

Her lips threatened to smile. "I've always pushed Annie toward men who are more cerebral than physical."

Zach waited with a predator's quiet patience.

"It was a conscious choice," Kimberly said without apology, "my way of ensuring she would never again be put in harm's way. I even rejected a brilliant engineer as a possible match because he frequently goes off to work on projects in remote locations. His humanity mattered less than the danger he might've exposed Annie to."

Her eyes met his. "To be quite blunt, changelings take that possible danger to the nth degree. Your very nature is one filled with the violence of the wild."

He was floored by her candor. "You're very aware."

"I know others might say I'm intellectualizing away prejudice, but I'm no bigot." She held his gaze with a strength he suspected had been honed by surviving a lifetime of hurt. "I simply want my daughter safe. I saw her almost die once—it's not something I want to witness ever again."

His cat detected no lies in her. "I'll keep her safe."

"I have a feeling you will. It seems I made a critical error—in thinking about how you could lead her into danger, I forgot that predatory changelings are also known for their willingness to protect to the death." Her eyes—Annie's eyes—clashed with his. "But that's not why I've decided for you."

"Oh?"

"It's because of the way you look at her, Zach. As if she's your sunshine." Her voice caught. "I want that for my daughter. Don't you ever stop looking at her that way."

Zach reached out and touched her lightly on the arm, sensing how very brittle her composure was at that moment. "I give you my promise."

A sharp nod. "Excuse me, I should go mingle."

As she walked away, Zach blew out a slow breath. It was becoming clear to him that he'd have a far harder road to travel with Annie than he'd initially thought. She'd grown up watching her mother love a man who, quite bluntly, didn't love her the same way. After only one meeting, Zach knew that Erik Kildaire was devoted to his work, while Kimberly was devoted to him. The insouciance with which Erik had crushed his wife's heart an hour ago—bussing her on the cheek and telling her he had something important to do at the lab—had angered Zach enough that he'd had to fight the urge to say something.

Annie would never have to worry about that kind of hurt with him. Once the cat decided on a woman, it didn't flinch. Devotion was almost obsession with those of his kind, and he was at peace with that. But words wouldn't convince Annie—she'd have to be stroked into trusting him, into relying on him. Because not only was she wary of loving, she'd become almost mutinously independent in her desire to avoid opening herself up to pain.

I like living alone. I intend to keep it that way.

That, he thought, the cat rising to a hunting crouch, was just too damn bad. But even as the predator in him prepared for the hunt, a vicious vulnerability grew in his heart. He *needed* Annie's trust, needed the surety of knowing she'd come to him no matter what. If she didn't . . . No, he thought, jaw setting, that simply wasn't an option. Annie was his. End of story.

"What magic did you do with my mother?" Annie asked, letting them into her apartment.

"That's my secret." He closed the door and prowled along behind her.

Her heart went into hyperdrive.

She was going to go to bed with him, with this man she'd met only yesterday. But it felt as if they'd never been strangers, it was so very easy being with him.

Careful, Annie.

Fear rose up in an insidious wave, showing her image after image of Kimberly's face as she watched Erik walk away. Was that what awaited her? Did the question matter now that she'd decided to take the chance and weather the hurt when it came?

"Hey." Zach brought her to a halt, nuzzling at her neck from behind as his hands closed over her hips. "Stop thinking so hard."

"I can't help it," she whispered. "I'm not . . ." She bit her lip, trying to think of a way to say this without betraying how incredibly important he'd become to her in such a short time.

"You're not the kind to kiss and walk away as if it meant nothing," he said, running his lips lightly over her skin, inducing a shiver. "Neither am I. This is no one-night stand."

"Changelings live by different rules."

He licked at her, and she felt her purse slip from her hand to drop to the floor. "Zach." A whisper, perhaps a plea.

He hugged her tighter against him. "We might be more tactile than humans, but it's nothing casual. It's about friendship, about pleasure, about trust."

"It sounds wonderful."

"It is." Another kiss pressed to the sensitive skin of her neck. "Trust me, Annie. I won't hurt you."

At that moment, she almost believed him. Closing her hands over his, she let her body melt into the hard masculine heat of his. "You make me feel beautiful."

"You're more than beautiful," he whispered, "you're sexier than sin."

"You're complaining?" She dropped her hands as he moved his to the side of her dress and tugged at the tie that held it up.

The tie came loose. "I didn't like the way Markson was undressing you with his eyes."

"He was not." Feeling the dress fall open at the front, she shifted so he could pull the tie out of the inner loop. He did . . . and the fabric dropped.

"Mmm." It was a murmur of utter pleasure as he began to pull the dress down over her arms. "I'm the only one allowed to undress you"—a kiss on her bare shoulder—"to pet you."

Pet.

The word reminded her that he wasn't human, wasn't anything tame. "You're very possessive." Air hit her back, her breasts. Then the dress was falling over her fingertips to pool on the floor.

Behind her, he made a sound strikingly close to a growl, one hand caressing the curve of her waist. "You already knew that, Annie."

Of course she had. A predatory changeling male, no matter how playful, had possessiveness built into his soul. For as long as she kept his interest, he would demand everything from her. She knew she'd give him what he wanted . . . everything but her faith. That, she thought, she no longer had to give. Her parents' marriage had shattered her belief in forever a long time ago. Sadness might've beckoned, but then Zach slid his hand up to lie flat over her stomach, big, hot, and darkly possessive, and her thoughts fractured. "Zach?"

"Shh. I'm looking."

The husky statement made her body clench inside, her thighs tremble. She was wearing black lace . . . for him.

"*Annie.*" He groaned and reached up to unhook her bra. "I want to see."

An instant later, she found herself standing there in nothing but her panties and a pair of strappy sandals. She was in no way ready for the boldness with which he moved to cup her breast. "Oh!" She trembled at the touch, at the erotic sight of his hand on her. His skin was tanned, rawly masculine against her creamy flesh. When he squeezed, it was all she could do not to collapse.

"You're so pretty, Annie"—he spread the fingers of his other hand on her stomach—"I could lap you right up."

Completely in his thrall, she raised her hand to reach back and touch his face. He nipped at her with his teeth, chuckling when she jumped. "I want to be in bed. This is going to take some time."

Her brain turned to mush right then and there, and when he shifted to scoop her into his arms, she was so startled, she squeaked and grabbed on to his neck. "I'm too heavy, Zach. Put me down."

"Questioning my muscles?" A wicked smile. "Kiss me."

Unable to resist, she obeyed, not stopping until he laid her down on the bed and rose. His eyes glittered the green-gold of the cat, hunger in every stark line of his face. She watched, heart in her throat, as he stripped off his jacket, then removed his shirt. He was built sleek and powerful, a predator in human form.

She sighed in unashamed pleasure and saw his eyes gleam as he bent down to get rid of his shoes and socks. "Now yours," he said, moving to the bottom of the bed and tugging off her sandals one by one, following each removal with a long, slow look up her body.

By the time he finally got on the bed beside her, she was so aroused that she rose to claim a kiss of her own. When he nipped at her lips as he seemed to like doing, she nipped back. He raised his head, his hand closing possessively over her breast. "Do that again."

Eyes wide, she did. He purred into her mouth. She broke the kiss to stare at him. "What was that?"

A feline smile. "Nothing." He reclaimed her lips, and a second later she felt that vibration again, that sign that he was something other, changeling to her human. It made her shudder with the need to crush her breasts against him.

"You purr," she accused when they parted.

"So do you." Coming over her, he began to kiss his way down the line of her neck. He seemed to get distracted between the curves of her breasts, leaving her to clutch at the sheets in unadulterated pleasure as he sucked and kissed. When teeth became involved, she cried out, feeling her body tighten into a fist so tight, a single touch would send her over.

He blew his breath deliberately across one wet nipple.

She shattered, and the pleasure was a tidal wave that demanded everything she had. When she finally resurfaced, Zach had recommenced his sensual exploration of her body, the dark strands of his hair sweeping over her like a thousand stroking fingers. She ran her hands through the rough silk of it, feeling sated and content. And happy.

He looked up, a lazy smile in his eyes. "Yes?"

"Come kiss me." She'd never imagined she would one day make such a brazen demand, but Zach listened to her. Even if he didn't always give her what she wanted.

He shook his head. "After."

"After what?"

His answer was to keep on kissing her, going steadily lower. When his lips pressed over black lace, she trembled. He did it again. Then she felt the whisper of something on her outer thighs—glancing down, she saw her panties being thrown off the side of the bed. "How?"

The eyes that met hers were wild, exotic. "I used a claw to cut them off."

"Oh." She looked at his human hand. "Like a very small shift?"

"Hmm." He wasn't paying attention, more concerned with pushing apart her thighs and raising her legs to put them over his shoulders. She'd never felt so exposed, so vulnerable. She waited, stomach tight.

But nothing could've prepared her for the ecstasy of his touch. Zach liked to take his time—he pushed her to insanity over and over. It might've terrified her except that he made no effort to hide his own arousal, murmuring his pleasure with every slow lick. "Sweet, pretty, Annie," he said. "My Annie."

She discovered she was raising her body to his mouth, moving with a sensual bliss that was scandalous in its eroticism. He liked it. She knew, because he told her so, his voice close to a growl.

"I am definitely going to bite," he whispered. And then he did.

By the time she could think again, he was getting off the bed. She exhaled in pleasure as he stripped off to reveal a body hard with arousal.

"Look what you do to me," he whispered, moving to kneel between her legs. He stroked his hands under her thighs. "Come here."

She swallowed at what he was asking, knowing it had far more to do with trust than sex. But she couldn't refuse, had the strangest feeling that any hint of rejection from her would wound him incredibly deeply. Rising, she held on to his shoulders and let him support her bottom as her body brushed over the tip of his erection. "Zach," she whispered, drowning in the intimacy of his eyes, "you undo me."

His eyes flickered from cat back to human. "Hold on to me, baby. I won't let go."

Breath coming in jagged bursts, she lowered herself onto him. He stretched her to the limit. But she wanted him inside her, wanted to possess him as absolutely as he'd possessed her. She drove down and shuddered. "It's too much." The angle was deep, the penetration intense.

He kissed her. "We'll practice until you get used to it." It was a husky promise as he laid her back down, bracing his body over hers using his hands.

"How much practice?" She wrapped her legs around the lean beauty of his hips, no longer shy with this man who treated her as if she was a goddess.

He groaned, pulled out a little, then thrust, as if he couldn't help himself. "Lots." Though sweat-damp hair hung over his forehead, and sexual need was an inferno in his eyes, he waited to give her time to adjust.

She felt a violent tenderness grab hold of her heart. He was, quite simply, *wonderful.* Raising her arms, she pulled him down and kissed him, telling him without words that it was okay to let go.

He groaned. And began to move.

Annie looked down at the male sprawled by her side the next morning and felt her body sigh. He was fast asleep and gilded dark gold by the sunlight sneaking in through the blinds. He'd kept her up half the night, loving her so thoroughly that she felt possessed. Taken. Branded.

Refusing to surrender to panic, to give him up to protect herself, she reached out to trace the tattoo she'd discovered on his back sometime during the night.

It linked to the one on his biceps, which was actually the stylized tail of a dragon. That dragon's front claws rested on his left shoulder, the mythical creature's sinuous body stretching across his back. It was a stunning design . . . and another example of the wildness in him.

That wildness brought her alive, made joy sear her blood.

It also frightened her—the depth of what she felt. Finally, she truly understood why her mother had stayed with her father all these years. Her mind filled with the echo of Kimberly's voice from a rainy night more than fifteen years ago.

Your father used to call me his heaven.

That time had passed long ago, as would Zach's interest in her. Yet even after the spark faded, Annie now knew that the temptation to stay . . . to hope for another moment when he might look at her as he once used to, would be overwhelming. It was that futile hope that kept her mother tied to her father, but, though she understood it, it wasn't a path Annie would ever allow herself to follow.

It would break her heart to see Zach look at her with disinterest in his eyes. She'd leave before that, at the first insidious signs of fading passion. It was bound to happen . . . but not yet, she prayed. *Please not yet.* Heart tight with a mixture of joy and pain, she lay down beside him, content to trail her fingertips over his tattoo and watch him sleep.

That was when she noticed his lips were curved.

"Zach." A whisper.

Cat eyes looking into hers. "Mmm?"

"How long have you been awake?"

Chapter 9

"Long enough to enjoy you petting me." Unrepentant mischief in his eyes. And desire. The desire was still there.

Relief made her melt from the inside out. "You're such a cat."

"Want to see?" he asked.

"See what?"

"My cat."

Her eyes went wide. "Really?"

He yawned, every inch the indolent feline. "Hmm." Without warning, color shimmered all around him, sparkles of light and shadow, beauty and eternity.

She held her breath until it ended. The leopard lying on her bed looked at her with familiar eyes. Swallowing at her proximity to such a dangerous creature, she struggled up into a sitting position, sheet held to her breasts. The temptation to touch was blinding. She lifted a hesitant hand—it was one thing to know intellectually that this was Zach, quite another to believe it.

When she didn't touch, the leopard raised its head to butt at her hand. Shuddering, she gave in to temptation and stroked him. He relaxed, closing his eyes in bliss. It made her awe morph into delight. "I think I just got conned." But stroking him, adoring him, was no hardship.

When the shimmer came again, she went utterly still. A few moments later, her hand lay on the muscular back of a man so sexy, he made her heart trip simply looking at him.

"So?" he asked.

She snuggled up to him, positioning her body so that they lay face-to-face, her hand now on his shoulder. "You're gorgeous, and you know that."

For once, he didn't smile. "Is it too much to handle?"

"No." She frowned. "Did I give that impression?"

"Just checking." She got a smile this time, a slow, lazy thing that tugged at things low and deep in her. "Some women like the idea of being with a changeling but find the reality harder to accept."

"Some women?" A prickly flare of jealousy.

His smile widened. "Not that I would know."

She felt her lips twitch. "Of course not, Mr. Innocent."

"Hey, you're the one who led me off the straight and narrow." He ran his hand down to her bottom in a possessive caress. "I seem to recall you demanding I do 'the licking thing' one more time."

Her body ignited to sensual life. Deciding to fight fire with fire, she said, "You never gave me my winnings yesterday."

Sensual mischief in his eyes. "Yes, I did. With interest. And then again."

"Cat." Wrapping her arms around him, she rubbed her nose affectionately against his. It felt natural, easy. He made a sound of contentment and shifted until she was under him, skin-to-skin contact all over. It was sexual, but it was also something more. Touch for the sake of touch, cuddling because it felt good.

"How long does the affection last?" she asked half-seriously. Making love with him was so stunningly beautiful, but this kind of simple contact . . . it was somehow deeper, going beyond pleasure and into a kind of trust that left her breathless.

Zach kissed her cheek, her jaw, her chin. "Always. *Not* touching is abnormal for us."

She remembered the easy affection she'd witnessed at the picnic. "I'm guessing that doesn't apply to strangers."

"No."

"That's good," she said, swallowing an unexpected pulse of hurt at the idea of being outside the circle of his pack. If she'd been his mate— She cut off that thought at once, more than a little panicked at the idea of being locked into a relationship that offered no escape . . . no matter if the love died. "I'm not easy with people I don't know well," she said to cover the sudden burst of fear.

"You're in charge of skin privileges, baby." He traced circles on her shoulder. "The pack will pick up the cues."

" 'Skin privileges'?"

"The right to touch." He kissed the corner of her mouth.

She wondered if she'd ever get enough of this play. "I guess you have total skin privileges then."

A sound of smug male pleasure. It made her laugh, he was so shameless about it. And that was when she knew. She was too much her mother's daughter. She'd love only once. And she'd love forever.

Zach was it.

For him, she'd break every rule, allow him into her home, into her very soul. For him, she'd jump into the abyss and worry about the bruises later. Because sometimes, there were no choices.

"Hey." His voice was a husky murmur. "What's the matter, Angel?"

She shook her head, glad that he wasn't Psy, that he couldn't read her mind. "Love me, Zach."

"Always."

But she knew he hadn't understood what she'd asked, hadn't promised what she needed. It didn't matter. He was hers, if only for now, and she would treasure every moment of that joy. The pain could wait until after he was gone.

Chapter 10

A month after he'd first met Annie, Zach sat on one of the car-sized boulders scattered around Yosemite and wondered what the hell he was doing wrong. He'd spent every night since the day of the picnic with her. She was fire in his arms, warm, beautiful, and loving . . . but she continued to withhold a part of herself.

Most men wouldn't have noticed. But he wasn't most men. Every time she waved off his offer to help her in some way, every time she pulled her independence around her like a shield, he noticed. It wounded the cat, confused the man. "Mercy, I can hear you."

A tall redhead jumped down from a branch a few feet in front of him. "Only because I let you."

He snorted. "You were making enough noise for a herd of elephants." He threw the sentinel a spare bottle of water.

"I didn't want to bruise your masculine ego by sneaking up,"

Mercy said, perching on a boulder opposite him. "Not when you already looked so pathetic."

"Gee, so thoughtful of you."

"I can be a right peach." She drank some water. "Let me guess—you've mated with the little teacher?"

He raised an eyebrow.

"Oh, puhleese," Mercy drawled. "As if you'd bring anyone but your mate to the Pack Circle."

"She's fighting the bond," he found himself saying.

"Why?"

"You're the female. You tell me."

"Hmm." Mercy capped the bottle and tapped it against her leg. "Did she say why?"

He stared at her.

Mercy rolled her eyes. "You did *tell* her that she's your mate, didn't you?"

"She's a bit resistant to the idea of commitment." That resistance frustrated the hell out of him, but he was trying to be patient. Not only did he care about her happiness, he wanted her to trust him enough to make the choice—even though there was only one answer he'd accept. "I don't think she'd react well to the whole 'till death *really* does us part' bit."

"So you're making the choice for her?" She raised an eyebrow. "Arrogant."

Anger flared. "I want to give her time to become comfortable with me."

"Is it working?"

"I thought so, but the bond hasn't snapped into being." The mating bond was an instinctive thing, but the female usually had to accept it in some way for it to go from possibility to truth. "It's tearing me up, Mercy." The leopard was lost, hurt. What was wrong with him that Annie didn't want him?

"Talk to her, you idiot." Mercy shook her head. "Has it crossed your little male mind that maybe she's protecting herself in case you decide to indulge in some hot sex, then flick her off?"

He growled. "She knows I'd never do that. It's about the commitment—she's scared of trusting someone with her heart." He couldn't blame her, not after what he'd seen of her parents' marriage.

"Correct me if I'm wrong," Mercy said, "but haven't you two been joined at the hip for the past month? Pack grapevine says you've all but moved into her place."

"Yeah, so?"

"Geez, Zach, I thought you were smart." Trapping the bottle between her knees, she raised her hands to redo her ponytail. "Sounds to me like she's already committed to you."

She'd given him a key to her apartment, to the place that was her bolt-hole. His heart slammed against his ribs. No, he thought, he couldn't have made that big a mistake. "But the bond—"

"Okay," Mercy interrupted. "Maybe you're right, and your Annie's going to freak about the mating, but let's say your amazing Psy mind-reading abilities are wrong—"

He growled.

"—and she's ready to risk everything for you. What would keep her from taking the final step?" She raised an eyebrow. "You know the rep we have. Humans tend to think of leopard changelings as affectionate but casual."

"That's not it," he insisted. "I told her this was serious right at the start."

"Let me share a secret with you, Zach. Men have been telling women things for centuries. Then they've been breaking our hearts."

Zach's mind filled with the memory of Kimberly Kildaire's

shattered face as Erik Kildaire walked away. Promises, he thought, lots and lots of broken promises.

"Only way," Mercy continued, "for you to gain her trust, might be to forget the pride that seems to come embedded in the Y chromosome. You ready to wear your heart on your sleeve and hope she doesn't crush the life out of it?"

He met her gaze. "You got a streak of mean in you, Mercy."

"Thank you very much." Finishing off the water, she threw him the bottle. "I'd better head off—have to meet Lucas."

He watched her climb back up into the trees, her words beating at him. Had he really been that much of an idiot, thinking he knew what was going on in Annie's head while being so very wrong? More importantly, was he willing to swallow his need for dominance, for control, and put the most important decision of his life into her hands? What if she rejected him? The pain of the thought was paralyzing.

Annie finished putting away her things with eager hands. It was five on Friday, which meant she had the entire weekend to spend with Zach. He'd promised to show her some of the secret treasures of his forest, and she couldn't wait. Of course, she thought with a smile, even if he'd told her he wanted to watch the entertainment network all weekend, she'd have had the same reaction. She flat out adored being with him, wicked teasing and all. Especially since she'd gotten pretty good at teasing him back.

"Hey, Teach."

"Zach!" She walked over to hug him. "What're you doing here?"

His expression was solemn. "I need to talk to you."

Her stomach knotted. "Oh." She stepped back, trying to appear calm.

"Mercy was right," he said.

Annie knew who Mercy was, having met the sentinel at the picnic. "About what?"

"You're waiting for me to leave you."

The world fell out from under her feet. She trembled, unable to move, as he closed the door and walked to her. "I will never leave you, Annie." Cupping her cheeks in his hands, he bent so his forehead pressed against hers. "Not unless you ask me to." He frowned. "Actually, I won't leave you then, either. Just so you know."

"Wh-what?"

"You're my mate," he said simply. "You're in my blood, in my heart, in my soul. To walk away from you would cut me to pieces."

The room spun around her. "I need to sit down."

He let her go, let her lean against her desk.

"Mate?" she whispered.

"Yes." His face grew bleak. "It's a lifetime commitment. Mercy was right about one thing, but I'm right about this—you're not too keen on that, are you?"

She didn't answer his question, her mind spinning. "Are you sure that I'm . . . ?"

"Baby, I was sure the first day we met. You fit me."

It brought tears to her ears, because he fit her, too. Perfectly. "Zach, I . . . ." She blinked, trying to think past the rushing thunder of emotion. "I never thought I'd marry," she admitted. "But it's not the commitment I have a problem with. It's what comes after." A confession made in a voice that threatened to break. "It's this cold terror that the promise, the love, will one day turn into a trap."

"I know."

"She still waits," Annie found herself saying. "For a Valentine, or a birthday present, or just a loving word. *She still waits.*"

"Oh, sweetheart." He tried to come closer, but she held up her hand, fighting to think, to understand.

"I could survive you leaving me," she said, "but I couldn't survive you stopping to 'see' me." And the mating bond would leave her with no way out. It truly was forever.

"That's something you never have to fear," Zach said, the declaration resolute. "It's not possible for mates to ignore each other."

"But . . ."

"No buts," he said, slashing out a hand. "I will never stop seeing you, never stop loving you. Mates *can't* shut each other out."

Part of her wanted to grab that promise and never let go. But another part of her, the part that had been trapped first by injury, then a mother's fear, was hesitant. Was she ready to take this chance on the faith of a man's promise? Was she ready to give up the freedom she'd fought a lifetime to attain? "I'm so afraid, Zach."

"Ah, Annie. Don't you know? My cat is devoted to you. If you asked me to crawl, I'd crawl."

It shattered her, the way he'd just ripped open his heart and laid it at her feet. Trembling, she placed two fingers against his lips. "I would never ask that."

"Neither would I." His lips moved against her touch. "Trust me."

There it was, the crux of it. She adored him, loved him beyond reason, but trust . . . trust was a harder thing. Then she looked into that proud face, into the wild heart of the leopard within, and knew there could be only one answer. She refused to let fear cheat her out of the promise of glory.

"I do," she said, cutting the last safety rope that had held her suspended above the fathomless depths of the abyss. "I trust you more than I've ever trusted anyone." Something tightened in her chest at that second and then snapped, leaving her breathless. She clung instinctively to Zach, and he held her tight, burying his face in the curve of her neck. When she could breathe again, she tangled her fingers gently in his hair. "Zach?"

He shuddered. "God, I was so scared you were going to say no."

She felt it then—his terror, his love, his devotion. It was as if she had a direct line to his soul. The beauty of it staggered. "Oh my God." There was no way this bond would ever let either of them ignore each other. "Zach, I adore you." She could finally admit that, needed to admit it, needed to tell him that he wasn't alone.

"I know." He squeezed her even as a wave of love flavored with the primal fury of the cat came down the bond between them. "I can feel you inside me."

So could she, she thought in mute wonder, so could she.

A week later, Annie sat down in Zach's lap, blocking his view of the football game. He reached up to kiss her. "Want to play, Teach?"

She always wanted to play with him. But they had things to discuss. "No, this is business."

He turned off the game. "So?"

"So we have to have a wedding."

"We're mated." A growl poured out of his mouth. "Why the hell do we need to have a wedding? Those things drive everyone crazy—last year, I saw a grown man cry during the buildup."

Once, she would've wondered how on earth changeling women dared stand up to their mates when the men got all growly. Now she knew—just like her, those women knew that heaven might fall and the earth might crumble, but their mates would never hurt them. "Didn't you say we were going to have a mating ceremony?"

"It's not really a ceremony." He scowled. "More a celebration of our being together."

She couldn't help it. She reached out to stroke her fingers through his hair. "It's getting stronger," she said.

"It'll keep doing that." His scowl turned into a smile that hit her right in the heart. "Even when we're a hundred and twenty, I'll still want to crawl all over you."

"Zach, you're a menace." And she loved him for it. Was starting to truly see what she'd gotten when she accepted the mating. It was a powerful, almost vicious need, but it was also a bond of the deepest, most unflinching love. Even when he wasn't with her, she felt him loving her deep inside. "We need to have a wedding," she said, coaxing him with a slow kiss, "because my parents need to see me married, and Caro's already picked out a matron of honor dress." Then she dealt what she knew would be the deathblow to any further objections. "Their happiness is important to me."

He blew out a breath. "Fine. When?"

"I was thinking spring for both ceremonies."

"That's a while away." He slid his hands under her sweater, touching skin. "We could do it at Christmas. A present for both of us."

"No," she said, stroking his nape with her fingertips. "It has to be spring. I want everything alive and growing." As she felt she was growing, opening, becoming. "And I already have my present."

Eyes the color of the deepest ocean gleamed with feline curiosity. "Yeah?"

"A long time ago, during the Christmas I lay in hospital," she told him, retrieving a memory that had once been painful, but was now full of wonder, "I wished for someone who would be mine, someone I could play with and share all my secrets." Never could she have imagined the astonishing final outcome of that long-ago wish.

He moved his hands down to close over her thighs. "Are you calling me your gift?"

"Yes." She smiled. "How do you feel about that?"

"Like it's my turn to be unwrapped." He nibbled at her mouth. "Do it slow."

Her laughter mingled with his and the sound felt like starlight on her skin, like the promise of forever . . . like a lick of "majick."

Christmas Bree

ERIN McCARTHY

Chapter 1

"The love of my life is not going to wear a pink shirt." Bree Murphy looked in disbelief at her little sister Abigail, who was waving what remained of the tarot deck in her hand with total confidence.

"It's right here in the cards, Bree." Abby tapped the Empress card lying on the kitchen table.

Bree fought the urge to roll her eyes. Teaching Abby the tarot had been her own idea, apparently a stupid one. Abby couldn't divine her way out of a paper bag if suggesting Bree would date a man in pastels was any indication. It wasn't going to happen. Ever. Besides, the Empress was an indicator of her own destiny, her own strength, not about a man.

"No men in pink. I like men in black who read poetry. You know my type."

"Your type usually looks like they need a flea dip," Bree's older sister Charlotte commented.

That was a total exaggeration. "Hey, no one I have ever dated is unclean. Give me some credit. But being empathic makes me sympathetic. I sense when men need my support and emotional counseling, and I can't help but respond."

"That's actually kind of creepy," Abby said, her lip curling back. "Who wants a guy who's that needy?"

Hey, Bree knew it was a bad pattern. She could admit that. That was why she had stayed away from men for the last two years, which suddenly seemed like an incredibly long time. A long, celibate, lonely time. But she did not need her eighteen-year-old sister passing judgment. "And you're the expert on men, how?"

"I have a boyfriend," Abby said, tossing back her dark hair.

Now Bree did let loose with an eye roll. "Whatever." Bree didn't think Abby's boyfriend was any sort of model of male attentiveness, but there was no point in arguing. "But seriously, no men in pink shirts."

"He does something corporate," Abby added, as if she hadn't heard a word of protest. "I see him in an office."

That got Bree's attention. Not because she would ever date someone corporate, because she so wouldn't, but because Bree was speaking with such total confidence, and there was nothing in the tarot spread in front of her that should be giving her a clear visual of any man, let alone a candidate for the corner office. "Abby, where are you seeing this?"

Despite Charlotte's lifelong protests, Bree knew that all three of them were witches. It was a trait of Murphy women, going back as far as Bree could trace. And she knew that she was empathic, meaning she could see and feel people's emotions almost as clearly as if they were her own. She also knew that Charlotte could move objects when she really focused, and that Abby could insert herself into her sisters' dreams. She'd been doing it since she was a toddler. But until now, Bree had never thought Abby could be psychic.

"I don't know." Abby shrugged. "It's just like there. In my brain. I thought that's what happens with tarot."

"No, not really. The tarot is an interpretation based on the spread of the cards." Bree lifted her cat Akasha off the floor as she walked by and settled the feline's warm bulk in her lap. "What else do you see?" She was curious to know if Abby was in truth seeing anything, or if she was just projecting her own thoughts and imagination out onto the cards.

If Abby were psychic after all, she clearly had Bree mixed up with someone else because she was not, repeat not, going to be falling for a man who thought money was the ultimate goddess and treated his overpriced car like a high-class hooker to stroke.

"Um. I see him walking up to the house and ringing the doorbell."

Because the love of her life was actually just going to stroll up to her very own house and ring the bell. Like that ever happened to anyone, let alone Bree. No one came to her front door but the mailman, and he was fifty and happily married.

Then Abby cocked her head to the side, staring off into space. "He wants to have sex with you."

"Okay, that's enough. This is ridiculous." Abby was either making fun of her for not dating in twenty—count them—twenty months or she was fishing to know about her sister's sex life. Either way, Bree wasn't biting.

Charlotte didn't look thrilled with the conversation either. "You know, we should probably get started if you want your Christmas tree up by the end of the day."

Bree wasn't really dying for a Christmas tree at all since she usually burned a Yule log, but it made Charlotte happy to provide her with one, and Bree could always put a witch's spin on it. "Sounds good." She moved to put Akasha down and paused. "What's in her mouth?" She tried to reach for the cat, but Akasha twisted her head in protest.

"Oh, my God," Charlotte said, reaching out and snatching something from the cat's mouth. "It's the mistletoe. From last Christmas. The one we put the spell on."

As her sister waved it in the air, staring at the greenery like it was possessed, Bree winced. "Whoops. I meant to destroy that." It was nothing more than a sprig of mistletoe, but she and Charlotte had loaded it with symbols of lust so Charlotte could lure her friend Will to make a move on her.

It had worked, forcing the longtime friends to confront their intense feelings for each other, resulting in Charlotte with a wedding ring and a new house to live in, but Bree knew she never should have left that mistletoe just lying around. Last she remembered, she had tossed it on her dresser a solid twelve months earlier, which meant Akasha had probably dragged it off and under the bed or something. No wonder Bree had been plagued with sex dreams for months. She had a powerfully charged hexensymbol hanging out under her bed.

And no man to satisfy her.

Ugh. She hated feeling discontent. And in a constant state of arousal.

"It's probably not a big deal," Charlotte said, carefully laying the loaded mistletoe on the kitchen table. "Will said it didn't work. He already was lusting for me way before we made this thing."

Bree had known that, which was why she had encouraged Charlotte to go for it with Will. "Yeah, but you can't just leave magick lying around."

Especially anywhere around her bed.

"The doorbell's ringing," Charlotte said. "Want me to get it?"

"No, I can get it." Bree stood up, noting that Akasha had already leaped up onto the fourth empty chair and snagged the mistletoe again. Bree was going to have to grab that thing and stuff it into a drawer until she could destroy it bit by bit.

Abby was two steps behind her.

"Why are you following me?" Bree asked her sister, darting a glance at her over her shoulder. "I can answer the door by myself."

"It's him," Abby said in an awed whisper. "The guy I saw."

"Sure. Or it's my mailman letting me know I have a package." Bree went down the hallway of the big Victorian house she had inherited from her grandmother. It was a lot of house for her now that Charlotte had moved out, but maybe Abby would want to move in after high school. Living with their parents was sometimes nausea-inducing since they were engaged in a perpetual lovefest. It was sweet and warming to see from a distance, but on a daily basis all the groping got old. Abby would probably appreciate some space.

Bree pulled open the front door and almost had a heart attack.

Have mercy, it was a man, about thirty years old, and very clearly wearing a pink dress shirt under his winter coat, the collar peeking out above the zipper. He was just standing there. On her front step. With snow on his shiny black shoes.

She knew this man. He was Amanda Delmar Tucker's lawyer, from Chicago.

Bree had only met him once, for a brief minute in the coffeeshop with Abby, the previous December, and he had clearly thought she had been sniffing her black nail polish given the look of disdain on his face at the time.

Now he was standing on her doorstep, with nary a smile in sight.

Abby was whispering loudly in her ear, "It's him. Told you so. Right on up the sidewalk to the front door. Ringing the bell. I'm so right."

Caught between wanting to muzzle her sister and slam the front door shut, Bree just stared at him. He stared back, his compelling chocolate brown eyes boring into her.

And suddenly she knew that her sister was right, as her empathic ability picked up on the feelings he was projecting, unaware that she could sense them. This man, this lawyer, wanted to have sex with her.

Yikes.

Ian Carrington was seriously annoyed with himself. He had told himself that seeing Bree Murphy again was the perfect opportunity to eradicate her from all of his thoughts. That the woman in the flesh, who he had only met once for such a short span of time, couldn't possibly live up to the sensual fantasies his sick mind had conjured over the past year.

He had been wrong.

The minute she opened the door and stared out at him, her dark hair falling past her shoulders, her pale, smooth skin a sharp contrast to the crimson of her bright lipstick, he had felt a gigantic kick of lust. He had an instant erection and wanted nothing more on earth than to have her naked in his bed, eyes glazed with passion, lips swollen from his kisses, voice begging him for more.

It was illogical. She was completely not his type in any way, shape, or form. He went for corporate women, not the kooky kind like Bree, who wore a witch pendant around her neck and did tarot readings for a living. He had never bought in to any of that sixth-sense crap, and he lived his life logically, with a plan. It was what he attributed his success to, despite his unusual and impoverished childhood. Living by logic and hard work had brought him to where he was.

But there was no denying that he was attracted to Bree in the most basic way, whether it made sense or not, and had been dreaming about her virtually nonstop from the second they had met. Both while awake and asleep.

Now she was staring at him like he was a bug she'd like to squish.

So even though this trip technically hadn't been necessary for the business he had to conduct, he had taken it with the intention of getting over his little lust crush on Bree Murphy and restoring his life to its former equilibrium. Only now that he had seen her again, in all her delicious flesh, he knew he wasn't over his crush, not by a mile. And he was going to stay in Cuttersville, Ohio, until he either had sex with Bree or regained his sanity, because he could not return to Chicago and face another twelve months of X-rated dreams that featured him and Bree Murphy rocking the house. He would spontaneously combust if he had to endure any more of the graphic dreams that were soaking him in sweat every other night.

"Hi, I'm Ian Carrington," he said, holding out his hand.

She took it for about a microsecond before she dropped it. "I've met you before. You're Amanda's lawyer."

Bree said "lawyer" with the disgust generally reserved for con artists who bilked seniors of their life savings. But he ignored that. At least she remembered meeting him. A blank look from her would have been a serious blow to his ego. "Exactly. It's great to see you again, Bree. Do you have a minute? I have a business proposition I'd like to discuss with you."

"Uh . . . sure. Okay." Bree looked confused, but she did step back to let him in, bumping into a girl in the process who Ian recognized as her younger sister. "Abby, give me some breathing room," she said in annoyance. Then to him, "Come on in."

As Ian stepped into the entryway of the house, Abby was grinning from ear to ear, which was a little distracting. Ian offered her his hand as well. "Ian Carrington."

"Abigail Murphy," she said, still smiling. "I'm psychic."

One of Ian's eyebrows shot up before he could stop it. "That's nice," he said, for lack of anything better to say. Kookiness obviously ran in the family.

"Abby," Bree said, her voice laced with warning.

"I just told Bree not fifteen minutes ago that a guy with a pink shirt was going to ring her doorbell and that you—"

Bree's hand clapped over her sister's mouth, cutting off Abby's words. Bree gave him a sheepish look, her cheeks tinting with embarrassment. "Sorry. She's sweet but delusional."

Ian glanced down involuntarily at his pink shirt. Why did he get the feeling he'd just been insulted? What the hell was wrong with pink anyway? It wasn't like it was hot pink, it was a very faint, light, barely there pink. It was a very now color in corporate circles. It was *GQ*, damn it.

But something about Bree Murphy and her Goth clothes suddenly made him feel . . . unmanly. Not a good feeling, given the dreams he'd been having, which all involved her running her fair-skinned fingers with those black nails over his chest, down his navel, and landing on his . . .

Ian dragged himself back to reality. "I won't take up a lot of your time, I just wanted to discuss this house with you. You're the owner, correct?"

Bree frowned at him. "Yes. Why?"

A blonde came down the hall and gave the women a pointed look. "Maybe he would like to sit down and have a cup of tea."

"Oh, that's not necessary," he protested, when Bree gave the woman a look of horror. "I just need a minute."

"No, no," Bree said, looking flustered and embarrassed and damn adorable. "We should at least sit down. This is my other sister, Charlotte, by the way."

"Charlotte Murphy-Thornton," the blonde said, sticking her hand out and giving his a firm shake.

"Ian Carrington."

Charlotte's type he understood. She was the kind of woman he normally interacted with. She was dressed in a twin sweater set in a shade of green that flattered her complexion, and she wore tasteful gold jewelry, enough for a flash, but not so much that it was gaudy. If he was going to lust after a Murphy sister, Charlotte should be the one. They were a logical fit. Of course, his client Amanda had told him Charlotte was newly married, and there was nothing logical about what he was feeling anyway because he wanted Bree in all her black. And then out of all of her black. Naked. Dark hair tumbling over her bare flesh.

He was insane, absolutely completely out of his normally practical mind. And horny. With no explanation for either.

Charlotte and Bree led him down the hallway to the kitchen, and Ian fought the urge to look at Bree's sexy backside. He lost. It was a good view, and he didn't want to miss it. She was wearing a long, stretchy black skirt that hugged her curves in a way that made him sweat.

Abby patted him on the arm as she walked next to him. "It's okay, you can't help it. It's destiny."

"What?" The youngest Murphy sister definitely freaked him out. He had no idea what to make of her.

"It will all make sense soon," she told him.

He could only hope. Because so far his preoccupation with Bree made no sense whatsoever, nor could he figure out why all his sexual dreams involving her took place in a Christmas setting. It was weird as hell, and said questionable things about his psyche.

"What about the house?" Bree said, after they were all seated at a vintage table.

It was painted in a soft shade of pink that surprised Ian. He wouldn't have expected that to be her choice in décor. Then again, he really knew very little about her at all. He needed to remember that. Own it. Eat it, damn it. There was no reason to be attracted to Bree Murphy.

"I have a client who would like to make an offer for the house." There. That sounded professional and completely lacking in lust.

"An offer? What does that mean?" Bree was looking at him with total suspicion, her fingers playing with the edge of a rich blue place mat.

"Someone wants to buy the house?" Charlotte asked, her lip curling up in horror. "Grandma's house?"

Ian didn't know the particulars, but he did know that Bree had inherited the house from her grandmother. He had assumed she would be reluctant, but he was obligated to make the offer for his client. And it had given him a legitimate excuse to ring Bree's doorbell. "Yes." Ian pulled out the contract that detailed the offer and passed it across the table. "It's a generous offer."

Bree took the paper, glanced down at it, and blanched. "Who the hell thinks my house is worth this much money?"

"My client does." Ian leaned back in his chair and tried to project casual. It was likely he wasn't succeeding because Bree was glaring at him, and all he could think about was leaning over the table and kissing her. Running his hands down her sides, raking his fingers through her hair, and licking every inch of her. It made focusing on real estate damn difficult.

"What's his name? What is he going to do with the house?"

"You're not going to actually consider this, are you?" Abby looked at Bree in disbelief.

"No, absolutely not. But I'm curious who this person is and why he wants my house."

All Ian heard was that she wasn't interested. "If you're not going to accept the offer, I don't see any reason to tell you his plans for the property." Then they could disregard what had supposedly brought him there initially and move straight to his asking her out for dinner, which was what he planned to do now that he realized there was no possibility of his attraction dissolving on sight. It had actually increased now that he was sitting close enough to touch her, and he would have thought that was impossible.

She obviously wasn't feeling the lust, if that sniff of disdain was any indication. "Why the hell can't you tell me who he is? What difference does it make? Is he some kind of pervert? A drug dealer? Was he planning to turn my granny's Victorian into a whorehouse?"

"Uh . . ." Ian was momentarily caught off guard. A whorehouse? Did they even have those anymore? "No. I believe he intended to use it as a private residence since that's the way its zoned, but it's not really my job to grill him on his specific intentions."

"What is your job anyway? I thought you were a lawyer. Why are you selling real estate?"

Ian shifted in his chair, annoyed. He wasn't there to present her with his résumé. "I'm not selling or buying real estate. I am a properties attorney. My client uses me to do his contracts instead of a real-estate agent."

"Why?"

Ian wasn't exactly sure how to explain that he worked for millionaires, who had no patience for real-estate agents, but he was saved from having to answer when something brushed against his leg. He glanced down and saw a black cat. Big surprise that Bree would make that her pet of choice. But he liked cats, so he reached down and scratched behind the feline's ears and was rewarded with a purr.

"Abby, get Akasha!" Bree said, nudging her sister. "You know she hates men."

Ian glanced down at the cat, who was nuzzling his pants and weaving in and out between his legs. "It's fine. I don't mind."

"She'll bite you. I'm serious. She hates men."

Ian kept scratching, and the purring kicked up a notch. "She seems to like me." And damn if he didn't feel a little sense of triumph over that.

"She does," Abby said, eyes wide. "Bree, do you know what that means? It means—"

"That you need to stop talking," Bree said, glaring at her sister. "Akasha is probably just waiting for the right minute to sink her claws into his leg."

Bree jumped out of her seat and got down on the floor next to him, reaching for her cat. It was an interesting twist on the current situation, and Ian didn't move, curious how the moment would play out. He just sat there with Bree moving closer and closer to his knees as she crawled around on the floor, reaching for the elusive cat, who darted away from her and around the back of Ian's chair.

"Akasha!" Bree frowned. "I'm really sorry, she really doesn't like men and I really need to get her before she—"

Bree stopped talking when the cat jumped up on his lap, kneaded her paws into his thighs, and sat down. Ian scratched Akasha again with one hand and used the other to play a little tug-of-war with the sprig of greenery in her mouth. It looked like mistletoe, oddly enough. Ian stared at it, a little unnerved. Funny how much mistletoe had factored in all of his sexual dreams about Bree. They always started with mistletoe, either hanging in a doorway, or in Bree's hands, teasing him to kiss her. And he always did, and it went to really happy and horny places after that.

It was crazy that the cat, the black cat, belonging to the self-proclaimed witch he was so attracted to, was chomping on mistletoe. In fact, it was disturbing enough that Ian decided it was time to leave.

"So you're not interested?" he asked her, very aware of the fact that she was on her knees right in front of *his* knees and under different circumstances, that would be a beautiful thing.

"Uh . . . what?" Bree looked up at him in confusion, her pale cheeks tinted pink again.

He thought it was damn cute that she blushed. Witches shouldn't blush, but he liked it when she did.

"The house," he prompted. "You're really not interested in selling it?"

"The house. Right. Yes. I mean, no. No, I am definitely not interested in selling it. Sorry." She snatched the cat off his lap.

Only Ian was still holding the mistletoe, as was the cat, and Bree wound up effectively stretching Akasha out to her full furry length between the two of them. She gave him a pointed look, so he dropped the mistletoe.

She stood up and cuddled the cat against her chest.

Ian didn't think a dinner invitation would have any chance whatsoever of being accepted, so he stood up as well. "Thanks for your time. I'll let my client know you're not interested."

"Thanks." Bree's mouth opened like she was going to say something, but then she closed it again.

The silence hung awkwardly for a second while they stared at each other for no apparent reason other than that Ian was having a hard time making his feet move him to the door. He really needed to come up with another excuse to see her. Tomorrow. But his brain wasn't cooperating and creating any plausible reason. Just when he was about to give up and save face by exiting, Abby stepped between them, breaking Ian and Bree's eye contact.

"You don't need a reason, Ian," Abby said. "You can totally stop by tomorrow."

Ian started. Had the kid read his mind or what? His feet lost their paralysis, and on that note, he waved good-bye to the women and got the hell out of there.

Chapter 2

"Abby, what are you doing?" Bree stood in her front hall watching Ian Carrington head down the snowy walk to an expensive-looking black car. "Are you just trying to embarrass the hell out of me or do you have a death wish?"

The whole ten-minute encounter with Ian had been an exercise in mortification. She couldn't even fathom why she had been so intent on getting Akasha from him. But she had thought the cat would bite or scratch him, and the thought of the meticulous Ian Carrington having his pricey pants torn into by her cat had panicked her. Of course, it had wound up being far more embarrassing to be crawling around on the floor in front of him, her eyes level with his crotch. She should have just let the damn cat sink her claws into his thigh.

"What?" Abby looked entirely unremorseful. "He's the dude I saw in the cards, and you're just blowing him off. I had to try and do something so you don't screw up the whole rest of your life."

Bree shuddered, a lifetime of attachment to such a pompous overachiever too horrific to contemplate. Though she had to admit, if she were honest, the way he stared at her, like he wanted to take off her clothes and devote all of his intensity to her body, was hot. Just a little. Okay, a lot. It was bizarre, given she didn't really like him, but her naughty bits seemed to think he could do a thing or two for her, because he turned her on, no doubt about it.

"I am not going to fall in love with that guy. But you were right about one thing—he does want to have sex with me. I picked up on that empathically."

Charlotte snorted. "You don't have to be empathic or psychic to figure that out. He was virtually drooling over your butt."

Bree involuntarily grabbed her backside. "He was? Ohmigod, are you serious?"

Her sisters both nodded, Charlotte solemn, Abby gleeful.

"When did he do that?" And more importantly, how had her butt looked?

"When you were walking down the hall to the kitchen," Charlotte said.

Damn herself for wearing such a tight skirt. "Did I look okay? I mean, am I having a good-ass day or a bad-ass day? God, this is awful."

Charlotte laughed. "What the hell is a good-ass day?"

Bree saw nothing amusing about it. "You know, when your butt looks good in whatever you're wearing, when it's sort of living up to its fullest potential, being the best your butt can be." Duh.

But her sister looked at her like she'd lost her mind. "That is the freakiest thing I've ever heard you say, and you've said a lot of weird things over the years."

"Your butt looked great," Abby told her.

"See? Abby gets it." And Bree was marginally reassured. She

didn't want to want Ian, and she didn't want him looking at her and not wanting *her* either.

"So we all know he wants to have sex with you, but the question is, do you want to have sex with him?" Charlotte pinned her with a hard stare. "And be honest."

Did she have to be? Bree bit her lip, something she never did. Exasperated with herself, she crossed her arms over her chest. "I don't know. Maybe. He's totally not my type, and I know I don't want to date him, but I can admit that I find him attractive in the most basic animalistic sort of way." And his intensity fascinated her, but she was not going to say that out loud.

This was not the way she had pictured her day. It was supposed to be a normal day, in which she lamented her celibate status but simultaneously applauded her independence, when she spent time with her sisters putting up a Christmas tree and ate those satanically delicious butter cookies Charlotte insisted on baking.

"So just do him," Abby said. "It's a good jumping point."

When had her baby sister become so outrageous? Wait. Abby had always been that way. Maybe it was the result of being conceived on a grave in the cemetery, but Bree should realize that literally anything could come out of Abby's mouth at any given moment.

"I can't just 'do him.' "

"Why not?" Charlotte asked.

And that was her conservative sister speaking. It boggled the mind. "Because," she said in exasperation. "I can't."

"Why not?" Charlotte asked, shrugging.

"Well . . ." That was a good question. Why couldn't she really? She knew he wanted her. Lust was radiating all over his aura. She really was attracted to him, too, for whatever random reason.

But it seemed like such a risk, such a messy situation to walk into voluntarily. How would they even get from where they were to *there*, and if they did, what happened afterward? It sounded like a potential disaster.

"Because . . ."

Akasha rubbed against her leg, the mistletoe still in its mouth. Inspiration struck. "Because it was the mistletoe that made him think he's into me. It's not real."

That should get her out of having to deal with it, and it might even be true. Even if Ian had arrived at the door looking like he wanted to eat her way before he'd had any contact with the lust-spell-loaded mistletoe.

"That's lame. When he comes back tomorrow I think you should go for it," Abby said.

"He's not going to come here tomorrow. He's probably going back to Chicago."

And she could forget all about Ian Carrington and his sexy brown eyes.

Except he didn't go back to Chicago.

Bree's stomach dropped when twenty-four hours later her doorbell rang and a peek out her front window showed none other than Ian standing on her doorstep again. Damn. How was that even possible? And she was totally alone. Charlotte was at work, and Abby was at their parents' house. Alone was bad. Dangerous. A test of her self-control, which—she had to admit—didn't seem all that intact.

At least she was wearing a loose skirt and a very unsexy black cardigan. That would help her feel less naked when he looked at her. Taking a deep breath, she pulled open the door. The cardigan was insufficient armor. She still felt naked under his intense scrutiny.

"Hi." She tried to smile, but didn't quite manage more than a tight-lipped upturn.

"Hi. Sorry to bother you again, but my client has countered with another offer. Can I come in?"

That threw her off. Another offer on her house? That was random. "Sure."

It was a long walk down the hall to the kitchen, and Bree's cheeks burned as she wondered if Ian was looking at her butt. It made her self-conscious, torn between wanting to put some effort into rolling her hips to show off her assets and wanting to cover herself with her hands. In the end, she tried really hard to just walk normally, but doubted she succeeded.

"Another offer? What does that mean exactly?" she asked him, gesturing for him to have a seat.

"It means that when I told my client you were not interested in selling, he upped the amount of his offer." Ian pulled out a piece of paper and pushed it over to her.

Bree's mouth went dry when she saw the dollar amount in black-and-white. "This is insane." It was a lot of money. She never would have guessed her grandmother's house was worth that much.

"It's a very respectable offer."

Bree glanced up at Ian. She couldn't tell if he cared one way or the other if she agreed to the offer. He had a poker face that was unnerving. Even his emotions, his aura, revealed nothing to her of his opinion about the house. But the sexual interest was there again. It was intense and vibrant, and it made her want to run away at the same time that it fired up every neuron in her body. He had the most compelling and intense eyes, and she felt seriously off kilter around him.

"I think it's actually too much. But that's irrelevant because I'm not going to sell. It's my grandmother's house." Bree couldn't part with the remaining piece of her grandmother, the woman who had taught her tarot and witchcraft. Charlotte had inherited their grandmother's tea shop, and had promptly turned it into a profitable coffee shop. That had been the smart, practical thing to do, but Bree couldn't help but miss the tea shop and its pleasant memories. She was sentimental in the extreme, and she wasn't going to sell the house just for the cash. She'd rather have that connection to her grandma indefinitely.

"I know."

"You know that it's my grandmother's house?"

"Yes. And I know that you won't sell it. But my client is wealthy and stubborn and used to getting what he wants. He'll keep making offers, and I'm obligated to deliver them. I'm sorry."

Ian didn't look sorry, exactly. He looked more ambivalent than anything. Like he was used to doing his job, following through on rich men's whims, and the outcome didn't much matter. It unnerved Bree a little, made her wonder who exactly Ian Carrington was and what he stood for. "It's okay. He can keep offering, but I'll just keep saying no. Seems like a waste of time, but I understand people are irrational."

As was her attraction to the man in front of her.

But she could also admit that she had spent most of her life living by emotion, not logic, so maybe her sisters were right. Maybe she needed to just embrace the idea of an affair with Ian. See where it led, if anywhere. Even if it went nowhere, she had a sneaking suspicion the sex would be well worth it.

"Well, I won't take up any more of your time then." Ian tucked his paper away and stood up.

That was it? Bree frowned. Here she had virtually just decided that she could have sex with him, and he was just going to leave without asking her out or at least hitting on her or flirting?

She knew he wanted her. Knew it. It was irrefutable.

Yet he wasn't going to act on it? That was all sorts of wrong.

As was the fact that she was offended by his lack of action. The whole thing was ridiculous.

"Okay. Thanks." She had no idea what the hell she was thanking him for, but she was at a loss as to what else to say.

In sixty seconds he was down the hall and pausing on her porch right outside the front door. "Good-bye," he said. Then he smiled at her.

It was the first time she'd ever seen him smile, and it was devastating in its charm and sensuality. It revealed straight and white teeth and crooked up a little in the corner. It was a smile that said he knew what she was thinking, the kind of smile that could bring women to their knees, and most of all, it was the smile of a man who knew how to please a woman.

So Bree shut the door on his sexy face.

She didn't feel like playing games.

Or maybe she was offended that he could want her physically but had reservations about liking her, as a person.

Of course, she was doing the same thing about him. Wanting his body but not necessarily him.

Which made the whole damn thing too complicated. She was letting it go. Done with it.

But she still found herself wandering back into the kitchen and pulling out her tarot cards. Maybe they would reveal to her why, exactly, a sexy lawyer from Chicago had popped into her life, only to pop right back out.

Only all she could seem to see in the cards was a future real-estate transaction, which was totally boring, and totally wrong. She was not going to sell her house to Ian Carrington's rich client.

"Never," she said out loud to the spread in front of her, pushing all the cards back into a pile and wondering if she had any ice cream in the freezer.

Cold outside or not, she could use a little comfort from the carton.

Chapter 3

Ian was pulling in the driveway of the bed-and-breakfast he was staying in, annoyed with himself for wimping out and not asking Bree to dinner, when he sensed movement in the car with him. He glanced over to the passenger seat and slammed on the brakes.

"What the hell?"

Bree's cat was sitting on the seat, staring up at him calmly, mistletoe dangling from her mouth.

"How did you get into my car?" The doors had been shut at Bree's house. Locked. He was positive of that. Even if he had, just this one time, inadvertently forgotten to lock it, it wasn't like the cat could open car doors by herself.

But Akasha wasn't answering him, thank God, and he had no choice but to put the car in reverse and drive back to Bree's. Ian glanced over at the cat every few seconds, wary of her. He didn't believe in magic or witches or the power of black cats.

Nonetheless, he had a feline Houdini miraculously sitting next to him at the end of a five-minute drive, and it was weirding him out. Especially since the cat just stared at him, that sprig of greenery dangling from her mouth, her big green eyes unblinking.

"What?" Ian asked her in irritation. "You look stupid with that thing hanging from your mouth, you know."

Akasha dropped the mistletoe onto the seat.

Ian felt the hair on the back of his neck rise. Man, he needed to get out of this town. Cuttersville billed itself as Ohio's Most Haunted Town, and he had always thought it was a ridiculous designation. Now he was struggling with the illogic of certain things, like the dreams he'd been having and this crazy-ass cat.

"Okay, you're home. Bree is probably wondering where the hell you are." Ian parked his car in Bree's driveway and gave a sigh as he glanced up at the big Victorian. It was a cool house, totally different from his streamlined, modern apartment, reminding him a bit of the house in which he'd grown up, though his mother's farmhouse had been more shabby than architecturally intriguing. But this Victorian was pretty and complicated, somewhat brooding and mysterious. The alleged witch who lived there shared the same characteristics with her house, and Ian doubted she was going to be thrilled to see him again. She didn't seem to like him, nor did she seem to be suffering from the same overpowering lust that he was. Unfortunately.

Grabbing the cat in a firm grip, Ian carried her up the walk and rang the bell.

Bree answered the door with a frown. "What are you doing with Akasha?"

Not much of a greeting. Yeah, she so wasn't interested in him. She held her hands out for her pet, and Ian turned the cat over.

"She was in my car . . . it was the weirdest thing. I drove all the way through town and looked over, and suddenly she was just sitting on the passenger seat." He still couldn't imagine how it had happened, but there it was.

Bree's eyebrows rose. "You can't be serious."

"Totally. I have no idea how it could have happened, but I swear to God, she was suddenly just there with me."

"Yeah, because cats just open car doors and jump in." Bree rolled her eyes.

Ian frowned back. "I know it's insane," he said in irritation. "But she was in my car, and I didn't put her there."

"Whatever."

There was no single word more designed to incite Ian's anger. He couldn't *stand* it when people said that to him. It catapulted him back to childhood, when his older sister would toss "whatever" at him a hundred times a day. It made him feel dismissed, humiliated. So he immediately reacted. "What, you think I swiped your damn cat or something?"

"That certainly seems more plausible than my cat somehow opening my front door *and* your car door—and closing both again, I might add—in the five minutes you and I sat in my kitchen. It's ridiculous."

"So is the idea that I would steal your cat, and then bring her right back. What kind of moronic theft is that?" Ian's indignation rose. What, like he'd steal a freakin' cat? "And why would I want your cat anyway?"

"I have no idea. Nor do I know why your client wants my house. But neither of you can have either."

She started to close the door on him yet again, but Ian stuck his palm out and held it open. Bree tried to push harder, but he was stronger. He was not a cat thief. "I didn't take your cat. I don't want your cat." Really. He didn't.

"What do you want?" she asked acidly.

"You," Ian said. Hell, he figured he hadn't risen to success from poverty based on being passive. He had always been aggressive in going after what he wanted, and Bree shouldn't be any different.

"Excuse me?" She blinked, looking more shocked than outraged.

Ian met her gaze. "I am attracted to you, and I'm hoping you'll agree to go to dinner with me."

There was a long pause, during which Ian was aware that he was still standing on the front porch and his nuts were going numb while she stared at him, and he was just about resigned to rejection when Bree nodded.

"Okay."

"Okay?" Ian was shocked into parroting her, but he rallied. "Okay, great. Fabulous. I'm only in town for a few more days, so are you busy tonight?"

"Tonight would work."

Said she with zero enthusiasm. Very ego-boosting. But she had agreed to dinner, so he was going to roll with it. "Let me have your number . . . I'll make some reservations and call you." Ian pulled out his cell phone.

Bree gave a smile. "You don't really need reservations in Cuttersville."

But she gave him her number anyway, reciting it quickly, testing the speed of Ian's typing.

"I'd take your number, but my phone is upstairs."

"I'll call it," he said. "So it's in your phone." He hit send for the number she had just given him and let it ring until the voice mail picked up. He smiled at her as he spoke into his phone. "Hi, this is Ian Carrington calling for Bree Murphy to see if we can change our dinner plans to a late lunch. I'd rather not wait to see you."

It was a risk, throwing his interest so clearly out there, and he watched her reaction closely, but Bree didn't balk. She just raised an eyebrow. He continued, "So let me know what you think, and I look forward to hearing from you." He hung up his phone.

"You don't have a lot of patience, do you?" she asked, still holding her cat. It didn't sound like a censure, just curiosity.

"No, I suppose not. I want what I want."

And he wanted her. The unspoken words hung in the air between them.

Finally, Bree gave an exasperated sigh. "Would you get into the house? We're letting out all the heat while you come on strong."

Ian stepped forward. "Too strong?"

Bree shut the door behind him. "I haven't decided yet if I'm appalled or if I like it. I'll let you know."

Ian laughed. "Well, that's honest."

She didn't laugh with him, just stared searchingly at him. "Why did you ask me out? I'm not your type at all."

"You're not like women I usually date, that's true. But that doesn't mean I can't look at you and think you're beautiful . . . it doesn't mean I can't look at you and be intrigued as to who you are." And maybe there was logic to his attraction after all. It was the fascination of someone who lived so differently from him, who embraced her different perspective of the universe and didn't apologize for it. He wanted to learn more about her, maybe even craved the sense of "realness" that she offered.

"I have no idea what to say to that," she said. "I want to say something witty and flirtatious, but that's not really me."

"What are you then?"

"Brutally honest. I say whatever the hell I'm thinking."

"Nothing wrong with that." Ian watched Bree standing in the hallway with her cat still tightly held in her arms. "What are you thinking now?" This was uncharted territory for him. It was 2:00 p.m. on a Tuesday, and he barely knew Bree at all. He had no idea where to go from there, and he didn't think she would appreciate it if he did what he really wanted to do, which was kiss her.

She shrugged. "I'm actually desperately wishing I had brushed my teeth after I ate a cottage-cheese snack because I have a feeling you're going to kiss me at some point before you leave."

Ian laughed. "I'd certainly like to. And a little cottage cheese won't stop me." He put his hand on the small of her back, wanting to be closer to her. "But why don't you give me a tour of the house? I'd really love to see the whole place, and you can make a quick pit stop for your toothbrush if it will make you feel better."

Bree glanced up at him over her shoulder, her eyes dark and mysterious under her long lashes. "This is a very strange and random date."

"Is it freaking you out?"

"Not particularly."

"Well, it is me," he told her truthfully. "This isn't the way I usually initiate a relationship."

"Then why are you doing it?" she asked.

Bree had put the cat down finally, and she was facing him. Her hair was sliding across her cheek and sticking to her moist, crimson lips. Ian reached out and pulled the hair free and tucked it behind her ear, reveling in the satin slide across his fingertips. It had been a while since he had touched a woman, and there was a paradoxical quality to Bree that he loved. She was strong and bold, yet wonderfully feminine and vulnerable at the same time.

"Because I can't stop myself." And he ignored the fact that he had just told her she could sneak off and brush her teeth before a kiss, and he went for one anyway. A hand on the back of her neck, Ian leaned forward and pressed his lips to hers, lightly. They fit together well, comfortably, and he felt her acquiescence, felt her lean toward him to meet his mouth.

Ian forced himself to keep it short, to just linger for a fleeting moment, then pull back. He didn't want to go any faster than he already was and have her balk on him. Bree gave a delicious sigh when he stepped away from her, her eyes dark and mysterious, her lips shiny. Wiping away the lip gloss that had transferred from her lips to his, Ian said, "I'm ready for my tour of the house. Starting with . . ."

Her eyebrows rose in censure as if she clearly expected him to say the bedroom.

"The living room. I'd like to see the fireplace." He smiled broadly.

They'd get to the bedroom eventually.

Bree watched Ian carefully. She wasn't used to men like him at all. Her ex-boyfriends had all been profuse in their attentions and loud about their neediness. None had been smooth or charming. Ian was both, and she was having trouble seeing what was coming around the corner with him. He kept startling her, and it was starting to annoy her that she constantly felt off-kilter, out of control. The advantage to the men in her past had been that she had always been the strong one, not vice versa. Ian and she were more evenly matched, and she didn't know quite what to do with it.

So she sucked in a breath, gathered her resolve—because she was now determined to have sex with Ian Carrington on her own terms—and said, "Sure. I assumed the fireplace was the first thing you'd want to see."

He laughed as he followed her, Akasha trotting along beside him.

So much for feline loyalty. It obviously didn't exist because Akasha, who to that point had never tolerated a man in her house, was clearly smitten with Ian.

Bree stopped just inside the main living area on the first floor, the room her grandmother had always referred to as the parlor. It was a large room, with two stained-glass windows and a fireplace with a very ornate carved mantel from which Abby had hung three sprigs of mistletoe. Bree said, "The house was built in 1888. All the woodwork is original, and so is the fireplace, though we can't burn wood in it. It's not up to code."

Though she had to admit she burned her Yule log there every Winter Solstice and so far no one had seemed to notice, and she hadn't burned the house down. But she wasn't really willing to take a chance on a roaring fire.

Ian had wandered into the middle of the room and stopped, turning a full 360 slowly. He looked puzzled, and Bree waited for a response, content just to look at him. He was so freaking good-looking, oozing confidence and success. His hair was very short yet somehow still managed to convey a sense of style, the front sticking up slightly. He was dressed more casually than the day before, his jeans distressed in all the right places, his shoes well-worn leather. He still had his coat on, but she could see his wine-colored button-up shirt with a subtle stripe, untucked, casual, but not the slightest bit sloppy. Bree had never been to Chicago, but she could picture him there, living in a high-rise apartment, walking down busy streets at a fast clip, talking on his cell phone.

"Wow," he said.

"Wow what?" The room wasn't that exciting. Bree was well aware the furniture was old and worn and that the overcast December sky lent a gloomy aspect to the room despite its being midafternoon.

"I'm having a serious case of déjà vu." Ian moved to the fireplace and fingered one of the mistletoe bunches hanging there.

Bree fought the urge to smack his hand away. Mistletoe, with all its sexual implications, was not what either of them needed at the moment. Or maybe it was.

"I don't believe in déjà vu," she said. "I think it's really that our sixth sense sometimes glimpses pieces of our future, then when we see them in actuality we recognize them as familiar, as if they're part of the past. But they're really our recognition of what our subconscious already told us was going to occur."

She expected him to disagree, since Ian didn't seem like he believed in anything but the present, but he surprised her.

"That's an interesting theory. But for me, this is déjà vu because I've seen this room in a dream. Right down to the three sprigs of mistletoe over this very fireplace mantel." He touched the grapevines that had been carved in the wood. "These grapevines. It's unreal how clearly I saw it all."

Bree sucked in her breath. "You saw this room in a dream? With mistletoe?" What the hell did that mean?

"Yes." Ian turned and looked at her, and those dark eyes studied her. "I don't believe in anything but logic, but I can't explain this. I've been dreaming about this room, not once, not twice, but over and over."

"For how long?"

"A year. And it always looked just like this, decorated for Christmas. The tree, the mistletoe."

A shiver raced up Bree's spine. It had been a year since they had met. "We just hung the mistletoe yesterday."

"That's really weird," he said, his voice thoughtful, his mouth turning down in a frown. He peeled off his jacket and tossed it on the sofa, moving around the room, studying all angles, all objects.

It was clear he wanted an explanation, and Bree had none to give him. "What happens in the dreams?"

But Ian just shook his head. "It's personal."

Whatever the hell that meant.

His hand was on an ornament on her tree, an innocuous sparrow that had no particular meaning to Bree other than it was meant to represent the power of nature in the smallest things, and he pulled it forward, stroking the faux feathers. Recognition hit Bree in a powerful wave, and she couldn't prevent a gasp from escaping her mouth.

"Ohmigod," she whispered.

"What?" He glanced back at her.

Now it was her turn to shake her head. She couldn't say it out loud. She couldn't admit that this was in fact her recurring dream as well, that it always started with the back of a man's head bent over her Christmas tree. That he always turned, his face in shadow so she couldn't see his features, and he came over to her and did delicious things to her body. That he shattered her with orgasm after orgasm, and she always woke up frustrated and aching with want for the reality of her dream.

"This is an unusual tree," he said, touching a pinecone ornament. "It's very natural-looking. I like it."

"It's a family tradition, based on witchcraft. You fill the tree with ornaments that appreciate nature, but also with ornaments that represent all your hopes and aspirations for the upcoming year. You fill it with symbols of that which you want to bring into your life." Bree swallowed hard, still reeling from the realization that it had in fact been Ian that she had been dreaming about so intensely. It had to be him. He was doing just what the man in her dreams did, and her body was already poised, anticipating a touch.

He murmured, "Really? That's very cool. I like that. What does this one mean?"

Bree squinted to focus, not really caring about conversation but striving to find normalcy in the situation. Ian was pointing to a diploma ornament.

"That's Abby's. She's graduating this year and hopefully heading off to college. She's incredibly book smart and I think she'll do well in college."

"And this one?" Ian fingered a baby carriage.

Bree touched her throat, a sudden tightness forcing her to breathe deeply. "That one's Charlotte's. She and Will would like to have a baby."

"I hope they're successful."

"Thank you. Me, too. They'll be fabulous parents."

Akasha came over to Bree and rubbed against her leg, dropping something from her mouth. Bree bent over absently and picked it up, unnerved by the surreal quality of being there with Ian, knowing that in her dreams she had felt him inside her, known the slide of his tongue over her most intimate places. It wasn't until she was standing again that she realized she had retrieved the battered mistletoe that Akasha had been dragging around.

Of course.

Ian turned to her. "Which ornament is yours? What is it that you want to bring into your life in the new year?"

"I didn't have any specific needs or wants," she whispered, clutching the mistletoe to her chest. "I just wanted contentment, and personal growth." She would never admit that she had wanted a man, a partner, a fulfilling and satisfying relationship with someone who simply wanted her but didn't need her.

Ian looked at the mistletoe she was fondling desperately for lack of anything better to do with her hands.

He shook his head. "Damn it, Bree, this is unreal . . ."

"What do you mean?"

"That's what you do in my dream."

"In your dream?" she asked stupidly, well aware that he was now walking toward her, and she was equal parts aroused and terrified. "I'm in your dream?"

"Yes." Ian stopped in front of her and ran his fingers down the side of her hair. "You hold that mistletoe, just like that, right before we make love, right here, in this room, in front of that fireplace."

Whoa. That was the way her dream always went. "Ian . . ." She had no idea what to say, and her tongue suddenly felt six sizes too big for her mouth. How the hell could they, virtual strangers, hundreds of miles apart, have been having the same dream?

"Bree."

He kissed her, not like before, but with passion and purpose. It took her breath away, the feel of his hands in her hair, his body warm and close to hers, his mouth taking without hesitation, with delicious skill and a definite knowledge. He knew her mouth and she knew his. They fit together, as though their lips had pleasured each other many times before, and deep inside Bree, she felt the burning of desire, knowing that in some way they had. They knew each other from their dreams, and this wasn't new, but was destiny.

"You taste so good, just like I imagined," he said, his lips brushing across the corners of her mouth, up her jaw, and kissing her earlobe.

Bree shivered, her fingers digging into his shoulders, mistletoe still bunched and crushed in her left hand. He said that in her dreams. *You taste so good.* She had always believed in the power of magick, but this was unbelievable, scary, titillating. It was hard to accept that it was real, and yet it was so very easy to just roll with it, to accept the sensuality of the moment, to know where it was going to lead. They both knew where it was going, because they had both seen it, felt it already.

"Ian, I have a confession to make."

"Yeah?" He was breathing in the scent of her hair while his fingers slipped under her shirt to stroke the small of her back.

"I've been having the same dream."

He pulled back and stared at her. "Are you serious?"

"Yes." She nodded, playing with the collar of his shirt nervously, her fingertips tugging then smoothing. "I didn't know it was you . . . your face is always in shadow. But when you bent over the tree and looked at me, I knew it was you. And you always walk towards me and kiss me."

"While you're holding mistletoe."

"Yes."

"And then we undress each other." Ian's eyes had darkened and his voice had lowered.

Bree swallowed hard. "Yes. Then you pull the quilt off the sofa . . ."

"And lay it down, then you down on it, in front of the fireplace. Then I kiss you from head to toe, and here." His knee touched between her thighs. "And you beg for more."

He did know this dream. "Yes, that's the way it goes."

Ian shook his head. "Amazing. Strange, freakish, weird as hell, incredible . . . and now we're going to live out our dream, aren't we?"

Absolutely. Or she was going to puddle to the floor in a mass of unrequited lust. "Yes."

"Is the dream good for you?" he asked, a small smile on his face.

"Oh yeah."

"Then let's make reality even better."

Chapter 4

Ian was shocked that Bree had been having the same dream, but at the same time it made sense, in its own very strange way. It wasn't even remotely logical, but it was obviously very real, that she knew exactly how his dreams played out, that he didn't even hesitate to take action.

He wanted her, a full year's worth of longing, and in that way he did know her. And she had said it had been good for her asleep, so he sure in hell wanted to live up to that awake. Ian kissed Bree, and this time she opened her mouth for him, so that Ian could take her with his tongue, taste her fully, and appreciate the rush of her excited breath past his ear.

Reality was definitely better than fantasy. He had never been able to fully feel the softness of her lips, the smoothness of her back as he held her, the press of her breasts against his chest. Bree was digging her fingers into his shoulders, and he could smell the evergreen scent as she crushed the mistletoe against him. He stepped back, panting, and marveled at how red her lips were naturally, now shiny and wet from his kisses. He had decimated all of her lip gloss, and yet her mouth was still plump and richly rosy.

God, she was just beautiful.

Reaching for her, Ian took her turtleneck by the bottom and pulled it up and over her head. It got caught on her head, and he laughed when she let out an indelicate curse.

"I'm stuck." She sounded more amused than angry as she shook her head back and forth and reached up to grapple with the shirt.

"I'm sorry, I've got it." Ian tugged harder, and the shirt finally popped up and off, leaving her hair plastered all over her face and sticking up with static. She looked adorable, and Ian smoothed the dark strands back down, cupping her cheeks and kissing her softly.

She unbuttoned his shirt while they kissed, and Ian sucked in his breath as she ran her fingers over his bare flesh.

"You're lean but it's obvious you work out," she said, rushing over the planes of his muscles and down his navel to the button on his jeans, making his body react enthusiastically. "You have definition."

"I should hope so after all the work I put into it." Ian leaned forward and sucked on the creamy flesh rising from the top of Bree's black satin bra. He loved that contrast of light flesh and dark clothing. It showed off the pureness of her ivory skin.

"I don't work out."

"I don't care." What he had seen looked beautiful to him, not overly thin, not buff, just soft female flesh, with the curves in all the right places. Ian found the zipper on the side of her skirt and yanked it down. A hand inside it, and he managed to knock the clothing off her hips and to the floor. Ian pulled back slightly to just drink her in, standing in front of him in her bra and panties, her hair sliding across her face and down over her shoulders.

"You're absolutely stunning," he said. "I don't have the words to describe your beauty, Bree, I really don't."

Even though her cheeks pinkened, she just said, "Thank you." Then ripped his shirt down his arms and tossed it to the floor.

Whoa. That was fucking hot. Ian had thought that was only his fantasy in the dreams, but apparently it was Bree's as well, because her eyes were burning brightly with desire. "Can you tear my jeans off like that, too?" he asked.

"I can try."

That was all a man could ask for.

The pants weren't as easy as the shirt, but Bree did manage to get them down to his ankles so he could step out of them. She also managed to grope across his erection along the way, and if the sly smile on her face was any indication, she damn well had done it on purpose.

"Does it meet your standards?" he asked.

"Mmm-hmm." Bree licked her bottom lip.

Ian groaned and reached back and yanked the quilt off the sofa. He dropped it on the floor in front of the fireplace and paused. He looked at Bree. "Is there a fire burning in your dreams?"

Her eyes widened. "Yes. But like I said, we can't use the fireplace. I don't even have any wood."

"Weird." Ian also didn't remember them using a condom in his dreams, but he retrieved one from his wallet and tossed it down on the quilt. This was real. Better. "It doesn't matter."

He stood in front of her for a minute, tracing his fingers down her shoulders, her arms, across her stomach and to the waistband of her panties. The anticipation was exciting, painful. He felt like he had waited, well, a whole year for this. So he kissed her, pulling her down onto the lumpy quilt, catching her head before it hit the floor. Part of him wanted to ask her if she was sure, but he didn't want the answer to be no, so he said nothing and trusted that she would stop him if she changed her mind or had second thoughts.

Ian went on his knees, one on either side of her legs, and kissed Bree, closing his eyes to savor. He kissed her neck, burying his hands in her silky hair, and breathed in her scent. She smelled exotic, like spices you'd find in the pantry, and he licked her shoulder, sucking her clavicle.

Bree made a small sound of surprise, but Ian didn't look up at her face. He cruised down to her breasts, which rose and fell in time with her quickening breathing. Reaching behind her back, Ian undid her bra and slid the straps down, pulling the whole thing to her waist and wrists. Bree was swallowing hard, her body moving restlessly, and he suspected it was nervousness, so Ian only allowed himself a brief glimpse at her rounded, pale breasts before covering a dusky nipple with his mouth.

He felt like he already knew her body in a weird sort of way since he had made love to her over and over in his dreams, so he went on instinct, the familiar tug and suck and pull garnering the same reaction from her in reality that it had so many nights in his sleep. Bree dug her fingernails into his back and made delightful moans of encouragement that spurred him on, and he switched from one breast to the other and back again until her nipples were shiny and taut from his attention. His erection was bumping against her inner thighs, and she moved against him, lifting her hips to grind them together.

Instead of giving her what she was asking for, he pulled back so they were no longer in contact, and he had the pleasure of hearing her disappointed mewl. But the sound cut off when he took her panties and peeled them down, then spread her legs by pushing her knees apart. He paused a moment then, just to check his control, and to look at her. She had her arms above her head, her eyes half-closed, her full lips open, black hair tumbling over her pale skin. When he bent over and kissed her, right on her clitoris, she jerked a little on the quilt. Glancing up the length of her, Ian moaned himself when he saw she had taken a finger and was biting the tip, the black fingernails of her other fingers splayed across her jaw.

She was the sexiest thing he had ever seen.

"I find you so beautiful," he said, and before she could reply, Ian buried his mouth between her thighs.

He stroked across her warm, moist flesh, and dipped his tongue inside her, the way he knew, just knew she would like.

When he pulled back, she said it just like she did in his dreams, "More. Please. More."

He could do that. He could do this all day and all night, taste her tangy sweetness and listen to her rhythmic cries of pleasure. When her thighs tensed, he pulled back, preventing her from an orgasm. Then he went back, licking and sucking, his body taut with desire, aching with the urge to possess her, but his control holding him back. He wanted to take her there again and again, so that she was insensible with want, then only then would he push inside her body. The floor was hard on his knees, a cool draft wafting over them, raising goose bumps on Bree's dewy skin, but he just pulled the quilt around her sides and kept going.

There was no awkwardness, no holding back, no first-time fumbles or strokes that caused zero reaction. Everything he did turned Bree on, and every sound, every move she made heightened his own arousal. They did know each other, they knew the steps to this dance, they knew where they were going and how to get there. Ian didn't stop to think about it, but just felt, just let it go, just focused on her body and its reaction and how to make the most of her acute pleasure.

When her moans were trailing off, her breathing and arousal so intense that her voice was raspy and losing projection, her thighs trembling, her eyes closed, arms slack against her sides, head turning restlessly from side to side as he ate at her, Ian knew it was time. Shucking his boxers, he used one hand to stroke her and the other to clumsily unroll the condom.

Then as he poised over her, he spoke the only words he ever remembered saying in his dreams. "Open your eyes, Bree. Look at me."

She did, her eyes a midnight blue, darkened with desire, glassy and bright in the waning afternoon light. "Ian," she said, voice husky.

Something about the way she said his name, the way she looked up at him, with trust and desire, twisted things inside Ian, and he felt a wave of possessiveness roll over him. This wasn't about just now, this was about him and Bree, being together, starting something powerful and intimate and sensual. He wanted her, in all the ways that mattered.

And it was real.

Bree's breath caught at the look on Ian's face. He looked fierce, a thin sheen of sweat on his forehead and upper lip, his biceps taut from holding himself over her. He had a sense of power about him, a control, a primal warrior quality about him. She never would have thought that, but now that she saw him, knew him on an intimate level, she knew it made perfect sense. He was successful because of those qualities, and right at the moment he was dedicated to driving her insane with want.

She didn't know how, or maybe she did in its unbelievable way, but he knew her body, understood what she liked without her speaking a word, and he had her primed and on the edge. If he had let her, she would have come six times already, but he had pulled back, kept her from an orgasm over and over, so that her body felt oversensitive, her mind liquid puree.

When he pushed inside her with a hard thrust, Bree knew it was over, that she couldn't stop it any longer, and she shattered, her back arching, her body clenching around him. He lengthened her orgasm by stroking in and out at the perfect pace, not too fast, not too slow, so that she could close her eyes and enjoy the pulsing ecstasy on and on, until she was fairly certain she had stopped breathing, had died, and had risen above her body to another plane of existence.

Could someone say holy shit? Bree pried her dry eyes open and stared up at Ian, her body jellied and slack on the quilt, his erection still hard and intimate inside of her, sparking little postorgasmic tremors. He was biting his lip, which she found endearing, and because he had done so right by her, Bree spread her legs farther and tipped her hips, so that he would go deeper.

In appreciation for her efforts, he gave her a low moan, then thrust harder, sliding her backwards on the quilt. She knew when he was going to come, saw it on his face, felt it in his pause inside her, understood that for whatever reason, she knew this man sexually, had a connection that was raw and intense and loaded with passion. When he collapsed on her chest, she welcomed his weight, enjoying the way he panted in her ear, and stroked her hair back from her face.

He stayed inside her while they both fought for air, and Bree tried to restore her heart rate to something less than a hummingbird's. She had no idea what to say, but the silence didn't feel uncomfortable. She could actually feel his smile, even without looking. It was there on his face, and she could feel it and hear it, and it made her smile in return.

It was three in the afternoon, and she was naked on the hardwood floor in front of her Christmas tree with a man she barely knew, and she felt nothing but contentment and a sensual satisfaction.

"Ow," Ian said, pulling out of her.

"Ow? Don't tell me that hurts."

"Well, it does, figuratively, but the reason I said 'ow' is because your cat just walked across my ass, claws out."

"Are you serious?" Bree tried to glance around Ian's shoulders for Akasha. "I didn't feel anything."

"That's because she walked on my ass, not yours." Ian kissed Bree's forehead and rolled onto his back next to her with a sigh.

Bree spotted her cat then, down by Ian's feet, looking up at her calmly, the mistletoe in her mouth. "Oh. She wanted what has become her new favorite chew toy."

"She definitely has a thing for mistletoe."

"I think I do now, too." Bree grinned at Ian. "It seems to be working for me."

He grinned back. "It's doing really positive things for me as well."

Bree would have been content to just lie naked with him for a while, but it was December, and she lived in a drafty old house. A wicked breeze was whistling in from the nonfunctioning fireplace and rushing over her flushed skin, making her shiver. The quilt was no protection since she couldn't pull it fully over them or they'd wind up on the bare floor. She was about to give in to the inevitable and tell Ian they needed clothes or a bed or a hot shower, when he spoke first.

"I'm sorry, you're cold, aren't you? Here, stand up, and we'll wrap you in the quilt." Ian stood up, giving her a hell of a view of his tight butt, and reached his hand out to help her up.

It was such a small thing. Such an obvious thing. He knew she was cold, felt her shiver, wanted to fix it. No big deal. Common courtesy, the sign of an observant man. It was no big deal. Yet Bree could count on one hand the number of times the men she had dated had paid attention to her needs or wants on that level. It just showed her that her baby sister was right—she had definitely been dating the wrong sorts of men, and no matter what happened with Ian, he had shown her that she was done fixing broken men. She wanted a partnership, a mutual respect in a relationship.

"Thanks." Before she could even consider the fact that she was standing naked in front of him and her giant picture window facing Main Street, Ian had her bundled up in the quilt papoose style, disregarding his own lack of clothes.

"Should we finish my tour of the house or do you want to go get that late lunch I promised you?"

He was holding the front of the quilt closed and dusting little kisses on the side of her mouth. Bree felt herself warming up, from the inside out. He was seriously cute, and she liked that he wasn't trying to run out on her now that they'd had sex. She was hungry, but somehow the idea of leaving her house with Ian, going out in public minutes after they'd touched each other in such intimacy, made her feel weird.

Which meant she needed to get a grip and just do it. She was a grown woman, and dating—if they could call it that—a lawyer from Chicago was not a dirty little secret. "Food is good."

"You're good." Ian gave her a searing kiss, the tangy taste of sex still in his mouth.

Bree freed her hands from the blanket and placed them directly on his bare butt. Nice and tight. She squeezed lightly, and he bumped forward against her.

"Can I pick up some stuff and spend the night here?" he asked. "Do you mind?"

Hell no. "I'd like that."

"Good. Now get off my ass or we'll never get out of here."

Bree pulled her hands away with a grin. "I don't know what you're talking about."

"Sure you don't." Ian turned and reached for his boxer shorts. He was holding them in his hand when he glanced back at her. "Hey, Bree?"

"Yeah?" She had no idea what he was going to say, but she wasn't worried. She trusted Ian, for whatever reason.

"How do your dreams end?"

"They always end right before, well, right before I have an orgasm." She refused to blush.

He studied her for a second, then nodded. "Mine too. So I guess we're on our own from here on out."

"Guess so." The reality of being with him felt too satisfying to worry about it though, and it was so much better than dreaming.

"Reality is definitely more satisfying than dreaming."

Bree felt that shiver run up her spine again as his words echoed her thoughts. She didn't understand what had happened, was happening, but she was too much a believer in signs to deny it or back down.

This, whatever *this* was, was meant to happen.

"Yes, it is. Infinitely more satisfying."

Ian pulled the condom off of himself with a wince. "Though messier."

Bree laughed. "True. But I'm willing to get a little messy if you are."

"I am. I absolutely am."

The look in his eyes was so fierce and sensual that Bree stepped back before they got messy all over again. She would spontaneously combust if he touched her again without a recovery period.

"Good."

And hopefully that one word would convey everything she was feeling, confused and mysterious and overwhelming as it was.

Chapter 5

Ian wasn't sure why he had ordered eggs and hash browns at four o'clock, but it just seemed like the appropriate thing to eat at a place called the Busy Bee Diner. The booth was sticky, the portions huge, and the waitresses sassy and efficient. He drank his coffee black and smiled across the table at Bree.

She still had a tousled look to her, her cheeks flushed and her hair erratic. He liked to see her this way, liked knowing he had satisfied her.

"This isn't exactly the fine dining you get in Chicago," she said, glancing around the restaurant.

"No. But I grew up in a town like Cuttersville, so I'm comfortable here."

Bree looked at him in amazement. "You did? I have a hard time picturing that."

That's because he had tried so damn hard to shed the dust of Prairie, Illinois, from his feet. Too hard. "Yep. I was the town poor kid who never fit in because we didn't live by the rules of a small farming community. We had a farmhouse but had no acreage. My mother had two kids by two different men without ever being married. She was an eighties hippie, growing our own food and living off welfare. None of those things were particularly acceptable to the locals."

"I can see that." Bree gripped her coffee cup. "I'm sorry, Ian. It doesn't sound like an easy way to grow up."

He shrugged. "It was fine. My mother loved us, and she taught us how to survive on our own. I owe a lot of my success to her lessons in tenacity." He really didn't look back on his childhood negatively, despite the poverty and the disapproval from adults toward his mother. If anything, he had been a cosseted town favorite because people had felt sorry for his lack of a normal life, as they deemed it. Ironically, though, his mother had been a better mother than any of them could have ever grasped. "In fact, in some ways I think I'm still a small-town boy at heart. I've tried to convince myself I love the city, but I get claustrophobic. I was actually thinking about buying a house in the suburbs and commuting downtown just to have some space to myself."

"I can't imagine not having my own yard or porch. Whenever you want to be outside you have to share it with other people."

Her grimace gave her opinion on that. Ian smiled. "You don't like to share, do you?"

"Not particularly. I like people, I want them around me, but I like the peace and quiet of being outside by myself. I like my big old house and my space. I like this town, in all its quirkiness. And I like that no one thinks anything of a Murphy girl being a witch. It's sort of expected."

Ian wasn't sure he wanted the answer, but he was too curious not to ask. "So what does being a witch mean exactly?"

Bree laughed. "I can hear the skepticism just dripping from your voice. It's kind of funny actually. But the thing is, I'm not professing to be capable of what characters in Harry Potter can do. Witchcraft is just harnessing the magick within all of us via spells . . . it's a nature-based religion that practices goddess worship. I was born with a sixth sense though. I can sense people's feelings and see their auras."

Yeah. He really hadn't wanted this answer. Auras weren't logical. "I'm trying to understand this, Bree, I really am, but I'm struggling. What the hell is an aura exactly, and how can you possibly see it?"

He didn't mean it as a slur, and she didn't take it that way. She just smiled. "I bet your mother knows."

"Probably. But unfortunately, she died two years ago. Cancer." And now there was a lump in his throat, damn it. His mother would have liked Bree, no doubt about that.

"Oh, I'm sorry." Bree reached across the table and put her hand over his. "That must be really difficult for you."

"It was. Is." Ian laced his fingers through hers and squeezed. "But I'm serious . . . what does an aura look like?"

"It's the energy that surrounds everyone. They're in colors, which indicates mood to me. Together with the emotion I can sense from their feelings, I can usually tell what mood someone is in and what they're generally feeling."

"What color is my aura?" Ian resisted the urge to pat the air around him.

"Right now it's white. You're content."

Now that was kind of cool. He was content. Relaxed. Enjoying the moment. "Very true. What was it when you met me?"

"The first time? In the coffee shop? You were radiating disapproval. You didn't like my nail polish."

Ian couldn't believe she even remembered meeting him, it had been so brief. But so very significant for him, setting off his year of erotic dreams. "That's not exactly accurate. It wasn't disapproval toward you, it was toward me. I was instantly attracted to you, and that didn't fit into my plan, so I was annoyed with myself."

"What was your plan?"

"To focus on my career and date corporate women who know their way around a boardroom and who understand my lifestyle." Now he wasn't even sure why he had thought that was a good idea. It wasn't really even who he was, and the idea of a high-profile romance with chichi dinners and expensive vacations held zero appeal. "You forced me to look at my plan and realize it was never really what I wanted."

"What is it that you want now?"

He wanted to say "you," but he had already said that to her once that day. And it wasn't the true, full picture. "I want to slow down. I want to have a life outside of my career. I want to date a woman whose company I enjoy, who is a friend, who appreciates the small things, and when I'm with her, I don't have to pretend that I grew up upper middle class." He thought Bree fit the bill, and that did crazy-ass things to his insides. "What do you want?"

"What do I want?" Bree held her coffee in front of her chin and sniffed it. "I want a relationship with a man who respects me as a partner. I want my part-time job at the library to be full-time, because I love working with the kids. I want just enough money to pay my bills but still have enough free time to be with my family, to take care of my house. That's not so much, is it?"

"No. It's not." And listening to her, Ian was having insane lunatic thoughts. Like maybe they could combine their goals and be together.

"Why did you come back to Cuttersville?" she asked. "You didn't really need to give me that offer on the house in person, did you?"

Busted. "No. I wanted to see you, to convince myself that the you in reality couldn't live up to the you in my dreams." Ian stroked her fingers. "I was wrong."

Bree's eyes had darkened. "When I opened the door and you were standing there, I was just about knocked out by the sexual intent rolling off you. I knew you wanted me."

Great. "Was it the erection that gave it away?" he asked ruefully.

She laughed. "No. I didn't look. But there was instant chemistry between us. You can't deny that."

"No, I definitely can't deny that." Ian was about to say something about them dating long-distance, having a future, and probably scare the complete shit out of her with his overeager aggressiveness, when the waitress saved him from himself by plunking a plate of eggs and hash browns down in front of him.

Bree had a chicken salad, which she didn't look all that interested in. While he shoveled eggs into his mouth to appease his completely empty stomach, she just played with her fork.

"Ian, why do you think we've been sharing the same dream?"

That was the million-dollar question to which he had no answer. "I don't know. I don't understand things like this, Bree. I've never been . . . spiritual." It was something he had neglected and ignored, frankly, in the need to pay the bills and achieve corporate success.

"But you're not close-minded to such things, are you?"

Ian thought about that. "No. No, not really. I have a hard time wrapping my head around it, but I do realize there are some things we can't really explain. They just are."

Like his rapidly growing feelings for her.

Bree studied Ian's face. He looked sincere, and he had been amazingly open to her discussing being a witch. He was definitely different from what she had assumed he would be like, and she was enjoying his company. It was odd how they weren't the polar opposites she had assumed based on each of their appearances. In fact, they had a lot in common when you got down to the basics, and she liked him.

Really liked him.

And she was about to say something crazy that maybe she shouldn't say, but she figured she acted out of emotion, always had, always would, and if he was going to be with her in any way, he would have to accept that facet of her personality. So she might as well come out of the gate being true to herself, and he could take it or leave it.

So she opened her mind and told him what had been rolling around in her head. "I think that the reason we've been sharing this dream in our sleep state, is because we're sharing a dream in our daytime lives."

His forehead furrowed. "What do you mean?"

"I mean that we have the same goals, essentially. We both want to hit the pause button, enjoy family and a house and a relationship. We're both lonely and looking for something with someone. With each other."

There it was. All laid out on the table in the Busy Bee. Everything she'd been thinking. If he thought she was a flake now, well, she'd save herself some time and potential heartache. If he agreed, then maybe, just maybe, it could be the start of something wonderful.

Ian did look like he'd taken a two-by-four in the face, but he wasn't running out of the restaurant screaming.

What he said was, "Maybe you're right, Bree. After today, I'm willing to believe just about anything."

"Really? You don't think I'm insane?"

He shook his head solemnly, setting his fork down. "No. I think you're amazing."

She'd take that.

* * *

Ian was holding her hand as they walked up her driveway. It was new and strange, but in a giddy, exciting sort of way. It was her house, and they were going to it, a messenger bag filled with his overnight things slung over his shoulder. It was easy and comfortable, like they were a couple, and he did this every weekend.

Her elderly neighbor Edith waved to her, myopic eyes wide with curiosity as she checked out Ian, studying their linked hands. Wonderful. The gossip that Bree Murphy was hooking up would be all over town by morning. Not that Bree cared, exactly, but it would mean a phone call from her mother, and unlike most mothers, there would be no censure. Instead, her mother would be gleeful that Bree was finally getting some, and she would press for details. Bree loved her mother, but she did not want to discuss her sex life with her. She didn't want to discuss her sex life with anyone except the man she was having sex with.

To that end, she glanced up at Ian and said, "You're making me the subject of town gossip."

He looked amused and even had the nerve to wave to Edith. "Do you care?"

"Yes," she lied. "So you had better make it worth my character defamation."

"Sort of like if everyone thinks you're being thoroughly debauched, I really should thoroughly debauch you?"

"You have to admit there's a certain logic to that," she told him as she fished in her purse for her house key.

"I'm all about logic." Ian held his hand out for the keys she had retrieved. "So I'll have to debauch you."

"Damn you." Bree gave him the key chain, letting her fingers slide across his bare skin. She wanted him again, immediately if not sooner.

"I'm going to start now, right here, on your porch."

"Don't do it," she warned him, in a voice that clearly conveyed she absolutely did want him to do it.

"You." He pulled her up against him. "Can't stop me."

Bree reached inside his coat and wrapped her arms around his waist. "I can scream."

Ian laughed softly. "In pleasure, maybe."

"Puh-leeze."

His hands were somehow miraculously on her butt, and they were sliding lower and lower, sort of stroking in a way that made her suck in a breath at the kick of desire that sideswiped her.

"Is that a challenge?" he asked, his head bent close to hers, his mouth inches from hers.

Duh. "Yes. Try to make me scream." Preferably not on her front porch in thirty-degree weather, but at the moment, she was even willing to give that a go.

"You're really asking for it, you know."

"Yes, I am." Bree was enjoying that Ian looked more than willing to give it to her. He had an erection pressing firmly into her thigh, and he looked like he could literally eat her from the bottom up right there with no encouragement. Perfect.

"Here it is then," he said, as he closed the distance between them and took her lips in a searing kiss.

Bree barely had time to open her mouth before Ian was slamming her back into her front door and burying his hands in her hair as he kissed her senseless. Whoa. Hello. Bree gripped the front of his jacket for support and gave as good as she got. There was definitely amazing chemistry between them, and he could make her hot in less time than it took to sneeze. Her mind went blank, and she forgot the cold, forgot the gawking neighbor, and only registered the heat, the pleasure, the intense desire to touch all of this man everywhere, to know him, to have him inside her.

The front door popped open suddenly from his hand turning the knob, hurtling her backwards. She would have fallen, but Ian held her steady before easing her carefully down onto the floor. He kicked the front door shut with his foot and Bree blinked up at him as he hovered over her, unzipping his pants.

"Are we having sex on the floor again?" she asked, spreading her legs slightly in invitation.

"I think so," he said, his fingers already shoving her skirt up. "I'm sorry, but there are just too many stairs in this house. It will take at least three minutes to get upstairs and I can't wait that long."

Bree gave a soft moan when he slid her panties down more quickly than carefully. "That is a long time to wait."

"And I am supposed to be debauching you."

"You're doing a good job of it." Bree would have added a comment about the view they were probably giving anyone who happened to wander up onto her porch and glance in her giant windows—like say Edith from next door—when her breath was literally taken away from his pushing inside her with an aggressive thrust.

Bree's eyes rolled back in her head and her entire body stood up and did the happy dance. "Oh, Ian."

She couldn't imagine why she had ever thought it was a good idea to go twenty months without sex. Sex rocked, and she loved it, especially with Ian. He knew every way to touch, every way to take, and she liked that he never hesitated, that he just knew his intentions would be well received.

He stroked in and out of her faster, then slower, harder, softer, teasing her until she was squirming beneath him and rocking her hips up to meet him, begging for more, for release, for him to never stop. The way she had in her dream. "Ian . . . please. God." Bree had no clue what she was even asking for, she just wanted everything, all of him, wanted him inside her indefinitely, and the blissful feeling of an empty mind to go on and on.

She was sliding backwards on the floor, her fingers jerking across his firm chest with each of his thrusts, and she couldn't react, could only feel, appreciate, breathe.

"What, Bree? What do you want?"

He had to ask that, when she was too steeped in pleasure, too insensate to articulate what she was feeling, so she just pried her eyes open and met his steady gaze. "You. I want you."

Ian groaned. "Bree."

She felt his orgasm, felt his muscles clench, his shoulders tense, felt the pulsing of him deep inside her, and she let go herself, came together with him, so that they were wrapped in pleasure together.

Ian dropped kisses on her forehead, her temples, her cheek, the corner of her mouth. "You are beautiful."

Bree smiled, her body and her soul incredibly satisfied. He had said she was beautiful at least four times that day. Not that she'd been keeping count, but it was nice to hear. "And you're hot."

"I'm going to carry you upstairs now," he said. "I need a twenty-minute nap, then the debauching will continue."

"You can't carry me all the way upstairs. There's like seventeen steps."

"Are you insulting my masculinity?" Ian pulled away from her and readjusted her skirt so it fell to her ankles again.

Rolling her eyes, but with no real irritation, she said, "I'm just being practical. We're going to fall if you try to carry me. And those steps are hard. Trust me, I've had the bruised knees to prove that running up them talking on your cell phone is not a good idea."

"I'm doing it."

"If you drop me, I'll curse you." Bree stood up and debated whether she cared if her panties were still lying on the floor. It seemed like a hell of a lot of effort to bend back over and pick them up when she was feeling so satisfied, sleepy, and tranquil.

Ian solved her dilemma by scooping her up into his arms, bouncing her a little to get a better grip.

"Ah!" She clung to his shoulders, off-balance. "Ian. I'm serious."

"And I'm tenacious. Get used to it." He started toward the stairs.

Bree was tempted to close her eyes so if she fell, she wouldn't see the floor rising up to break her nose and knock her teeth out, but she was too enamored by his cuteness to not take advantage of the closeness the position gave her to his face. She rubbed her lips over his jaw and the corners of his mouth.

"You think I'm going to drop you, so you go and distract me?" he asked. "Not a good idea."

"Sorry." Bree just watched him the rest of the way up the steps, studying the fine lines flaring out from under his eyes. Enjoying the length of his thick eyelashes and the strength of his jaw. "How old are you?"

"Thirty-two. In the best shape I've ever been."

His breath was a little ragged, and he had a death grip on her.

Bree laughed. "I can see that." At the risk of distracting him yet again, she brushed her finger over his lip. "But remember that you never have to prove anything to me. I know."

She wasn't entirely sure what she meant by that, but she could sense his feelings, could sense the contentment and happiness he felt with her, the wonder he had at his attraction, attachment to her. She sensed he was falling in love with her, and she was doing the same.

It was insane, but it was real.

"Thank you." Ian hit the landing, and said, "Which way?"

"First door on the right."

He finished the odyssey by ungracefully dropping her down

onto her bed and collapsing beside her. "Now leave me alone, Bree, I need some sleep."

"I haven't done anything! This is all you, every time." She loved their banter, that he could tease and take it back in return.

"Witches shouldn't lie." Ian stripped off his T-shirt.

Bree laughed, and shed her own skirt and sweater before pulling back her comforter. "Why not? Not that I'm lying, but if I was, why can't a witch lie?"

"I don't know. It seems deceptive." He punched the pillow to fluff it up and smiled at her.

"Such is the nature of a lie."

"Very true."

They both laughed. When Ian reached for her, she gladly went into his arms and fell asleep.

Chapter 6

Ian woke up, the dream still fresh in his mind, so real that he glanced around the room to figure out where he was. Still in Bree's room, the light from the bay window was gone. It was night already. He reached for her, needing and wanting to feel her warmth. He didn't understand the dream he'd had, didn't know where they had been in it.

"Bree?" he whispered, aware that she was probably still asleep, but not caring. He wanted to hear her voice in the dark.

"Yes?" she said immediately.

"Did you dream?" he asked cautiously. When he had planned this trip to Cuttersville, it had been his intent to end his dreams of Bree. Get over them, move on. Now that he'd had her, now that he was getting to know her and he saw how truly fabulous she was, he didn't want the dreams to end. In his sleep or awake. Bree had come into his life for a reason, and he wanted to explore the full length and breadth of that meaning.

That was why the dream he'd had bothered him.

It hadn't been sexual. Nor had it been in her house.

"Yeah, I had a dream. Not the same one as before though, so it must have just been some jumbled thoughts cramming together." She rolled over and snuggled closer to him. "We were in some house I didn't recognize. It was kind of dirty in the living room, and there was no furniture, just a card table and a bare artificial Christmas tree. Who knows where my mind pulled that all from, but it's probably pure exhaustion." She kissed him, her tongue sliding along his bottom lip. "You wear me out."

Ian would have liked to give that kiss and her innuendo the response she was clearly asking for, but he was too unnerved. "Bree, I had the same dream. It was the same house you're describing. There was some woman there I've never seen in my life, and I could swear you and I were actually upset with each other. What the hell could we have been doing?"

It had been as vivid and real as his more pleasant sexual dreams, only in this one, instead of the scent of Bree's perfume, he had smelled the mustiness of a house that had been empty. He'd seen the dust on the floor, felt the cold of a room that was only being minimally heated. He'd known the sharp agony of Bree's disapproval. Toward him.

He didn't like it, any of it. He wanted to stay together, warm, in her bed all winter, content with exploring each other's bodies and minds and hearts.

"What? You saw the same house? Are you sure?" She went up on her elbow and looked at him in the darkened room. "That's weird. It was like it was abandoned or for sale or something."

Ian was about to say he'd thought the same thing when his cell phone rang on Bree's bedside table. He reluctantly pulled himself away from Bree and grappled for the phone to check caller ID.

Damn. It was Darius Damiano, his eccentric millionaire client who wanted to buy Bree's house for indecipherable reasons. "I really should answer this, babe. It's a client. Do you mind?"

"No, go ahead. I have to go to the bathroom anyway."

Ian said, "Ian Carrington," into the phone, distracted as he watched Bree walk across the room naked before pulling on panties and a T-shirt retrieved from her dresser. It was dark, but not pitch-black, and he could see the outline of every one of her delicious curves as she moved.

"Carrington, it's Darius Damiano. I figured out how to get that house I want."

"What?" That snapped Ian back to reality. "What do you mean?"

"The Victorian monstrosity in Ohio's Most Haunted Town. I know you said the owner isn't going to sell, but I did a little digging, and she's going to want to unload it after she hears what I found."

Ian gripped his phone tighter, glancing toward the doorway through which Bree had disappeared. This didn't sound good. "What did you find?"

"She owes eighty grand in back property taxes. Turns out her granny had a little arrangement with the appraiser and her house value was frozen at 1989 prices. I suggested this was illegal and might land him in some trouble if he didn't reevaluate the property and go after back taxes, and he agreed with me."

"Holy shit." It was all Ian could think to say. He was sitting in Bree's bed in the very house Damiano was talking about. Bree was going to be furious, and somehow Ian doubted she had a spare eighty grand lying around. He felt a measure of responsibility in that he should have known Darius was a wealthy businessman—he went after what he wanted, and usually got it. Ian should have seen some kind of maneuver coming, but he had been too busy undressing Bree to pay attention to the signs.

"And I'm reasonable, you know that. I don't want to screw her. I'm perfectly willing to still give her my last offer. It's significantly higher than market value, and she'll be able to pay the tax bill and still have the same cash that she would have if she sold the house in an open market."

It was reasonable, and wouldn't leave Bree out any actual money. But Ian couldn't support the way Darius had gone about securing himself a purchase, nor could he ever put a price on Bree's attachment to her grandmother's house. It wasn't about money, it was about emotion. And Bree's ran high. God, she was going to be devastated, and that devastated him.

"I'll inform the owner of her options," Ian said carefully. He heard the toilet flush down the hall, and he wanted off the phone when Bree returned to the bedroom. "And I'll get back to you as soon as possible."

"Thanks. I think we can have this locked up by Christmas. I'd like closing on January 1, and have her out of the house by February 1."

"Okay, I'll present that request to her." Ian really wanted to ask Darius why the hell he was so determined to have a house in the middle of nowhere four hundred miles from his penthouse in Chicago, but Bree had walked back in and was settling down onto the bed beside him. There was no way he wanted to ask that question in front of her. It was going to be hard enough to tell her what was going on. "I'll call you as soon as I have an answer, Darius."

"Great. Thanks, Ian."

Ian turned off his phone and set it back on the nightstand. He stared at the table and tried to formulate words for what he had to tell Bree. He had none. The situation sucked, plain and simple.

Bree touched his back. "What's the matter? Who was that?"

"That was Darius, the client who wants to buy your house."

Bree felt a tremor of alarm disrupt the calm contentment she had been feeling. Ian was acting strange. He wasn't looking at her, but was staring intently at her nightstand, his back arched. "What is this Darius like? And what did he want now?"

Ian finally glanced at her over his shoulder. He was biting his fingernail. "What's he like? Well, he's . . . brisk. Efficient. He's twenty-eight and worth close to $50 million, so he has a certain confidence."

Bree still wasn't sure why Ian looked and sounded so stiff, so she leaned against his bare back and kissed his shoulder blade. "How does someone get fifty million dollars by the age of twenty-eight? That's unreal. Did he inherit it?"

"No. He investigates hauntings for a television show, and he's made some wise investments."

She forgot all about her desire to squeeze the warmth of Ian's rock-solid biceps and sat straight up. "Wait a minute. Do you mean Darius Damiano? The guy who stays overnight in haunted houses on camera?"

"Yes."

Sure she'd seen Ian wince, Bree crawled around until she was off the bed and standing in front of him. "What is going on here?"

"Well. He still wants to buy your house."

"No!" Bree put her hands on her hips. "I wasn't going to say yes before but now that I know who it is, it will never happen. He's a total freak." Just the thought of his walking into her house and putting in some weird modern furniture gave her hives. She had no idea why she thought he would go for contemporary decorating, but he seemed cold, like gray and black and steel would appeal to him.

"How can you say he's a freak because he investigates hauntings? You're a witch."

Bree frowned, offended. "Totally different, Ian. I am not sensationalizing my beliefs, nor am I making money off them."

"Reading tarot isn't putting cash in your pocket?"

Damn it, he had her there. "Okay, that's true, but I don't do it on camera. His show is like a circus act, an illusion. And you have to admit, he goes for drama. I mean, he sleeps in freshly dug graves! Who does that?" She wasn't sure why his show bothered her so much, she just knew that it did, ten times more now that she knew he wanted her house.

Ian put his forearms on his thighs and shrugged. "Twenty-eight-year-olds worth fifty million."

"So why did he call?" Bree was getting cold from standing in her underwear, but she knew there was bad news coming. She could feel it from Ian. There was guilt leaking off him.

"Well, the thing is, he *really* wants your house. So he did a little poking around and he found out that you owe $80,000 in back property taxes. I'll have to contact the county, but I suspect they're due by the next tax quarter deadline, which is January 15."

Bree stared at Ian. She could have sworn he had just said something as insane as that she owed eighty frickin' thousand dollars in taxes. That had to be wrong. Had to be. She wouldn't see eighty grand just lolling around in her bank account anytime in her life. "Excuse me?"

Ian launched into an explanation about her grandmother and something about property values being frozen and some other stuff that didn't register at all because her ears were ringing and her heart was racing and she was pretty damn sure she was going to faint. "Are you actually saying that I have to come up with *eighty grand* in the next three weeks?"

"Yes. You can take a home equity loan against the house to pay for it, Bree. Since you own the house, it won't be a problem securing the loan, and your payments would only be about six hundred a month, I'd think."

"Only? Only six hundred a month. I can't afford that, Ian! I can't afford half that. I work part-time in a small-town library and read tarot cards for tourists. I'm not exactly rolling in it here." Bree clutched her throat, wondering why it felt like she could no longer swallow. "Crap, crap, crap. What am I going to do?" She couldn't even think.

"Is there someone you can borrow the money from?"

Was he smoking crack? Bree looked at him in disbelief. "Not $80,000! I don't know anyone who has that kind of money, except for my little sister Abby. She inherited over $200,000 from my grandmother, but she can't touch it until she turns twenty-one, which is in two and a half years."

"Maybe you can take the home equity loan and take in renters to pay the loan."

Oh, that sounded like fun. Sharing her house for the next fifteen years with a revolving door of strangers. "Eew," she said. "That sounds horrible."

"Well, you can always sell the house to Darius. He is willing to give you the last offer he made, which is way above market value. You'd have enough to pay the taxes and pocket a substantial amount of cash. You'd actually end up better off than if you tried to sell the house yourself."

Bree felt slapped as she listened to his words. So there it was. The source of his guilt. He knew that was the most viable option for her, and he was trying to list the benefits of it because if she sold the house, it made his client happy and him money. "Oh my God," she said. "You knew this all along, didn't you?"

To his credit, he looked shocked. "No! Of course not. He just told me on the phone."

"But you think it's a good idea?"

"I think it's a logical one, but I know how much this house means to you."

"You have no idea." Bree felt tears pricking her eyes. She felt panicked and, frankly, betrayed. Ian could talk his client out of wanting her house. He could find another one for him, even right there in Cuttersville. There were alleged haunted houses all over town, and hers wasn't even one of them. But Ian clearly had no interest in talking Darius out of his underhanded offer. And how did she even know that it wasn't Ian who had dug up the knowledge about the taxes at Darius's request?

All while sleeping with her.

Ugh.

She just wanted to be alone. "Okay, you need to leave. I'm going to get dressed and go talk to Charlotte." Bree glanced around for her skirt. She needed a shoulder to cry on and some advice, and she didn't think it would be wise to do that in her panties, though she just might if she didn't find clothes in the next two seconds.

"I'll go with you." Ian stood up.

"No. No, you won't." Bree grabbed her skirt off the floor and stepped into it.

"Why not?" He gave her a wounded look.

"Because I just want to talk to my sister alone." She yanked off her T-shirt and pulled a turtleneck on. "Is there anything else about this Darius and his crappy offer that you need to tell me?"

"Just that he wants to close on January 1 and he wants you out by February 1."

Fresh tears filled her eyes, and these actually spilled up and over and slid down her cheeks. "Are you kidding me? What a total bastard."

"He's just a businessman, Bree. It's nothing personal."

She could not believe he was coldhearted enough to say something so callous. "Not personal? Not personal! This is my family *home*, Ian. I've been manipulated into a corner and I'm going to lose everything and you're acting like it's not a big deal. Oh my

God. Just get out of my house. Now. Or I will scream, and I am seriously not playing this time." In fact, she felt like she might just start spontaneously screaming regardless of whether he left or not.

"Bree . . . calm down. We'll figure this out. I'll loan you the money."

He reached for her, but Bree dodged him. She couldn't stand the thought of him touching her, and she really, really wanted to be alone so she could break down in private. She hated feeling vulnerable, hated feeling like she was being patronized, hated worrying and wondering if he had manipulated her all along.

"I don't want your damn money. I want you out of my house." She was crying for real now, and it pissed her off.

Ian tried again to touch her, but she just threw his pants at him, hitting him in the face. "Get. Out."

Maybe she was being totally irrational, but she was overwhelmed and hurt and panicked. She wanted to be alone to think, and he was not listening to her or respecting that, which said volumes about him.

"You don't mean that," he said, pulling his pants off his head.

Hello. "Yes, I do. Leave."

He stood there for a minute, and Bree stared him down, her heart pounding and her palms sweaty. His jaw was locked, his shoulders tense.

Finally, he said, "Okay. If that's what you want." He tried to step into his jeans and tripped over Akasha. "Damn it, this fucking cat is always under my feet."

Bree gasped and bent over to grab her cat. "Do not swear at my cat."

Ian rolled his eyes. "I wasn't swearing at the cat. I was swearing *about* the cat."

She bit her tongue before she said something utterly childish. Instead, she just turned and walked out the door.

"Bree!" Ian called after her. "Please, don't do this. We need to talk. We can figure this out."

Except that at the moment she just didn't want to.

Chapter 7

Bree sat in her living room in front of the fireplace the next day, her Yule log resting on the grate, red candles all around it. She felt much calmer than she had the day before. Discussing the bleak situation with Charlotte and Will had helped. The tax bill was a huge problem, there was no doubt about it. Her sister and her brother-in-law had echoed Ian's suggestions for how to handle paying the tax bill, but somehow coming from them the logic was way less irritating.

She felt bad about the way she had handled the situation with him. She was fairly certain she had overreacted, but she had just been so blindsided by the horror of potentially losing her house that she had lashed out at Ian. He had been an easy target, and she wasn't necessarily proud of that. But she didn't really know him well at all, and she had been falling for him. Hard. And that had scared her. So maybe she had found a reason to pull the plug. Which made her seriously annoyed with herself.

She was the one who always professed to believe in signs, to believe in destiny, to believe in her own empathetic ability.

Yet she had ignored all of those and reacted with fear and mistrust.

There was, or had been, something special growing between her and Ian, regardless of how short a time they'd known each other. She had been dreaming of him for a year, and she truly, genuinely enjoyed his company. When she was with him, she felt an ease and a comfort that she had never had with any other man.

Yet she'd thrown his jeans at him and tossed him out. Granted, he still had a little explaining to do as to why he hadn't tried to talk his client out of stealing her house from under her, but Bree understood that to a certain extent, Ian's hands were tied. She had reacted with pure emotion and now Ian was probably back in Chicago and she would never know the fulfillment of what they might have been together.

It sucked, basically. So Bree wanted to burn her log in solitude and ask her grandmother for guidance. She wanted to bring peace and more logic to her life in the new year. She wanted to stop acting first and thinking only later, and she needed to accept whatever was going to happen with the house. She needed to make a decision and be comfortable with it.

Closing her eyes, she visualized her desires, saw them as words and pictures in her mind. Peace. Answers. Ian.

Then she opened her eyes, lit her candles, and spoke softly, "*As you burn, this spell's set free; As I will so mote it be.*"

An hour later, Bree stood up from her fireplace and blew out the half-burned candles. She knew what she had to do. She didn't like it, but it was the option that made the most sense, and she was at peace with it.

She was going to have to sell her house to Darius Damiano. She couldn't ask anyone to lend her that kind of money, even if they'd had it, and she couldn't afford a loan. She had to let the house go, and somehow in her meditations, she'd felt in her heart that her grandmother was telling her it was okay to do the reasonable thing. That she understood.

So Bree went to her computer, found a phone number for the heiress turned real-estate agent, Amanda Delmar Tucker, and gave her a call on her cell phone. Amanda answered right away, and Bree explained to her the situation.

"So, I need to find a place to live, Amanda. Either a rental house or if there's something decent available to buy, I'd be interested."

"No problem, Bree. We'll fix this for you. I do actually know of one property for sale that you might be interested in. It's over on Evergreen Drive, and it's a little 1920s Victorian. Sort of like a mini version of your house, and it's been empty for a while since the owner died and the kids have taken a year to decide what to do with it."

Evergreen Drive. That struck Bree as fortuitous. Evergreens symbolized eternal life since they never went completely dormant during the winter. Bree could use any sign she could get because she was still feeling a little shell-shocked from the whole situation. "So when can we see it? I don't have a lot of time. The buyer wants me out by February 1."

"We should be able to see it tomorrow since it's empty, as long as you don't mind that I'll have my monkeys, aka children, with me. Today was Piper's last day of school before Christmas break, and Logan lives on my hip since he's only six months old. I don't think Danny will be able to stay home with them on such short notice."

"I don't mind. You know I've always thought Piper was a great kid. I'll bring a book for her from the library to compensate her for having to go house hunting on her first day of break."

"She'd love that. And I have to say that I'm damn curious why Darius Damiano wants your house so badly that he was willing to dig through tax records. I know Darius from my clubbing days in Chicago, and he never struck me as mercenary. I'm really sorry he's doing this to you, Bree. I know what that house means to you, and your sisters, too."

Bree swore she wouldn't cry, but her eyes did tear up. "Thanks, Amanda. I'm trying to tell myself that there is a positive reason for all of this, I just can't see what it is yet."

"Sometimes things just suck, you know."

That made Bree give a watery laugh. "That's true."

"And not to change the subject—okay, I am totally changing the subject—but there is a rumor running around town that you're shagging my lawyer. Please tell me that it's true."

She should have known that the Cuttersville rumor mill would be grinding out the news about her and Ian in no time. "It's sort of true. Ian and I spent the day together yesterday, but then he told me about Damiano's 'offer,' which basically forced me to have to sell my house, and I thought he bore some culpability, so I sort of lost it on him."

"Oh, I doubt Ian had anything to do with it at all. He was just acting under the direction of his client. Ian is a really good guy under all the button-up shirts."

Somehow Bree suspected that was the truth.

"So did you sleep with him before you kicked him to the curb?"

Leave it to Amanda to just ask straight out what she was thinking. And leave it to Bree to tell the truth. "Yes. Twice."

"Ooohh, *ma chérie*, that is *très magnifique*." Amanda sounded downright gleeful.

Bree felt the same when she thought back to the feel of Ian inside her. "But then I freaked out on him and threw his jeans in his face and kicked him out."

Amanda gave a short laugh. "Well, that's easy enough to fix, if you want to."

Bree knew she wanted to fix it. Or at least hear Ian's side of the story. "It's too late, Amanda. He went back to Chicago."

She was sure of it.

Ian pulled into the driveway of the house that was for sale and parked his car to wait for the real-estate agent. He considered it a good sign that the listing agent was willing to show him the house on such short notice, and the price was unbelievably low. Ian could afford it easily and still maintain his condo in Chicago. He was very attracted to the idea of having a house in the country, one so close to Bree. Maybe if he was around town, they could fix the rift between them, and God knew, he wanted that more than he wanted any piece of property.

It had been an accident that had led him to the house. After leaving Bree's house two nights earlier, he had taken a wrong turn in the dark and wound up in a part of town he had never seen. He'd turned around in the driveway of this house and seen the FOR SALE sign. Then he'd returned in the light the next day and had felt an immediate kinship to the shabby Victorian. It was calling for an owner, and he was looking to put down roots.

Maybe it was a way to ease the wound of losing Bree so quickly after finding her. He didn't know. But he had looked at that house and felt like Charlie Brown with his spindly Christmas tree. They needed each other.

The agent, Marcy Hancock, had pulled in behind him. "This house needs work," she said as a way of greeting when they both stood in the driveway. "It's been empty for a year, and the mice have made it home."

Ian stuck his hands in his pockets. "I'm aware of that. But it sounds like the price reflects that, and if it's structurally sound, I don't have a problem with a little grime."

"Okay, let's take a look then. Oh, and another agent is bringing a client by to look at it. We might bump into them."

They went in through the back, into the kitchen. It needed serious updating but it had a good layout, and Ian could see it would be an easy job to replace the existing cabinets and do a remodel. Not cheap, but no walls needed to be moved either. He liked the light and the woodwork and the hardwood floors. He was feeling cautiously optimistic when they headed into the living room.

There he just stopped and stared. Holy shit. It was the room, the house, from his dream. It had the same musty smell, the same dusty floor.

The same bare and lonely Christmas tree standing in a corner.

The agent was running on and on about the previous owner and how the house had such potential, but Ian barely heard a word.

It was the house.

And the front door was opening.

He turned and there was Bree, walking into the house.

She saw him, and he felt it, just like in his dream. Her disappointment in him, her longing. The mutual ache from both their hearts.

God, he was in love with her. It was crazy, impossible, but he was.

Just looking at her standing there, snow on her boots, coat bundled up to her throat, gloves on, nose red from the cold, he thought she was the most beautiful woman he'd ever seen, and he wanted nothing more than to pull her into his arms.

"Ian?" she said. "What are you doing here?" She stepped into the entry hall.

He cleared his throat, which was suddenly tight. "I was thinking I might like a place in the country. I found this one by accident."

"Really?" Bree moved into the doorway of the living room, pausing between the open pocket doors. She looked around the room and gasped. "Oh, Ian." There were instant tears in her eyes. "This is the house in our dream."

"Bree," he said, moving toward her, unable to stop himself from taking her hands in his. "I'm so sorry about Darius and the house . . . I swear I had no idea what he was doing. I'll give you the money, I'll do whatever you want me to do to prove that I would never intentionally hurt you. Please understand that. I really, really . . . love you." He couldn't believe he'd said that out loud, but it was true, and he wanted her to know. Ian cupped her cheeks in his hands and kissed her forehead. "You can think I'm insane, but it's true. I know you. Does that make sense?"

"Yes." Her hands wrapped around his wrists, and she kissed the inside of his palm. "I know you had no part in Damiano's offer. I'm sorry I overreacted. I was hurt and overwhelmed, and I always react with emotion."

"I understand."

Bree looked up at him, saw the love he had for her shining in his dark eyes and she felt the peace, the happiness she had asked for. This was the man she wanted, whether it made sense or not, whether it was too soon or not. Nothing ventured, nothing gained, and she knew that Ian was, quite literally, the man of her dreams. "I love you," she said. "And this is *our* house, isn't it?"

"Yes, it is." Ian smiled down at her. "Let's take the rest of the tour together."

"Yeesh, it takes forever to wrestle this car seat out of the car."

Bree turned to see Amanda Delmar Tucker stumbling in the front door in her jeans, a trench coat, and boots with two-inch heels, massive handbag over one arm and a baby carrier over the other. Amanda's son was nothing but a round bald head surrounded by fleece in his car seat. Her daughter, Piper, was standing behind Amanda, holding a diaper bag and peering curiously into the house.

Amanda stuck her sunglasses on her head and took a deep breath. "I feel like a pack mule." Then she seemed to finally realize what she was looking at. "Ian. What the hell are you doing here?"

"I'm buying this house, Amanda."

Amanda set the carrier down and slammed the front door shut. She came toward them, hand out. "No, you're not. Bree is. You've already let your client screw her out of one house, you're not screwing her personally out of another."

Bree thought it was awesome that Amanda was willing to go to the mat for her. But in this case, she didn't actually need to. Bree snuggled closer to Ian. "Actually, it's okay for Ian to screw me personally in this case."

Ian laughed. It took Amanda a second, but then she just said, "Hello. Not in front of my kids, okay? But what do you mean? What's really going on here?"

Ian said, "I think that Bree and I have decided to buy this house together, fifty-fifty. Am I right?" He looked to her for confirmation.

She had never been more sure of anything. "Absolutely."

"I'm confused," the real-estate agent who had been with Ian said.

"Hey, look," Piper said. The little girl had dumped the diaper bag on the floor and was wandering around the room. "There's still an ornament on this tree. It's a cat."

Of course it was.

Chapter 8

"Are you sure you want to do this?" Charlotte asked Bree for about the nineteenth time in the last two days.

"Yes, I'm sure. I'm absolutely one hundred percent sure." Bree held a potted plant in her hand in the hallway of Granny's house. She was almost done moving all of her stuff to the house on Evergreen.

Abby pushed her hair out of her eyes and sat on the chair she had been carrying. "Not everyone needs to know someone for eight hundred years like you and Will did. Most people figure it out a little sooner."

Charlotte stuck her tongue out at Abby. "It was more like eight years, not eight hundred."

"Bad enough. Bree can't wait eight years. She'll be old by then."

Bree smacked Abby's arm. "Thanks. But no, I'm not waiting. Ian and I are starting our life together now."

"I just want you to be happy."

Bree smiled. "I am."

"I can't believe someone else owns this house now," Abby said, her expression sad as she glanced around the empty front rooms.

Bree reached out and squeezed Abby's shoulder. "I know. Me either." It was the only sad spot in a bright future. She was going to miss the house, miss the memories that could be found around every corner. But somehow she knew this was her grandmother's way of telling her that it was time for a new phase in her life.

"Hey, look, Akasha left that mistletoe bunch on the floor." Charlotte pointed to the corner of the living room, by the fireplace. "We should probably grab that."

Bree stared at the mistletoe and smiled. "Nah. I think we should leave that for Darius Damiano. It sounds like he could use a little love in his life."

Abby scoffed. "Or someone smacking him upside the head."

"You're not talking about me, are you?" Ian appeared in the doorway, Will behind him.

Bree smiled. "No, we're just insulting Darius Damiano."

"Fair enough," Ian said.

"What else needs to go out?" Will asked, ever the efficient and brawny cop.

"This chair," Abby said, still sitting on it.

"Well, I guess you need to get out of it then, Squirt."

Bree would have expected Abby to make a smart-ass remark back to Will, but instead she just stared into the parlor. Then she said, "I'm going to live in this house, Bree. I just saw it. I'm older, and I live here. With a dude."

Bree wanted to dismiss it as Abby's melancholy over losing the house, but she remembered Abby's prediction about Ian, and she had to trust it. Or at least that it was a possibility. "I can see that, Abby."

Ian came over and whispered in her ear, "I love you. And I can't wait to debauch you in our new, freshly painted, remodeled house."

Bree turned slightly and kissed his cheek. "I love you, too. And I love the debauching in case you hadn't noticed."

"Oh, I've noticed."

Bree was wondering if they could get rid of everyone else for one last romp in the house, when her brother-in-law called over to them.

"Hey, Ian, give me a hand. Let's get the show on the road." Will was bent over, hands under the seat of the chair Abby was sitting in.

Ian went over and together they lifted the chair and carried a squealing Abby toward the front door. Charlotte hooked her arm through Bree's. "You okay?"

"I'm great." She had her sisters, her brother-in-law, a man she loved, a new house.

It was wonderful. It was magick.

Sweet Dreams

LINDA WINSTEAD JONES

Chapter 1

There were a dozen houses on Holland Court, and each household was represented at the annual Christmas party, which was, as usual, held on the afternoon of the second Sunday in December. Ruby had been tempted to skip the affair, to pretend to be sick or busy or antisocial, but weaseling out of anything Hester Livingston was in charge of was usually more trouble than it was worth.

Besides, she'd drawn a name, as had everyone else on the cul-de-sac. This year she was Secret Santa to Zane Benedict, the studly and standoffish professor who lived across the street from the house Aunt Mildred had left to Ruby in her will. Mildred had died more than six months ago, and the grief was still very sharp. When Ruby had buried her aunt, she'd buried all that remained of her blood kin, and the holidays only made her more aware of that fact.

"Did you lose a bet?"

Ruby glanced up from her seat in a chair against the wall to see that the professor himself stood before her, the box of cookies she'd made grasped in his hands. Large hands, she noted, with long, well-shaped fingers. She'd seen him from a distance more than a time or two, but never so close. She couldn't help but take a moment to study the details. His black hair was too long, curling just a little on his neck, but she suspected the style was a result of neglect, not design. His brown eyes were amazingly dark and deep. He needed a shave, this late in the day, and his clothes were the norm, for him. Jeans. Boots. A dark gray long-sleeved T-shirt. How tall was he, anyway? Six-three, she'd guess, but then she was sitting and he was standing.

Benedict hadn't been here for last year's Christmas party. He'd moved into his house shortly afterward—in February, if she remembered correctly. He'd skipped the early-summer picnic and made only a brief appearance at Aunt Mildred's funeral. She was actually surprised that he was here today. He didn't seem to be the neighborhood-party type. Mildred had loved these neighborhood affairs.

"What?" Why would he ask if she'd lost a bet? She blinked twice, fast, and pushed away the threatening tears that had crept up on her.

"The sweater." He gestured with the box.

Ruby glanced down at the holiday sweater Aunt Mildred had given her last year. Yes, it was gaudy and busy and too bright, but it was also festive, and she was trying very hard to feel festive. "It's Snoopy," she said. "You don't like Snoopy?"

"It's not becoming," the professor said. "The garment is too big for you and the design is garish."

"You came over here to tell me you don't like my sweater?"

Like her, Benedict was quiet in a crowd. He hadn't exactly been the life of the party thus far. Ruby wondered what Hester had threatened to get him here.

"No, not really." He offered the box of cookies to her. "I don't eat white sugar or white flour."

Ruby had thought nothing could take her mind off of her aunt today. This was Mildred's neighborhood, Mildred's friends, and it was impossible to be here and not be reminded that Mildred was no longer among the living. And yet somehow this odd man had turned Ruby's morose thoughts around. "I'm very sorry for you," she said, perhaps more coolly than was necessary.

"I'm not allergic," he responded, missing her subtle sarcasm. "I simply thought you'd like to give these to someone who will actually eat them. It would be a waste to throw them away. I'm sure those who eat this sort of thing will find them enjoyable."

Talk about ungracious! "The gifts are from Secret Santas," she said. "What makes you think I gave you those cookies?"

He tilted the box so that she could see the name of her business there. RUBY'S SWEET SHOP was emblazoned on white in bright, crisp crimson. "You're not particularly good at being deceptive, I would deduce."

Someone else could've bought them at her shop, but the professor was right, of course. "In that box there is an assortment of my best-selling cookies. Macadamia white chocolate chip, oatmeal cranberry, peanut butter chocolate chip, and orange-walnut. I understand eating healthy, I really do, but every man should indulge on occasion. Would it kill you to eat a cookie now and then?"

"Probably not," he responded seriously. "But refined sugars . . ."

"I don't want to hear it." Ruby snatched the offered box from his hands.

Instead of walking away from her, as he should have, the professor sat next to Ruby and asked, "What did you get?"

He couldn't have simply walked away once he'd returned her gift. No, he had to stick around and make awkward small talk.

Ruby placed the rejected box of cookies on the chair beside her and reached under her chair to grab the gift bag she'd stashed there. She held it out so he could see inside.

"Candles," he said brightly as he peeked into the bag. "Very practicable to have on hand in case the power goes out."

A loose strand of black hair fell across one eye. Ruby studied his face while he was peering at her candles. The professor was handsome but not cute; his features were more interesting than pretty. His face had the nice, clean lines of a healthy man who doesn't eat white sugar or white flour. His lips were just full enough, and he had smart eyes that seemed to notice everything. She had noticed it all before, but from a distance. Up close, there was a surprising power about him. An intensity she should have expected but had not.

"Yes, I suppose they are practicable."

He looked around the room—Hester's basement, where the Christmas party was almost always held—as if he were searching for someone. There was an almost instant disconnect. Was he one of those absentminded professors who sometimes forgot to eat and missed doctors' appointments and birthdays? It sure looked that way.

The other neighborhood bachelor headed her way, and Ruby sighed. Todd made the professor look downright normal, and that wasn't an easy task. His long gray hair was pulled into a ponytail, as usual. Today's tie-dyed T-shirt was done in Christmas colors. Red, white, and green swirls were stretched over a protruding belly. The shirt had seen better days. And the professor thought Snoopy was bad!

"Hey, Ruby! I found this under the tree." Todd waggled a small, square box in her direction. "It has your name on it."

"There must be a mistake. I already have my gift." She held the bag of candles aloft.

Todd looked at the tag hanging from the brightly wrapped box in his hands. "No, this says To: Ruby Kincaid, From: A Secret Admirer."

A chill walked up her spine. Maybe it sounded romantic, but in her mind a secret admirer was just one step away from a stalker.

"That's weird," she said softly as Todd offered her the gift. "I don't think I want it."

Todd and the professor both seemed surprised. "I thought women liked gifts," Benedict said.

"Me, too," Todd said.

It occurred to Ruby that the only two unmarried men in the room were with her, and if the box really did come from a secret admirer it was likely one of them. Oh, she hoped it wasn't Todd! Weird as the professor was, he wasn't a forty-four-year-old man living in his mother's house, living off of unemployment combined with money and prizes from radio and television contests and one long-ago moment of glory on a network game show.

"Fine." Curious, she offered her hand for the box. Best to open the thing and get it over with.

Both men watched curiously as she carefully unwrapped the box. She had never been one to tear into pretty paper, but instead picked away the tape with care and removed the wrapping paper in one barely wrinkled piece to reveal a sturdy white gift box.

She placed the paper aside and opened the box, finding that whatever was inside had been protected by white tissue paper. She removed the tissue as carefully as she had the gift wrap. At the bottom of the box sat a pale green figurine of a cat, perhaps two inches by three. She lifted the figurine out of the box and studied it carefully, noting the incredible detail and the heaviness of the stone. Jade, perhaps? Whatever it was, this was no cheap knickknack.

"Wow," she whispered. "This must be some kind of mistake."

"Interesting," the professor said. "May I?" He offered his hand.

"What is it?" Todd asked. "A doodad? Not very romantic, considering it came from a secret admirer. Perfume or jewelry would be better. I won some really expensive perfume when I was on television, but I gave it to my mom."

"I like it," Ruby said defensively as she finally placed the cat on Benedict's palm. Neither of the men acted as if they knew anything about the cat, which was odd. Who else would've gone to so much trouble to give her an anonymous gift? Who else would've signed the card "secret admirer?" It didn't make any sense. If the secret admirer was one of the married men who lived on the street—that really was creepy.

The professor studied the figurine as if it were made of solid gold. He turned it this way and that and studied all sides, taking in every aspect. "This appears to be quite old," he said. "The work is incredibly detailed. See the hairs here, and the shape of the mouth? Extraordinary." He lifted his head and looked at her, his dark eyes deeper than before. "Would you mind if I borrowed this piece for a few days?"

"Why?"

"I'd like to do a bit of research if you don't mind. Classes are out for the holidays, and I have some time on my hands."

"It's just an ornament," she said. "It's pretty and intricate, and I agree that it's interesting, but if it were worth studying I doubt it would've ended up in a box with my name on it."

"Please," the professor said softly.

"Hey, Ruby!" Todd called too brightly.

Her head snapped around. She had forgotten that he watched. "Yes?"

"I have tickets to a concert in Birmingham on Thursday. Won them in a radio 99.1 contest." He told her the name of the popular band and grinned. "I was the tenth caller. They're really good seats."

"Thanks, but I can't." At least once a month Todd won tickets to something, and he always asked her to go along. Maybe her love life was nonexistent. Maybe she did spend her nights alone. She had a feeling if she ever said yes to Todd, she'd be stuck for life. Lonely as she sometimes was, that was entirely unacceptable.

"Are you sure?"

"I'm sure."

"I don't want to ask someone else, then have you change your mind." It sounded almost like a threat.

The professor did not take his eyes from the figurine in his hand as he said, "For heaven's sake, Todd, she said no. Go away."

Todd looked annoyed, but he did leave. In the crowded basement, he didn't have far to go before he ran into another victim. He honed in on poor Mrs. Logan, the very shy widow who lived on the other end of the cul-de-sac.

"So, can I borrow this?" Benedict lifted his head and looked at Ruby expectantly.

He looked so anxious, so excited, she almost gave him an instant yes, but something stopped her. "Well, Professor . . ."

"Zane," he interrupted. "Call me Zane. We are neighbors, after all."

Her heart did a strange little flip. It was the expression in his eyes and the intimacy of calling him by his first name and the fact that all day she had been hyperaware that she was all alone in this world that made her insides react. Ruby took a deep breath. "Well, Zane, if you want it that badly . . ." She opened the box that sat on the chair beside her and reached in, randomly plucking out a cookie. Orange-walnut, she noticed as she held it beneath his nose. "Live a little. Eat a cookie."

Zane didn't hesitate. He'd worked too hard, given up too much to get to this point, to let a little dietary lapse get in his way. He didn't even bother to take the cookie from Ruby's hand but simply dipped his head and took a big bite.

He was prepared for the cookie to be tasty, and still the flavor that burst on his tongue and the way the sweet melted in his mouth took him by surprise. Yes, it had been a long time since he had indulged. In anything.

Watching his reaction, she smiled with evident satisfaction. It was a tempting look on a very pretty face, he admitted. The soft smile, the twinkle in her green eyes, they were very nice.

"More?" she asked softly, and he responded by taking one more bite from her hand. The second bite was as good as the first, but without the shock.

As he savored the second bite of the decadent cookie, he studied Ruby Kincaid. She wore her dark brown hair very short. At the moment it was shorter than his. On most women it might've been too severe, but the style suited her face and made her eyes look larger than they might've if she had a mop of hair. No, it was best that the neck and that pixie face be shown off to their best advantage. Not that he should be thinking about how she looked. Poor girl, she had no idea what was about to happen—if he was right and this was *her*.

It was a shame, really. Taste in holiday sweaters aside, she seemed like a very nice person. He did not understand why she was alone, when her looks and baking skills should have men lined up at her door. True, she was a few years too old for the college students who made up a large portion of the population of Minville, Alabama, and more than a few years too young for most of the professors at the college that was the heart of this small town, but there were many men in between.

Of course, in order to meet men, one had to be available. Ruby was not. She'd moved into the house directly across the street from Zane shortly after her aunt's death this past summer, and he had studied her, just as he had studied the others in the neighborhood. She left the house shortly after five every morning, headed for work. Ruby's Sweet Shop was located within walking distance of the college and did a brisk morning and lunchtime business. There were a number of part-time employees, all students, who apparently spent a good portion of their salaries on cakes, cookies, and pies. Ruby served coffee as well as sweets, but none of those fancy caffeinated concoctions that were served at the chain store down the street. No, nothing was available to compete with the taste of her scrumptious creations.

He understood why, now, as the flavor of the cookie lingered.

She closed at two in the afternoon and headed straight home—unless she stopped by the grocery store on her way, in which case she'd be home by 2:35. Once home, she worked in the yard, did laundry, cleaned the house she now called her own, perhaps grabbed a nap before dinner. Her lights were always off by nine at night, and sometimes as early as eight thirty. She was open six days a week. So, where was the time for a personal life in that schedule?

Zane took what was left of the cookie from Ruby and finished it in short order. By the time he was finished, she wore a wide smile that broke his heart. She had no idea what was coming. Maybe he was wrong. He could still hope that he was wrong.

"See?" she said as he swallowed the last bite. "A little bit of indulgence now and then isn't a bad thing."

He looked her in the eye, and she blushed. Ruby might push indulgence on other people, but he suspected she didn't practice what she preached. She led a structured, dull life, apparently of her own choosing.

If he thought telling her to run would save her, he would. Not only would she not believe him, he was convinced that running would not do her any good at all. They would find her; they would bring her back and keep her where she needed to be until the time was right. Time was running out.

The party was winding down. A few people had already left, and Hester busied herself picking up dirty dishes. Time to go. Zane reached past Ruby and grabbed the box of cookies. "Can I walk you home?" he asked as he stood, cookies in one hand, cat statuette in the other.

Ruby was momentarily stunned. It wasn't as if he'd been an overly friendly neighbor to this point, but until now he hadn't been sure. He hadn't known, until he'd seen the cat, that she was most likely the chosen one. He also hadn't realized that someone in this neighborhood was actively working against her. The fact that the jade cat was here at this party, and not left on her doorstep or sent by mail, hinted that one of Ruby's neighbors was involved.

If he didn't find a way to save her, she wouldn't live to see Christmas.

Chapter 2

One of the things Ruby most liked about Holland Court was that the houses were all different. Some were brick, others were clapboard. The colors of the houses were alternately bright and subdued, indicating the personalities of those who lived within. In newer subdivisions, the houses all looked alike and the yards were small and there was no character. This older neighborhood, built in the fifties, definitely had character. Even the Christmas decorations hinted at the residents of those houses. Some were tastefully done, others were garish. A few, hers and the professor's among them, sported no holiday decorations at all. She kept planning to take Mildred's decorations down from the attic, but she'd just not gotten it done. There weren't enough hours in the day. Besides, she was doing her best to avoid the holidays, so why should she torture herself with a tree no one but her would see?

Her house was a soothing pale yellow, and she'd worked very hard to keep up Mildred's garden and the profusion of plants on the front porch and the back patio. It wasn't a big house, not by any means, but it was lovely and warm and homey. And paid for. Zane Benedict's house was brick. It was solid and well kept, but his tastes in accommodations were as simple as his tastes in clothes. She suspected inside there were lots of bookcases and gray or brown furnishings.

Todd lived just south of Zane, and his house was just as his mother had left it when she'd moved to Florida and put him in charge of the family home. The split level was white with blue shutters, and of all the neighbors, Todd was the last to mow. She didn't think he owned a weed eater. Unless he managed to win free landscaping service, his lawn would never be great. He had strung up sloppy but colorful Christmas lights around the porch, and there was a large plastic Santa on his lawn. Inside she suspected there were lava lamps and beaded curtains and black-light posters. She hoped she never found out if she was right or not. All up and down the street, she could see the personalities of the homeowners in their dwellings.

In hers, she still saw Mildred. Would she ever put her own stamp on the place? Did she dare?

She was surprised that Zane stayed with her as home grew near. He'd shortened his stride to remain beside her, and actually seemed to be walking her to the door. The very idea made her heart constrict. Her cookies were good, but no man had ever taken a bite, then latched on to her as if he was staking a claim.

Later in the evening it would be cold, but right now the air temperature was pleasant enough, even though they were well into December. That was a benefit of living in the Deep South. Her Snoopy sweater was actually a bit too warm for the day.

After a moment of awkward silence, when Zane turned toward her house with her, Ruby blurted, "I'm not looking for a man. I don't want a man in my life. I'm perfectly happy being single and

I don't intend for that to change." She didn't add that she was not desperate because that would sound, well, desperate.

"Okay," he said, sounding not at all surprised or hurt.

"It's just, I don't want any misunderstandings," she explained. "The holidays have a tendency to make people weird."

"I get it," he said. "I'm not hitting on you, I'm just being neighborly."

"As long as that's clear," she said, trying to sound firm but not stern. She probably ended up sounding like a bitch, but better a bitch than a tease. She wanted all her cards on the table. "So, how long do you plan to keep my cat?"

"Just a few days," he said. "Is that all right?"

"Sure. I'm actually interested to hear what you can find out about it. The thing is definitely unique."

He made an absent and noncommittal sound in his throat as they stepped onto her front porch.

"Good night," she said as she put her key into the door and turned it.

"Thanks for the cookies," he said.

"Sure." She closed the door behind her and locked it, and for a moment she just stood there, back to the door as she took a deep breath, suddenly convinced that she should've skipped the party and stayed home and weathered Hester's wrath.

The rest of the evening passed as usual. She put on her pajamas and watched a show she had recorded on her DVR. She'd eaten so much junk at the party that she wasn't hungry, but around seven she ate a bowl of cereal. Tomorrow morning would come early, so she crawled into bed about eight forty-five and pulled the covers to her chin. Her alarm was set for four. Monday mornings were always a bear, and even though classes were out for the holidays, she had lots of orders for parties and gifts, and even the locals frequented her shop. She was lucky. Business was good.

Afraid that the day's excitement would keep her up too late, Ruby closed her eyes expecting to fight for sleep. Instead she drifted off almost immediately.

Callida wanted to fight against the bonds that restrained her, but she was too weak to move. He had put something in her wine, something intended to take away the last of her strength. She was helpless, bound and prone on a cold stone floor. She wanted to call for help, but even if she could manage to make a proper sound, who would come? No one. She had no one to rescue her, no one to miss her when she was gone. The one person she had believed to be her friend had put her in this position. Dezso had pretended to care for her, he had promised to show her the wonders of Rome, but instead he had kept her here, far from the great city, always promising tomorrow and tomorrow and tomorrow. He had clothed her in fine chitons and fed her an abundance of food and given her gifts of jewels and other pretty things. And now he had betrayed her; he had poisoned her and bound her hands and left her here. Why?

The door to her stone cell opened, and Dezso walked inside. He smiled at her, smiled with great warmth even though he had lied to her and made her his prisoner and drugged her so that she could barely move.

"What you are about to do is very important, Callida," he said in his soothing, pleasant voice. "You will make the ultimate sacrifice in the name of a power much greater than any you have ever known."

"Please, let me go," she whispered.

Dezso shook his head. "I cannot. It is time. Do you see the moon?"

Callida turned her head—it was a great effort to do so, as her head felt heavy and her vision swam—and she saw the full moon through the small window high in the stone wall of her cell. It was bright, and large, and it shimmered with power. "I see."

The man she had loved stood over her and began to chant, calling to a demon to rise. Callida tried to scream but could not. Dezso clasped some-

thing in his hand, and from that hand black smoke began to rise. No, this was not smoke it was simply blackness, a darkness so deep it looked bottomless. What began as a formless blackness grew and took shape before her very eyes. The shape was not that of a man but was of a large, black cat with tremendous paws and glowing red eyes. It was solid and yet was not, as if a great nothingness in the shape of a large cat floated on air.

With a mounting horror Callida realized that Dezso offered her to the blackness, he gave her to this monster that grew and took shape before her. Again she tried to scream, but no sound came forth, not even when the dark cat hovered above her, blocking out all other sights, and its red eyes captured and held hers.

She stopped trying to scream. It was too late for that. Much too late. And she was too terrified to make a sound or fight her fate. The demon—for yes, it was indeed a demon that Dezso had called forth to take her—placed its empty face close to hers. And it inhaled . . .

Ruby was jerked out of the dream with a scream. Her own scream, one that died quickly, caught in her throat. Good heavens, she'd never had a nightmare like that one! She'd been watching and participating at the same time, she'd been terrified as if she'd been the one sprawled on cold stone, sacrificed to a dark monster. Lying in bed, Ruby rubbed a hand up and down her arm. She still felt chills, as if her blood ran icy cold. What had she eaten at the party to bring on such a nightmare?

She glanced at the clock. Not quite 2:00 a.m. She had two more hours before her alarm went off but wasn't sure that she could sleep after that vivid dream. Great. What a way to start the week!

It was dark in her bedroom, the only illumination coming from the bedside digital clock and a decorative porcelain night-light on the other side of the room. What little light she had was enough to draw her eyes to the object that sat on her bedside table, an object that should not be there. The cat figurine, the one she had allowed the professor to borrow, stared at her.

Ruby muttered a curse as she sat up slowly, blinking hard, wondering if this was still a dream. She'd seen Benedict walk away from her house with the figurine in his hand. How had it gotten here? She reached out slowly and touched the pale green cat. Strangely enough, it felt warm. Alive. She drew her hand back. That nightmare had certainly revved up her imagination.

The damn cat had not been on her bedside table—had not been in the *house*—when she'd gone to sleep. It was here now, and that was fact, not the product of a bad dream. She shook herself into full awareness, throwing off the last of her dream along with the blanket that covered her and kept her warm. Had Zane Benedict broken into her house and placed the statuette there? What other explanation was there? She threw her legs over the side of the bed. Was this supposed to be some kind of sick joke?

No, this wasn't funny, it was creepy as hell. Studly or not, she did not want men she barely knew—or even men she knew well—creeping into her bedroom at night to leave signs of their visit. Ruby grabbed her bathrobe and stuck her feet into warm, fuzzy slippers. She snatched up the green cat and headed for the front door.

She stopped in the hallway between her bedroom and the living room, her step stuttering. What was she thinking? Her first instinct was to run across the street and confront Benedict with the evidence, but maybe that was just what he wanted. Maybe he was waiting for her by his front door—or in the darkness somewhere between her door and his. Two in the morning. Holland Court slept. There would be no one to see her, and no one to hear, if anything went wrong.

Ruby fell into the wall for support, and when her knees went weak she gave in and sank to the floor. Until this moment she hadn't thought to be afraid of the professor. Why should she? He was a known factor, a quiet neighbor who ran every evening and kept odd hours and mowed his yard when it needed to be done. She'd always suspected he was one of the very smart people who lived in his own little world, which was odd, perhaps, but odd in a normal way. He was a well-respected member of the academic community. A couple of her employees had mentioned him a time or two, not only bringing up the fact that he was cute but that they loved his classes. A while back she had heard one student mention that he taught some kind of psychology.

She remained on the floor for a few long moments. Her luck with men had never been the best. They turned out to be unfaithful or dishonest or else they lost interest in her and her workaholic schedule. Not that she'd had a slew of serious relationships in her twenty-eight years, but there had been a few. None of them had panned out, and in the past couple of years she'd been content enough just to drift alone. It was easier that way.

But now, sitting in the dark with a nightmare still on her mind and the proof that a man she barely knew had been in her bedroom, she didn't know whom to call. A year ago she would've called Aunt Mildred, but Mildred was gone.

She could call Todd, she supposed. He'd love that, wouldn't he?

No, she should call the police. With that in mind, Ruby pushed herself to her feet and walked toward the living room and the phone there. Of course, by the time she reached the couch and grabbed for the receiver, she realized that she *couldn't* call the police. She could swear up and down that the cat figurine had been in Zane's possession when she'd gone to bed, but she had no proof. She wasn't hurt.

A quick check of the doors and windows showed that everything was locked tight. The dead bolts were engaged on the front door and the back. To all appearances, it looked as if it would be impossible for Zane or anyone else to have broken into her house to leave the cat.

That statement alone was enough to keep her from dialing 911. *Someone broke into my house to leave this cat figurine, then sneak out, leaving no other sign that he was ever here, and somehow locking the dead bolts behind him.*

Deflated and wondering if she was losing her mind, Ruby collapsed on the couch, the figurine still clutched in her hand. She carefully placed the green cat on the end table, grabbed the phone book out of the table drawer, and snatched up the phone.

Zane hadn't been asleep very long when the phone rang, jerking him out of a deep sleep. Shit. Phone calls that came in the wee hours of the morning were never good. Never. He lifted the receiver and glanced at the caller ID. Shit, again. He barked hoarsely, "What's wrong?"

The voice he expected to hear responded, "What makes you think anything is wrong?"

He breathed a sigh of relief. Ruby sounded okay, at least. "It's almost three in the morning," he said. "No one calls at three in the morning unless something is wrong."

She breathed steadily, perhaps more deeply than was normal, but did not immediately respond. After a couple of minutes that dragged on too long, she said, "I have to know. How did you get this blasted cat into my house?"

Zane threw off the covers and leapt from the bed, cordless phone in hand as he ran into his office, which was set up in the spare room across the hall from his bedroom. Sure enough, the figurine he'd left sitting on his desk was gone. He had studied it for quite some time before retiring, but he was positive he'd left it *right there*.

Obviously, the cursed thing had found its way to Ruby's house.

He couldn't tell her the truth. Not yet. She would never believe him, and he wouldn't be able to do what had to be done.

"Well?" she prompted sharply.

"I don't know what you're talking about," he said, forcing a yawn she was sure to hear.

"The little cat knickknack that was left under the tree by my secret admirer," she said testily. "I let you have it to study, but when I woke up after having a bad dream, the thing was sitting on the table by my bed. Don't play dumb with me. You put it there, and I want to know how and why."

"You changed your mind, don't you remember?" Zane said, trying to sound sympathetic. "I was going to study it. It's quite an interesting piece, and I think it might be jade, and there are small markings that I'd like to magnify and study."

"I didn't change my mind," she said softly. "You took it home with you."

"No, you kept it. If you've changed your mind I can pick it up tomorrow . . ."

"I . . . brought it in with me?"

Zane leaned against the doorjamb and took a deep breath. Guilt was an unaccustomed and uncomfortable feeling for him. He was usually unfailingly honest and forthright, but now was not the time. A lie that made Ruby question her sanity was better than the truth. "You did. Listen, are you all right? You don't sound like yourself. I can come over."

"No," she said quickly. Too quickly. "I'm just tired, I guess, and the bad dream shook me more than it should've." She laughed uncomfortably. "And apparently my memory is starting to go."

"Want to tell me about the dream?"

"No," Ruby whispered. "I'm sorry I woke you. Good night." With that she ended the call. Zane walked to the front of the house without turning on a single light. There he pulled back the curtain to look across the street to Ruby Kincaid's yellow house. Every light in the house, every light he could see from this vantage point, was on. Living room, bedroom, dining room. The nightmare, and waking to find an object she knew had not been in her possession when she'd gone to sleep, had shaken her.

"I'm sorry," he whispered to the well-lit house. "I wish I could make this go away." Unfortunately, it was much too late to make Ruby's troubles disappear.

Chapter 3

Five hours of sleep weren't enough for Ruby. She could get by on seven, but she loved to get eight good hours. When those five hours were followed by a rude awakening and a questioning of her sanity, it made for a bad day.

Fortunately, many of the students who made up her clientele were home for the holidays, and business was slow. No business-woman should hope for business to slack off, but she could use a break, so she was allowed. A couple of her part-time employ-ees were also away and unable to work, but Marielle, the one who had been with her the longest—three full years, now—was still in town. Marielle was perfectly capable of running the front part of the shop, especially on a slow day like today.

Ruby kept herself busy in the kitchen, only occasionally giving in to a yawn. She had lots of baking to keep her busy; in addition to the usual cookies, cakes, and pies, she had a special order for three pumpkin cheesecakes with cranberry glaze to fill.

She glanced at the clock often. Usually the day flew by, and she was surprised when two o'clock came around. Today, she kept glancing at the big clock on the kitchen wall, wondering if two would ever arrive. She wanted to go home and take a nice, long nap.

It was just past one thirty when Marielle, who wore a huge smile on her young and pretty face, stuck her head into the kitchen. "Oh my God," she whispered. "Professor Benedict is here to see you."

Ruby's first thought was, "You're kidding, right?" But judging by the awestruck expression on Marielle's face, there was no joking involved.

"I'm busy," Ruby said, returning her attention to her work. "Tell him to go away."

Marielle's blue eyes went wide. "Come *on*. It's Professor *Benedict*, and he wants to talk to *you*."

Ah, such youthful exuberance. The way she said "Benedict" was so filled with awe she might as well be whispering "Johnny Depp."

"I heard you the first time," Ruby said. "If you think he's such a big deal, you talk to him."

Marielle pursed her lips. "No wonder you don't have a social life."

After the door closed, Ruby made a face at the cheesecake. "I could have a social life if I wanted one," she whispered.

Too soon, the kitchen door swung open again. "He said if you don't come out he's coming back here, and he's not wearing a hairnet just to talk to a stubborn woman even if she is pretty and likely the best baker this side of the Mississippi."

Ruby lifted her head and glared at Marielle. "Did he really say that?"

"Yes!"

She took a deep breath and exhaled slowly. This was a complication she did not need, but she couldn't make herself brush Zane off again. "I'll be right out." After Marielle was gone, Ruby washed her hands and removed her chocolate-stained apron. She made sure she removed the hairnet before pushing against the door and leaving the kitchen that was her domain.

"Everything here is filled with white flour and white sugar," she said, pinning her gaze on Zane. "You won't eat any of it."

He lifted the disposable cup of coffee he cradled in his hands, then he smiled. Good Lord, he had a dimple! "I'm thinking of giving up my refined sugar and flour ban for the holidays. Your cookies have been a bad influence on me."

Marielle had to step away to wait on a customer, a fact that obviously annoyed the curious woman to no end.

Ruby stepped around the counter and moved closer to Zane. Like yesterday, like always, he was dressed in blue jeans and a loose-fitting T-shirt. The T-shirt was a dark, dull green, today. It was almost as if he purposely dressed so as not to call attention to himself. It didn't work. "You didn't come in here to buy cookies," she said in a lowered voice.

"No. I still have a few left."

"Just a few?"

"I told you, those cookies have been a bad influence." He looked at her with expressive, dark eyes. "But no, I didn't come here to buy anything but a cup of coffee. I wanted to check on you, make sure you're okay."

"I'm fine," she said.

"You weren't fine this morning."

"I'm sorry I called you in the middle of the night. I guess I freaked."

He smiled again. "A little."

"I think someone spiked the punch, and the liquor went straight to my head."

"Don't tell Hester," Zane said, a hint of teasing in his soothing voice. "She'll surely hunt down the cretin who dared to spike her Christmas punch."

She was losing her mind. Other than that one small detail, her life was nicely settled. She had a routine that suited her, and when she'd told Zane last night that she was not looking for a man, she hadn't been exaggerating. Romance meant drama, and she didn't want any drama in her life at the moment. Maybe her life was boring, but she *liked* boring. It was easy. No one got hurt.

The expression on Zane's face changed. The easy humor disappeared. "What are you doing for dinner?" he asked, taking her by surprise.

"What?" Ah, the snappy comeback.

"Dinner. I thought we could eat. Together. Food," he added when she remained silent.

Ruby gathered her courage and said, "I'm kinda tired. I didn't sleep well last night."

Again, that smile and the dimple. "I know."

"Sorry."

"We still have to eat, and I won't stay late," he said. "Promise."

Stay? His invitation to eat was supposed to mean dinner at *her* house? Boy, did he have a lot to learn about wooing women. That was what he was attempting to do, right? She hadn't been wooed in a long time. She'd gotten really good at shutting down even the simplest advance long before it got to the wooing stage.

"I'm a lousy cook," she said. "I can bake sinfully sweet and decadent treats you'll never eat, but I can't cook a meal to save my life."

"I'm a good cook, but my stove's on the fritz. I'll bring the food if you'll provide the stove, pots, plates, and silverware."

"And dessert," she said, not sure she wanted to agree to his invitation until the words were out of her mouth. She still wasn't looking for a relationship, but she realized as she looked ahead that she didn't want to be alone. Not tonight.

This was a very bad idea. He wasn't supposed to get involved with the woman, he was simply to watch and wait. But he wanted to get a look at the layout of her house, and he really wanted another look at *Il Colletore Di Anima.* The Soul Collector.

There were those who called the dark spirit that lived within the innocuous-looking statuette *Il Gatto Nero*, the Black Cat, but the Brotherhood of Madani preferred a more fitting name. Soul Collector was definitely fitting.

Once upon a time the thing had had a name, he supposed, but as far as Zane or any of the Brotherhood knew, that name had been lost sometime in the past three thousand years or so—give or take a century. If the information that had been gathered by the Brotherhood during those centuries was correct, Ruby's would be the last soul *Il Colletore* claimed. She would be the ninth, and once her soul had been taken the demon would live again. It would live for more than the few hours it normally enjoyed after taking a soul. The dark thing would walk the earth, immortal and indestructible and bringing an unimaginable darkness to an unprepared world. He couldn't allow that to happen.

Zane wished he could convince himself that he was wrong and it was coincidence that someone had given Ruby a cat knickknack, but the fact that the jade statue had made its way from his house to hers on its own made that theory impossible to swallow. Someone in this neighborhood—someone who was aligned with The Order of Runhura, no doubt—had left the cat under the tree for Ruby, specifically. The jade piece had transported itself to Ruby's bedside table. No, he could not even wish to be wrong.

The Brotherhood that was dedicated to stopping the darkness and the Order that worshipped the demon had both existed since sometime long before a Brotherhood wizard had cursed *Il Colletore* to be captured in stone. Three thousand years of sacrifice, of training, of secret warfare, and it all came down to this place, this time, and this woman.

Zane watched as Ruby set the places at the small, round kitchen table. She had a formal dining room, but had chosen to set out their plates here, in the warm, yellow kitchen. Maybe she was afraid eating in the dining room would make this feel like a date, and dating was definitely not on her list of things to do. The kitchen was for neighbors and friends, and he could fit comfortably into that category.

This would be so much easier if he didn't like her. Emotions were only going to get in the way, before all was said and done. Still, while *Il Colletore* wasn't human, Zane most definitely was. He felt that humanity now more than ever. Ruby tried to be tough, but she radiated a very feminine vulnerability that had crept beneath his skin and aroused his most primitive protective instincts. He was also attracted to her sexually, which was ludicrous given the circumstances but undeniable and growing stronger with every passing moment. It wasn't as though his attraction was new. In months past he had thought about how he might live his life after this final crisis had passed. If the demon they fought rose elsewhere in the world and was stopped, then Zane would be free to ask his neighbor on a date. His life was so centered on the Brotherhood, he could not even remember the last time he'd had a real date, a real relationship. There had never been time for such indulgences.

He should've already called in the Brotherhood. There were agents posted in at least twenty sites around the world; there were men like him watching over vortexes where *Il Colletore Di Anima* might rise, one last time. As soon as they knew where the event was to take place, they could converge and see that the final collection did not happen, not here and now. Defeated, *Il Gatto Nero* would be forced to return to the jade and wait another two hundred and eighty-seven years before trying again to rise, and at that time the demon would be someone else's problem.

If the Brotherhood could keep the statue in their possession, perhaps they could find a way to destroy the demon before that time passed.

All possible scenarios had been studied and discussed, and Zane was well aware of the most favored scenario. The Brotherhood would find the next victim. Ruby. They would watch over her closely, just as he was doing now. A group of well-trained warriors would wait for the demon to rise, and they would kill the intended victim, robbing her of her life and robbing the collector of the soul he required to take form. By that time it would be too late for the collector and those who served it to choose another victim, to appear in the heart of another vortex in another town or another country. The time for the taking of a soul was very precise and inflexible. There would be no second chances for the demon, not if the timing was right.

It was a coldhearted but workable plan. Unfortunately, Zane liked Ruby. He liked her a lot. For the first time since joining the Brotherhood and dedicating himself to the destruction of *Il Colletore*, he was having serious second thoughts. There had to be another way.

The demon would rise on one of the three nights when the moon was at its fullest. It was impossible to know which one. In any case, Zane had a matter of days to find an alternative.

Dinner was simple. He didn't want to scare her off with anything too unfamiliar, so he made chicken teriyaki with pineapple salsa and brown rice. Zane actually enjoyed cooking. The simplicity of the task took his mind to a quieter place. Usually. Tonight his mind would not rest. There was no quiet place within him.

He filled their plates at the stove, then carried them to the table where two tall glasses of ice water sat on cheerful Christmas place mats, along with matching cloth napkins and good silverware.

"Looks good," Ruby said as she took her seat. "And healthy."

"It is." Zane sat, after she was settled. Since the table had been pushed into one corner, there were only two spaces available, and they were side by side. "Do you have something against eating healthy food?" He forced his voice to be light, almost teasing. He even managed a smile.

"As long as it's in moderation," she responded. And then she took her first bite. The look on her face was one of surprise. "Oh, this is good," she said after she'd swallowed.

"You sound so surprised."

"Don't get me wrong, it's not exactly an English toffee cheesecake, but it's very tasty."

They managed to eat and talk, and the conversation was very nice. Even though he could and did on occasion cook, Zane was accustomed to eating alone, whether he grabbed something quick or made a full meal. He couldn't even count the number of meals he'd eaten mindlessly while reading a book or working on charts or doing research on the Internet. This was nice, and made him wish the circumstances were different.

They were almost finished with the meal when the doorbell rang. He couldn't help but note how the sound of the bell made Ruby jump out of her skin. She was skittish, as if she instinctively realized something was wrong.

She stood and headed for the front door, and Zane followed. Someone in this neighborhood had given Ruby the jade cat. Someone in this neighborhood was aligned with the Order of Runhura and offering her up to *Il Colletore Di Anima*. That someone would not take kindly to a disruption in her routine, and Zane intended to be a disruption.

Todd stood on Ruby's porch, his tie-dyed T-shirt not quite enough to keep out the December chill, not even here in Alabama, where the winters were mild. He hunkered in slightly and rubbed at his arms to ward off the chill, as he looked past Ruby's shoulder. The man was obviously surprised to see Zane standing there, making himself at home in Ruby's house. Usually friendly eyes hardened, for a moment.

"I didn't know you had company," Todd said.

"Yeah," Ruby said. "What can I do for you, Todd?"

"I won a drawing for a free dinner at Captain Ron's Seafood, and I thought you might like to join me." He waved a piece of paper that was clutched in his meaty hand.

"That's very nice, but I've already eaten," Ruby said kindly.

Zane wondered if Todd's interest was normal and sexual or abnormal and deadly. It was impossible to tell. He had been the one to deliver the anonymous present at the party yesterday, and he did seem to hang around Ruby's house more than he should, but that didn't mean he was in league with the demon. It only meant he was a creep.

"Tomorrow, maybe." Todd grimaced. "It expires on Wednesday, so I need to use it soon."

"I really . . ." Ruby began.

"We're busy tomorrow," Zane said, stepping forward and placing his arm around Ruby's shoulder. It was a pose that said, very clearly, *mine*. His eyes communicated the same, as they met Todd's. "You're going to have to find someone else to take to dinner."

Todd grimaced. His nose twitched, and he rubbed his hands along his meaty arms. "Do I smell coffee? It sure is cold out here."

Ruby was just about to invite the creep in when Zane reached past her to grab the doorknob. "Good night, Todd," he said as he swung the door closed. And locked it.

"That was rude," Ruby said, tilting her head back to look up at him.

"You're welcome. Now, tell me why you jumped out of your skin when the doorbell rang."

Ruby felt silly telling Zane that a dream had made her jumpy, but he did teach psychology, so maybe he could shed some light on the meaning of the vivid nightmare. All day she'd expected the dream to fade, as they usually did, but this one had stayed with her. If anything, it had grown more vivid in her mind, more real.

They'd cleared off the kitchen table, and she'd placed her contribution to the meal in the center of the table. Dessert tonight was Death by Chocolate Cake, her best seller at the shop, and a pot of freshly brewed decaf. Zane was eyeing the cake as if it might come to life and bite him.

"There are only two of us."

"You can take some leftovers home, if you can get past the fact that it's not at all healthy." She cut him a huge slice and put it on one of Aunt Mildred's favorite Christmas dessert plates, then cut herself a smaller piece. He poked at the cake with his fork as if he still expected an attack.

"Tell me about the dream that spooked you," he said, eyes on the cake.

Ruby took a bite to delay. She chewed slowly. Maybe if she told the dream aloud, it would sound silly and she could laugh and dismiss it and tonight she'd sleep well. She began, and as she told the dream it did not sound silly at all. By the time she was finished, she had chills all over again. She'd never sleep tonight!

Zane didn't make fun of her or make light of the dream, but instead listened intently. He didn't so much as take a taste of the cake, so when she was finished with the telling—the last bit being the sight of a fathomless black face sucking the very breath out of her—she reached for his fork and cut off a big piece that had moist cake, chocolate chips, white chocolate chunks, and thick frosting. When she led the fork to his mouth, he automatically parted his lips, and she slipped the cake inside.

Zane closed his lips, and an expression of sheer ecstasy flashed across his face. "Good God," he said, taking the fork from her and cutting off another bite, then taking a swig of hot coffee. "This is decadently delicious."

He was always so surprised when her treats tasted good. "Didn't your mother bake?"

"No. She did on occasion buy the generic brand lemon cookies or Twinkies, but I never developed a taste for either."

"Bless your heart," she said sincerely. He literally didn't know what he was missing!

He shrugged. "Your dream," he said, changing the subject. "It's quite interesting. Did you write down the details?"

"No."

"You should. Do so tonight before you go to bed," he instructed. "And if you have any more dreams like that, write them down as well."

"I hope there are no more dreams like that one, not ever again." She shuddered and sipped at her decaf, wondering if she'd sleep at all tonight.

"Dreams often have meanings we must take time to decipher. Yours was definitely unusual. I want to hear immediately if there are more like it."

"I'll call you at three in the morning again," she said, trying for a lighthearted tone.

"Do," he said seriously. "Anytime."

"So," she said, pushing a half-full cup of coffee back. "In your expert opinion, what do dreams like that one mean?"

"Expert?" he asked, taking one more bite of the cake before setting it aside, as she had her coffee.

"You teach psychology, right?"

For a moment he looked confused, then chagrined. "No. I teach *para*psychology."

"Parapsychology," she repeated.

"It's the study of phenomena which have not yet been explained by conventional science. You know," he said when she did not respond. "Extrasensory perception, clairvoyance and clairaudience, telepathy, psychometry, remote viewing, precognition."

Ruby felt deflated. Shit. Zane Benedict was good-looking and smart and sexy, and she had really enjoyed his company tonight. She was even beginning to forgive his insistence on eating healthy and shunning her favorite food groups. Too bad he was a flake.

Zane knew this look. He'd seen it many times in his lifetime. It wasn't as bad for him as it had been for his father. These days there were a greater number of people willing to admit that there was more to life than what could be seen and explained in a rational fashion. Of course there were skeptics. He should've known Ruby was one of them.

"You're not a believer."

"In woowoo stuff?" she asked. "No."

Woowoo was one of his least-favorite words. "I could try to convince you, but I suspect we don't have enough time for that, not tonight."

"Nope. I'd be a hard sell." She did smile a little, which assured him that while she was not a believer, she wasn't afraid of him, either. Sadly, she would be a believer before all was said and done, but by then it would be too late.

Shortly after that awkward moment, he said good night and accepted a huge piece of chocolate cake she insisted he carry home. Death by Chocolate, she called it. Normally, he might find that an amusing name for a dessert, but at the moment there was nothing at all amusing about death.

While Zane did not claim to have any psychic ability of his own, he felt as if eyes were watching him as he crossed the street. Curious neighbors? A jealous would-be suitor? Or a servant of *Il Colletore* who was watching over the latest sacrifice?

Ruby was so tired she didn't have any trouble falling asleep. After placing the anonymous gift on the bookcase in the living room and double-checking all the doors and windows, she crawled into bed, pulled the blanket to her shoulders, and almost instantly dropped into a deep sleep.

Aiyana ran, cutting into the deepest part of the forest to make her escape. Her long black braid whipped as she ran. Her bare feet had been battered against the harshest part of the path, and already her legs were scratched. They bled, a little, they stung horribly. She did not slow down.

When she had found the pretty rock in the creek, she had thought it a gift from the earth, and she had treasured it, hiding it among those few things she called her own, taking it out and stroking it when she could not sleep. The stone was shaped like an animal and had the face of a small panther. Many nights she had passed studying that face, feeling as if it were alive. Now she knew that the stone was not a gift but a curse. A terrible curse. It had come for her soul. Helaku had told her so, right before he'd unleashed the darkness.

She grabbed the protective totem she wore around her neck and squeezed tight, and as she did so she heard the movement behind her. Footsteps crashing through the forest she called home came closer and closer, stealing the last of her hope. She looked up to the full and brilliant moon, which she could see through an opening in the limbs above. The moon was too large, an omen that all was not as it should be. She had always thought the moon was her friend, but tonight it was not. It shone down upon her, offering no place to hide.

Helaku grabbed her from behind and threw her to the ground. He held the cursed stone on the palm of his hand as he pressed her body to the ground with his foot.

Aiyana gripped the totem that lay against her chest. It would protect her from darkness, as it was meant to do. Helaku reached down and pried her fingers apart. He forcibly took the totem from her, throwing it aside to land on the littered forest floor, where it would do her no good at all.

*"*Il Gatto Nero *has chosen you," Helaku said. "Your soul will feed him well."*

"Why, Helaku?" she asked. "Why do you do this to me?"

The old man who had been her father's friend for all of Aiyana's too-short life did not answer. Instead, he looked to the moon and began to speak in a language she did not understand. From the green stone in his hand a dark shape rose.

Aiyana screamed, realizing that the darkness was coming for her. That blackness would take her spirit, it would take all that she was, and she would be no more.

It hurt . . .

Ruby sat up sharply. There was a pain in her chest, a deep pain just like the one that had made a young girl scream for help that had not come. She glanced at the bedside clock. One fifteen in the morning, and she was wide-awake and terrified of returning to sleep. Drugs. She needed drugs to knock her out, so she would not dream.

Unfortunately, she had no such drugs, and besides, that might make matters worse. What if another dream came and she couldn't wake up? She shuddered and rolled over to face the window.

The moon was not quite full, but it was getting there. Just a couple more days. Both of her disturbing dreams had included a full moon. Was it a warning of some kind? Was something going to happen during the full moon?

All was silent, so she could not mistake the soft sound that captured her attention. A deep purr resonated from the very walls, as if a large, satisfied cat hid within them. A large, satisfied *black* cat?

No, just a cat. One of Hester's kitties must've crawled under the house and gotten stuck. Great. Ruby rolled over, intent on grabbing her bathrobe and a flashlight so she could check under the house for a stray cat. She didn't get far before her plans changed.

The jade cat was sitting on her bedside table, in front of the clock. It had not been there two minutes ago, she was certain of it.

Chapter 4

Zane hadn't been able to sleep, but had hours ago settled in front of his computer to study a file of Brotherhood documents. Over the past several years he had read it all, and now he was looking again to see if he might've missed something. There had to be a way to stop *Il Colletore* without sacrificing Ruby.

According to their carefully kept records, the victims were always female and young. Those who had been properly identified had been between the ages of fifteen and thirty-two. There had been no male sacrifices, but that didn't mean a male sacrifice would not be accepted. If he had to get Ruby to a safe place and take on the demon himself, he would. Was there a safe place? Was there anywhere in the world those who served the demon would not find her?

He wasn't surprised when the phone rang. After hearing about Ruby's dream, he'd suspected there would be more. Somehow, the demon had already begun tormenting her.

"Are you okay?" he asked, not bothering with a greeting.

For a moment, she didn't answer, then she breathed a "No," that made the hairs on the back of his neck stand up.

He ran.

Again, all the lights in Ruby's house were on. She lit up the dark street when she opened the front door long before Zane leapt onto her front porch. She was pale, and even from a distance he could see that she shook. Her hair was mussed, and it was so short that meant it stood on end. That style should've been amusing, but was not. She was terrified.

"Tell me you hear it," she said in a hoarse, sleep-roughened voice.

Zane listened carefully. "I don't hear anything."

Ruby laughed sharply, then clapped a hand over her mouth.

Zane closed the door behind him and instinctively gathered her into his arms. She fell there easily, accepting of his comfort. She continued to shake, but the trembling soon eased.

"Better?" he asked softly.

She shook her head. "It's stopped," she said, relief evident in her voice.

"What's stopped, Ruby?" he asked. "Tell me."

"Sounds from the walls and the floor. Cat sounds. Purring, with the occasional mewing." She pulled her head away from his chest and looked him in the eye. "Tell me the truth," she said.

"If I can."

"I didn't change my mind and bring that damned jade cat home with me Sunday night, did I?"

"No, you didn't." He could at least be a little bit honest with her.

"It came here on its own," she whispered.

"I believe so."

"It moved again, from the living room to my bedside table, then from the garbage can to the coffee table. Explain that!"

"I can't," he said, running his hands through her hair to smooth a particularly wayward strand. And to comfort her, too, he supposed.

"I think I'm losing my mind," she said. Though she no longer clung tightly to him, she did not let go.

"I doubt that. Did you have another dream?"

She nodded.

"Want to tell me about it?"

The shake of her head that followed that question was fierce. "Not yet. Aren't you cold?" she asked, wrinkling her brow slightly.

"No." Zane glanced down, just now remembering that all he wore were faded flannel sleep pants. No shirt. No shoes.

"I woke you up again," she said, then she offered him a poor attempt at a smile. It didn't last.

"I wasn't asleep," he said. "I was working on my computer."

"Woowoo stuff?" she asked.

"Woowoo stuff."

Ruby let her head fall against his chest again. "I haven't heard the purring sound since you walked through the door. I don't understand what's going on, but will you stay? Please?"

After half an hour of sitting on the couch watching an old movie with Zane, it was almost possible for Ruby to convince herself that she hadn't heard anything. She'd been the one to put the jade cat on her bedside table. She had never thrown it in the trash can, only to have it reappear in the living room, front and center on the coffee table.

But only *almost*. She had heard the purring. She had thrown the blasted thing in the garbage, but it had refused to stay.

Having Zane sitting in her living room shirtless and warm was a nice distraction, and for a moment she allowed herself the luxury of thinking about something other than her fragile mental state. The no-white-sugar, no-white-flour thing had its benefits, apparently. Beneath those loose T-shirts he always wore, Zane Benedict was fine. More than fine, he was muscled, cut, strong and well shaped. Oh, the ridges and sharp angles were tempting. She wanted to reach out and run her hands along those muscles, she wanted to test them all with her fingertips, to see if he was as warm and hard as he looked.

The fact that she didn't want to be left alone had nothing to do with her attraction. Yeah, right.

She did, eventually, tell him about the newest dream. He seemed concerned, he listened intently and nodded and wrapped his arm around her when her voice trembled. Once he even leaned down and kissed the top of her head, an impulsive move that seemed to take him by surprise as much as it did her.

When she was finished, he said, "Tell me about the totem. Did this girl really think it could protect her?"

"Yes, and the man who brought the dark thing to her, he snatched the totem away from her before releasing . . . whatever it was." She shuddered.

"What did it look like?"

She tried to remember, but that part of the dream was unclear. "I don't know. It was fairly small, and I think there was a crescent-moon-shaped thingie attached to it." Moons again. She shuddered.

"Anything else?"

Ruby shook her head. "What do these dreams mean? And what the hell is going on with that damn cat knickknack?"

Zane didn't answer for a while. "You don't believe in my field of study."

"If my walls keep purring, that's going to change pretty quickly," she muttered. "First things first. How do I get rid of the cat?"

"I'm sorry to say, I don't think you can. Not easily, at least," he added. "I'm going to have to study this a bit before I have any definite answers for you."

"Study tomorrow," she said, burrowing into his side. "If you leave I'll . . . I'll . . ." Go mad, eat every bite of the leftover cake, cry, scream—maybe all four.

"I'm not leaving," he assured her.

Ruby took a deep breath and sighed. On her television screen, men in top hats were dancing in black and white. A woman in a flowing white dress drifted across the screen. It was an odd scene to fall asleep to, but she did, falling hard.

Olwen stopped fighting. She was tired, and she was frightened, and she now knew that there was no escape from this. Her beloved husband Arlin had tied her to her own bed when she'd told him about the dreams. At first she had been afraid he thought her a witch, but now she knew that was not true. He simply didn't want her telling anyone else about the warning dreams.

She'd been here for two days, now. Arlin had seen that she was fed, and he had even given her a washing and dressed her in her best linen shift. The man she loved, the father of her child, made sure she could not escape, but he also cared for her. And then, when he said the time and the stars and the moon were aligned, he offered her soul to the demon he worshipped.

The dark cat stood on her chest and placed its snout close to her nose. It purred, deep and rumbling, so that it seemed the entire world shook. When she had first seen the feline rise from the pretty stone cat her husband had given her, it had been made of nothing. It had been a hole where there should've been none, darkness where there should've been light, but now it was solid, heavy on her chest. It was real. She could see the fur on its skin and the burning red of its evil eyes. Using the power of its mind, the cat forced her mouth to open, and it inhaled, stealing her breath, sucking her life and her soul from her body. She could see her life escaping, white and blue streaks flowing from her mouth into his until there was nothing left of her but what lived inside the darkness.

Olwen, devoted mother and wife, saw her betrayer husband through the eyes of the demon who had killed her. She did not wish to gaze long upon her own lifeless body. She looked so scared in death, so horribly empty.

Arlin dropped to his knees and praised this demon who had taken his wife's soul. The large cat who had once been nothing but a dark hole now had a beating heart and a deep hunger for flesh. He would not be like this for very long, she knew, as she was now inside the demon in all ways and shared his thoughts. A part of this night was all the time he had to feed his hunger of almost three centuries.

The curse that kept the demon trapped in stone for all but a few hours out of nearly two hundred and ninety years was not unbreakable. When he woke the demon took souls, and when the ninth soul was his, he would live again. He would be whole and he would make the world pay.

Arlin looked up, a love and admiration in his eyes. Olwen had once thought such expressions were reserved for her, but apparently his love for the demon was greater than his love for his wife. "I have been promised much for my great sacrifice." Arlin opened his arms wide. "I am your humble servant, Il Gatto Nero*."*

A great black paw swiped out and sliced open the betrayer's throat. A cat's scream filled the small hut, and the baby began to cry. The demon who had taken Olwen's soul could not take another, not until he was whole again, but while he lived he craved flesh, and he started with his most humble servant . . .

Not my baby! Olwen screamed.

The gruesome scene went black, and a soft voice, the voice of the woman who had been sacrificed, whispered in Ruby's ear, "While his heart beats, he can be taken. Do not hesitate, or he will take your soul.

"Trust no one."

Ruby awoke with a cry and all but threw herself at the man who shared the couch with her. Zane, too, had slept, and when he came awake his arms instinctively wrapped around her.

"Are you okay?" he asked.

"Not even a little," she confessed.

"Another dream?"

She nodded, then she pressed her face to Zane's chest and closed her eyes. Another movie was on the television in front of them, this one more somber than the musical that had been on when she'd fallen asleep. There was no singing, no dancing. Lots of angst, judging by the expressions on the faces on her television.

If she believed in curses and living statuettes and telepathy and all that other nonsense, she might be able to make herself believe that the dreams were a kind of warning. Whatever had killed the women who visited her as she slept was coming for her.

She shook off that thought; it made no sense. No more sense than a piece of jade that seemed to move on its own and make the walls of her once-peaceful home purr like a satisfied panther. No more sense than the urge to lose it all in the earthy and pleasurable distraction of sex with a man who was willing to sleep on her couch so she wouldn't have to be alone. Ruby was tempted to lift her head and kiss Zane Benedict and see where that kiss took them. She hadn't been attracted to a man this way in a very long time, and it would be nice, very nice, to enjoy something real and solid and *reasonable*, like sex. He could make her forget, she knew he could, and right now she very much wanted to forget.

After being alone for much too long, she wanted someone to hold. She wanted the complete connection that would come with Zane inside her, when pleasure would wipe away the fear. She had told him so fiercely that she was not looking for a man, but having him here, feeling his skin against hers, it was wonderful. She wanted more.

Ruby didn't consider herself a brave person, but she lifted her head and very slowly moved her mouth toward Zane's. She didn't attack him; she moved so slowly he had plenty of opportunity to move away or turn his head. He didn't. Instead, his lips parted slightly right before hers touched them.

Eyes closed, they let their mouths linger against one another. Immediately a riot of sensations was set into motion. What she felt was strong enough to wipe away the fear of her dreams, to allow her to forget the impossibilities of purring walls and figurines that moved on their own.

Her hand rested on his side, and she allowed her fingers to stroke there, learning the unexpected muscles and strength he usually hid beneath baggy T-shirts. They moved a bit, adjusting arms and legs, getting more comfortable and closer on the couch. She was oddly twisted but didn't care. The kiss took her beyond the terror of inexplicable sounds and terrifying dreams, and she wallowed in it.

Ruby was so hot she didn't mind at all when Zane loosened the belt of her robe and parted it. She enjoyed the rush of cool air, the extra bit of freedom, the feel of his hand slipping up her pajama top and finding one welcoming breast. They kissed and touched, caressed and learned one another, until Ruby found herself lying on her back with Zane Benedict cradled between her legs.

Reality intruded. She didn't have any sort of birth control in the house. Hadn't needed any for about two years, sad to say. Zane had come running to her house wearing elastic-waisted flannel pants. Unless there were hidden pockets with condoms in those sleep pants, they were out of luck.

"We have to stop," she said, then she kissed him again, unable to help herself.

"Why?" Zane asked gruffly.

She could use a lack of birth control as an excuse, but more than that concern stopped her. There were ways they could offer one another pleasure that wouldn't risk pregnancy, and there was a twenty-four-hour drugstore five minutes from her house. No, she had to tell him the truth. "This is happening too fast for me," she whispered.

"It is rather unexpected," he agreed without anger or even a hint of frustration. There wasn't going to be any sex on her couch—not tonight—so she half expected Zane to pull away and sit up straight, putting an end to the comfort. Too bad. But he didn't go away. He held her. He stayed.

"You are perfectly symmetrical," he whispered.

Ruby had not thought it possible to laugh tonight, but she did. "What?"

"Symmetrical. True beauty is in symmetry, and you have it."

"I'm not beautiful," she said. Cute, maybe, when she worked at it, but not beautiful.

"You are." He demonstrated, first with both hands on her face, slowly tracing and measuring in between kisses, then lower, hands on her breasts. Thumbs rocked gently against sensitive nipples beneath the thin fabric of her pajamas, as he weighed and tested shape. Then lower, to her hips, where his hands gripped and held her, thumbs rocking against her pelvic bone.

If she had one iota less control, she'd strip him naked in a heartbeat and he'd be inside her and it would be so good. It would be symmetry; it would be true beauty. They were so close. She was lying on the couch, and he was on top of her. There wasn't much in the way of clothing between them. A shift, a push, and she could so easily dismiss all her reservations. Without warning, Ruby twitched as the final words of her latest dream came back to her. *Trust no one.*

"We should sit up, I suppose," she said.

"Yes." Zane slowly and reluctantly moved up, taking her arm and pulling her with him until they sat side by side. Her head rested on his shoulder, and he didn't make any juvenile attempt to hide the fact that he was aroused. "So, tell me about your latest dream?"

It was still too clear, too vivid and horrible, and those final words haunted her. What had happened to the baby that had been in the next room as his father offered his mother to a demon? It was only a dream, and yet the child seemed so real. It had been a little boy, she knew. How did she know?

Trust no one. "I don't want to talk about it," she said.

"Perhaps later," Zane said, sounding more disappointed than he had when she'd made him take his hand off her bare breast.

Even when dawn came, Ruby refused to tell him about the latest dream. She said she'd forgotten the details, but Zane didn't believe her.

She was white as a sheet and refused to try to get more sleep. She was exhausted but afraid of another nightmare. The nightmare had just begun, he knew that, but he couldn't tell her, not until he knew what could be done to stop *Il Colletore.*

By now the others would be frantic, wondering at which location the collection would occur. He should've reported his findings yesterday, but he had not. It was unfortunate that he liked Ruby so well. What if it wasn't possible to save her? What if only her death saved the world from destruction at the hands of a demon that had been locked away for nearly three thousand years?

He watched Ruby make coffee and shuffle to the refrigerator for eggs and bacon. She moved like a zombie, slow and heavy and without emotion. Only her eyes hinted at life, and they revealed her terror. Last night, he had seen more than terror in those lovely green eyes, and he had liked it. They were at a critical juncture. Her life was literally at stake, and if she had not called a halt to their explorations last night, they would've ended up having sex on her couch. He needed to protect her, and he could not even protect her from himself.

"Don't go to work today," he said.

"I have a business to run."

"You also have employees. Call one of them and let someone else run the bakery for one day."

"Most of my people are out of town." Ruby wrinkled her nose.

"But I really don't feel like going to work today. I haven't missed a day since I opened the place four years ago, but . . ."

"You can't work like this," Zane said.

"I know." Ruby made her way to the kitchen phone and dialed a number from memory. "Marielle?" She paused, while the girl on the other end of the line spoke. "I know it's early, but I can't make it in today. I'm sick." She looked pointedly at Zane. "Can you run the store today?"

Apparently Marielle agreed, because Ruby told her employee where the special orders were stored, and that with the students out of town business would be slow, so they could get by with the inventory on hand. If they ran out of anything . . . well, there was nothing to be done.

Zane knew that Ruby needed sleep, but it was likely any sleep she got would be filled with terrifying dreams. How many days did they have left before *Il Colletore* rose? Two? Three? Four?

"Let me make you breakfast," Zane said, walking into the kitchen intent on taking the eggs and bacon from her. In her current state, she was likely to burn herself. He hadn't gotten any more sleep than she had, but he was used to getting by with little sleep. She was not, obviously.

"No," Ruby said sharply. She looked at him with suspicious eyes. "I really appreciate your coming over, but I'm all right, now. You can go home."

Zane's jaw tightened. "You are not all right, I assure you."

"I don't need anyone to take care of me."

"I beg to differ."

Her face hardened. "Go home, Professor."

Professor? She hadn't called him that in days. "I'd rather . . ."

"This is my house, and I'm asking you to leave." She looked him up and down. "As it is, you're going to raise a few eyebrows crossing the street half-dressed at dawn. Wait an hour, and everyone in the neighborhood is likely to see."

"You care what the neighbors think?"

She hesitated, then said, "No, but you need to leave anyway."

This was her house, and he could not insist on staying. "I thought we were . . ."

"You thought wrong," she said, long before he was finished.

As he walked through the living room toward the front door, Zane looked at the jade cat, which remained on the coffee table. Ruby hadn't wanted to touch it after it had made its unexplained trip from the garbage can to the living room, so there it had remained all night. He could offer to take it with him, but when it reappeared close to Ruby, where it should not be, she would only be freaked out all over again.

"I'll check on you later," he said as he opened the front door on a cool morning.

"Don't!" she called, and Zane wondered what had happened in her most recent dream to make her afraid of him.

Chapter 5

After a breakfast of bacon and eggs, Ruby showered, hoping the spray of water and the familiar routine would wake her up and chase away the lingering dreams. It didn't work. She dressed in a faded pair of jeans and a lightweight blue sweater, trying for normalcy even though at the moment her life felt anything but normal.

In all three of the dreams, it had been a friend or lover who offered a woman's soul to the demon. They had all been betrayed by men they loved or cared for. A husband, a lover, an old family friend.

She sat on the couch and stared at the jade cat. It seemed to stare back at her, but there was no purring, no distant and creepy meow. Not yet, at least. The feline's green face was pointed and sharp, primitively feral, not at all like a normal cat. Ruby didn't believe in ghosts and demons, she didn't believe in Zane's woowoo. But something was going on, and this damn cat was at the center of it.

Trust no one.

The only man Ruby trusted, the only man she had trusted in more than two years, was Zane Benedict.

She was *not* going to sit here and wait to see what might happen next! It took her no more than three minutes to grab her coat, her keys, her cell phone, and her purse. She had credit cards and some cash, and she was, by God, going to get as far away from Holland Court as she possibly could.

As Ruby locked the front door, Hester Livingston was walking up the driveway with a loaf wrapped in foil grasped in her hands. "Hellooo," the older woman called, and she flashed a smile. "Did I catch you going to work? You're later leaving than usual. When I saw your car in the driveway, I thought you might be ill, so I brought you a loaf of my homemade cheese bread."

"I'm just on my way out," Ruby said.

Hester was not deterred. "This will just take a minute. I know you make your own baked goods, and you're quite talented, but my cheese bread is special."

Intent on taking the bread from the old woman and just carrying it with her, as that seemed the simplest and fastest way to end this encounter, Ruby met Hester on the driveway. "Thanks," she said.

The nosy neighbor did not leave; did not even move from her position between Ruby and the car. "I was up early this morning, and I could've sworn I saw Professor Benedict leaving your house in nothing but his skivvies."

Ah, so this was the reason for the visit and the cheese bread. "They were flannel pants," Ruby said. "Not skivvies."

Hester waved a dismissive hand. "He was hardly dressed at all. Unsavory situations like this can give the neighborhood a bad reputation."

So could demons, Ruby thought. "Zane and I are two fully

grown unattached adults. What we do indoors is really none of your business." Letting the old woman believe that Zane had been at her house for a little recreational sex and nothing more was much better than the truth. "Now, if we start hooking up in the middle of the street . . ."

Hester's eyes got wide. "There's no reason for sarcasm."

"There's no reason to be meddlesome."

In a huff, Hester reclaimed her foil-wrapped bread and turned to stalk toward home. Any other time, Ruby would've felt guilty about being short with her neighbor, but today she only had one thing on her mind. Escape.

She got in the car and threw her purse on the passenger seat, started the engine, and let it idle for a moment to warm up. When she put the car in reverse to back out of the driveway, she looked into the rearview mirror and saw the front door to Zane's house open. He stepped onto the porch as she backed into the street, but she didn't give him another glance or another thought. She had to get away from here, and she suspected if she gave him the chance, he would try to stop her.

She didn't know where she was going, but the interstate would be a good start. Twenty minutes to the interstate, and from there she'd go to Birmingham or Huntsville or beyond. Maybe she'd just keep driving until she couldn't keep her eyes open, then she'd find a motel and crash for the night, so tired she couldn't possibly dream.

Not five minutes from the house, Ruby pulled up to a four-way stop. She looked to her left, and saw nothing. She looked to her right, and there on her dashboard, where a moment ago there had been nothing, sat the jade cat. It appeared to be smiling.

Ruby screamed as she instinctively hit the gas and raced impulsively through the empty intersection. She could feel herself losing control, inside and out. She didn't see the telephone pole until it was too late.

Amalie smiled as she stretched her naked body across the fine sheets of her lover's bed. She had never known such pleasures existed, but then, until Henry had claimed her body and soul, she had known very little pleasure in life. An orphan since the age of eleven, a ladies' maid who served others and answered to others' demands, she had never thought to know such indulgence for herself.

"You are incredibly beautiful," Henry said. He was naked, too. She liked his body. It was hard and strong, and so very different from her own. She could not keep her hands off him.

He said they would soon be married, but he had family business to see to first. His wealthy merchant father would not approve of his taking a woman who had once been a servant as his wife. Henry was planning a charade. By the time all was said and done, his family would think she was a fine lady just recently arrived in the colonies from France.

"I think he will like you happy," Henry said.

"Who will like me happy?" Amalie asked, smiling as she ran her hands along his fine chest. "Your father?"

"Il Gatto Nero," *Henry said, taking her wrist and wrapping a length of fine red-silk fabric around it. She did not protest, not even when he tied her wrists together and tethered her to the bedpost. His sexual tastes were sometimes a bit odd, but he never hurt her, and he always saw that she found her own pleasure before he found his. Amalie didn't like being tied up, but if it made Henry happy, it was a small price to pay.*

"The black cat? I did not know you had a cat."

Henry took a nipple into his mouth and suckled it, and Amalie forgot about cats and charades. Nothing else mattered but this. She closed her eyes and savored the sensations. She wished to be able to touch Henry, to wrap her arms around him, but she could not. Her lover took his time, kissing and licking and arousing . . . then he was gone.

Amalie opened her eyes to find Henry standing beside the bed. He still smiled with great warmth, so she was not concerned. "Is everything all right?"

"Yes," Henry said. "Are you happy, love?"

"Ecstatically so. Come back to bed." She wanted to gesture to him, but could not with her hands bound and tied to the bed.

*"That is good." Henry reached beneath the mattress and withdrew a small jade figurine. A cat, she saw right away. "*Il Gatto Nero *takes greater enjoyment from a soul filled with pleasure as well as fear. Such a soul tastes sweeter, and he has waited a very long time for that taste."*

"What are you talking about?" Amalie pulled against the bonds. She did not like the expression that crossed her lover's face.

"No one will miss you," he said softly. "Are you truly surprised? Did you not hear Il Gatto Nero *speaking to you in days past?"*

The soft purring, the echoing meow, the distant roar of a large cat in the woods surrounding the remote cottage where Henry kept her . . . she had heard it all but had thought the sounds to be those of normal animals around her newly claimed home.

Henry began to chant, and a black smoke rose from the head of the jade cat. Amalie pulled at her bonds, but that did no good. She was trapped. Trapped by the man she loved . . . a man she had been so certain loved her. The blackness grew, and she jerked her head to the side and stared at Ruby.

Trust no one.

Ruby opened her eyes sharply. The scream that escaped was short and weak, but it was enough to catch the attention of a nearby nurse. Ruby glanced around, recognizing the place. She'd been here before, with Aunt Mildred. Minville had one small but well-equipped clinic set up to act as a small ER, and she was in one of the beds.

"What happened?" Ruby asked, and as she finished her question she remembered the damned cat, the telephone pole, and the dream.

"There's someone here to see you," the nurse said.

Ruby suffered a rush of fear. Somehow Zane had found her. He was here and he was going to seduce her and tie her to a bed and offer her soul to a piece of rock. Is that why he'd aroused her last night? Was he making her tastier for the demon? She shook her head and immediately wished she had not. It hurt.

The curtains parted, and Marielle stepped through. Even obviously concerned she looked perky, with her long blond ponytail and heart-shaped face. "Oh my God, I was so worried about you," the girl said. "The police called the shop looking for family, and I came right over."

"Who's running the store?" Ruby asked.

Marielle pursed her lips. "The shop is closed and will remain closed until I'm sure you're okay. I thought you were sick. Why were you out driving around? What were you thinking?"

It was a question Marielle didn't expect an answer to, which was good because Ruby didn't have one.

"Take me to Nashville," Ruby said, sitting up carefully. She was suddenly certain neither Birmingham nor Huntsville was far enough from Minville.

"You're addle-brained," Marielle said as she offered a steadying hand. "I'm taking you home."

"I don't want to go home!"

Marielle didn't ask why, which was just as well since she'd never believe the truth. "Well, my place is too small, and it's a mess. I wasn't expecting company so we can't go there. I'll take you home, and I'll stay with you until you're feeling better."

"The shop . . ."

"Ruby's Sweet Shop will still be there when you're recovered. If there's someone else you can call to sit with you I'll keep the place running, but if not, then your loyal customers will just have to make their own cookies and cakes for a few days."

There had been a time when Ruby would've crawled on her hands and knees to keep her business open, but now her little shop seemed unimportant. She didn't want to be alone. She couldn't call Zane. She didn't have anyone else.

Zane had been keeping an eye on Ruby's house all morning and all afternoon, waiting for her to return. It was after three when a strange car pulled into the driveway. The blonde he had seen at Ruby's shop stepped out of the driver's side door. Ruby, not instantly recognizable with the white bandage on her head, stepped carefully from the passenger side.

He was tempted to rush over there to ask what had happened, but she'd made it clear this morning that she no longer wanted him around. He wasn't sure why, but he suspected it had something to do with the most recent dream she'd had. She no longer trusted him, that much was clear. She had gone to sleep in his arms and had awakened afraid of him.

What if he couldn't save her? She was the ninth, the last, and he could not allow her to become a part of the demon. The males of his family had been important members of the Brotherhood for generations. Stopping *Il Colletore* was a purpose he had lived with since the age of fifteen. Twenty years devoted to research, training, and waiting for this moment. No matter how much he liked Ruby, he could not allow the demon to live.

He waited for the blonde to leave, but she didn't. The car remained in Ruby's driveway. The curtains to the cheerful yellow house remained shut. Night fell, a few lights came on, and still the blonde remained in the house. A bad feeling crept down Zane's spine. This was it. It had started.

For a few moments he hesitated, his hand on the telephone receiver, his heart physically heavy as if it were weighing him down. Not Ruby, please. He would not wish for anyone to be taken as a sacrifice for *Il Colletore*, but of all the possibilities in the world—why her? She was good and fragile and had only begun to live her life. If the situation were different, he might ask her on a real date, make love to her, make her laugh.

But his time for pretending the situation could be different was done. He lifted the receiver and dialed, and snapped out a crisp "This is Benedict. It's here."

The older man on the other end of the line actually tried to argue with him. Apparently there was a gathering of known members of the Order north of London, near a particularly powerful vortex. Many warriors of the Brotherhood were gathering there.

"I'm telling you, it's *here*," Zane said. "The UK assembly is a distraction."

Still unconvinced, the dispatcher reluctantly agreed to send a few men to assist, just in case. When that was done, Zane closed his eyes. A moment later, he threw the phone across the room.

Chapter 6

Ruby was not surprised to see the jade cat sitting on her bedside table when she crawled into bed. She hadn't slept well in two days, her head hurt, and Marielle had prepared a very nice chicken soup that had really hit the spot. Now Ruby could barely keep her eyes open, and for the first time all day she didn't feel as if she needed to run as if the devil were on her tail.

Marielle had been very attentive since arriving at the clinic, and Ruby was thankful to have such a good friend. When the younger woman had insisted on spending the night, Ruby hadn't protested. Maybe if someone else was here, the walls wouldn't purr.

With her blond ponytail dancing, Marielle walked into the dimly lit room to make sure her patient was settled for the night. She even straightened the covers. Ruby didn't mind.

"Take that damn cat out of here," Ruby said, her eyes barely opened as she pointed to the night table. "Throw it in the trash." It wouldn't stay, but there was something satisfying about plunking the thing into the garbage.

"This?" Marielle lifted the jade cat and studied it casually. "It's pretty, and it looks kinda old and expensive. Why would you want me to throw it away? Shoot, if you don't want it, sell it on eBay. Or I can just keep it."

"No!" Ruby tried to get up but couldn't. Her head was so heavy. "Stay away from that damn thing," she said, wanting to protect her friend from whatever had ruined her own life.

"Okay." Apparently forgetting the original request, Marielle placed the figurine on the bedside table.

Ruby thought about reissuing the order to take the thing away, but she didn't have the energy to speak, and besides, if the cat wanted to be there, watching her, it would find its way back. Her fear was no less sharp than it had been when she'd tried to flee, but somehow Ruby felt safer than she had earlier in the day. She was not alone; Marielle was here. There was no more mewing, and Zane Benedict wasn't going to get anywhere near her.

She heard the front doorbell ring, and thought nothing of it. Marielle went to answer and was back shortly, wearing a big grin on her pretty face. "Some guy in a tie-dyed T-shirt wants to take me to a concert on Thursday. I think he wanted to ask you, but I told him you were under the weather. He won the tickets and is desperate for a date."

"Todd wins everything," Ruby said, her tired voice slurred.

"He really wanted to come in and check on you, but I wouldn't let him." She shuddered. "What a loser."

"Yeah." Ruby closed her eyes, aware that Marielle remained by the bed, standing guard.

There was snow all around. Freya felt cold, but that cold was the least of her worries. Her hands and wrists were tied, and she had been staked to the ground. A full moon made the night bright white, and the icy cold cut to the bone as surely as the fear that gripped her.

She did not want to give up her soul. All beings died, but the soul was eternal, and she feared for what would happen if hers was taken.

"Sister, no," Freya said softly.

Her own sister, older by two years and the beauty of the family, was the one who had drugged and bound Freya. It was Maeva who offered Freya's soul to the evil spirit. Since the rest of the family had died in the fire last winter, it had been just the two of them. They were close, especially so since the deaths of the others. It had been Maeva who'd saved Freya from the fire.

Freya had a horrible thought, one that rivaled her fear for her soul. "Did you kill them? Did you start the fire that killed our parents and our brothers?"

Maeva smiled, and her long blond hair whipped in the wind. She seemed not to feel the cold that tortured Freya. "All for a good cause."

Ruby stirred but did not entirely awaken. This was different from the other dreams. A sister? Such a betrayal seemed worse even than the betrayal of a lover or a friend. She was vaguely aware that her house was purring again, but she didn't care much. Why didn't she care?

Amalie watched from her new home inside the demon, as the monster panther took the heart of Henry, the man who had pretended to love her, the man who had trapped her soul in this dark place. She was not alone, she knew. There were others. Women, girls, souls trapped as hers was trapped. There were seven others, she sensed. Seven who had been betrayed by those they trusted most only to be trapped inside this blackness for a very long time.

Through the demon's eyes, Amalie saw the door to her bedroom burst open. Four men, all of them armed with swords and hatchets, tried to surround the big cat. The cat moved so fast. Two of the men fell almost instantly, their throats ripped apart by deadly and unnatural claws. The two others did not flee, as sane men would've, but continued to fight. One of them managed to thrust his sword through the panther's heart.

The demon slowed, wounded but not yet ready to forfeit what little time it had to live. One of the men shouted, Benedict, look out! *just as the demon swung again. Benedict, a black haired young man with intense brown eyes, moved lithely to the side and avoided the attack. He used his sword again, and this time he moved close and swung mightily, taking the panther's head.*

And still, Amalie watched. The two men who had survived searched the room for the piece of jade where the demon once again hid, but they could not see it. Amalie tried to shout here *but she could not make a sound. The jade cat that housed the demon and eight betrayed souls hid. The cursed stone was invisible to the men who had come here to stop the demon. They had taken the head of a living being, but the demon still survived.*

Too late. They had arrived too late.

Amalie's eyes met Ruby's. "You are the ninth and last. Do not let him take you. Remember, he is vulnerable for seconds before he sucks your soul from your body, when he is solid and yet still hungry. Take him then, if you can. If not we are all doomed.

"You cannot escape this," Amalie whispered. "Fight, fight with all you have. You cannot avoid what is coming. You cannot trust her." In the way of dreams, there was no face, but there were large blue eyes and large warm tears. "Save us, Ruby. Save us all."

Ruby came awake slowly, not with a start as she usually did after one of the horrible dreams. It was morning, she could tell by the way the light was coming through her window. The pieces of the dream fell together as she woke, claiming consciousness slowly.

Watch out, Benedict!

You cannot trust her.

Her?

Ruby rolled over to see that Marielle sat in a chair beside the bed. The younger woman smiled brightly, and the pieces of this twisted puzzle came together in a heart-crushing burst of reality. The one person she could depend on; the one person she truly trusted. Marielle. Could she slip past Marielle without revealing what she knew? If she could get to Zane, would he help her?

Could she be helped?

Ruby attempted to swing her legs out of the bed, but could not. Her ankles were very loosely bound, and the length of fabric that was wrapped around them was attached to the bedpost.

"They've been talking to you, haven't they," Marielle said.

Ruby tried to play dumb. "Who? What?"

Pretty coed Marielle just smiled. "The eight women who have fed *Il Gatto Nero.* The eight souls you will soon join. You must be a touch clairvoyant; otherwise, they would not have been able to reach you. I'm clairvoyant myself, though the talent was dormant until *Il Gatto Nero* awakened my abilities and spoke to me." Marielle bit her lower lip. "I have had my own special dreams, dreams that led me to this special place and time."

Ruby sat up awkwardly. She could continue to play dumb, but judging by the dreams and the expression on Marielle's face, arguing would be a waste of time. "He's going to kill you too, you know," she said. "First me, then you."

Marielle shook her head. "No, he loves me. He's going to give me everything I've ever wanted, and we are going to live together forever. No one will be able to stop us." Her eyes were bright but unfocused, feverish and distant. Reasoning wasn't going to work. "Besides, I've already worked so hard and done so much to come to this point. Why would I give it all up now?"

Ruby didn't think her heart could sink any more. "What have you done?"

"Well, your aunt had to go, so you could be in this house. It's built on a very special bit of land, which allows *Il Gatto Nero* to come alive. Fortunately, Mildred wasn't in the best of health, and all I had to do was hurry things along with a few carefully measured drugs administered slowly and diligently."

"You poisoned her."

"With the same drug I put in your soup," Marielle confessed without regret. "That was actually easier than breaking into the house down the street to drop off your anonymous gift." She grinned. "Breaking into a house to leave something beneath a Christmas tree is just as hard as breaking in to steal. It will all be worth it when he comes to life again. We're going to have everything, including an army of servants who will do anything we ask of them." The pretty girl was downright giddy at the prospects.

"The demon who has been speaking to you in your dreams is a monster," Ruby whispered angrily.

Marielle's eyes hardened. "Then so am I."

Too late, again too late! Twice before since the founding of the Brotherhood they had come close to stopping the taking of a soul, but both times they had arrived too late. In each case the sacrifice had taken place, and the Brotherhood had lost members to *Il Colletore*. They had *once* managed to kill the demon's solid form, but only after he had taken his chosen soul. On one other occasion they had arrived in time to save a child—an orphaned Welsh boy who was ultimately taken in by Zane's own ancestors—but in saving the boy they had allowed the demon to escape to wipe out an entire village in the hours he had to feed.

This was why Zane had fought so hard to avoid getting personally involved with the woman across the street. He should be concentrating only on killing the demon, and yet he was distracted, thinking only of saving Ruby—a task that was likely impossible. He hadn't fought involvement as hard as he should've. When he'd kissed Ruby, he had not been fighting at all. In truth, he had barely been thinking.

Three other men had gathered in Zane's living room. Those in charge still believed that the collection would take place north of London, where the Order had gathered. Would four men be enough to stop the demon? During the night these warriors had parked on a nearby street and walked through backyards and climbed over fences to reach Zane's back door secretly. They couldn't know who might be watching.

Marielle had been in Ruby's house all night. Was she the one, the servant of *Il Colletore*? Likely. It had been foolish of him to think one of her neighbors had been the one. That was too simple, too damn easy. Still, one or more of them could be with the Order, so they had to be careful.

Though he was itching to rush across the street now, they would wait until nightfall before making their move. Zane did not like it. He was so tempted to rush across the street, break down the door to the little yellow house, and kill the girl who held Ruby hostage. But the research was indisputable. If he saved Ruby now, the jade cat would disappear. It would reappear in another house on another vortex, somewhere in the world where another servant to the demon would be waiting. Another vulnerable woman would die, and the demon would take its form—forever, this time.

The other men in his living room were, like him, members of the Brotherhood through family connections. Their fathers, their grandfathers, their great-grandfathers and in some cases ancestors much farther back, had dedicated their lives to researching and planning for this night. If they succeeded, there would be no more need for a Brotherhood, thank the heavens. If they failed . . . well, they could not fail.

The latest research suggested that there would be a moment—just a moment—after the cat took form that he would be vulnerable. He would not be easy to kill, but he would not yet be indestructible. One of Zane's own ancestors had killed the body of the living demon, some two hundred and eighty-seven years ago. It could be done.

This was the time they had all waited for, if their records were correct. *Il Colletore* was about to take his last soul, the soul that would give him eternal and terrifying life. Would the opportunity to kill the demon come before or after he had taken Ruby's soul? Why did it have to be Ruby?

"We have always been told that the timing has to be precise," Zane said to his companions as he once again parted the curtains and peeked out the window. Ruby's yellow house looked as it always did, offering no outward hint that a true darkness lurked within it. "If we can stop *Il Colletore* from taking the ninth soul, and if we can keep him from transporting to another vortex until it's too late, then it will be over. His chance for immortality will pass until another two hundred and eighty seven years have gone by."

"I'd like to get my hands on that jade cat and destroy it," Terence said softly.

"Aye," Aiden agreed.

"Ruby is a good person," Zane said, revealing more than he should to these Brothers.

"So were they all, I imagine," Julio responded darkly. "And so will be those the demon takes if we do not stop it tonight."

Chapter 7

The passing of the day was too fast to suit Ruby, as she realized that it might very well be her last. A couple of times she tried to go to sleep, hoping for more instruction from the women she had begun to think of as one very strong entity. Marielle, however, wouldn't allow Ruby to sleep. Did that mean there was a way to stop the plans? Why else would Marielle work so hard to keep Ruby from making contact?

The eight were inside that piece of jade as surely as the demon was. Perhaps together they were stronger than anyone knew. Perhaps they could communicate with Ruby when she was not asleep if she got her head in the right place.

She should've taken one of Zane's classes, she supposed. Or at least not laughed at him.

Ruby stared out of her bedroom window. Once during the day Marielle had allowed her to go to the bathroom, but her ankles had remained tied together, which made for short, awkward steps. Her hands were free, and maybe she could try to fight. *Maybe* she could get away, but whatever drug Marielle had given her last night still had Ruby woozy, and she knew a failed escape attempt would get her more tightly bound. She did not want her hands trussed as her ankles were! Maybes were not enough.

She sat up, her back against a thick stack of pillows, and stared out of the window. It was a cool day, but the sun shone through the thin curtains. Ruby focused on the light. She tried to dismiss everything else—Marielle, the jade cat, the possibility that this day would end very badly. If she did have a gift of some sort, if she could hear the demon's previous victims in her dreams, then why could she not hear them now?

Deep, even breaths lulled her, and in her mind she did her best to picture the women who had come to her. She remembered their faces. She had not dreamed of all eight, but there were five she could remember very well. Five victims. Five souls who only wanted to help her. Had those five been a touch clairvoyant, as she apparently was? Was that why they had been able to reach her in her dreams?

In her mind she asked, *How can I fight?* For a long while there was nothing. Not an idea, not a word, not a shimmer of light to hint that someone—or something—heard her. She asked again, How can I hurt the demon? *What was it about that totem that made the demon's flunky snatch it away? She remembered the shape of a crescent moon, and something else that dangled there. What was she searching for? What did she need?*

A single word finally came to her. *Silver.*

Ruby blinked hard. Of course! In every horror movie she'd ever seen, silver did the trick. Vampires and werewolves. Silver crosses and silver bullets. She didn't know *why*, and at the moment she didn't care. It was something to work with.

She turned to look at Marielle, who was staring at the jade cat with a dreamy expression in her eyes. "I have a request," Ruby said.

Annoyed to be interrupted from her admiration of the demon's current home, Marielle snapped her face around to glare. "Why should I care what you request?"

"Because no matter what, we were friends. Good friends, Marielle." She reached back into her dreams for more, she asked for guidance from the eight. "Besides, I suspect a happy soul is tastier and more filling than an unhappy and hungry one."

"You want something to eat," Marielle said.

"There's a Death by Chocolate cake in the fridge, and double chocolate chunk ice cream in the freezer."

"You want both?" Marielle asked, her blue eyes widening.

"I don't exactly have to worry about how many calories I'm getting today, now do I," she snapped.

Marielle relaxed. "That's true." As a precaution, she quickly bound Ruby's hands and tied them to the headboard.

"Since this is my last hurrah, let's do it right," Ruby called before Marielle left the room. "I want the cake and ice cream on Aunt Mildred's best china, and I want a *good* fork and a *good* spoon. I feel like such a putz, saving all that stuff for special and never using any of it."

Marielle huffed a little, making Ruby wonder if she'd get what she'd asked for, but then the girl asked, "Will I find all that in the dining-room buffet?"

Ruby nodded, trying not to give away the surge of hope that filled her. Marielle couldn't be allowed to see even a hint of that blessed hope.

Maybe she couldn't stop what was coming—maybe she couldn't kill the demon that was coming for her. But she wouldn't go easily; she was going to fight.

* * *

The sun set, and the four soldiers of the Brotherhood armed themselves to the teeth, said a prayer, and positioned themselves by the door to Zane's house, waiting for the correct moment. The moment of attack had to be precise—not too soon, not too late.

They had always known that even if all went well, they could end up dead or behind bars for the rest of their lives. Four men rushing into a house armed with guns and swords was bound to call attention. They would probably have to kill the demon's servant, and no one would know—or believe—that a pretty young girl like Marielle was actually an evil bitch who deserved killing.

Not that deserving killing was a defense. In that respect, the old days had been much better. Now there were fingerprints, telling fibers, blood evidence—all that CSI shit. Still, if Ruby was saved, it didn't matter. He would happily spend his remaining days in prison if she could be safe.

"Now," Zane said, reaching for the doorknob.

"Too soon." Julio reached out and covered Zane's hand with his own.

The cul-de-sac remained quiet, but in Zane's mind he could hear Ruby screaming. He could see and feel the soul being ripped from her body. His heart pounded too hard, his mouth was so dry he could hardly speak, and still he said—somehow knowing that he was right—"*Now.*"

"Accept, and this will go easier," Marielle said as she took the jade cat on her palm and began to chant, using sharp, decidedly unfriendly words Ruby didn't understand.

Ruby's heart pounded hard, and beneath the sheet that covered her she clutched a fork in one hand and a spoon in the other. She was quite sure Aunt Mildred had never intended for her good silver to be put to use this way, but knowing all that she knew now—she didn't think her aunt would mind.

Just as in the dreams, a darkness rose from the jade cat. It looked like a hole, a vast nothingness, and Ruby choked back a scream. The eight had warned her, and still here she was, tied to the bed and offered as sacrifice to a demon. Offered by a friend. A fork and spoon seemed precious little in the way of defense, but she would, by God, fight with all she had until she could fight no more.

Just as in her dreams, the blackness began to take shape. The eyes were fiery red. Marielle was so excited, so overjoyed at the appearance of the demon who had seduced her with dreams of forever, that she trembled from head to toe and smiled like a woman on the verge of a big orgasm.

"Wacko," Ruby muttered. Marielle either didn't hear or didn't care.

The darkness drifted to the bed to hover over Ruby. More and more it looked like a cat. She gripped her weapons tightly.

Not yet, a serene blending of soft voices whispered.

The thing Marielle called *Il Gatto Nero* began to look solid, not so much a hole in the world as a large, fierce cat. There were likely claws—she had seen the claws in her dreams—but at the moment she had eyes only for the face above hers. The eyes were hideous, red like fire and blood. The teeth were wicked, white and sharp and hungry. The fur was black as night, and did not look soft like a kitten's coat but was instead thorny and rough, as if it would cut like shards of glass if touched. Not that she wanted to touch.

The image above her occasionally shimmered, shifting from almost real to insubstantial illusion and back again. Suddenly, Ruby could not resist the urge to open her mouth. She had seen this in her dreams, too, and knew what would happen next.

Not yet, those comforting voices called.

Were they kidding? She didn't have much time left!

The cat placed its mouth close to hers, as if moving in for a kiss. Oh, what a horrible, rotten smell! She had not been subjected to the stench in her dreams. Her heart was pounding so hard and fast she could feel it. Her heart wanted to escape, but there was no escape, not that Ruby could see. Now? she thought.

There was a pause, as the cat above her inhaled and with that breath began to draw Ruby's soul from her body. It hurt! She felt as if a part of her was literally being ripped from deep within her. Eight voices whispered, *Now!*

Ruby swung her hands up as hard as she could, burying the fork and the handle of the spoon into the flesh of the demon. What she struck was not entirely flesh. There was no blood—but the thing howled as if in pain, and it drew away from her. Ruby took that opportunity to shift her weapons. She stabbed at the ghastly face, aiming for the eyes. The tines of the fork pierced the demon's left eye, while the spoon glanced off the side of its face.

The thing growled and screamed, and Ruby was vaguely aware that Marielle was protesting, too, though not as loudly as the big, solid cat, which was now very annoyed. Great. She'd only made it mad.

The door to her bedroom burst open, and four men rushed inside. One of them grabbed Marielle and pulled her away from the bed. Another snatched up the jade cat. Two moved toward the demon.

One of them was Zane.

"Silver!" Ruby shouted. "He doesn't like silver!"

* * *

The noise coming from Ruby's bedroom had drowned out the sound of four men breaking down her front door. Zane's heart had almost come through his chest, as again he had thought they were too late.

They followed the unnatural din, and without hesitation Zane kicked in the door. Ruby was tied to the bed, offered as an unwilling sacrifice, but her hands were free. She clutched a fork in one hand and a spoon in the other, and when the demon cat turned toward the intruders, he had only one eye.

Il Colletore. He was solid, and Ruby was alive.

Julio grabbed Marielle and dragged her toward the master bathroom, throwing her into the windowless room and closing the door on the hysterical blonde. Terence grabbed the jade cat and placed it in a leather sack, which was tied to his belt. This time it would *not* hide!

With Aiden beside him, Zane faced the demon—and Ruby shouted, "He doesn't like silver!"

Zane shifted his sword to his left hand and drew a silver dagger that was hanging from his belt. He heard the others making adjustments, as well. Julio fired a bullet at the demon, but it had no effect. Surely no one had thought to bring silver bullets. In all their research, there had been nothing about silver!

Research or not, silver made a difference. In the demon's one red eye, Zane saw frustration and confusion. Time was running out; his ninth soul was fighting; and for once, for *once*, the Brotherhood was not too late in arriving.

Zane used the silver dagger to swipe out, aiming for the place where the heart should be. The demon's shape was that of a panther. Did that mean the heart was in the same place? Was there a heart? The demon screamed, emitting a loud, catlike shriek that cut through Zane's brain like a hundred burning needles. A mere four warriors of the Brotherhood fought against *Il Colletore* with whatever silver they had available. Knives, mostly, though while the demon howled in protest, Julio jerked the silver cross from around his neck and threw it into the gaping, tooth-filled opening.

The cross flew into the demon's mouth, and while *Il Colletore* howled, Zane took careful aim and swung his sword with all his might. With the head and body separated, the black cat fell to dust. It had not taken a soul this time, and so was weakened. The demon had not retreated into the jade, where it would be frustrated but safe until the proper moon came again, but was destroyed. As what was left of the terrifying thing fell, several bits of bright light rose, separating from what remained of *Il Colletore*, rising to the ceiling of Ruby's bedroom.

Zane looked to the bed, where a bound Ruby sat still clutching her silverware. She used the fork to gesture to the streaks of light, and he realized that she was counting. She counted twice, then breathed what seemed to be a sigh of relief as she looked at him with wide, tear-filled eyes. "Eight," she said. "All eight are free, now." And with that, she collapsed onto the bed.

Ruby took a deep breath and tried to calm herself while Zane untied her ankles. Everything had happened so fast! She was alive, she had her soul, and Zane wasn't one of the bad guys. He was a good guy. A very good guy.

She had just fallen into his arms when the doorbell rang. One of his friends went to answer, and after a loud argument, a handful of neighbors rushed into the bedroom.

Hester was in the lead. "What's wrong? What was making those awful sounds? Who are these men?" No one paid any attention to the innocuous and almost invisible sprinkling of dust on the bedroom carpet.

Zane and his friends remained silent, and in the bathroom, Marielle cried hysterically. The neighbors watched and waited.

The truth was impossible. "I can't believe my screaming sounds awful, but I was scared." She sat up, swinging her legs over the side of the bed but not trying to stand. Not yet. "In a nutshell, Marielle murdered my Aunt Mildred. Poison." Her lower lip trembled. That part of it was so unfair. "She planned to kill me tonight."

One of Zane's friends, the big blond, opened the bathroom door and dragged Marielle out. She looked at the dust on the floor and screamed in pure agony.

"Thank goodness Zane and his friends heard me. They were just about to start a poker game, but they rushed right over."

"With swords?" Todd asked, scratching his head.

"Zane's collection," Ruby explained. "They scared Marielle sufficiently, I'm happy to say."

"I called the police!" Hester said, and at that moment Ruby heard the distant wail of sirens.

Zane and his friends stiffened, but Ruby found herself patting Zane's arm in offered comfort. This could all be explained away, and Marielle would end up in jail. "Good," she said.

"They'll kill me," Marielle said softly. "I failed, I screwed up, and they'll kill me."

The neighbors all kept a distance from Marielle. Anyone could see that she wasn't quite right. The good people of Holland Court just didn't know how out of her gourd the pretty blonde was. She yanked away from the man who held her and dropped to the floor to run her hands through the dust—all that remained of the demon who had seduced her with dreams and promises.

"I actually asked her out," Todd whispered to the nearest man. "Thank goodness she told me to ask another time. I might be dead right now!"

The excitement over, Ruby's neighbors peeled away. More than one of them told her she had a scary-ass scream. She had a feeling that scream—the cat-demon's screech—would haunt her for a long time. Fortunately, she wouldn't have to face it on her own.

Before all the onlookers had departed, Ruby fell into Zane's arms. "I want a cookie," she whispered. "No, that's not enough. Maybe a cupcake, one with really thick frosting." Frosting, that was an idea. She'd choked down a huge piece of cake and a bowl of ice cream not so long ago, but that didn't count. Choking down food in order to keep the silverware did not compare with snuggling beneath a blanket with a warm man and a sweet dessert. "No, wait, I want a cake. I want a whole chocolate cake with fudge icing. Nothing fancy. Aunt Mildred's recipe, the one she used to make when I was a kid."

"You can have whatever you want," Zane said, smoothing her hair.

"Can I?" she asked. "Can I really?"

"Yes."

She pulled away and looked up into fierce brown eyes. Life was too short for her to be so damn careful all the time. "Remember when I said I didn't want a man?"

"I remember."

"I've changed my mind."

He gave her a tired smile. "Good, because I'm planning to ask you out."

"On a date?"

"Yes, on a date."

"I'm a little rusty," she confessed. "I haven't dated in a while."

"Neither have I."

Ruby allowed her head to rest against Zane's chest. She held on to him more tightly than was necessary, and it felt good. She listened to his heartbeat, which was almost as fast and hard as hers. She took a deep and stilling breath, and when his hand settled on the back of her head she almost cried. It felt so right.

"Get me out of here, Zane," she whispered, and without hesitation he slid his arms beneath her legs and lifted her.

"I can walk," she said, resting her head on his shoulder and making no attempt to make him put her down.

"Not tonight."

The neighbors had not really left. They milled about in her yard and on the street. They all watched as Zane carried her to his house, and no one said a word, not even Hester Livingston. There were still police questions to handle, and Ruby had no desire to ever again set foot in that house—even though she knew the demon was gone. She didn't have any idea when she'd reopen her shop, and even though Marielle had turned out to be a fraud, Ruby had lost a friend today. And still, at this moment she was content.

CHRISTMAS EVE

Tomorrow there would be a big family Christmas celebration at the Benedict home place, a rambling farm-style house on a horse ranch in Tennessee, just past the Alabama state line. Zane was looking forward to seeing his parents and his brothers, to introducing Ruby to them and celebrating the fact that *Il Colletore* was no more. Since she'd moved in two weeks ago, he had not doubted for a moment that Ruby would celebrate the holiday with him. She was a part of the family, now. She was a part of him.

Ruby had already made four desserts to take with them, as she was horrified at the very thought of generic lemon cookies or Twinkies for the holiday meal. He didn't think she was trying to bribe her way into his family's heart, but if anything would do the trick, it would be the English toffee cheesecake, or the Death by Chocolate Cake, or the Mile-High Lemon Pie, or the huge box of homemade cookies that would feed his brothers for a week.

But tonight was for them alone, and he liked it. He liked it very much. With the demon destroyed and Marielle's assumption about the status of her safety having been proved correct—she'd been found hanging in the Minville jail two days after her arrest, dead from an apparent suicide—life was normal. For the first time since Zane had turned fifteen, he didn't have to worry about saving the world.

He just had to take care of Ruby.

That actually meant that for him life was no longer *normal* at all. He was going to have to get used to a different kind of normal. So far, that experiment was going very well.

Ruby put a few finishing touches on the small Christmas tree they'd put up earlier in the day, then they settled together on the floor by the tree, entwined and comfortable. Dressed in a wonderfully skimpy Christmasy red nightgown, she fed him cookies and the most decadent apple pie he had ever imagined. If this was what most people considered normal, he would very quickly get accustomed to normalcy in his life.

While a piece of a rich sugar cookie melted on his tongue, Ruby moved onto his lap and draped her arms around his neck. "Do you think it's possible I only love you because you saved my life? And my soul," she added, making a face and shuddering a little. "And the world, of course. For the purposes of this discussion, let's just stick with my life."

"I don't know. Do I only love you because you feed me increasingly decadent sweets?"

"Don't forget the sex," she said with a smile.

"As if I could."

She rested her head on his shoulder. "The sex is very nice, but I thought you loved me because I'm symmetrical."

"There is that."

It was too soon for love, perhaps, but they both felt it, and neither of them had been shy about saying the words. Almost losing everything would do that to a person, he supposed.

For a few precious moments he tested Ruby's symmetry with his hands. Face. Shoulders. Breasts. Hips. Thighs. Lovely.

"What am I thinking?" he whispered.

For someone who had so firmly denounced "woowoo" a couple of weeks ago, Ruby accepted her own clairvoyance very easily. That talent had saved her; it had allowed her to communicate with the women who had been sacrificed to the demon in years past. She was no psychic, but she did have telling dreams, and more often than not she knew what was on his mind. They'd been "dating" for two weeks, if you could call spending every moment together "dating," and already she was finishing his sentences for him. After the first of the year, when she reopened her shop and he went back to teaching classes, they would have less time to study her abilities, so they had been doing all they could to test and refine it. *What am I thinking?* had become a game of sorts. She was quite good.

It was too easy, of course, since lately his mind had been quite one-track, and still Ruby played along. Sitting in his lap, leaning toward him possessively, she closed her eyes.

She did best with visual images, they had discovered. It was very easy for Zane to vividly imagine what he wanted from Ruby. He didn't want to make it too easy for her this time, so he didn't picture her naked on his bed. Instead, he imagined her naked here, lying beside the Christmas tree, red and green satin ribbon wrapped around her torso, her hips, her thighs. She was the best Christmas present he had ever imagined, so it was fitting enough to see her this way.

"This is no longer much of a challenge," she said softly. "Must I always be naked?"

Practice was making her ability stronger. Day by day, she saw more, she saw more clearly. Though she could guess "naked" and be right more often than not.

"All right," he said, "Let's try something else."

He pictured another Christmas in another year, perhaps five years or so down the road. They were still in this house, and someone else, someone who had no idea what had happened there in the past, lived in the yellow house across the road. He was still teaching; Ruby still had her shop though she no longer worked there every day. She had her hands full with the kids. Two, he thought, maybe a boy and a girl. The Christmas tree was larger than the one they'd bought on clearance this year, and it was heavy with decorations, some purchased but many made by the kids.

And they were happy and still in love. Whatever the reasons they had fallen in love so quickly, it was going to last. They were going to enjoy the only real forever that existed in this crazy world.

Ruby's smile faded a little, and she placed her head on his shoulder and shifted closer. "Is that what you want or are you teasing me? Don't tease me," she added quickly. "Not like this."

"It's what I want," he said honestly.

She shifted, moving her body closer to his. "Me, too."

He took her face in his hand and tilted it toward his so he could kiss her. "Merry Christmas, baby," he whispered with his mouth against hers.

The kiss lingered for a while, then Ruby moved just far enough away to reach for the messy pile of wrapping supplies. She snagged the red and green spools of ribbon and proceeded to make all his Christmas wishes come true.

Christmas Heat

LORA LEIGH

For my early readers, all of you.
For saying, Hey, this just doesn't work.
Or, OMG this is working so great.
For telling me when it's going wrong
and when it's going right.
Each book is a combined effort, a creation
of my imagination, my early readers' imaginations,
and all the hard work my editors put into it.
You all make the difference.
And I couldn't do it without you.

Foreword

They were created, they weren't born.

They were trained, they weren't raised.

They were taught to kill, and now they'll use their training to ensure their freedom.

They are breeds. Genetically altered with the DNA of the predators of the earth. The wolf, the lion, the cougar, the Bengal tiger; the killers of the world. They were to be the weapons of a fanatical society intent on building its own personal army.

Until the world learned of their existence. Until the council lost control of their creations, and their creations began to change the world.

Now they're loose. Banding together, creating their own communities, their own society, and their own safety, and fighting to hide the one secret that could destroy them.

The secret of mating heat. The chemical, biological, emotional reaction of one breed to the man or woman meant to be his or hers forever. A reaction that binds physically. A reaction that alters more than just the physical responses or heightens the sensuality. Nature has turned mating heat into the breeds' Achilles' heel. It's their strength, and yet their weakness. And Mother Nature isn't finished playing yet.

Man had attempted to mess with her creations. Now, she's going to show man exactly how she can refine them.

Killers will become lovers, lawyers, statesmen, and heroes. And through it all they will each cleave to one mate, one heart, and create a dynasty.

Prologue

Haley McQuire was hiding in Sanctuary's extensive, beautiful library the night of the pre-Thanksgiving party. She didn't do parties well, and she didn't enjoy them. Jonas Wyatt, Director of Breed Affairs, had given her permission to peruse the extensive collection of first-edition classics, but he had warned her that if one of his enforcers caught her there, they would drag her back to the party.

If she was found, she hoped that it wasn't by Noble Chavin. She smiled a bit at that thought. Noble loved books too, though. He would understand.

He was always at the library, choosing books she would never have expected him to read. Carpentry books, books on world history. He devoured them, it sometimes seemed. And when he returned them, she could quiz him playfully, and he always had the answers.

And he talked to her about the books. She liked that. Perhaps too much. And though he would probably talk to her, she doubted he would let her stay.

So when the door opened, she hid quickly. She expected the breed entering the room to smell her instantly. She was a human, and fairly easy for a breed to detect. Haley didn't understand why she didn't.

Maydene Brock was a breed older, a nurse in the labs. With her graying brown hair and pinched expression, Haley had never really seen her as much of a caregiver.

And perhaps she might have sensed Haley if the men following her hadn't overpowered the room with the scent of cologne.

Haley wrinkled her nose at the smell. Even across the room, hidden behind a low shelf as she peeked between the books, she could smell the obnoxious scents.

"Do you have payment ready?" Maydene snapped.

"We need the code," Phillip Brackenmore, the head of Brackenmore Pharmaceutical Research, informed the nurse dangerously. "No code, no payment, breed."

Maydene sniffed. "We'll meet you at the hotel with the code. We'll slip it out when Dr. Morrey arrives at the party. Everyone will be busy with her," she told them smugly. "When you transfer payment, we'll hand you the code. I don't trust the two of you as much as you would like to think I should."

"As long as you're there," Horace Engalls, president and CEO of Engalls Pharmaceuticals, replied. "Don't bother trying to betray us. We have our own spies watching you, Maydene."

Maydene growled at that. "I know who your little bitch is. She can watch until hell freezes over. All we care about is the cash."

"And all we care about is the information to complete our own research. The live trials on the breeds you suggested aren't working out as well as we had hoped."

"I warned you." Maydene's voice was smug as Haley felt chills race up her spine. "Even Morrey isn't responding as well as you had hoped, is she? I told you, you need us."

"So we do," Brackenmore drawled. "We'll meet you at the hotel and transfer the money to your account, but we'll see what we're paying for first. Understood?"

"Quite well," Maydene sneered. "Return to the party now, before you're missed."

Haley peeked over the top of the books that lined the shelf she was hiding behind. She could barely see them, and as the door opened, she eased back down carefully, certain that if Maydene looked back, she would sense her.

She waited. She waited so long. She could feel her muscles cramping, feel the sweat that eased along her spine, but she could still feel the danger.

She looked up at the vent above her and inhaled slowly. Was that why Maydene hadn't smelled her? The vent pulled the air out of the library and circulated it, while another vent fed dry air into the library to protect the expensive books. That combined with the scent of men's cologne must have hidden Haley's scent.

But Maydene must have suspected that someone was in the room. As Haley began to consider the risk of peeking over the books again, she heard movement, a doorknob turning, a muttered curse.

She took a chance and watched as the breed made her way from the library.

Just a few more minutes, she told herself. If Maydene was suspicious, she might watch the door from outside. She might be waiting for whoever she had sensed.

My God, what were they talking about? Drugging breeds? Selling information? She had to find Noble. The breed enforcer would know what to do—he would know how to handle this. She had to find him before Maydene and whoever was helping her managed to slip from the estate.

Carefully, she moved from behind the shelf, thankful that someone had made the little hidden reading nook that Merinus had shown her a few weeks before. It had possibly saved her life.

Now, to sneak out of the library and get to Noble.

There was something about librarian Haley McQuire and her staid little outfits that just made Jaguar breed enforcer Noble Chavin insane.

He should be watching the ballroom, keeping his eyes trained on the two men they knew would make an attempt tonight to gain confidential breed information from a source within Sanctuary.

Breeds betraying breeds, for money. For greed. And the humans determined to destroy them. Several breeds had already been killed in the past day, and if they didn't stop that information from going out, then more would die.

It had to be insanity, he decided again, as Haley stepped into the ballroom from the direction of the ladies' room down the hall, because nothing else could describe his reaction to how completely luscious she looked in the simple black, long-sleeved ball gown. Or how she snagged his attention against all his best efforts.

The gown swept the floor, the hem floating around her like a dark, sexy dream as he tried to keep his eyes off her. He was there to increase security, not to ogle the little librarian, who seemed to hug the wall more than she danced.

But his eyes had a will of their own. His gaze swept over the full skirt of the gown, lifted to her curved hips and trim waist, and he had to swallow as he came to where the material draped from her shoulders and barely hid the hint of curvy, sweet breasts beneath. She might have believed she had succeeded in hiding those curves with the folds of material that draped over them, but he could have assured her, nothing was further from the truth.

He should have stopped there. Dammit, he had no business looking further. But he did anyway. He let his eyes caress the smooth, creamy flesh above the material, the graceful arch of her throat.

A stubborn chin. There was fire in her. Soft rosebud lips, a pert nose, and eyes that mesmerized. Dammit to hell, he knew better, but there he was, staring into eyes that seemed to be looking right back at him. Dove gray and ringed with the merest hint of blue. Thick chestnut lashes surrounded them, and they stared back at him as though as helpless as he to break the connection.

Fiery red hair surrounding a gently sculpted face, added spark and fire to her eyes, and the look of her had his back teeth clenching as he fought unsuccessfully to drag his gaze away.

Back to her feet. Where the tip of one small black shoe peeked out beneath her dress. The dress flowed around her, drifted and moved like a whisper as though teasing him, tempting him to brush it from her legs to see all the pale, beautiful flesh he knew it hid.

Damn, if she didn't draw his gaze like a hidden flame, one he was certain would erupt into a conflagration.

He forced his gaze away then, far away, not even looking at her feet but at her slender, graceful fingers. She wore no rings. No adornments. As though proclaiming to the world no ties and no bonds. She was as free as the wind yet restrained by some force inside her.

And she was moving toward him.

Noble let his gaze move to her face once again, a frown edging at his brows, a sense of foreboding rasping at the back of his neck at the look on her face.

Perhaps he should have paid more attention to her face. Because there was an edge of fear in those odd, blue-ringed gray eyes and the pinched line of her lips. Her face was pale, but her chin was lifted in determination and purpose.

His gaze moved around the room then. She had come out of the hall and into the ballroom no more than minutes after Phillip Brackenmore and Horace Engalls had entered, the two pharmaceutical and drug-research magnates.

"Noble." She all but whispered his name, and he heard the sound, that soft hint of longing he wondered if she even knew was in her voice, at the same moment he glimpsed the entrance of the ballroom from his peripheral vision.

He gripped her arm and jerked her behind him, ignoring her soft little cry as orders began to snap into the communications link at his ear.

"You stay!" He jerked her to the corner and pushed her into the little alcove created by the fronds of several potted plants. He pushed her to the floor and pointed his finger to her pale face. "Stay till I come for you. Understand?"

She nodded quickly even as he turned away and began snapping orders to other guests, herding them quickly from the confrontation brewing at the ballroom's entrance and into the buffet room.

Why he hadn't pushed little Miss Haley McQuire into the more secure room, he couldn't explain. It was something about her eyes, that edge of fear, and the fact that she had entered after Brackenmore and Engalls more than anything else.

Or it could have been that niggle of insanity that he had been trying to ignore for months.

"Librarian Haley McQuire is secured in the far left corner of the ballroom, leave her in place," he spoke into the small mic that curved along his cheek as he helped secure the ballroom.

"She's a hazard in the ballroom," he was told, Rule's voice cold. "Get her with the others."

"Negative," he refused the order. "Something isn't right with that, Rule. I want her separated for her own safety."

He heard the tension in the line. "For now," Rule finally snapped.

Moments later, several things happened at once. A breed female enforcer distracted Dr. Ely Morrey, and Jonas jerked the gun from Ely.

"Move in on Brackenmore and Engalls," Rule ordered through the comm link. "Secure them and get ready to move them out."

Noble moved toward the two, staring back at them with cold, brutal determination. They were involved with whatever was going on. Involved in trying to control and kill breeds. The bastards needed to die now, not later.

"Please come with me, Mr. Brackenmore, Mr. Engalls," he requested, his voice carefully bland, unemotional. He wanted to kill rather than react politely.

Those damned animal genetics. He could feel the blood he needed to spill for the threat this man represented to the breeds.

"What the hell is going on here?" Brackenmore blustered, as Noble gripped his arm and began to move him, his wife, and Engalls to the entrance, waiting for the final go-ahead from Rule to escort them from the estate.

"Director Wyatt will discuss this with you soon I'm certain." Noble flashed his canines in a tight, hard smile as he watched the other breeds filling the room, keeping a careful barrier between the guests and the clean-up of the situation that had just arisen.

Felines weren't the only ones in attendance. Noble watched as Wolf Gunnar, pack leader of the wolves, conferred with Del-Rey, pack leader of the coyotes, to direct their own security forces in concert with the felines'.

The pre-Thanksgiving party Sanctuary hosted every year had never been so exciting. Now if they could just make certain they kept the damned journalists contained.

"Noble, give Brackenmore and the others to Mordecai. I want you to contain your librarian and get her sequestered," Jonas said into the link seconds later. "We have a security report from surveillance that she may have been close to a meeting between Brackenmore, Engalls, and one of the lab assistants earlier in the hallway."

Noble's head jerked in her direction. He could still see the very edge of her skirt peeking out from where he had pushed her.

The Coyote breed, Mordecai, his face scarred, his icy blue eyes filled with death, took Brackenmore and the others, and Noble strode across the ballroom quickly.

Haley was still huddled there and stared back at him, her eyes wide and touched with courage and trepidation. He held his hand out to her and watched as she lifted hers, her fingers trembling as he gripped them.

"They're monsters," she whispered, and though her eyes were dry, sorrow filled them. "Noble, they're monsters."

The fine hairs along his body lifted in warning, but even worse, the spots along his shoulders began to tingle in foreboding. She knew something. In that moment he knew, she had seen or heard something that could possibly get her killed.

Chapter 1

THREE WEEKS LATER
DECEMBER 7

"The winter storm heading for the Virginia mountains is slated to pile on the snow. We're looking at up to ten inches possible before nightfall, with another ten to fifteen over the next two days. The moisture we're tracking . . ."

Haley turned off the television and stared at the black screen in satisfaction as she forced herself not to smile in glee at the thought of snow.

She tugged at the snug cuffs of her cheery red cotton blouse instead and turned to her assistant, Patricia.

Nearing fifty, but as spry as a woman fifteen years younger, Patricia looked displeased over the weather forecast. Dressed in dark brown tailored slacks and a matching sweater, Patricia had a smile that always brightened the darker hues of the clothing she wore.

"I'll never get out of that damned lane the county refuses to pave with that kind of accumulation," Patricia pouted, her brown eyes sorrowful. "I hate being stuck."

Haley frowned. Patricia's little sedan would never handle such a heavy snowfall, nor was it equipped with the same traction sensors and tires that Haley's four-wheel-drive truck had.

Living in town, Haley didn't worry as much about getting out as she did about the inconvenience of the snow itself. They hadn't had a storm like this move in for years, and the dump of fluffy white stuff almost had her rubbing her hands in glee.

But she knew Patricia, and her friend hated the snow, just as she hated the way it confined her in her little house outside of Buffalo Gap.

"Take my truck." Haley moved to the counter behind which she and Patricia worked and lifted her purse from the floor.

She pulled the car keys from the inside and tossed them to her friend.

"Are you serious?" Patricia stared back at her in surprise.

"They'll have the roads here in town clear before noon, and Sanctuary will make certain the main road is clear before then. All you'll have to worry about is getting out of that little hole you live in."

She almost shuddered. Patricia lived in one of the small hollows that dotted the mountain terrain. The mile-long track between her house and the main road was rough at all times. Filled with snow, it would be impossible for Patricia to navigate in her little car.

"You'll take my car then?" Patricia worried. "I'd hate to leave it just sitting in the parking lot." She gripped Haley's keys like a lifeline.

"The car will be fine for me until they get the snow cleared to your house." Haley shrugged, then stared back at Patricia worriedly. "But please be careful. I just bought her, and she's still unscratched."

The pristine cherry red pickup had been her dream vehicle, with big tires, the standard shift—and the advanced electronics was her pride and joy.

"Don't worry, I'll take care of your baby." Patricia was almost as gleeful over driving the truck as Haley was over the coming snow.

Haley looked around the nearly deserted library. The two-story glass-and-metal building was incredibly beautiful. Donated by an effort between Sanctuary and several of its supporting companies, the building had the look and feel of beautiful wood, without the cost. Even the metal-and-steel shelves had that old-wood look, and housed the thousands of paperback and hardback books beautifully.

The electronic books were housed in the main data boards and e-readers were plentiful for those who needed to check them out if they didn't have their own. But it was the paper feel of the books that Haley cherished. The history and the bridge between the past and the present that always drew her.

The library was deserted this evening. The last college student had left more than an hour before, and no one else had come through the heavy glass doors.

"Why don't you go home, before the storm hits," Haley suggested. "It's only another hour before closing, and I can take care of that myself."

"Or that handsome Noble Chavin, should he arrive before closing," Patricia teased her. "When do you think he's going to get up the nerve actually to do more than follow you home every night?"

"With Noble, who knows." Haley turned away from her friend, tucked the keys to Patricia's car in her purse, and hid her expression.

Noble, unknown to the curious, wasn't courting her in any way, and she knew it. He was watching her, just as breeds from Sanctuary often watched her. Just to be on the safe side, she had been told after she had told Callan Lyons and Jonas Wyatt about the meeting that had taken place in the library room of Sanctuary the month before.

Jonas had promised her it was a precaution only, but that precaution still had the power to make her mouth dry with fear.

"I think I'll head home early then," Patricia decided, as she moved behind the counter and pulled her coat on. She flipped her shoulder-length gray-and-brown hair over the stiff black collar and stared back at Haley worriedly. "You're sure you don't mind about the truck?"

"As long as you don't scratch her," Haley reminded her, but her smile was quick. Patricia was excessively careful with everything, no matter to whom it belonged.

"Should I throw a quilt over her before I go to bed?" Patricia laughed.

"If you don't mind. And don't forget the pillows for her tires," she reminded her playfully.

Patricia rolled her eyes as she grabbed her purse and headed for the door. "I'll be sure to remember both," the assistant teased her. "Perhaps I should park her where she can watch television as well."

Haley laughed. Okay, so she loved her truck. Everyone teased her about it.

As Patricia left the library, Haley moved from behind the counter, picked up the remote, and flipped the news on again. There was all that fat fluffy stuff headed her way. Piles and piles of snow. A snowman in her yard, the Christmas lights around her house twinkling against it, it was going to be the best Christmas ever.

A smile was curving her lips when the world exploded around her. The blast filled the air, glass shattered as a wave of heat knocked her from her feet and flung her several feet away to where the children's reading nook was sectioned off. She bounced over the low shelves, cried out in shock and pain, and crumpled on the floor as a wash of red seemed to fill the library.

Sirens were howling. Something red was flashing, flickering and the scent of burning paper filled the air. It was hell on earth.

Haley dragged herself to her knees, shaking her head as she felt the ground shake again, and another explosion rock the air.

She cried out, covering her head with her hands as more glass exploded, and the cold seemed to battle with a surge of heat.

She staggered to her feet, shock, disbelief and horror filling her as she realized the books were burning. Piles of books. Flames licked at them, consumed them. The tables, counters, and much of the interior of the library was wood or a facsimile of it, and it was all burning.

Smoke poured around her, choking her, making it nearly impossible to see as she fought to get her bearings. She stumbled through the debris-littered section, nearly falling as another, smaller explosion ripped across the earth.

What was happening? A strike? Some sort of attack? Sanctuary wasn't far from Buffalo Gap, and she knew that it was prone to attacks from several different racist societies, but no one had ever attacked Buffalo Gap.

She choked and stumbled again, falling to her knees as her eyes burned, and she fought for breath. She wasn't going to get out of here. Tears filled her eyes, and fear filled her mind as she tried to crawl, fighting to figure out which way to move, which way to go.

"I have her!" someone yelled, a second before strong arms wrapped around her and dragged her to her feet..

A moment later she was slung over a broad shoulder.

"Was anyone else in there?" another voice called out.

"No one," she choked. She couldn't breathe, even as the cold outside wrapped around her, and she tried to blink the stinging pain from her eyes, still fighting to breathe.

"Haley, where's Patricia?" She was deposited on the hood of a car as someone shook her shoulders. "Is Pat in there, Haley?"

Haley shook her head, blinking as the fierce visage of the sheriff filled her vision. She shook her head again.

"Gone," she coughed. "She left."

"Her car is still here," Sheriff Zane Taggart barked into her face.

"My truck," she coughed again. "Gave her my truck."

Silence met the information. She coughed again, blinking, gazing around frantically until her eyes found where her truck had been parked. Right there, in front of where the big windows had been, where a fiery blazing hulk sat in the middle of melted pavement and the burning vehicles left in the parking lot by several city workers that worked nearby.

Her truck. Her truck had sat right there. And Patricia had been in her truck.

"No," she whispered, horror filling her, streaking across her mind. "No!" she screamed. "Oh God, Patricia."

She tried to jump to her feet and ended on the ground. Her legs folded beneath her as the sheriff tried to catch her.

Her nails dug into the frozen earth, and she stared at the blazing vehicle in disbelief and agony. Oh God, Patricia had been in her truck.

The report came across the radios within seconds of the blast. Noble was just coming off a twenty-four-hour shift and heading to the barracks when it crackled across the comm links.

"All available enforcers, be aware. Explosion at the Buffalo Gap Library. One dead, one injured. Officers en route. Sheriff Taggart requesting enforcer backup."

He didn't wait for the order. He heard the names called to backup, the enforcers being pulled in to head to Buffalo Gap, and he didn't care if his name was on the list or not.

"Comm one, this is Chavin," he reported to the dispatcher. "I'm heading from Sanctuary en route now." He jumped on his motorcycle, revved the motor, and shot out of the driveway next to the barracks. "Advise Alpha leaders one through four, we have a compromise."

"Enforcer Chavin, order received and being forwarded. You'll be met by enforcers Warrant, Savant, and Crayven. Be advised, Director Wyatt will be en route."

Sanctuary's heavy metal gates swung open as he approached, the headlights of his motorcycle piercing the darkness and highlighting the faces of the ever-present protesters.

He shot through the opening, hit the gas, and tore through the press of bodies that threatened to surge against him.

"Heli-jet is being prepped and en route," the dispatcher reported.

"Any report of the casualty?" he yelled into the link.

"No report as of yet," he was informed.

He hit the accelerator with one hand, felt the power surge beneath him and, with the thumb of his other hand, hit the integrated traction control and advanced speed protocols before he pushed the specially designed all-terrain cycle to its limits.

Thankfully, the curvy mountain road was more or less free of traffic. The cycle's warning system alerted him to traffic and allowed him to streak around it safely.

As he sped to the town, all he could see were Haley's wary gray eyes and pale, worried face the night she had overheard the plans Brackenmore and Engalls had discussed with the breed attempting to sell them information. All he felt was the echo of the knowledge that there was the chance that someone besides himself and the Breed Cabinet would find out what she had overheard before the hearing she was due to testify at.

He powered down as he hit the city limits, though he still pushed the cycle faster than the posted speed limits allowed.

Haley, with her bright red hair, her soft scent of desire, couldn't be gone. He knew he should have never left her protection to any other breed. Something had warned him, some strange foreboding had told him that her life would be in more danger than one silent bodyguard could defend her against.

Damn Jonas. Noble had warned him they couldn't keep her safe like this. She needed to be sequestered, at the very least pulled into Sanctuary until the hearing next month against Brackenmore and Engalls.

The bastards. The drug they had created to attempt to control breeds had resulted in two deaths in the past few weeks, and they had nearly lost Dr. Morrey as well.

And now, they could have lost Haley.

He couldn't imagine a world without Haley in it. He refused to imagine such a thing. It was impossible, it couldn't happen.

He hadn't kissed her yet. He had barely even touched her. He hadn't yet figured out why she drew him as no other woman ever had, though in the past week, he had begun to suspect exactly why.

He hadn't yet had a chance to decide if he could risk taking her, making her his, or if he should force himself to leave the situation as it stood.

The hunger eating at him was still controllable. The need driving him could still be buried in another woman. The heated lust could still be pumped from his body, and though satiation was never complete, it was satisfying.

He was still his own man.

For the moment.

Once he knew Haley was safe, once he made her life his primary objective, he would no longer be able to claim that singular independence. And he knew it.

He raced into town, slowing the cycle and easing it around traffic, bending over the padded chest rest and gearing down as he glimpsed the flames that blazed around the library.

And he felt the roar that discharged from his chest at the sight of the twisted, ruined, blazing hulk of Haley's truck. A roar of bloodlust and animalistic rage. Someone was going to pay. Dear God, if she was in that truck, if she was gone forever, then blood would flow.

Chapter 2

Haley shuddered in the blanket Zane Taggart had wrapped around her. The sheriff was kneeling in front of her as she sat sideways in his cruiser, her feet on the ground, the heat from the vents blasting over her upper body. Still, she shuddered from the cold and the fear.

Zane was one of those men in Buffalo Gap Haley had known almost since the cradle. He was a few years older than she, so he had always been a little protective of her. Zane was protective of all women though. He wasn't in uniform, so he must have been off duty when the explosion happened. He was dressed in jeans, a dark flannel shirt, and a heavy quilted overshirt.

He was staring at her silently as she gripped the cup of hot coffee he had pressed into her hands seconds ago, his expression concerned.

"You should let the paramedics look at you, Haley." He reached out and brushed her hair gently off her forehead.

"I'm fine." A sob hitched her breath, shuddered through her body. "Patricia's not okay, Zane." More tears leaked from her eyes.

She couldn't seem to hold them back. Patricia was gone, and it was all her fault. Because she had let Patricia borrow her truck, had given her the keys because it was going to snow.

Lazy fluffy flakes were already drifting through the air, but they no longer held the magical appeal they had only a few hours ago.

Flames still burned inside the library. The fire blazing around the building and the vehicles that had caught fire were more important than the books inside a building that would contain its own flames.

"No, Patricia's not okay, Haley." Zane sighed and stared through the windshield before turning back to her. "You have to tell me what happened, honey."

"I don't know." She stared back at Zane in shock. "It was going to snow. You know how pitiful Patricia's car is in the snow." Another sob tore free. How pitiful it had been. The explosion had destroyed several other vehicles as well, Patricia's being one of them.

She lowered her head, fighting the sobs that shook her shoulders as Zane patted her knee.

"Come on, Haley." He lifted her chin until he was staring back at her. "You gave Patricia your keys, right?"

She nodded unsteadily. "So she could get to town after the snow. She hates being snowed in."

"Yes, she hates that." Zane nodded. "Go on."

"That's all," she whispered. "She went out to leave. I turned the television back on. I wanted to see the snow." Her lips trembled. "They were showing the snow in other states, and I wanted to see it. And then . . ." She blinked and shook her head.

She had to stop crying. She had to remember what Jonas Wyatt and Noble had told her. She couldn't tell anyone what had happened at Sanctuary until the hearing. But she knew, oh God, she knew Patricia had died because of it. Somehow, some way, the Breeds' enemies knew what she had seen and overheard. She knew it. She could feel it crawling over her skin, digging its way inside her brain.

"Haley." Zane stared up at her, his blue eyes sharp, concerned, but knowing. "You have to tell me what's going on here, honey. Someone blew up your truck. That wasn't an accident. You and I both know it wasn't an accident. Now, you have to tell me why."

She shook her head. She couldn't lie to Zane. She was a horrible liar, and she knew it. And she couldn't look him in the eye when he was staring at her like that. Determined and worried, compassion and pain glittering in his eyes.

She looked at her truck, and her stomach ached with the sobs and the fear she was holding in. Her chest felt constricted, tight, and filled with pain.

There was nothing left of Patricia. She was gone, while the snow drifted through the air, and the flames billowed around them.

Firefighters were working to put out the blazes, several twisted hunks of vehicles were nothing but charred skeletal remains of what they had been.

"We found a breed, Haley," Zane told her then.

Her head jerked around in terror. Haley could feel the rest of the blood leeching from her body, agony tearing through her.

"No." Sometimes Noble came in late. Returned books, helped her lock up.

"He was shot behind the library. Someone killed him. Now tell me what the hell is going on, or I'm taking you in for your own protection."

"Who?" The word wheezed out of her as her stomach churned sickeningly. She was rocking, slowly, back and forth, and didn't notice as the coffee cup slipped from her grip and crashed to the ground.

She was going to throw up.

"Who was the breed?" She nearly pushed Zane back as she forced herself to her feet. The quilt dropped behind her. "Where is he?"

She was shaking so hard she had to grip the open door as Zane grabbed her shoulder.

"Haley, dammit, tell me what the hell is going on."

"Was it Noble?" she screamed back at him. "Tell me, damn you. Who was the breed?"

She tried to tear away from him, the sickening fear of Noble, gone, dead. No, it couldn't be Noble.

But it had been time for Noble. It had been. She had been waiting for him.

She stared around and jerked away from Zane.

"Where is he?" She sobbed again, stumbling around the door and gripping the side of the car as she tried to force her legs to move.

He had said behind the library. Dead behind the library. She wasn't crying now. The fear and the pain was going too deep for tears. If Noble was gone, she couldn't bear it. Not Patricia and Noble. It couldn't happen. Not like this. Not because of her.

As she forced herself around the front of the vehicle, she heard a sound so wild, so animalistic, her head jerked up. It was Noble. She knew it was. She couldn't accept anything else.

"Noble!" She screamed his name and heard the sound again.

It rocked the night. Like the wild lions that patrolled the borders of Sanctuary. If the night was quiet, sometimes, you could hear them. And now, it sounded as though one had stepped into the city itself.

Her head jerked around, staring into the parking lot, watching as the flames flickered around it. And she saw him. All that wild black hair blowing back from his savage face. His lips were pulled back into a snarl as he pushed a police officer attempting to hold him back to the side.

Black-leather pants and heavy motorcycle boots. A leather jacket that he was unzipping as his gaze caught hers. He moved like the jaguar he was bred from, a hard, graceful shift of muscle, a ripple of danger.

"Noble." His name tore from her lips again as he snarled. The sight of it, the sound of it, should have been frightening. The flash of his canines, the hard edge to his black eyes, should have frightened her as much as it did the officers and bystanders.

She tried to make her legs move. Tried to run to him but they weren't functioning as they should. She stumbled again and heard his throttled growl a second before he jerked her into his arms.

Warmth covered her. She was only barely aware of his jacket going around her shoulders, because he was holding her, jerking her against his chest and swinging her off her feet.

She wrapped her arms around his neck and buried her face against him to block out the sounds, the sight, and the smell of the fire.

He smelled like the night. Like winter. Like the snow that was drifting around them. There was no death around him. There was nothing of the nightmare and chaos around her.

For the first time since the night had turned into hell, Haley finally felt safe.

"Chavin, be advised of reinforcements landing," the comm link crackled with the information as Noble buried his face in Haley's hair and held on to her. His arms tightened around her as he let himself rest against the hood of the sheriff's cruiser and let himself soak up the knowledge that she was alive.

As he held her, he was aware of the breed heli-jet landing on the other side of the parking lot, and of the sheriff moving closer to them.

His head jerked up as Sheriff Taggart pulled the edge of Noble's jacket over her shoulder. He flashed a feral snarl at him, the thought of the man touching her finally sending him past the limits of what little control he felt he possessed.

Taggart lifted his hands, his eyebrows arching.

"She was afraid the dead breed behind the library was you," the sheriff told him, his blue eyes knowing as he watched Noble.

Noble tensed and let go of Haley just enough to activate his communicator.

"Jonas?"

"I have you. We're on scene."

"There's a breed behind the library, apparently dead."

Silence filled the line for long seconds.

"Fuck. We had Jason covering her."

Jason was young, but fully trained. He wasn't inexperienced.

"I want her out of the open. I'm bringing her to the heli."

"Negative. We have vehicles coming in and a civilian in the heli. Transfer her to one of the secured SUVs."

Noble grimaced. No doubt, the first Leo was in the helijet, the breed who only a few knew was a breed, and an interfering bastard at the moment, had decided to check things out himself.

That meant there was no way to transfer Haley to Sanctuary. Not and preserve the secrecy of Leo's identity from her.

He listened through the link as Jonas sent Mordecai Savant and Mercury Warrant to check the body and prepare it for transfer.

"You guys are going to fuck with my investigation, rather than just helping me secure the scene, aren't you, Noble." Zane tucked his fingers in the belt of his jeans and rocked back on his heels. "You know that's not going to go over with me. Right?"

"Talk to Jonas about it," he snapped. "My concern is Haley right now, Taggart, and where she's concerned, then your best bet is just staying the hell out of my way."

He turned and carried her to the vehicles pulling into the outer edges of the parking lot. The library was pretty much lost. The books had fed the flames that had whipped through the windows as they burst. It was a wonder she was still alive and relatively unharmed.

Relatively. He could smell her blood, her pain. He could feel her fear and her disbelief, and it was enraging him.

Clamping a firm hold on his control wasn't easy. As he carried her to the SUVs and slid with her into the backseat of the nearest one, he could feel that rage pumping through him.

Someone had dared to harm her. To attempt to kill her? The attempt was against her; otherwise, the young lion breed, Jason, wouldn't be dead, and her beautiful truck she so loved wouldn't be a hunk of twisted metal.

"They killed Patricia." Her head lifted from his shoulder as the door closed behind them. Her eyes, that dark ring of blue spreading into the gray, darkening them further.

He saw the pain and tears in her eyes. Noble let his arms tighten around her for long seconds as he watched Jonas stride to the SUV. Beside him, was the taller, broader form of the Leo, barely disguised in a hooded jacket, and his son Dane Vanderale. Evidently, neither of them were content to wait in the heli or at Sanctuary.

Behind them, the sheriff followed more slowly, his rugged face set in a scowl as breeds moved between them. That damned sheriff wasn't going to be content to let this go, he thought, as the others moved into the long seat across from Noble and Haley, and the doors closed behind them.

The combined stares of the three powerful men didn't bother Noble, but evidently, there was something about them that made Haley self-conscious.

Her head lifted, her expression flickering with wariness.

"Someone found out, didn't they?"

Haley stared back at Jonas Wyatt, knowing exactly what had happened. Brackenmore and Engalls had somehow learned that she would be testifying against them during the January hearing.

"We don't know that, Ms. McQuire," Jonas answered carefully, his expression carefully blank.

She moved, forcing herself from Noble's lap and sliding onto the seat beside him.

"She hasn't been seen by a medical professional, Jonas."

The younger of the other two men leaned forward. She knew him. The vice president of Vanderale Industries and beside him was the president, CEO, major shareholder, and whatever other title anyone had ever found to attach to him. Leo Vanderale.

And she had a feeling she knew why they were there.

She glanced out the front window to where the flames were finally dying down within the library.

"All the books are ruined," she whispered, looking back to the elder Vanderale. "You were so kind, Mr. Vanderale, to help donate all those lovely books." Her breathing hitched. "I'm very sorry."

His head tilted just slightly, his amber eyes staring back at her curiously. "Why would you apologize to me, Miss McQuire?" he asked her.

She sniffed back her tears, aware of Noble brushing back the side of her hair to examine the gash she could feel against her temple.

"Because it was my fault. Someone killed Patricia and destroyed the library because of me."

"Ridiculous," Dane Vanderale snapped, a frown veeing his brows.

"My dear, the choices others make because of your kindness is not your responsibility." Leo sighed. "And Dane is right, you need to be attended to. You're bleeding, my dear." He turned to Jonas. "Have her taken to Sanctuary."

"That's not possible." Jonas shook his head sharply.

"And why would this be?" Leo's tone was dangerously smooth.

"Leo, you know exactly why." Jonas bit out. "Let's not air our disagreements in front of Ms. McQuire and see what we can do to help her out here."

There was a tension brewing in the vehicle now, wrapping around her, tightening her nerves to breaking point.

"She's obviously in danger because of her courage in coming to you about what she saw and heard," Leo pointed out imperiously. "She should be taken to Sanctuary."

"No one is asking me," Haley pointed out, watching as the two Vanderale men glared back at Jonas.

"I don't think they believe you should have an opinion." Dane leaned back in his seat with a grin.

Haley ignored him, glancing to Noble instead as he spoke into the mic that curved around his tough, angled cheek bone.

"We need to get her to a secured site, one way or the other," Noble growled. "She's bleeding, Jonas, and she's scared out of her damned mind. Sitting here glaring at her isn't helping the situation."

"And you think taking her to Sanctuary will?"

"No," Noble snapped. "Her home will be easier to control. I want a team under my command, men I choose. I want the area declared off-limits to any other breeds, and I want full security protocols placed around it."

Jonas stared back at him blandly. "Those are a lot of wants for an enforcer," he said softly. "A low-ranking one at that, Noble. You've barely been within the hierarchy a year now."

"And I was invited in," Noble reminded him. "I didn't apply."

Haley blinked as Jonas grunted. She felt light-headed, uncertain. She lifted her hand to her temple, where the pain seemed worse, and touched dampness. Drawing it back, she saw her own blood.

"Choose your team," Jonas suddenly stated. "We'll cover you until they get there." He pulled the mic wand to his cheek. "Lawe, Rule, pull everyone to Haley McQuire's home. I need a medical attendant and the sheriff to follow."

Immediately, three of the breeds standing outside were sliding into the front of the SUV limo. The engine started, and the vehicle was pulling out as the snow began to fall faster.

Haley stared at her bloodstained fingers before lifting her eyes to Noble. "I'm bleeding," she whispered.

"Not bad." He laid a folded gauze pad that Dane handed him from a first-aid box he had acquired from beneath one of the seats over the wound. "Everything's okay, Haley."

"It's not okay," she whispered, staring into his dark eyes, his savage face. "Everything's not okay anymore, Noble."

Chapter 3

Haley's little brick house was strung with multicolored Christmas lights outside. In the front yard sat two wire deer covered in white lights. The two conical evergreen trees at each side of the front of the house were well lit, and there was a large fir wreath on the door.

Inside the large living room, across from the fireplace was a six-foot Christmas tree that glowed with lights reflecting every color in the rainbow. An angel perched at the top, a small light in her folded hands, her wings spread, a serene expression on her face.

The fireplace was laid with fresh logs and ready to light, and four stockings dangled, two on each corner of the mantel.

A television screen hung on one wall, a coffee table between it and the couch, and two chairs sat to the side.

It was a large, simple room. It led into a large kitchen and a smaller dining room. There were two bedrooms down a short hall, each with an attached bath, and a cramped attic above.

The house seemed to reflect her. Gently welcoming, a sense of restrained excitement filling it with all the Christmas decorations. As though someone here truly believed in the Santa nonsense.

Noble stood in the entrance to the kitchen, his eyes narrowed as a female breed, Shiloh Gage, checked Haley's injuries where she sat in the living room. Shiloh was the closest thing they had to a medic outside Sanctuary's labs. But with Dr. Morrey still recovering from the attempt to destroy her with the drugs Brackenmore and Engalls had tried to develop, that left only the council scientist, Amburg, whom Jonas had kidnapped months before, to treat injuries. And Noble knew he would rip Amburg's throat out before he allowed that bastard to touch Haley.

"I think I'm okay." Haley had her head turned as Shiloh treated the narrow gash at her temple.

The once-white blouse Haley had worn was torn and stained with blood. There were scratches on her arm, one of which looked deep. Her hands were red, almost blistered. The dark pants she wore were in the same condition as the blouse. Her bright red hair was mussed around her face, singed in places and darkened with her blood.

"You're fine." Shiloh patted her knee kindly, her round face filled with sympathy as she lifted a piece of gauze and taped it to Haley's temple. "You'll be good as new in a few days."

Shiloh pulled the surgical gloves from her hands and dropped them into the small waste can that sat beside her. Rising, she adjusted her black uniform pants and turned back to Noble.

Dressed in the enforcer uniform, her dark auburn hair secured in a French braid, Shiloh looked more like a playful teenager than a full-grown, fully trained breed enforcer.

"I need to clean up." Haley came to her feet, and Noble barely caught himself before jumping for her.

She swayed a bit, and he had to force himself to remain in place as she moved to the hallway.

"You should rest a bit more, Haley," Shiloh warned her, following her.

Haley held up one hand, waving her back. "No. I have to clean up, Shiloh. Just . . . Just let me clean up."

Her voice was stronger than it had been earlier. The shock was wearing off. He could see the anger flickering in her gaze even before Shiloh had finished.

When the enforcer looked back at him, he nodded toward Haley, indicating that she should follow and cover her until Jonas, Leo, and Dane were finished with the meeting in the kitchen. Noble then joined the others in the kitchen.

The sheriff wasn't exactly pleased with the information he was getting. He didn't like being excluded from the investigation, and if Noble could read the man, and he liked to think he could, then he was guessing Zane Taggart wasn't going to be as easy to control as Jonas was hoping.

"Wyatt, you're pissing me off," Taggart retorted at Jonas's suggestion that the sheriff leave the investigation in their hands. "A friend of mine was just killed, and you want me to just back off?"

"Your friend has just lost one friend," Jonas reminded him. "Let's not add to the count. The further you stay away from this, the safer it will be for her."

There was taut silence as Noble turned back to the meeting taking place at the kitchen table.

Jonas stared at the sheriff coolly, while Leo and Dane watched the confrontation silently. Leo hadn't said much, nor did his expressions show his opinion either way as to how the meeting was going.

"Forget it." Taggart crossed his arms over his chest and stared back at Jonas with steely determination.

"The agreement Buffalo Gap has with Sanctuary requires you to step aside in this investigation," Jonas reminded him.

The sheriff snorted at that. "Look, Wyatt, we both know the city council. They're gonna talk out of both sides of their mouths and smile real pretty for both of us. They'll tell you they'll restrain me, they'll tell me they'll cover for me. So let's just cut the shit here and come to an understanding. This is my county, like it or not, hate me or whatever. I'm sheriff, that makes it, and the people living in it, mine. And that includes breeds. I have two of my people dead tonight. From all appearances, it was a professional hit. Your boy was shot in the back of the head at close range. An explosive device large enough to blow a hole in the parking lot and take out the library went off no more than half an hour later. Now you want to tell me what the hell is going on, or do I want to find the answers myself?"

"You want to let this go, Zane." Haley stepped into the kitchen from the washroom.

Damn, he'd forgotten about the door that led from her bathroom and into a small washroom, then the kitchen that he'd found earlier while securing the house. Shiloh was moving through the hall from Haley's bedroom, a scowl on her face.

"Miss McQuire, this meeting can be conducted without you," Jonas told her, his frown fierce as Noble moved towards her.

"Like hell," she told him.

She had changed clothes and washed her face and arms. She was dressed in soft cotton pants resembling pajama bottoms and a long T-shirt. She looked like a kid. A hurt, frightened, angry kid.

"Haley." The sheriff came out of his chair as Noble passed him and shot him a warning glare. "Honey, are you ready to talk to me now?"

Honey? Noble's head jerked around as he barely caught the growl in his throat. What the hell was the sheriff doing calling Haley, "honey"? She wasn't his honey, period.

"I'm obviously in a bit of trouble, Zane." Her lips trembled for a second before she tightened them, seeming to ignore Noble as he moved behind her.

"No shit, little girl." Zane sighed. "Come on, tell me about it, so I can fix it."

"You can't fix this." She shook her head. "I want you to do what Jonas suggests. Let him handle it. I couldn't bear it if I lost you, too."

Noble could feel his jaw tighten at the emotion in her voice, at the statement. As though that damned sheriff was something to her. He wasn't. Noble watched her, he knew her. She wasn't dating anyone. She wasn't sleeping with anyone. She was free. He knew she was because if another man had fucked her recently, he would have smelled the bastard on her.

Noble stared over her head at the other man, his lip twitching as he fought to hold back a silent snarl.

"Haley." Sheriff Taggart shook his head. "You know I'm not going to do that. And what's going to happen when your brothers find out about this? Your daddy? The McQuires are going to descend on Buffalo Gap like a Scottish hunting party, sweetie, and they'll likely bring reinforcements. Do we really want that to happen? They'll talk to me first. If I have answers, they might listen and stay home."

It was a bribe, and a warning. Noble heard it, but he didn't appreciate it. He could feel the worry rising inside her now. She needed rest. She needed to put some distance between her and the events of the night, to allow her to deal with the loss she had suffered.

"The boys are still in California," she said. "And Daddy flew to France last night to help broker a deal with the airlines. I have a few days before I have to deal with them."

"And then?" Zane asked.

"And then, perhaps Mr. Wyatt will have the answers you need. But I can't give them to you right now, Zane. Right now, they aren't my answers to give."

"But it's your life to give?" Zane suddenly snapped, despite Noble's warning growl at the tone of his voice. "Son of a bitch, Haley, you were nearly killed. Don't tell me they aren't your answers to give."

"Son of a bitch, Zane." She was in his face, anger pouring from her. "I've already lost one friend tonight. Do you think I need nightmares of losing another?" She pushed against his shoulders, as broad as they were, even despite the height he had on her. "Go home. I can't deal with you."

"I'll call your daddy myself," he bit out furiously at that point.

"And risk his life? Or my brothers'? I don't think you will, Zane. But you will leave this alone for now. And so will you." She swung around to Noble. "Get the hell out of my house and out of my life. I don't need you here."

Silence filled the kitchen. Noble was aware of Jonas, Leo, and Dane coming warily to their feet. Tension spiked hard and fast, thick enough to cut with a knife as her gray-blue eyes pierced his.

Noble smiled at the demand, the angry exclamation. He was aware that it wasn't a pretty smile. He didn't do smiles well, unless they were the sort that came seconds before killing.

"You must have mistaken me for someone who obeys your orders," he told her softly. "Sorry about your luck there, sweetheart, but it's not happening. You're stuck with me, whether you want to be or not."

Haley stared back at him furiously before swinging around to Jonas.

"He's your enforcer." She shoved a trembling finger in his direction. "I don't want him in my home, period. Get him out of here."

Jonas dragged his hand over his face, muttered something about women and heat that made absolutely no sense whatsoever before staring back at her.

"It's not that simple, Miss McQuire."

"Don't you 'Miss McQuire' me," she snapped back at him, ignoring Noble as well as Zane. "This is your mess, now you can fix it. And you can fix it without him being here."

She couldn't bear the thought of something happening to Noble. For one blinding minute tonight, she had felt the overwhelming pain of believing he was dead, because of her. She knew what that would have meant—a sorrow so bleak, so deep that she had almost sunk beneath the waves of pain.

"Well, looks like you're being thrown out in the cold too, lover boy." Zane's laughter was mocking. "We can share a beer and discuss her stubbornness, then we can get to the best way to protect her," he suggested.

"Stop being a smart-ass, Zane," she ordered him roughly, her eyes still on Jonas. "I helped you," she reminded Jonas. "You know I did. You owe me."

"Yes, ma'am, I owe you." He nodded. "But I don't owe you the chance to die. And Noble won't walk away from this. He has his team, and he knows what the hell he's doing. He's your best protection."

"And the breed that died tonight," she yelled back at him. "Did he know what he was doing? Did you have an untrained man watching me, Jonas? Did you send a boy to do a man's job?" She knew better. "I knew him. Jason Lincoln. Do you know why he chose that name? Do you know he picked the name Lincoln because of a president who died before any of us was ever born? Did you know he liked comics? That he was flirting with one of the college girls who comes to the library?" Tears were filling her eyes. "Did you know that he wanted a Christmas present?" she whispered painfully. "I bought him a Christmas present." She wrapped her arms around herself and turned away from all of them.

Lifting her hand, she covered her lips and shook her head.

"Patricia has a grandson. He was coming for Christmas. Now he'll be coming to bury his grandmother." She wanted to scream with the rage filling her. "I have to see two friends buried because of me." She turned back to all of them. "I won't see any more. I won't bury more friends. Now get the hell out of my house. All of you."

She stalked out of the kitchen, knowing none of them would pay any attention to her, and that only made her madder. The helplessness that rose inside her was like a tide of red, bleak fury. Whoever wanted her dead knew what the hell they were doing. They knew how to get to her. How to hurt her friends, how to make her suffer.

That bomb that killed Patricia would have killed her if she had gotten into that truck herself. Patricia always parked right beside Haley because she didn't like walking to her car alone in the dark. And Jason. She shook her head as she slammed her bedroom door and locked it.

Jason Lincoln. And he had chosen that name because he'd admired all he knew about Abraham Lincoln.

Jason has asked her once if she saw breeds as mankind. Haley had told him she saw them as the best of what man could accomplish, and the best of humanity. His brown eyes had lit with pleasure as he nodded, took his books, and left the library.

And now, she would never see him again. His shy smile would

never touch her heart again, just as Patricia's laughter would never again fill her day.

She couldn't bear the thought of never hearing Zane give her another smart-ass comment, or of Noble never reading another carpentry book, or never reading another book of "mistakes" as he always called them. Because history was filled with mistakes, had been his reasoning. And he wanted to learn from them.

She sat down on her bed and stared around the neat, pretty room. The canopied bed, with its thick, heavy curtains that she could draw around her when it was really cold. The bedroom set, which had been given to her by her father's parents. The writing desk across the room, which her mother's parents had given her. Bridges to the past, just as her precious books had been.

The thought of dying filled her with terror. The thought of Noble dying, especially for her, filled her with cold, bleak agony.

She couldn't bear it. He would have to leave. She would make certain they all left. The breeds didn't have enough power to invade her home, or her life, without her permission. If they weren't out of her house by dawn, she would call the state police. She would pack her bags and leave town. And then she would figure out exactly what it was going to take to survive.

Because dying wasn't in her plans. At least not for a while. Living was. And there had to be a way to live without risking everyone she loved.

Noble stared at the closed washroom door and silently opened it a crack to make certain Haley wasn't there. Motioning to Shiloh, he sent her inside to watch for the fiery little librarian before he turned back to the others.

"Well, that was interesting," Dane commented as he turned to

Noble. "She does do orders quite well. Too bad she wasn't born a breed."

He smiled, a mocking little smile at odds with the cold fury in his brown eyes.

"Contact the state police," Noble warned Jonas. "Inform them we have a situation here. I want Haley placed under the Bureau's 'persons of interest' mandates."

Persons of interest, meaning anyone, breed or human who might have information pertaining to or involving an open breed case under investigation.

"That's pushing it," Jonas pointed out. "If she gets a lawyer, she could beat it within forty-eight hours."

"Then let's not tell her that," Zane warned them before Noble could speak up. "Listen up, boys, let me tell you a little something about Haley. She's more stubborn than those mountains out there, and she's sure as hell got more fire in her than that explosion that nearly killed her tonight. You're not going to bully her as easily as you think you can."

"I have no intentions of bullying her," Noble ground out. "I'll protect her. With your help."

"Noble," Jonas's voice was warning.

"Do you believe you're going to keep him out of it?" Noble stared back at him coolly. "You're not. And you're not going to keep him from trying to protect her. Let's at least use him wisely."

Man or breed, sometimes one had to go with gut instinct. Gut instinct warned him that Zane Taggart would walk through fire for someone he cared for, and for whatever reason, he cared for Haley.

"Smart boy." Zane's smile was hard.

"Jonas will give you details, you will stay out of the perimeter he lays out to you. This house is fairly sheltered. No neighbors too close, no reason for them to be on her property. Anyone moving within her property line is fair game. Do we understand each other?"

Gut instinct and trust were two different things. The sheriff might get information, but he wouldn't be aware of the security protocols Noble intended to set up.

Haley's home sat at the end of a block. She owned a little over an acre, the boundary of which was fenced and thick with trees. Across the street were several clear lots, the street that ran by the side of the house was an occupied lot, enclosed by a privacy fence. Behind her property were more homes, closer together.

Protecting her might not be easy, but at least here he would know the breeds who should be in place. In Sanctuary, at the moment, there were too many suspects and not enough space to ensure no breed but those he trusted were within sight of her.

"We'll have the information we need on this soon, Noble," Jonas promised, his voice hard now.

And they would. Noble knew that the number of people with the information of the witness who had overheard that meeting was small. One of them told someone, or had personally done the killing. Either way, they would be found.

"You have two weeks," Noble warned him. "After that, she disappears." He stared back at Jonas, knowing the director understood exactly what Noble was telling him.

"That won't be enough time," Jonas growled.

"It's all the time you have." Noble shrugged before turning to the sheriff. "As of tonight, call before you arrive here. Call before your deputies arrive here. Don't try to surprise me, Sheriff Taggart, and don't try to piss me off. I get mean when I'm pissed off. And trust me, you don't want to see that side of me."

The sheriff's gaze locked with his for long moments before the other man cursed and scowled. He got the message. He wasn't just dealing with a breed, he was dealing with one that didn't mind killing someone for stupidity. If the sheriff was stupid enough to try to blindside him, then he would die. Nothing mattered at this point but protecting Haley. No matter from whom he had to protect her.

Chapter 4

Haley's bedroom door opened slowly, and Noble stepped into the room.

She stared at him from her bed, watched the way the dim light from her lamp followed and loved the hard, strong angles of his face.

His thick black hair fell to his shoulders and framed the hard, sharp contours of his face. High cheekbones, deep-set, slightly tilted eyes, and a strong, sharp nose. He could never be called handsome, not really. Noble was anything but a pretty boy. He was a man, rugged, tough, certain of himself and his abilities to the point that his confidence gleamed in his black eyes.

She remembered, several months before, the report that he had been wounded on a mission. He had been away from Sanctuary for several long weeks. She had waited, and she had worried, and she had promised herself that the next time she saw him, she would push past the wariness inside herself and do something about this "almost" relationship they seemed to share.

Yet, when he had returned, she had retreated again. And it wasn't that she lacked confidence, or even daring. Everyone knew Haley could be daring. No, there was something else that had held her back, a certainty, a knowledge that any woman who took Noble on would be taking on much more than a lover.

And there was always the chance that the "mating-heat" rumors and gossip trash stories in the rags had enough truth to them to be dangerous. Haley was a great believer that where there was smoke, there was fire. And where there was Noble, things would naturally get hot.

She flinched as he closed the door quietly behind him, still watching her, his black gaze cool and shuttered.

"You're not supposed to be here," she told him. "I asked you to leave."

"Are you that anxious to die, Haley?" He leaned against the door and crossed his arms over his chest. "Strange, I never saw you as a quitter."

His lips quirked at one corner as she stared back at him silently.

"You can't run, and you can't hide. Not from this."

She was already realizing that. That didn't mean it was any easier to accept.

"Jonas can assign someone else to protect me then," she told him. "I don't want you here."

She wanted him with a need that sometimes bordered on a craving. From that first meeting a year before, when he had walked into the library, she had known a need for him unlike anything she had known for anyone else.

And her need was going to cause complications, she could feel it. She had made the mistake years before of having a short affair with Zane until he realized his need for the job was stronger than his need for a woman. But that relationship had taught her how to spot a problem male. And Noble was definitely a problem male.

"I'm your best bet to stay alive," he told her.

"And what was Jason?" she asked, her tone biting. "You didn't even warn me you had anyone else watching me. He died needlessly."

"All breeds die needlessly," he informed her roughly. "It's a war out there, Haley, and you're smack in the middle of it now. Get that in your head. You will not survive alone. You will not survive without me. Period. Until we figure out what the hell happened, you're stuck with me."

She came off the bed, denial raging inside her.

"Find someone else. I told you, I don't want you here."

"And I told you, sorry 'bout your luck," he snarled, those wicked, wicked canines flashing at the sides of his mouth.

Haley fantasized about those teeth sometimes. Fantasized about watching them rake over her breasts, nip at them. Sometimes she dreamed of them at her neck, her shoulder, biting against her, holding her in place as he took her.

The animalistic quality of those dreams had always shocked her to her core and left her wet and hungry for days on end.

As she faced him, she felt that arousal, a constant companion anytime he was near, and forced herself to back away from him.

"You act as though all you need to do is place distance between us to alleviate the sweet smell of your hunger for me," he bit out, shocking her. "Do you think I can't smell your desire a mile away?"

She shook her head. She couldn't face this tonight, not on top of the blood and death that surrounded her. She felt as though her body and her soul were stained with guilt.

"This is why you can't be here," she whispered. "I'm not stupid, Noble. I'll distract you, and you'll end up dead."

He shook his head and moved closer. Just a few steps, just enough to warn her that he wasn't going to pay attention to her.

"We'll definitely distract each other," he promised her, his voice low, vibrating with lust. "There's no help for it. And that will be our advantage."

She shook her head fiercely. "It's not an advantage. You know better than that."

She backed farther away from him, jerking in surprise as she came against the wall behind her. She watched, her breathing harsh, heavy as he came closer, stalking her, his expression becoming intent, heavy with hunger.

"You're my mate, Haley," he told her, his voice heavy. And it didn't sound like a good thing. It sounded much too close to the stories that were devoured in the magazines that featured the breeds prominently, with stories of lust-crazed hungers and desires that defied believability.

"I can't handle this from you," she whispered, as he came closer, almost touching her, his chest inches from the rapid rise and fall of her breasts as she stared up at him beseechingly. "Can't you see that, Noble? I can't deal with fairy tales tonight, or with you here."

"And I can't deal with another man watching over you." He reached out and touched her cheek, his knuckles rasping over it.

He rarely touched her. In the year he had been coming to the library, she could count on one hand how many times his skin had actually touched hers.

"Do you know what a mating is?" His head lowered until his lips caressed her ear.

Haley let her head rest against the wall, her body feeling weak now while the blood began to pump hard and heavy through her body.

"The tabloids," she whispered. "They're not true."

"Not precisely." He rubbed his cheek against her.

The curiously gentle stroke of his cheek against hers did more to her than she could have imagined possible. Her lashes drifted closed, sensual weakness invaded her body as her sex began to heat, to clench with empty need.

"Not precisely?" she whispered, as his head lifted, and he stepped back slowly. "What does 'not precisely' mean, exactly?"

"It means, soon, you'll find out, there's no escaping me, Haley. And there's no escaping what you need from me. Soon."

He stepped back farther. "You need to rest. The next few days won't be easy for you, and I don't want to complicate that. But there's no forcing me out of here, there's no running from me any longer. We will see this through together."

Haley bit back her protests. She had been raised by her Scottish father and two older brothers, she knew male determination and arrogance, and if she wasn't mistaken, then Noble had more than his fair share of both.

As he left the bedroom, she slumped against the wall and breathed out wearily. Fear was like an animal trapped inside her, as was her grief. And like the desire she felt for Noble, she had no idea how to handle either emotion.

Noble stepped from the kitchen hours later, after Haley slipped silently through the house, like a wraith in her long white gown and robe, her soft red hair a fiery cloud around her pale face.

He watched as she moved to the huge Christmas tree and slowly, silently, collected two presents from beneath it and walked to the couch.

He was careful to stay within the shadows. He knew grief. Sometimes, a person had to be alone with it, and sometimes a woman needed to be alone with her tears.

She opened the first, which he knew must have been Patricia's. The finely made wrap was a blend of russets and dark golds. He remembered that Patricia liked darker colors.

Haley brought the wrap to her cheek, closed her eyes, and let her tears fall. They fell to the material as her shoulders shook, and she whispered her sorrow against it.

Long minutes later, she smoothed the wrap over her lap and stared at the other, smaller present in front of her. Regret sliced across his chest. He wanted to go to her. He needed to hold her through her pain. Yet, a part of him sensed, knew, that for Haley to survive, she had to say good-bye in her own way.

She reached for the box and set it on her knee as she opened it slowly. She lifted the lid of the wide, black jeweler's box and stared at what she had revealed for long, silent moments.

"I'll miss you, Jason Lincoln," she whispered. "I'm sorry you never found out what freedom truly was."

Then she set the box on the table, pulled the wrap around her, and curled herself onto the cushions of the couch. She stared at that box as the tears whispered over her cheeks, and finally, just before dawn peeked over the horizon, Haley drifted into sleep.

Noble stepped farther into the room, moved to the table, and stared down at what she had bought Jason Lincoln. It was a bracelet. Hammered silver and engraved with a single word. FREEDOM. Beside the word was a lion's paw print.

She'd known Jason wanted a Christmas present. He wondered if she knew that the women of Sanctuary made certain every breed had a Christmas present at Christmas whether they wanted one or not, whether they believed in the holiday or not.

He bent his knees, resting on the pads of his feet as he stared at the present and at the woman. The wrap she had bought Patricia was snug around her shoulders, and the tracks of her tears still dampened her cheeks.

He would give her her time to grieve because he knew she needed it. If he allowed that to be stolen from her, she would never walk into his arms as he needed her to. And he needed her to do that. To come to him. To need him. To ache as he ached and to want as he wanted.

Shaking his head he straightened, drew the light blanket from the back of the couch, and spread it over her before moving to the chair beside her.

He needed a few hours to doze himself. He would catch sleep as he could, and as a breed, he would adapt until they caught the person who had wounded her so deeply. And when they caught him, Noble promised himself, he would exact vengeance for her.

Three days later, they laid Patricia to rest next to her husband and the daughter who had gone before her. Noble stood behind Haley through the service and the burial, and as her pain overwhelmed his senses, he pulled her against his chest.

Her tears soaked into his shirt, branded his flesh, and broke his heart. He rubbed his cheek against the top of her hair, and across the small area his gaze met that of the sheriff's. Noble's eyes narrowed at the flash of jealousy in the sheriff's gaze and the anger when he looked at Noble.

There was more than friendship in that sheriff's eyes when he stared at Haley. And perhaps hatred when he looked at Noble.

Later, as they attended the small service held at Sanctuary for Jason, Noble found himself frowning. The priest who presided over the funeral was compassionate, he didn't judge, and he spoke of

Jason's love for books and his abiding need for freedom. The priest assured them, Jason was free now.

As they approached the casket, Noble watched as Haley slipped the silver bracelet in beside the young breed, and his heart clenched.

Until Sanctuary, breeds had never had a burial. They were incinerated, turned to dust and ashes and, in the minds of their creators, forgotten.

This ritual that nonbreeds practiced made little sense to him, just as the ritual of Christmas still confused him. Breeds participating in either ritual almost seemed against the laws of nature to him. They weren't human. They hadn't been born, and the God that sanctioned the lives of others hadn't sanctioned the lives of breeds.

If their lives hadn't been sanctioned, could they still claim His benevolence?

Noble shook his head and followed Haley as she left the small chapel. He kept his arm around her, kept her to his chest as his team surrounded her and led her back to the black SUV limo that would return her to the warmth of the home she had made for herself.

Her grief was easing, but he had felt her determination rising. She had been quiet the past few days, but something was strengthening inside her. He could sense it. He could feel it. And the animal part of him stretched in anticipation.

"We need groceries," Haley stated later, as they neared the outskirts of Buffalo Gap.

She was aware of the six breeds who rode with them, their silence, their watchfulness. Just as she was aware of their suspicion each time they checked to see if Zane Taggart was still following them.

Zane wouldn't let go easy. He had imagined himself in love

with her years before, and during that brief affair, he had driven her crazy with his protectiveness. It was always very subtle, very warm, but he would have tried to wrap her in cotton if they had stayed together.

And as much as she cared for Zane, the rest just hadn't come as she had hoped it would. As he had been certain it would. Breaking off their relationship had hurt both of them, and she had tried to ensure that she never placed herself in that position again.

"You can make out a list when we get to the house," Noble stated. "Someone will deliver the items you need."

Of course, why hadn't she thought of that?

Her fists clenched in her lap. She couldn't even risk going to the grocery store.

"Jonas will be waiting for us at the house," he continued. "We need to discuss what he's learned in the past few days. He's finally managed to gather enough information to give us an idea of what we're looking at."

She looked up at him in surprise. "He's going to tell me?"

"It's your life." His sensual lips tightened, and his black eyes flared with anger. "I need you to help me protect you, Haley. To do that, you need the same information I do."

"At least you're not going to try to lock me in a box then." She sighed.

The past three days had been hell. Of course her brothers as well as her father had eventually learned something was going on. Concerned neighbors, nosy citizens, someone had made certain they got hold of them.

Her father was screaming on the phone the night before as her brothers vied to be heard over him during the four-way call.

She still had a headache and she doubted Noble's conversation with them had done much to allay their concerns or their threats to head straight to Buffalo Gap.

"It wouldn't do any good to lock you in a box, would it?" He sounded mildly interested at the prospect, enough so that she shot him a warning glare.

"I know how to pick locks."

His lips quirked. "Now, why didn't I guess that?"

"Probably because you were considering the box," she muttered.

She ignored the amusement in the breeds across from her.

They were an interesting lot. The three in the driver's area and the three sitting across from them. They were hard-eyed, tough, and strong. Long hair, numerous scars, and all of them looked like men who could fight their way through an army single-handedly.

And they had all put their lives on the line for her. It was a terrifying thought. It was the reason she had promised herself that whatever Noble needed her to do, she would do. Because it was apparent he wasn't going to leave. Nor would he let her leave. That didn't mean she had to like it. And it didn't mean she had to accept the very sensual invitation he extended each time their eyes met.

"A box was never under consideration," he finally admitted. "We'll find out who is behind the bombing soon. We know the why of it, we just have to identify the who. Once we've done that, you'll be safe. And once you've testified at the hearing against Brackenmore and Engalls next month, then they'll no longer have a reason to want you dead. They'll be too busy trying to save their own skins."

She didn't know if she agreed with him on that one. It seemed to her that the hatred Brackenmore and Engalls would feel toward her would be reason enough to kill her. Thankfully for the breeds, she wasn't the only proof they had against the pair.

"Jonas has arrived at the house," Mordecai Savant, the Coyote breed enforcer who had arrived at Sanctuary six months before, told Noble as he glanced at the handheld PDA he pulled from the heavy uniform pocket at his thigh. "It's clear. No signs of unwanted visitors. The lions have canvassed the area, and everything's clear."

"The lions?" She glanced at Noble again. "You have lions at my house?"

"The natural lions can sense things we don't," he told her. "If they hesitate, then we know there's a problem. They're our best first defense."

"Proceed in," Mordecai told him. "Jonas is waiting in the kitchen."

Haley had to bite her tongue to keep from commenting on that one. No doubt he had sniffed out her stash of cookies again. She was going to have to bake more before long. Breeds could find the cookies faster than her brothers could.

"Is he eating all the cookies?" Blade Travers could never, in anyone's imagination, look boyish. But the anxiety in his eyes reminded her of just that. A kid's concern that he wouldn't get his share.

"If there are cookies around, then Jonas is going to find them," the breed simply known as Crayven snorted from the front seat. "And I bet Mercury, Lawe, and Rule are taking more than their share, too."

Yes, she was going to be making more cookies soon, she thought as she heard Noble sigh, almost with longing beside her.

"I know how to bake more," she finally gritted out between clenched teeth.

And why she was that insane, she couldn't imagine.

"You would bake us more?" Mordecai's eyes narrowed on her, as though he suspected her of lying.

She was definitely going to have to add to that grocery list.

"I always bake at Christmas." And it seemed this year, she was going to be baking a hell of a lot more than she imagined.

Breeds. Why hadn't anyone warned her it wasn't just their sharp teeth, biting words, or flare for killing that she needed to watch out for? Someone should have warned her to watch out for their craving for sweets as well.

She wondered if it went to their hips as fast as it did to hers.

She glanced at each one, then grimaced. She couldn't get that lucky.

Chapter 5

Hours later, Haley was baking cookies out of sheer desperation. Chocolate chip cookies, chocolate oatmeal cookies, and chocolate drop sugar cookies.

Haley baked to feel good, to think, and to hide. Tonight she was hiding.

Uriel. She'd heard that name before, she'd read that name before. One of the names associated with a god of death. The Grim Reaper. The taker of life. In this case an assassin.

According to Jonas, the assassin was suspected to be a breed still under the control of the Genetics Council that had created him.

The explosion had all his signatures, but the really telling mark was the so-far-untraceable e-mail sent to Jonas at his Bureau of Breed Affairs e-mail address. It stated that he really didn't want to kill more breeds to get to her, but he would if he had to. And it was signed, Uriel.

She had a professional assassin out to kill her. So what was she doing? She was baking.

The moment Jonas had given Noble the information the demeanor of the breeds guarding her had changed. The six under Noble's command turned hard and cold.

Mordecai had demanded Jonas have his pet released from Sanctuary. So, a full-grown, malevolent-eyed natural coyote was now on her property. Great. Just what she needed.

Weren't they supposed to be impossible to tame?

Noble had changed as well, and that change made her more nervous than the others. The look he had given her had held a promise, a dark, almost forbidden promise, that shook her to her core.

As he and Jonas retreated to the living room to discuss security, Haley retreated to the kitchen to bake. And to try to forget that look she had seen in Noble's eyes. The one that promised her he had given her enough space, and that soon, he would be crowding in even closer.

"Jonas is leaving, Haley." Noble stepped into the kitchen, his black gaze hooded as he flicked over the last sheet of cookies she was pulling from the oven.

Haley nodded slowly. "Fine."

She turned and faced Jonas as he moved into the kitchen.

"We'll have this taken care of soon," Jonas promised her. "We have several leads. Uriel was careless this time. Uriel has been erratic in the past few years anyway, so the successes could barely be counted because of it."

"But someone still ended up dead, right?" she pointed out.

"Only because the victims didn't know they were targets," Jonas stated. "We know. Now, I'll leave you with Noble. You have six men guarding you outside as well as that bloodthirsty animal Mordecai carts around with him. Nothing gets past any of them."

He moved to the back door, shrugging his suit jacket on over the white dress shirt and shoulder holster he wore. Once he had the jacket on, he seemed like any other powerful businessman, until you looked in his eyes.

"Noble, I'd wish you luck with the other thing," Jonas suddenly turned back to them, his gaze amused, his hard face almost smiling. "But I have a feeling you have that covered as well."

He left the house, and Noble secured the door behind him before Haley could comment.

"What's the other thing?" she asked, as he turned back to face her.

"Something more personal," he finally stated.

His voice was different. There was a rasp to it, a brief roughness that sent a chill up her spine.

She rubbed her hands together, ignoring the tingling warmth that filled her palms. Her hands tingled every damned time he was around her. The need, the desire to touch him often nearly overcame her common sense.

She nodded rather than asking about it. For a few minutes anyway—while she transferred the cookies from the baking sheet to the wire rack for them to cool.

"What is something more personal?" She laid the spatula down beside the rack and turned to him.

Facing him across the distance of the kitchen, she somehow felt braver than she had in days. Someone was trying to kill her. Someone who knew how to kill. Excuse me for taking a little initiative here.

"Are you sure you want to know?" Sensually curved lips quirked knowingly.

"Is it about that mating crap you tried to pull on me the other night?"

She hadn't forgotten. It had been in the back of her mind, teasing her, taunting her, and following her into her dreams when she managed to sleep.

His brow arched. "Mating crap?"

She lifted her hand, indicating he should stay in place, then stomped to her bedroom, jerked several tabloids from beneath her bedstand, and moved back into the kitchen and slapped them on the table.

MATING HEAT SWEEPS THROUGH
THE BREED COMMUNITIES.
BREED APHRODISIAC RUMORED
TO CAUSE UNSTOPPABLE LUSTS.
ARE THEY MORE ANIMAL THAN WE IMAGINED?
MATING HEAT RUMORED
TO PRODUCE ANIMALISTIC RESULTS.

The headlines were ridiculous, but they all reported nearly the same phenomenon.

"You read this trash?" he asked her, flipping his fingers over the magazines.

She crossed her arms over her breasts. "How much of it is true?"

He flipped through the magazines one by one. His brows arched a few times. Mockery tugged at his lips before he tossed the last one back to the stop.

"I'd say ninety percent of it is fairly accurate."

She blinked, then narrowed her eyes suspiciously.

"You're lying to me."

His grin was slow, and did nothing to still the nervous feelings rising inside her.

"Yeah, I am." He shrugged. "Probably more like eighty percent."

He pushed his hand into the pocket of his jeans and withdrew a vial. Within it were several oddly colored pinkish pills. He tossed the vial to the table and stated. "One a day, starting tonight."

She stared at it, wondering if the breeds were into poison.

"For what?"

He moved around the kitchen then, stalking closer as she refused to retreat. He came behind her, brushed the hair from her shoulder, and his head lowered, his lips brushing her ear.

"When I kiss you, the taste of that kiss is going to make you crazy for more. The hormone in the small glands beneath my tongue will be released into your system, and the mating hormone will begin to fill your senses. It's like a drug for sex. It's like a need that only one thing will ease, and that's my semen pumping inside you. When that happens, a small, thumb-shaped extension will become erect from beneath the head of my cock. It will lock me inside you, spill another hormone into you, then, together, they'll prepare your body for the few viable sperm breeds possess. That pill will ease the effects of the heat. It might even ward off the pregnancy that will come, eventually. It takes a while sometimes for fertilization, for a child to be created. But it always happens, eventually. And the heat never goes away entirely. It grows, day by day, year by year, until mates are bound so closely together that life without each other is unimaginable.

"Breeds only mate once, Haley. One time only. A breed has one chance, and one chance only to claim something in this world that belongs to him and to him alone. And my body is claiming yours."

"You're crazy." She forced herself away from him, rounded on him incredulously, and stared back at him in shock. "That's not true."

"Why do you think I kept such a careful distance between us?" he asked her, his expression imposing, his black eyes gleaming, glittering with hunger. "A year. I've tasted the need to kiss you, to fuck you, for a year. I've tried to drown my lust, ignore it, fight it. Nothing works, Haley. Nothing is going to work until I share it. With you."

Her eyes were wide, shock resounding through her. His expression was tortured, almost agonized, almost convincing.

"Why are you doing this?" She stared back at him furiously. "I like you, Noble. Have I ever been cruel to you? Why would you do this to me?"

She was hurt. She stared back at him painfully, wondering why he would want to play with her in such a way. Okay, she gave the tabloids credit, there might be a glimmer of truth to some of it. But what he was saying was unreal.

Noble stared back at her, his jaw clenching furiously, the muscle at the side ticking in a resounding rhythm of restraint.

"You want me," he growled. "I can smell it. More than you've ever wanted another man, Haley. I'm betting on it."

She pushed her fingers through her hair and fought back her embarrassment.

"I know you can smell that I want you," she said uncomfortably, feeling the flush that worked up her neck and face. "I don't expect anything from you, but you don't have to lie to me."

His expression tightened, the flesh seemed stretched over the bones and angles of his face, giving him a darker, more animal-like appearance.

"Come here." He reached out for her.

Haley stared at his hand suspiciously. It was broad, darkly tanned, strong. His fingers were powerful and graceful, and she couldn't stop the clenching of her stomach at the thought of his touching her.

"Give me your hand, Haley." His voice hardened.

She lifted her hand to him. Slowly, he took the tip of her finger and brought it to his mouth. "Let me show you."

His lips parted, the heat of his mouth flushed over the tip of her finger and seemed to wash into her flesh. Then his tongue was curling around it, and there, beneath it, she felt the small, enflamed glands. They were hard, pulsing against her finger, hot and rasping against her.

His thick, black lashes lowered, sensuality and hunger suffused his face. And all he was doing was suckling at her finger, licking it.

Her finger heated, and she swore she felt a tingle of something more than simple pleasure move into her flesh. When he pulled her hand back, she stared at the dampened flesh, then back to him.

"Give it an hour," he told her then, his voice rasping. "It doesn't take a kiss to make the hormone move into you, Haley. Something that simple." He nodded to her finger, and in his expression she could see a need for more of her. "A kiss to your neck. A gentle taste of your flesh, and it will burn inside you, it will warm your desire more than ever before. And the sweet, sensual smell of your cream will make me crazier." His hands clenched into fists at his side. "I want you. I've wanted you since the moment I laid eyes on you a year ago. Want you until the need for you overwhelms everything else. That's why your security team is so large. Why you have six breeds rather than two working to make certain you're safe. Because here, in this house, the world outside isn't going to exist for either of us soon. Soon, nothing is going to exist except the hunger."

She stared at her finger and back to him. She licked her lips nervously, her breath catching as his gaze sliced to the action.

"I want to lick your lips, too." His voice sounded torn from his throat. "I want to lick your lips, your breasts, and the sweet wet heat between your thighs. I want to take you until you can't deny me, or deny the hunger feeding us both. And it's going to happen, Haley. Very very soon. The only question is, can you accept it?"

Could she accept it?

She stared back at him. "I'm not in love with you."

She wanted him. She had wanted him for a year. She was fascinated with him, fantasized about him constantly, but that wasn't love.

"Then we're in for a rocky ride, Haley." He sighed regretfully. "But it's very possible that I am in love with you. And I've never in my life had anything or anyone that belonged to me. Knowing you're my mate makes it damned hard to give you a warning, or a choice. But I'm trying to do that. In the next few hours, I want you to remember that. I'm trying, and for me, that's a hell of a concession."

He turned and walked away from her then, his broad shoulders straight, his head held high as he moved back into the living room.

There was so much pride in every movement of his body. Strength and determination, confidence definitely.

Haley collapsed into one of the kitchen chairs beside her and stared at her finger.

Was it a virus? Whatever that mating thing was? Just a hormone surely couldn't do what he said it could. She turned her gaze to the vial of pills on the table. There weren't a lot of them. One a day he had said. To help minimize the effects?

There were so many questions pouring through her mind now. And so many sensations filling her. It wasn't the hormone he had licked onto her finger that had her heart racing. And it couldn't be causing her thighs to tingle. It was a mind game. And she wasn't so simple that she was going to allow herself to be played so easily.

She rose from the table and moved quickly, angrily into the living room. He wasn't there. His bedroom door was open, and she moved there, determined to question him, to get the answers she needed. She stepped into the bedroom, where she came to a halt just inside the doorway.

For some reason, he had pulled his shirt off. God, why had he pulled his shirt off? Because before he could turn to face her, she had glimpsed his back. There, across his shoulders, were spots. Not freckles. Not scarring, but a unique, fascinating pattern of dark rings, rather like the spots of the Jaguar whose DNA she knew he shared.

She stepped forward. Her hands were tingling again, more strongly, the need to touch him almost driving her past common sense.

"I need a shower." He faced her, and across his shoulders and upper chest those spots continued. They were faint, patterned across his chest and arrowing down into his jeans.

She stepped forward and stopped. Then moved again. She had to touch them.

As she got closer, she could see that it was more than just spots. It was a pattern of the fine, almost invisible hairs she knew covered the breed bodies. But they were darker in areas, creating the pattern of spots.

Breeds appeared hairless, except for their eyebrows and the hair on their heads. Actually, according to her research they were covered in a thin, fine pelt almost undetectable, even to touch.

"Haley, you don't want to touch me right now," he told her softly.

She couldn't help it. She touched. She reached out, letting her palm smooth over his chest and feeling her breath catching in her chest as she felt the heat, the hard muscle rippling beneath his tough skin, and the ultrasoft feel of that darker pelt against her flesh.

"It's beautiful," she whispered, lifting her gaze to his as she lifted her other hand and touched him more.

"Don't. Haley, please." His hands gripped her wrists, but he held her in place, he didn't move her, didn't pull her from him. "You don't understand what that hormone does to me. You don't know how I burn for you."

"Why me?" she whispered. "Why did you choose me?"

His gaze was heavy, black eyes that swirled with dark color and hints of emotion. They gleamed with life, with hunger, and with more than lust.

"I saw you," he said. "A smile on your face, your pretty eyes lit with laughter and hope and joy. And you dazzled me, Haley. You always dazzle me. Confuse me. Draw me. It doesn't take love for mating heat to begin, but if love truly does exist, then I knew that feeling the first moment I saw your smile. I claimed you, when I never meant to claim anything or anyone that could be taken from me. *I claimed you, Haley*. Now if you don't get the hell away from me, all choice I would have given you is going to be taken from you."

Chapter 6

Noble never would have believed that he had the strength to hold back as he did. To allow Haley to touch him, despite his hold on her wrists, to allow her to pet him.

And she was petting him. Stroking her palms over his flesh, feeling the slight rasp of the darker hairs that made the spots covering his chest and arrowing down his abdomen before spreading out over his thighs.

They weren't large spots. Some were oddly shaped, some smaller than others. They were not human, a glaring reminder of what he was. Part animal. Bred from the DNA of the jaguar.

And at the moment he had never felt more like an animal. His cock was swollen in his jeans, thick and hard, throbbing in a hunger unlike anything he had known before he hungered for Haley.

His fingers circled her wrists as he forced himself to watch her, to stare down at her. Watching the latent sensuality in her expression as she touched him. She was enjoying it. Touching him with stark innocence, discovery, and joy.

"You're so warm," she whispered.

"Haley, I'm burning," he warned her roughly.

He didn't want her to stop touching him. He wanted it to continue forever. But he knew that wasn't possible. Not yet. He couldn't let her strip his control, because if she did, then he would take the choice from her. He would mate her, even knowing it was possible she didn't love him.

She said she didn't. But he could smell her. He had smelled the emotions, the pheromones breeds and mates created together, and he could smell the subtle scent of it on her. It made him crazy, smelling it, knowing he couldn't have her, that she wouldn't understand the animal he was and that he couldn't force her into the mating.

The animal that stretched inside him didn't care though. It wanted. It ached. It snarled relentlessly for the taste of her.

"If you keep stroking me, you know what's going to happen," he told her.

"Maybe I don't believe you." She looked up at him through her lashes, her gray eyes nearly blue as her features flushed with arousal.

With true, pure arousal. This wasn't heat-induced. It wasn't hormone-induced. It was her hunger for him. Pure and sweet and filling his senses.

"You believe me, Haley." He could see it in her eyes, in her expression. She didn't want to believe him, but she knew it was there. "You think I'll hold back. That I'll let you pet and stroke me and keep the need I have for you under control. What happens when I break? When I take that choice from you?"

And he didn't want to. He wanted to luxuriate in the sensations of her hands on his flesh, touching him, stroking him. If only this.

She stared up at him. "Is it that bad?" Worry filled her eyes and he saw her intentions to draw back, to move from him, to leave him.

"I'll warn you when it gets that bad." Ah hell. He was insane. He had passed that point minutes ago, and he was encouraging her to go further?

"Are you sure?" Hesitation filled her now, and he didn't want her hesitation.

"I'm sure." He was crazy. That was exactly what he was, insane. The need for her touch outweighed everything else and made him insane to think he could control his response.

"I've been dying to touch you," she whispered as he released her hands and reached behind him to the footboard of the bed, gripping the wood tightly with desperate fingers.

He tipped his head back. He wasn't going to watch. He couldn't watch her.

"Touch me then." He could feel the sweat gathering on his back.

Her touch was like electric pleasure. It shimmered over his flesh, dug talons of exquisite need beneath it, and left him tight, tense, torn between stopping her and begging her for more. He would probably end up begging her for more, that was how damned crazy he was, a true glutton for punishment. Or for pleasure.

"Tell me when it's too much," she whispered.

"Gotcha." He gave her a sharp nod.

Too much had already been done and gone. Too much was the feel of his balls drawn excruciatingly tight and the head of his cock flaring thick and hard, and throbbing like a damned wound.

Too much was when he felt her lips touch his chest and her hot little tongue licking over a spot. That was too damned much.

Haley let her senses become immersed in the need to just touch him. Touching should be okay, she told herself. It wasn't a kiss, at least, not his kiss. It was just his flesh, just those intriguing little spots and the dampness of his flesh as she felt his flesh heat.

It was moving slowly, hesitantly into the desires that had never made sense where he was concerned. As though without even trying he touched a hidden part of her, drawing it free, and teasing it to be wild with him.

Without saying a word. Without touching her, without tempting her with anything more than a look or the quirk of his lips. He tempted that unknown something inside her.

"I love how you feel." She touched his hard, rippling abs with her hands, smoothed over them to the band of his jeans and back up.

She tasted him. She kissed his chest, licked at several spots, feeling the ultrasoftness of the tiny hairs against her tongue. Then, in a move more daring than she had ever considered, she raked her teeth over the flesh beside a stiff, hard male nipple.

As though she had flayed him with fire he jerked, a hard, primal growl tearing from his chest as his head jerked up, and he stared down at her.

His eyes were like black velvet, studded with even darker glimmer of lights. How could anything be darker than black? But something was, and it flickered in his eyes, the color overtaking the pupil and giving him a primal, primitive look.

As though the animal were so close to the surface that it would be hard to tell where human and jaguar separated. And she was tempting it. She knew she was.

"Is it too much?" She didn't want to torture him. She just needed to touch him.

"No." The word was short, the rasp in his voice was deep as his hands moved from behind him. "But if you can bite, then I can touch you as well."

She hadn't counted on that. Just as she hadn't counted on the throbbing growl in his voice as he said the words.

"How?" She needed to know. "No kisses."

"No kisses. No little bites." He bared his teeth, and she should have been frightened of those canines, which flashed at the sides of his mouth. Instead, they intrigued her.

How would they feel on her flesh? Raking over it, creating a flash point of pleasure and heat?

She swallowed tightly as he gripped the hem of her shirt.

"Let me take it off."

Her breath caught in her throat. "Is that a good idea?"

"Is any of it?" He tugged the hem upward. "Take it off or walk out of here. I can't stand here and not touch you as well, Haley. That's asking too much."

"No kisses?" She was almost whimpering with the need for his kiss though. Her lips tingled, her tongue ached to twine with his.

"No kisses," he promised.

She lifted her hands from his chest and raised her arms slowly, allowing him to draw the shirt from her. Sensuality wrapped around them heavily, saturating the air with lust and hunger as he tossed the material aside and stared down at her.

The white lace camisole she wore in place of a bra adequately covered her, sort of.

"That's cheating." There was no grin, there was only need in his eyes to see her. "Let me take it off, too."

She could feel her nipples rasping against the lace, urging him to do just that. She licked her lips nervously and lifted her arms for him again.

He drew the lace covering from her, the material stroking over her nipples drawing a ragged groan from her. As he tossed the material aside, his hands caught her wrists, holding them over her head as he stared down at her.

"I want to suck your nipples." The blunt, blatant hunger in the words caused her womb to clench in response. Like a punch to her stomach, firing her nerve endings and sending pleasure streaking through her body.

She wanted him to suck her nipples. Her nipples wanted his mouth on them. She ached for it. The flesh between her thighs heated for it. She felt weak, dazed, arousal pouring into every cell and whipping over her nerve endings.

"If I weren't a breed," he told her then, "if I were just a man, I'd lay you down and tempt you with my mouth. I'd suck your pretty nipples until the dark pink blushed a pretty rose. Then I'd go between your thighs and lick the sweetest cream, and know your arousal is just for the pleasure I can give you."

Haley watched the regret that filled him as he stared down at her. He held her wrists easily in one hand. With the other, he cupped the rounded mound of a breast, the tip of a finger stroking over the ultrasensitive, hardened peak.

Haley shuddered. She leaned her head against one of her arms as he held them both over her head and stared up at him.

"I'm going to melt to the floor," she whispered. "We need to stop this."

"I'm still in control," he rasped.

"But maybe I'm not," she gasped.

"I'll keep you in control."

His hand lowered from her breast to the elastic band of her lounging pants.

"Let me." He pushed them over her hips.

Haley stared up at his face. No man had ever stared at her with such need. Even in the height of sex, the few lovers she'd had hadn't looked at her like this.

She trembled as she let him push the loose material over her hips. She watched his face as he stared at the white-lace panties she wore. The French-cut, hip-high panties matched her camisole, and they were damp, wet with her need.

"Ah, Haley." His tone was guttural as she watched in shock as he knelt in front of her.

He had released her hands, but what the hell was she supposed to do with them? The bed. She gripped the footboard as his hands clasped her hips. His face was only inches from her, her flesh covered only by the lace of the panties.

"You don't shave here?" One hand lowered, the backs of his fingers stroking over her mound.

"No." Shock gathered in her voice that he would ask her.

She had tried it, once, and hadn't liked the sensation.

"Good." He crooned, his fingers stroking over her again. "So good. I want to feel your soft curls against my face. Can I do that, Haley? Can I feel your sweet damp curls against my lips? I promise, no tongue."

And she stood there. Stared down at him. And like a woman who enjoyed walking the edge of insanity, she let him draw the panties down her legs.

"You have spots, too." His voice was nearly strangled as he stared at her. And she did have. Freckles over the tops of her thighs and her hips. Not many, a few here and there. But enough.

"I want to lick them."

She watched his jaw bunch.

"I want to taste you."

He leaned closer, both hands gripping her hips now as he neared the dark red curls between her thighs. Haley had forgotten how to breathe, she was certain of it. Why else did she feel so light-headed, so dazed? So aroused. It was like a fire burning beneath her flesh now, searing her, destroying her senses.

"Haley," he breathed her name against the damp curls, against the engorged bud of her clit, and she jerked, much as he had when she rasped her teeth over his chest.

She knew that pleasure now. Like a strike of brilliant, white-hot heat tearing through her.

"Haley," he breathed again. "Get the hell out of here."

It took long, disbelieving seconds to understand what he was saying.

"What?"

"Go," he growled, his eyes still on her as he licked his lips, his tongue swiping over them. "Get away from me, Haley."

"Noble."

"I'm going to lick that sweet cream. I'm going to bury my tongue inside your pussy and to hell with your anger or your hatred later. Get the fuck away from me."

She shuddered, shaking with the need she couldn't seem to control. She couldn't move. How the hell was she supposed to get away from him?

"Go!" His voice hardened.

The deliberate control in his movements as he released his hands from her hips was frightening. His expression, his eyes as he stared up at her, sent her stumbling back from him.

There was lust and hunger, then there was the pure, unbridled desperation she saw in his face. He would do it. And he was close, so close.

What had she done to him?

She jerked back farther, bending to snatch her clothes when he crouched over them, his gaze brimming with fiery, intent lust.

At that point, Haley all but ran from his bedroom. As she glanced back at the doorway, she nearly changed her mind. Nearly went to her knees in front of him and took everything he had to give her.

In one hand he held her lace panties to his mouth and nose, his eyes were closed, and his expression, his expression was pure, wicked pleasure.

She had to force herself to turn and go to her own room. Had to force herself away from him. And she had a feeling running was only delaying the inevitable. He was going to end up in her bed. And he was going to be there soon.

Chapter 7

The night was hell. The next morning was an exercise in restraint that had Noble's control stretched to its limits. The day was gray, the clouds lying heavy as more snow drifted over the mountains.

There was more than two feet out there, and the city was struggling to keep up as more snow was forecast. Winter was driving in hard and heavy, unlike anything they had seen in years. The winds swirled and moaned as the icy cold tried to penetrate every crack and pore of the house.

Haley had lit the fire that morning. Noble had carried in the firewood from the back porch and watched as she efficiently set fire to the tinder, building the coal bed with the smallest logs before placing the larger ones on it.

She did it the old-fashioned way. She used untreated firewood, preferring, she said, the scent of the wood over the fumes of the chemicals.

And as the afternoon progressed, he found her more and more often in front of the fire, her legs curled beside her as she sat on the thick, heavy rug before the hearth and leaned into the fat, fluffy pillows she'd had stored beside the couch.

She watched the fire as though it held the answers to every question she had ever asked.

Behind her, the Christmas tree twinkled with a million lights, the gaily wrapped presents beneath it gleaming with brilliant colors.

He'd never experienced Christmas. He'd been out of the labs for ten years, but it had been ten years struggling to aid the survival of the breed communities. The feline compound of Sanctuary as well as the Colorado-based wolf breed compound, Haven.

Christmas had been just another day for him, until now. Until he saw all the careful planning and the joy that would have gone into it for Haley.

Decorations filled the kitchen and living room as well as the outside of the house. From the groceries that were delivered that morning, he knew she planned to bake. He knew she was praying the danger would all be over before her family arrived on the twenty-third. He knew there were more presents in her bedroom to be wrapped. A pile of them. And he knew she was fighting the same needs, the same hungers he was fighting.

He stood just inside the living room, having just finished a call from Jonas. They were moving in on the person responsible for the leak in Haley's identity. The information they were tracking through their own servers as well as spyware slipped into Brackenmore's and Engalls's computers was turning up some interesting information.

Information that might end this sooner than any of them imagined.

There was a reason why Uriel had been so erratic in the past years. A reason why Brackenmore and Engalls had found the information about mating heat and ultimately the aging decrease. Mating heat always slowed aging in mates. Because Uriel was definitely a breed, and obviously in mating heat. That damned phenomenon was enough to make any breed slightly off center, but for a hired killer, it could be more dangerous than to most.

"They've had a break in the investigation." He kept his voice low, kept a careful distance between them. "Jonas is certain he'll have the identity of the person behind this within days."

She tensed. The fiery scent of her arousal seemed to intensify as he spoke to her.

As she turned, her hair fell over her shoulder, the flames gleaming over it, turning it to fire as well. The sight of it was nearly mesmerizing. Dazzling.

"Within days," she said softly. "That's pretty fast."

Jonas was pushing. He was breaking mandates and laws and working silently to identify Uriel, the hired assassin who had attempted to kill her. Not that he would get caught, even if the spyware was eventually detected.

"Jonas made you a promise to protect you, Haley. He'll keep it."

She lowered her head, staring down at her fingers as she twined them together.

"And when it's over?" She lifted her head and stared back at him somberly. "What then?"

"Sanctuary and its backers rebuild the library, restock it, and you get your life back," he told her.

"The way it was?"

He inhaled heavily, staring back at her, uncertain how to ease the pain he could sense inside her.

"That's up to you," he finally told her.

The memory of her touching him seared him then—a flash of heat hotter than the flames as the glands beneath his tongue made it feel thick, unruly. The hormone was growing more potent, torturing him. The arousal was building inside him, and he knew he had only a short amount of time before he was forced to walk away from her or risk destroying her trust in him.

Trust was such a fragile commodity, especially for a woman. He'd known of matings that had worked when that choice was removed. Love had grown, and it had thrived. But he had sworn he would never take that choice from his mate. That he would never take that choice from Haley. But time was running out for him.

The choice had been taken from him a year before, when he first saw that smile. When he first scented her, first felt the glands swelling beneath his tongue and realized what was going on. And he hadn't left. He had stayed. If he had left, he might have had a choice.

"My choice," she whispered before shaking her head and lowering it again. "You don't make things easy do you, Noble."

"Was I supposed to make it easy?" he asked her, feeling the growing tension rising inside him. "Did you want me to take the choice from you, Haley? Would you have hated me for it?"

Haley stared back at him, having no answers. All she knew was the need that didn't go away, the knowledge it was never going to go away. She had somehow always sensed that. That Noble would be the one man she would never be able to forget, never be able to get over if she fell in love with him.

And that had been what had held her back.

"I wouldn't have hated you," she finally whispered. "But it's too late for that, anyway. I do know. And knowing changes things."

"It didn't change anything last night," he bit out. "You loved touching me, Haley. Tasting me. I saw it in your face."

And she had seen it in his as well. The pure pleasure, the hunger and the overriding primal lust that had filled him. A part of her was drawn to it. A part of her was terrified by it. And she knew, she couldn't walk away from it again.

He pushed his fingers through his hair before gripping his neck and glaring over at her. She stared at him with those solemn, stormy eyes, and he knew that the same torments plagued her. Not as intently, not as strong. But she needed him, she ached for him.

"I want you until I don't know how to breathe without thinking of it anymore," she finally whispered, her voice echoing with the ache he felt inside his chest. "And I don't know what to do, Noble. I never expected this. And now, I don't know how to handle it."

"I'm not asking you to handle anything," he stated harshly. "Look, don't worry about it." He forced a tight, hard smile to his lips. "I've lived with it for a year now and survived. It won't kill me."

Maybe.

He moved through the living room into the spare bedroom he used. The communications and sensor equipment was set up there. Thankfully, the snow wasn't interfering with it too severely.

The satellite imagery was a little corrupted, but it still pinpointed his team's position. Three breeds on twelve-hour shifts, three resting but prepared for backup. Mordecai's coyote paced the grounds, and there was nothing in the immediate vicinity to cause any alarms.

Even more, whoever the breed was that had targeted her for Brackenmore and Engalls, they had no idea that Jonas was moving in. That would make it easier. And none besides himself, Jonas, and Callan were aware that there was a six-man force on constant detail.

The mission rosters were listed and Blake, Shiloh, and Flint were listed as operational and out of country. Mordecai was listed as patrolling Buffalo Gap, which he did, sometimes. And John Talon and Micah Jones were listed as Noble's outside security team only.

The careful deception wouldn't last for long, but perhaps long enough for the assassin to feel safe and confident enough to move in for the kill. Because Noble was also listed as "compromised," the term used for a breed entering mating heat.

Mating heat was known to compromise a breed's ability to detect more subtle scents. The senses were so involved with the scent, the taste, and the need for the mate, that most breeds weren't even operational during the first months of the phenomenon. Only after the mating heat had leveled off, allowing both mates to function without the near-constant need for sex, were mated breeds returned to operational status.

They had laid the groundwork, and the opportunity for the assassin to show up. And he would, soon. Noble could feel it. And when the bastard made the move, they would be ready for it.

"How bad is it for you?"

He tensed as she stepped into the bedroom. He had been aware of her movement through the house, the scent of her, like summer in the mountains, flowing toward him.

"Like I said, I'll survive." He shrugged.

"Can I touch you then?"

Agony ripped through him.

"No." He had to force the word out. "Not yet, Haley."

"If it's not that bad, then you could stand for me to touch you," she whispered. "Why are you lying to me, Noble?"

He clenched his jaw as she moved closer.

"Wrong time to push this," he growled, turning on her, glaring down at her.

There was no fear in her eyes, though he knew he must look more like an animal than the man he tried to be. The hunger was nearly out of control. As long as he kept a careful distance between them, then he survived it, but Haley wasn't keeping that distance.

She flowed toward him, dressed in soft pants and a softer sweater.

She looked like an angel coming toward him, and he wanted her with a force that had nothing to do with innocence.

"The wrong time to push it?" she asked him then. "You're hurting, aren't you?"

He'd gone past hurting last night. He was to the point that if she touched him, if she pushed him, he was going to take. And he wouldn't stop taking until all the need burning inside him was sated.

"Do I look like I'm hurting?" He wanted her, not her pity.

"You look just as arrogant and as forceful as you ever have," she told him as she trailed her fingers over the footboard of the bed and stared back at him. "Maybe I'm the one hurting, and I need to know if it's the same for you."

He could smell her arousal. It wasn't yet scented with mating heat, but the alluring scent of her, the sense of her need, the pulsing tension that seemed to throb through her body snared his senses like a carefully laid trap.

"I ache to my back teeth to touch you," he snarled back at her. "Is that what you want to hear? My cock feels like someone's sliced it open I want you so damned bad. Is that hurting enough for you, Haley?"

Her stormy eyes darkened, her breathing hitched. "I need . . ." she swallowed tightly. "I need you, Noble, and that need terrifies me. I've never ached for anyone like this. I've never wanted anyone like this. And I'm scared. I'm terrified you'll walk away, be taken away, or decide later this wasn't what you wanted, despite what you say about the hormone. I'm scared of reaching out to someone who might only want me because he has to protect me, or who may grow tired of having a woman weaker than he is. I'm not a breed." She shook her head as her eyes glittered with dampness. "I'm not strong like a breed woman is, and I'm not as courageous, or as adventurous."

He jerked her to him. "Not courageous or adventurous?" he rasped. "What the hell are you then? You risked your life for Sanctuary, and now you're standing here with me, knowing what I could do to you. What is that, Haley?"

Her lips trembled. "Insanity. And I've been crazy about you since the moment you walked in the library and stared at me as though you knew me. As though you felt that same sense of knowledge that I did."

He stared back at her in shock.

"I've never wanted anything, never needed anyone like I need you," she told him, reaching up, her fingers touching his lips. "Show me, Noble. Show me how to be your mate."

Chapter 8

She had spent the day going over it. She had thought it to death, reasoned it around every corner and curve she could reason it around, and come to the same ending each time. If she walked away from this, if she let him walk away, she would never forgive herself.

Like Noble, she had feared for so long that she would never find that feeling that something or someone belonged just to her. That one heart beat for her, her heart for him.

For a year she had kept her distance, but only because Noble had kept his. It would have taken very little for her to go into his arms.

The mating heat was a frightening prospect. The tabloid stories, if they were even 80 percent true, were enough to make any woman pause. But at least she had an idea what to expect, she told herself as she stared back at him. At least she had a chance of finding that unknown something she had been waiting for so long.

"This isn't like last night, Haley," he warned her. "There's no stepping into this and pulling back. Do you understand me? Once I kiss you, it starts. I promise you, stopping won't be a part of what comes later."

"I understand that." She nodded. And she did, she hoped. Yet he still stood there, staring at her, his expression tight, arrogant, fierce.

She gripped the hem of her sweater and, as he watched, pulled it over her head and dropped it to the floor. She wasn't wearing a camisole today. She wasn't even wearing a bra. Her breasts were swollen with need though, her nipples standing out, hard and desperate for his touch.

She licked her lips and gripped the elastic band of her cotton pants.

"Not the panties," he growled. "Leave them on."

Her heart raced in her chest as she remembered the sight of him holding her panties to his face, inhaling the scent of her the night before.

Gripping just the waist of the pants, she eased them over her legs and stood before him in nothing but the thin silk-and-lace panties she wore now.

She shivered as the winds howled outside, and inside, the bedroom filled with steamy, erotic lust. His black eyes moved over her body as he sat down in the chair next to him slowly and lifted one booted foot to his knee.

He unlaced his boots slowly, watching her, simply staring at her, stroking her body with his gaze as she felt her breathing constrict in her chest.

No, no man had ever stared at her like Noble did.

His boots thumped to the floor.

"Do you ever touch yourself?" he asked her as he began unbuttoning his shirt, obviously forcing himself to do the chore slowly.

Haley flushed at the question. "Sometimes."

"Do you think of me?"

She licked her lips nervously. "Yes."

"You play with your nipples?"

Oh Lord, she was going to melt to the floor. Each time he spoke, his voice was thicker, rougher.

"I do," she whispered through a moan.

"Gently or rough?"

She was going to turn into one huge blush at this rate. But she answered him, her breathless, "Both," filling the room with another layer of tension.

"Show me." He shrugged the shirt from his shoulders, and she wanted to lick his spots rather than touch herself. "Let me see you touch your breasts, Haley."

She stared at his body as he slowly undressed, watching avidly as her hands lifted to her breasts. She cupped the mounds and imagined his hands. She fluttered her fingers on her nipples, rubbed against them, pinched them lightly as he loosened his belt and pulled the metal buttons of his jeans loose.

She saw his cock before he shed his pants. It eased from between the flaps of his jeans, the flesh dark, thick veins raised along the shaft as the mushroomed head throbbed fiercely.

She pinched her nipples and moaned. Between her thighs she felt her moisture gathering, saturating her flesh, dampening her panties.

She wanted that. Wanted him. She could feel the ache in her sex growing now, the heat and the need almost painful as he quickly shed his jeans and socks.

Another moan slipped past her lips as his fingers wrapped around the shaft, stroked it, once, twice.

"I want to do that." She couldn't hold back the breathless words. "I want to feel you in my hands."

The need rising inside her was unlike any other she had ever felt. She had never wanted anything as she wanted to feel Noble inside her now.

"On the mattress." He nodded to the bed. "I'm not going to take you standing up, Haley. And if I touch you before you get in that bed, then that's exactly what's going to happen."

"I want to touch you." She moved to the bed, staring at him as she eased onto the mattress. "Just for a minute, Noble. I need to touch you."

She had to be kidding. Noble stared back at her, feeling the wash of white-hot arousal tearing through his system, and prayed to God she wasn't a virgin. He couldn't handle it. Right now, he wasn't a fitting lover for a virgin.

"Have you had a lover?" he asked moving closer to the bed.

She blinked back at him. "I'm not a virgin." She frowned then. "Does that matter?"

"Thank God," he muttered. "Move onto the bed. The middle of it."

"You're not just going to take me, are you?" she whispered though she did as he asked.

"Get real, Haley," he growled. "I've waited a year for this. Do you think I'm going to do anything but take hours loving that sweet, hot little body of yours?"

"First, I get to touch." She reached out to him, her hands touching his hard abs, feeling them tighten painfully against her palms. As he knelt beside her, she ran them to his thighs and stared at the thick, heavy length of his cock.

It only made sense that the dark flesh, fully engorged and ready for her, would be so damned sexy. He was sexy all over. He just couldn't help himself.

"Haley, the edge is close," he warned her. "Trust me, you want me to love you before I do this."

"Yeah, I do," she murmured absently, sitting up, her hands moving to touch him.

"Fuck. You're not listening to me." His voice was strangled. She couldn't breathe.

She looked up at him, opened her lips and licked over the thick cock head.

His response was almost violent. A primal growl tore from his throat as his hands went to her head, fingers threading through the strands of her hair, and he leaned his head back.

She parted her lips farther, sucked him inside, and moaned again. Because his taste could be addictive. He tasted like a mountain storm. And she loved mountain storms. Like the lightning rolling over the forest and the wind picking up through the trees. Earthy and clean, natural.

"Damn you." He breathed out the curse, his voice harsh as his hips jerked. He buried the head inside her mouth as she sucked him, tasted him, and loved every second of it.

She licked and consumed, sucked and moaned around his flesh and never knew a pleasure so great. As she sucked, she felt, tasted, the drops of pre-cum that beaded on the head. She consumed them eagerly. If it felt as though each taste warmed against her tongue, then she ignored it. If after a few minutes she could feel the need inside her raging hotter, then she went with it. Whatever his touch brought her, she would accept.

"Touch yourself," he snarled above her.

Haley lifted her lashes and stared up at him. He was watching her, his gaze fierce, demanding.

"Let me watch," he groaned roughly. "Give me something to hold on to, Haley, or I'm going to lose control here."

Her hand lifted to her breast.

"No," the word snapped from between his teeth. "Not your

breasts. Your pussy. Spread your legs. Let me watch you touch yourself."

She had never done that. Never allowed a lover to see her touch herself.

"Lean back."

She moaned around his cock. She didn't want to stop tasting him.

"Lean back, Haley. So I can watch you. I promise, I won't take away your pleasure."

The skin was stretched tight over his face, and as she leaned back, she realized the pillows of the bed cushioned her shoulders and head perfectly. She was elevated enough that she could still pleasure him, still touch him, and he could watch her touch herself.

The eroticism of the act was nearly too much for her. Her fingers moved over the fabric of her panties as she touched herself through the silk and lace. She stared up at him, caught by his expression, held suspended by the hard jerk of his hips as he buried the head of his cock in her mouth.

"Yeah. Stroke yourself," he snarled, lust tightening his expression further as she stroked her fingers over her panties. "I can smell how hot that makes you. You're wet, Haley. So wet and so sweet I can almost taste you on the air."

He held her head with one hand, moving against her, his eyes trained on her fingers.

She gripped the elastic that circled her thigh, pulled it to the side, and touched her flesh. The tips of her fingers eased over the narrow slit as she pulled her panties farther to the side to allow for the careful circular strokes around her clit.

It was too much. Noble nearly roared with the surge of lust that shot into his system. He pulled back from her, forcing her mouth from his cock, his other hand pulling her fingers from between her thighs and pushing those glistening tips to his lips.

And he tasted. Soft, sweet cream. Haley's cream.

He tore the pillows from beneath her head and lowered his head to her as he pushed her arms over her head. His lips covered hers, his tongue sinking into her mouth.

He heard her soft cry in a distant part of his brain. The cry of a woman who knows she has no more room to run. The cry of a woman immersing herself in the hunger feeding into her system.

Her lips closed over his tongue, as though instinct guided her. Her tongue stroked against his, rubbed against it, and then, the soft, sweet suction as the taste of the hormone began to fill her senses.

His cum nearly pumped from his body as she began to suck his tongue. He felt his balls clench, spasm, and wrapped his fingers tight around the base of his cock to hold it back.

Not yet. He wasn't coming yet. Not until he could spill inside her. Not until he could feel the barb locking him to his mate, marking her, making her his. Just his. No matter what happened after tonight, she would always be his.

Haley paused as the taste of his kiss hit her tongue. A wild, lust-filled taste, dark and potent, spicy and filled with heat. And tempting. Tempting her to sate the sudden need for more that whipped through her senses.

She drew on his tongue, feeling his lips slant over hers, the hard, drawn contours of his larger body moving over her. Had he just ripped her panties off her?

He had, and she moaned at the sheer eroticism of the knowledge.

He held her hands over her head as he kissed her, refusing to allow her to touch him. But that was okay, the taste of him was making her insane. She couldn't think past the need for more of his kiss.

To say the hormone pumping into her system now was potent was an understatement. She could feel it sinking into her, digging talons of need inside her and stoking the flames of arousal past an incendiary point.

"Ah, Haley." When he finally drew back, she was writhing beneath him, her legs clamped around the hard knee pressing between her legs as she moved against it. "I can feel you burning for me now."

"I've always burned for you," she whimpered. "For too long, Noble."

And that had been the deciding factor in her decision. Noble had fascinated, drawn her, and held her attention, solely, for a year now. Each day, each time he spoke to her, each time she saw him, the fascination had only grown. She couldn't walk away, not when so much of her had already become invested in this one man.

Was it love? At this point, she suspected she had been wrong the night she told him she didn't love him. What she felt for him went so far beyond what she knew love to be that she just hadn't recognized it.

And the night she thought she had lost him? Had anything ever been more agonizing in her life? She knew it hadn't been.

But nothing could have prepared her for the hard pulse that shook her moments later. Her eyes widened, her gaze locking with Noble's as he pushed her thighs apart with his leg and moved between them.

She licked her lips slowly, a hard groan shaking her as the next pulse of need shuddered through her body. She could feel her juices spilling between her thighs. Felt her nipples aching and throbbing, her clit swelling tighter, harder.

"Oh. This is different," she moaned, arching against him as the broad contours of his chest lowered and stroked across her nipples.

"It's different?" His voice was strained, his expression tense as she stared up at him. "How's it different?"

His hips settled between hers, the thick length of his erection pressing into her sex, rubbing against her clit. His cock was hard and hot, like living iron throbbing against her.

"It's like . . ." she gasped, arched again as sensation speared through her womb. "Like pleasure and hunger all mixed up." She could feel perspiration beading on her body. "It's like being . . . like becoming, a living flame."

She arched again, gasped, and felt the sensual contractions in her vagina tightening and building into her womb as Noble gave a low, ragged groan and lowered his lips to her neck.

She shuddered at the sensation of his rough kiss there. The light nip of his teeth, she had so wondered what that would feel like. His tongue stroked over the arch of her neck, her collarbone, then his body shifted against her, moving lower as his lips caressed over the rise of a breast.

"I've been dying to suck your nipples," he groaned, his hair falling over his face to caress her skin along with his lips.

Silken, feather-soft, his hair brushed against her skin, adding to the harsh strike of pure pleasure that raced there when his mouth covered the hard tip of her breast.

He sucked her into his mouth. His tongue rasped against the ultrasensitive tip, and Haley felt herself sinking beneath a tidal wave of pure sensation. Pleasure was a haze of exquisite agony and ecstasy.

It raced over her flesh, filled her with heat and, long before his lips began to spread a path of burning kisses down her stomach, she was begging him for more.

"God how I've wanted to taste you." His voice was a growling purr, dark and rough, as he pushed her thighs wider apart, and his kisses moved closer to the burning, tight center of her body. "I've wanted my tongue inside you, Haley. Licking all your sweet cream. Loving you and tasting you."

He rubbed his cheek against her curls and she nearly orgasmed from the sensual, erotic expression on his face.

He had released her hands, but she kept them above her head and stretched against him. She couldn't touch him yet. She didn't dare. If she touched him, she was going to beg. She was going to sink completely beneath the waves.

But her body and her need had minds of their own. Within seconds, her fingers were tangled in his hair, her thighs opened wide, hips arching, and she was pressing his lips into her.

"Oh yes!" Her fractured wail filled the room as he kissed her clit. Kissed it, as though he were kissing her lips. Soft, gentle, sucking little kisses that had her head thrashing against the bed and any thought of control or restraint dissolving beneath the pleasure.

They were wild together. She could feel it, their pleasure and their need blending and merging, creating something she couldn't have imagined as he began to devour her flesh.

He licked and stroked with his amazingly adept tongue. It flickered along the tender slit, circled the entrance to her body, then plunged inside her with destructive results.

She had burned before. But now, as his tongue licked and thrust inside her, she was blazing, consumed, arching, and crying out at the exquisite agony of pleasure. It tightened inside her, expanded, and before she could draw breath or prepare for it, the explosion of exquisite sensation tore through her.

Haley felt her shoulders jerk from the bed. Her eyes opened, widened, unseeing, her senses dazed as the most exquisite feelings tore through her. Sharp and vibrant, a race of liquid flames, white-hot destruction and dark, primal pleasure.

Noble snarled as he felt her release tearing through her. A year. He had waited a year. He couldn't wait any longer. He straightened between her spread thighs, stared into her dazed feature as he lifted her hips, bracing her rear on his thighs, and tucked the head of his cock into the tiny, spasming entrance to her pussy.

Fiery damp curls surrounded the engorged head as he watched, holding her hips still, determined to see this. To watch her body take him, open for him.

His teeth clenched as he pressed inside her. Sweat ran down his face, burned his eyes, and dampened both their bodies.

He had to hold on just a few more seconds. Just a little bit of control. He had to watch. Watch as he worked his cock into the furnace heat of her rippling pussy and felt his senses incinerate with the sensations.

She clenched around the throbbing head, so tight, so hot he wondered if he would survive taking her. Or if he could hold back his own release until he had felt hers once again.

Beneath the head of his cock he felt the ache of the barb pressing beneath the skin. It matched the ache in his balls as he pulled back, worked in farther, then in one involuntary thrust, the pleasure dimming every thought of control, he impaled himself within her to the hilt.

Her scream of pleasure rocked his soul. It was ragged, feminine, throttled. As though she could barely draw in the air to cry out.

Noble shook his head and fought. He tried logic and reasoning, he thought of fishing and cleaning his weapon, but the thoughts disintegrated even as he tried to concentrate on them.

He came over her, feeling her legs cross above his hips, and gave in to the need striking hard and heavy to the painful erection buried inside her.

Nothing mattered but this. He had to fuck her. He had to take her. Hard and deep. And he took her hard and deep. His arms slid beneath her shoulders, his lips covered hers, and his hips jacked against her, burying his cock inside her with rapid, delirious strokes as she sucked at his tongue and moaned into his kiss.

Her nails were raking his shoulders, biting in and creating an ecstatic burn. Like a cat, clawing at him, demanding more. And he gave her more. He gave her everything he had as he felt her exploding beneath him.

Burying inside her once, twice, he let his release pour from him. Pumping into her, his semen spurted hot and thick as the barb stretched from beneath the head of his cock, locked inside the fluttering muscles of her pussy, and spilled its own, tremulous release into her.

He was shuddering with the pleasure. Jerking against her as his head lifted from her kiss, his lips lowered to her shoulder, and before he could still the need, his teeth bit into her tender flesh.

He tasted blood and heard her scream. He couldn't pull back. His tongue raced over the little wound, licking and spilling the hormone into the marks, sucking at them as he felt another, shuddering orgasm tear through her.

He had marked her. He had promised himself he would hold back, that he wouldn't mar her creamy flesh, that he wouldn't leave that telltale animalistic wound on her. But even as he remembered that promise, his teeth remained in her flesh. The violence of his need rocked inside him, the primal possessiveness tearing through him until nothing mattered, nothing eased it, until he was taking her again.

Chapter 9

"What happened here?" It was dark, the faint light that spilled into the room was courtesy of the bathroom light Haley had left on earlier. Just enough to allow her to see the amazing spots on his body, and the scars.

The scars made her ache. Especially the one on his chest. It wasn't very old, the healing flesh still looked tender to the touch.

"Bullet." He yawned as though it were nothing. "We were on the Lawrence estate a few months ago, and I took a bullet covering one of our enforcers."

She remembered the news reports of that. Callan Lyons had been wounded as well, and Cassie Sinclair, one of the wolf breeds who was often in Sanctuary.

The emergence of the wolf breeds and their Colorado compound had aligned two powerful forces. Journalists were forever covering the compounds, the strikes against them, and the struggle for freedom in the two areas.

"What about here?" There was a long, jagged scar on his side.

"Knife." His tone was lazy, still unconcerned. "Council soldier almost managed to gut me there."

She flinched.

Noble opened one eye and stared down at her. "I'm more careful now than I used to be."

She stared back at him in disbelief. "Why don't I believe you? You wouldn't lie to me, would you, Noble?"

"Course not." His hand stroked down her back, his fingers playing against the rounded curves of her rear as his lips twitched playfully.

"Uh-huh." She rolled from him, aware of his gaze on her, the lazy sprawl of his naked body, and the erect length of his cock.

She glanced at the clock. It was nearly midnight.

"I'm hungry." She was starving. "There's a roast in the slow cooker, if I throw some cut-up potatoes and stuff in, we could have a meal within the hour."

"Let me check the house first."

He was out of the bed in a bound. Smooth dark flesh rippled with muscle as he moved to the surveillance equipment. He checked the screens, then grabbed his weapon, and moved from the bedroom naked to make his rounds through the house.

Haley pulled on the gown and robe that he had collected for her earlier, when she had meant to finish dinner. He had distracted her that time. When he returned, she was belting the robe and pushing her feet into warm house shoes.

"I'll shower." He entered the bedroom moments later.

She almost grinned at his decisive statement. She had showered earlier, then had allowed him to convince her to lie beside him a little while longer.

While he petted her. Just stroked and touched her. For the moment, the incredible biting need that had filled her had eased, leaving her warm and languorous, a glow of satiation filling her.

Another unfamiliar feeling she thought as she moved into the kitchen and checked the roast in the slow cooker. Opening the refrigerator she pulled out the potatoes and carrots she had cut earlier that day. Emptying the water from them, she rinsed them and placed them in the pot.

Half an hour, she decided as she turned the heat up on the food.

She moved into the living room and refueled the glowing embers of the fire, watching as the smaller logs caught, and the flames began to lick over them greedily.

She turned and stared at the brightly lit Christmas tree before moving and rearranging a few of the presents beneath it. The bottom of the tree was surrounded by gaily wrapped boxes. Hanging on the limbs were small, Christmas-patterned bags that held much smaller presents. A silver ring for her mother. A necklace for one of her sisters-in-law, a bracelet for another. There were earrings for several of the college students who helped out at the library and almost always joined Haley and her family for a few hours on Christmas Eve.

The house was always filled on Christmas Eve. Her parents, brothers, and their families would arrive a day or two before, and laughter and joy always filled the air as they dragged mattresses from the attic and made room for ten extra people in the small house.

A smile tipped her lips at the thought of Noble's reaction to that. If he was even here.

She straightened one of the bags and frowned at that thought. Breeds weren't known for their Christmas spirit; she wondered if Noble would at least be patient with the friends and family who piled into her house that holiday week.

"What are you thinking of so hard?" His arms came around her as he pulled her against his bare chest. He'd donned jeans, but he was barefoot and sexy and tough and hard.

"Christmas." Her fingers curled around his wrists. "I bought you a present, you know?"

She looked back at him in time to see his surprise.

"Why would you do that?" he asked her, as though he truly didn't know the reason why.

"Because it brings me joy and always reminds me what Christmas is all about."

"It's all about giving presents?" he asked, his eyes narrowing.

"No, it's not about giving presents. Giving presents reminds *me* of what the season is all about."

"And what's it all about for you?" he asked her, still staring at the tree, his eyes narrowed, his expression thoughtful.

"It's about life. About celebrating my beliefs and my family. About the connections we don't always consider through the rest of the year. And it's about love. Our love for those who fill our lives."

"So you buy presents?"

"Or make them." She grinned. "Or bake them or cook them. Or simply stopping by to wish them a happy holiday and showing you care. For me, it's the joy in the giving, Noble. In remembering all the joys that have been given to me throughout the year."

He was strangely quiet then. He stared at the tree, then back at her. His gaze flickered. "What did you get me?"

She almost laughed. For the slightest moment, just the briefest breath of time, she might have glimpsed an almost boyish eagerness in his face.

"It's a surprise," she whispered teasingly.

He glanced down at her. "It's about tormenting those who receive, isn't it, Haley?" He growled. "Do you have any idea how curious a cat can get?"

"If you peek, then all you'll get is coal in your stocking."

Noble's head swung around, a completely involuntary act to

stare at the mantel. And there was another stocking. One that hadn't been there the day before.

Something in his chest constricted as he turned back to her.

"Why did you do that?" he asked her then. "I've not bought you anything."

"You gave me yourself." She stared back as though there were a question in her statement.

Noble nodded slowly. "Every part of me." And every part of him reached out to her.

"Then I don't need anything else."

"But you gave me yourself as well," he stated confidently. He knew she belonged to him. The mating had been strong, already she carried the scent of him mixed with her own, just as he carried her scent within him. They were bonding, perhaps now, only physically, but she would bond with him emotionally he knew, if she hadn't already.

He saw things in her. In her eyes, in her expressions, in her touch. Perhaps his little librarian just hadn't wanted to admit to what she felt for him. But he knew she did indeed feel for him.

"And I love giving presents." Her smile was soft and filled with happiness. "That's part of the fun, Noble. Knowing there's a present and wondering what it is."

He stared back down at her, faintly confused by that.

"Breeds never celebrate Christmas."

"I celebrate Christmas every year," she whispered. "And on Christmas Eve, my entire family descends. My brothers and their families, my parents, and on holiday nights friends and neighbors are always dropping in. Every Christmas Eve we go caroling in the park, and we laugh and drink hot chocolate and freeze our butts off walking back."

"And you do this why?" He fought the feeling of confusion that swept through him.

She was quiet then. The Christmas lights flickered over her face, multihued and giving her expression an almost otherworldly hue.

"Because I love doing it," she finally said, sighing. "Because I feel close to my family, my friends, and to my beliefs."

He nodded slowly. "You feel closer to your God," he said.

And she smiled.

"Dinner should be ready." She pulled from him slowly, catching his hand and drawing him to the kitchen. "And we have all these cookies. After we eat, I have about ten million paper Christmas bags to start filling with chocolate chip cookies."

"And those are for?" But he followed her, because her smile was teasing, warm and filled with joy.

"For the breeds at Sanctuary. Cassie Sinclair told me once that they go nuts for chocolate chip cookies. So Callan Lyons was kind enough to give me a number for the bags I needed, and I've been filling them for weeks."

He paused, ignoring the tug on his hand. "That's over three hundred breeds at the moment, Haley."

"And just think, over three hundred smiles when they taste my delicious cookies. I make very good cookies."

She did indeed. She made cookies that melted in the mouth and made a breed think of chocolate ecstasy. But Noble wasn't certain if he wanted to share those cookies, and her smiles, with other breeds. But one thing was certain, he wasn't about to dim the pleasure the thought of it brought to her eyes.

As they shared the late dinner, she managed to convince him, and how she did it he wasn't certain, to make sure those on duty were fed as well.

One by one they came in, ate a plate of heaping roast, potatoes, and carrots, with fresh-baked bread. They were sent off with a handful of cookies.

Even that damned mongrel coyote that trotted at Mordecai's

heels was given a bowl of fragrant roast. And he stared at Haley with adoration as he stuck his snout in the bowl and lapped it up.

It was nearly four in the morning before she loaded the dishwasher, and Noble noticed her hands were shaking. He'd smelled the heat building in her, surprised it had taken so long. Normally, the second phase struck must faster, and burned hotter.

"Enough." He closed the dishwasher and took the dish towel she held from her hand.

A fine film of perspiration dotted her upper lip, and the light sprinkling of freckles glared out from across the bridge of her nose, her face was so pale.

"I think I might need you." She was almost panting, her nipples so hard they were pointed into the material of her robe and the sweet scent of her desire filling the air.

The need had lain dormant inside her for nearly four hours, only to strike in a matter of minutes. Which was unusual.

"Have you taken the pills I gave you?" He pushed her hair back from her face.

Haley shook her head. "The first one made me feel funny. I didn't like it."

"Funny how?"

She shook her head. "It gave me a headache. I don't like headaches."

"It shouldn't have given you a headache." He frowned.

"Can we discuss this later." Her arm curled around his bare shoulders, her lips pressed into his flesh. "I'm tired of waiting."

"Why did you wait?" He glared down at her. "You fed every breed in the city rather than taking care of yourself."

She stared up at him somberly. "I wanted to know what you felt for the past year. You held back, even after you moved in here. I needed to see how it hurt you."

Noble stared back at her in shock. "Haley, it isn't the same for the males, sweetheart," he groaned, clasping her face with his hands. "The physical symptoms aren't as severe. Baby, why didn't you say something?"

The endearments slipped out naturally. He barely realized he had spoken them, concern filled him, driving past his lust as he stared into her nearly blue eyes. The gray had almost disappeared, to be replaced by a grayish blue that fascinated him.

"Noble, kiss me before I have to kill you," she groaned. "If you'd just kiss me, I'd be okay."

"It's the kiss that makes it burn," he reminded her, clasping her face and holding her still.

"Then make it burn."

He took her lips with a groan. He licked over the sweet curves and picked her up in his arms. Stilling her heat was the greatest pleasure he could know. But this time, it wasn't the bed he wanted to use to still that fire.

Still kissing her, he stumbled his way to the living room. There, in front of the light of the fire, he laid her down on the large rug.

"What are you doing?" She stared up at him as he stripped his jeans, then knelt beside her and eased her robe from her shoulders.

"I want to take you in the firelight," he growled. "With your Christmas lights shimmering around you and the light of the fire warming you. I want to see you right here, watching me as I take you."

She touched his hair, her graceful fingers threading into it before caressing the nape of his neck.

Her arms arched gracefully moments later as he pulled the gown from her, then she lay there, naked, wanting him, her gaze languorous and filled with desire.

"I used to fantasize about you right here," she told him, her voice low, throbbing with the power of her need. "I imagined you taking me while the fire burned beside us."

He knelt between her thighs, his cock pounding a desperate beat of hunger as he let his hands cup her breasts, let his lips and tongue lick over them.

Her nails bit into his shoulders, and he felt the purr that suddenly dug through his chest.

He had never purred in his life. But as her sharp little nails raked over his shoulders, the sound exploded from him.

And Haley shuddered beneath him.

Noble's head jerked up, his eyes narrowed.

"Just a little one," she panted, describing the orgasm he knew had just exploded within her. Yes, just a little one, but spurred by the sound of his purr.

"You liked that?" He pressed her breasts together and lowered his head again, licking over her nipples as she arched to him.

"A little bit maybe," she breathed.

He drew one of the ripe little points of flesh into his mouth again, restrained the grumble, and watched her face.

She was drifting in her pleasure, dazed by it. Exaltation filled him at that look. This was his woman. She carried his mark, his scent, she hungered for him. Only for him.

He dropped a scattering of kisses down her stomach, moved to the swollen bud of her clit, and drew it into his mouth. He suckled her gently, sweetly. He licked it, pursed his lips around it, and purred again.

And he watched her unravel for him. The sweetest expression he had ever seen in his life filled her face. She stared back at him, her eyes dazed and filled with emotion. Her expression almost serene.

"My Christmas present is right here," he whispered. He kissed her thigh, lifted his hand, and touched her face.

She surprised him then. Her lips parted, and she drew his finger in, suckling at it, nipping as he watched her.

The pleasure streaked from the tip of his finger to the head of his cock. Something that simple, a caress that should have never shaken him as it did. Yet it did.

Rising to his knees he pulled his finger back, then stroked his thumb over her lips. He smiled as he moved between her thighs, came over her, and felt the folds of slick, sweet flesh enclosing the thick crest of his cock.

"Watch." He glanced down along their bodies, holding himself up, allowing her to see.

Haley watched as he took her. She hadn't been able to watch the first time, only feel. She wanted to watch this time. Watch as he parted the sensitive folds, his thick flesh pressing into her.

She saw him and felt him. Felt him stretching her, burning her. She watched as he worked inside her, stroking her, pleasure tearing through her with each inch she took.

She couldn't breathe, and she needed to breathe. She needed to focus, to watch the penetration, to feel him possessing her.

"I dreamed this," she moaned, her thighs opening wider, her hips arching to him. "Dreamed of you taking me like this, Noble."

"I dreamed too, Haley," he groaned, his hips surging slow and easy, impaling her inch by inch with fiery destruction.

Pleasure whipped and tore through her. It burned with a white-hot intensity, cramped her womb, spasmed through her sex, and had her crying out his name. Her hips lifted with his, burying him deeper inside her, feeling the pleasure and something deeper, something binding and all-consuming tightening between them.

"Hard," she whispered, staring, watching her juices gleam on his heavy erection as he pulled back, only to press deeper inside her once again.

In his arms, that wild uninhibited woman she always dreamed of being fought to be free.

"Fuck me." The words passed her lips, words she had longed to whisper to a lover and had never had the courage. "Hard, Noble. Fuck me hard. Fast."

He surged inside her as she cried out at the pleasure. One hand clamped on her hip as she watched his cock draw back, penetrate, over and over, hard and deep, creating a friction, a pleasure she couldn't fight.

"Oh God yes." She writhed beneath him, pulling him to her, her lips at his neck, her nails on his shoulders as she scratched him in her need.

She tried to hold back, not to rake her fingers across his back. God knew, he had enough scars. But he marked her. He bit her. She could scratch. She could cry out his name, and when the rolling, rocking waves of pleasure began to cascade inside her, she could give herself to it, knowing he was there. Holding her, stilling the fear as she felt the extension becoming erect, the barb of the male breed pressing into her, locking her in place and spilling a fiery sensation inside her that flung her into another strong, deeper orgasm as his semen pumped into her, and his teeth pierced her shoulder.

And he held her. He held her close to his heart, his arms tight beneath her as he shuddered above her, growls rumbling in his throat as she felt something in her chest break free. As though her heart had expanded, as though heat burned from her very spirit, and Haley knew, in that moment, she had loved Noble Chavin far longer than she had ever realized she had.

The first time she saw his black eyes gleam with almost confused amusement. The way she felt when he watched her, the way she watched for him each night. The way her heart had shattered when she feared he had been lost to her.

"I love you," she whispered, and felt the tears that burned in her eyes. "Oh God, Noble, please don't be lying to me about this 'belonging' to you stuff, because I love you."

He jerked against her again, causing her breath to catch as the barb caressed nerve endings rarely subjected to touch. Miniexplosions cascaded through her, little releases that rocked her to the core. There should never be pleasure like this. Pleasure like this was addictive, it could become necessary.

"Mine," he growled at her ear then. "Always mine, Haley. My heart, my love, my soul."

And that was more than love, and why she hadn't known what had been staring her in the face for the past year.

"Mine," she whispered back.

More than love.

Chapter 10

"Aww, how sweet." The menacing drawl had Noble tensing as he pulled away from Haley, the air of danger, of death, filling the room as he turned his head and snarled.

Alaiya Jennings was propped against the doorway between the living room and kitchen. She wore her black breed mission uniform, which she had obviously not turned in when Jonas revoked her position as Enforcer. The utility-and-weapons belt was strapped to her hips and secured to her thigh. She was dressed to kill. And he knew, she intended to kill Haley. As well as him.

Noble felt Haley's nails pierce his side, felt the fear that began to flow through her, and the anger. She turned her head and stared at the breed watching them.

Smiling, Alaiya lifted a cookie and bit into it while she held the imposing, snub-barreled high-powered rifle she carried in one arm.

"The cookies are really good." She lifted her brows. "Such a shame. Not many people can make good homemade cookies anymore. And now we're going to lose another fine homemaker." She clicked her tongue and shook her head. "Pity."

"How did you manage to get into the house?" he snarled.

Noble eased up until he was sitting in front of Haley, watching the barrel of the powerful short rifle carefully. He knew the mark of that weapon, though it had only been seen rarely. When explosives didn't work, Uriel always found a way in, and the hole that gun made was not something men survived.

"Now, Noble, that would be revealing trade secrets. Assassins never do that."

"Uriel," he muttered, disgust filling his tone.

Alaiya smiled.

"Are my men still alive?"

"Alive. Sleeping, but alive. I'm not a total monster, you know. Jason wouldn't have died if he hadn't seen me." Her giggle was maniacal. The girlish sound scraped across Noble's nerve endings and lifted the hairs at the back of his neck. "Oh and your security system." She waved her hand negligently. "So trite Noble. Did you think any professional assassin would have missed the buried cameras? Really, darling. I thought you better than that."

He was better than that. The cameras inside the house were still working, and the moment another heat signature had been detected, the information would have been sent to Sanctuary.

The cavalry would be coming, but it could be too late if he wasn't careful.

"You're not saying anything." Alaiya frowned as Noble felt Haley's forehead press against his shoulder. "You should be congratulating me on how I managed to outsmart you."

"Yeah, congrats," he muttered, and she giggled again.

Noble could feel Haley behind him, shuddering. Fear was whipping through her, but not panic. She wasn't breaking down on him, she was sitting strong, staying behind him, not distracting him. And son of a bitch, he felt a gun press against his back. Where the hell had she come up with a weapon?

"What do you want me to say, Alaiya?" he asked her, keeping his hands in sight as he watched her. "We knew it was a breed, we just weren't certain who."

"Poor Jonas." She sighed. "He's been racing around Sanctuary, trying so hard to figure out who it is. I even helped him a time or two." Amusement gleamed in her brown eyes. "That was so funny. I, of course, played the distraught mateless mate. Very irritated, very saddened that I had lost Mercury to that bitch Rio. He never guessed, of course, that he was being played."

"He'll figure it out," Noble asserted. "Did you figure out who your mate is?"

Supposedly, she had believed another breed, Mercury, was her mate weeks before.

She stared back at him blandly then. "I've always known who my mate was. The act was merely that, an act to throw Jonas and his enforcers off-balance. To allay suspicion, it was much easier to walk into Sanctuary demanding a mate."

He felt Haley whisper *I love you* against his back.

He felt his heart pick up, race in his chest as she began to tense.

"Come on now, Noble, let's finish this quickly." Alaiya straightened from the doorway, finished her cookie, then gripped the rifle with both hands. "I do want you to know this wasn't easy for me. If the little bitch had just taken her pills as she was supposed to, then she would have been dead by now."

The pills. Noble tightened. "You messed with the hormonal supplement?"

"Of course I had it messed with." She smiled. "Ely Morrey made quite a few toxic batches for us while under the influence of those drugs, you know. It was easy to exchange them for the ones Amburg made up for your mate." She grimaced. "The breed butcher is determined to become the breed savior. I believe he just might find a way to help all that nasty mating stuff." Her lips tightened at the thought of it.

"Don't like being a mate, Alaiya? How sad."

She grimaced. "Such a nasty exercise, that mating shit. And disposing of the pregnancy is a pain in the ass. Those hybrid bastards don't want to die, and I'll be damned if I'll carry one of them."

The evil that poured from her sickened him.

"You're going to die with her, you know," Alaiya stated then, the barrel of the gun lining up with them. "And killing you will be a treasured memory, Noble. No other breed has kept up with me nearly so well."

He stared at the gun, careful not to tense before he moved.

When he moved, the rifle exploded. The blast tore into the fireplace as he threw Haley to the side, jerking the gun from her grip and firing.

There was no time to aim. He hit Alaiya's arm as she cocked the rifle to reload, throwing her back, causing her to lose her grip on it.

"You bastard!" she screamed, launching herself at him.

Noble fired again, and again. He could hear the coyote howling outside as Alaiya dropped to the floor, her gaze filled with shock.

"It's not over," she wheezed.

"For you it is," he stated, watching the life disappear from her eyes a second before an enraged snarl rent the air.

The attic. How the hell had they gotten in through the attic.

The ladder dropped nearly on his head as a shadow dropped from the opening into the living room. Noble was thrown to the side, ending in a crouch, his leg swinging out in front of him, lashing at his assailant's feet.

He wasn't dealing with a breed this time. But he knew who he was dealing with. Alaiya's mate. A human male and, from his moves, obviously a former council trainer.

Noble came to his feet, his eyes narrowing as he found Haley crawling into the kitchen. Somehow, she had managed to jerk her gown on and was finding safety. Good. If she could just get out of the house. Just get to safety.

Hazel eyes narrowed on him as the man crouched beside the body of his dead mate. He screamed again, rage and anger, insanity burning inside him as a knife cleared the sheath at his thigh and he jumped for Noble again.

The fiery slash against his thigh had Noble cursing, but not pausing. His fist cracked into the trainer's shoulder, his arm blocking the knife as he pulled back quickly.

He jerked Haley's robe from the floor, twisted it, and used it to deflect the blade as he fought for an opening in the man's defenses.

Alaiya's trainer had been one of the best the council had, he remembered that. Mark English was a former black ops agent before the Council recruited him. He was well trained and had a taste for blood.

"You killed her." Mark jumped back, glaring at Noble.

"She would have killed my mate," Noble snarled back at him. "Get a grip, English. You'll die tonight, too."

English rushed him. At the last second, Noble knocked the knife from his grip, twisted his arm, and threw him into the wall.

A hard kick to his stomach had Noble flying back, then the sound of an explosion had him freezing.

He saw the shock on the other man's face, the hole in his chest, blood splattering the walls around him as he slowly sank to the floor.

Noble swung around, expecting to see Mordecai, perhaps even Shiloh.

Instead, he saw his mate. Her gray eyes were wide, her face white. She held the short rifle in her hands and stared at the body of the trainer she had killed without pity, then turned back to Noble.

Noble looked back at English, then back to his mate. Son of a bitch. She was holding that gun like a pro.

"My daddy is a former soldier," she reminded him.

Noble nodded. Hell, he had to be in shock. "He taught me to shoot first, worry about the fallout later. If you're falling out, then at least you're alive."

She was shaking.

Noble moved to her and took the gun. "I could have taken him."

She frowned and looked at the gashes on his waist, thigh, his arms. "Yeah, no doubt." She breathed out roughly. "But he was making you bleed. I didn't like that. He was going to cut something important." She stared down in disbelief. "God, Noble, you really need to get some jeans on. I don't want all those female breeds that I know will be here soon seeing you like that."

He looked down, his lips twisting in amusement. He was still more than semiaroused. Mating heat could be a wicked bitch.

He moved back to the couch and grabbed his jeans before jerking them on. Just in time to hear the kitchen door crash in and all those breeds she was talking about pouring into the house.

He jerked her robe up. Some of his blood was on it, and wrapped her in it as she leaned against him.

Jonas didn't bother asking questions. He stared at Alaiya, then at English, and Noble saw the heaviness in his expression.

"I should have known it was her," he finally said, sighing. "She managed to slip away from me. Stayed just out of range. But I should have known."

And Noble knew he should have suspected. They had all known she was lying about having mated a breed the month before when she arrived at Sanctuary. They had known she had influenced several of the tests that indicated she had mated a breed.

"She was good." Noble exhaled as he held Haley closer, his nerves still taut, still amazed by the sheer courage his mate possessed.

"Yes . . ."

"Don't you tell me I can't come in here!" A booming voice filled the house as Haley jerked in Noble's arms. "Son, you want to get out of my way before we jerk your head off your shoulders and rip your guts out your throat."

"Oh God. It's Daddy."

Noble stared down at her, then into the kitchen. Flaming-haired, gray eyes dark in anger, and followed by two more just like him, it appeared the McQuires had finally made it back to Buffalo Gap. All six-foot-five or better, powerful, red-haired, with blazing eyes and furious expressions. The three warriors stood glaring at him as his arms tightened around her.

Haley turned in his arms and faced her father as he shoved his way past the breeds filling the kitchen. He stopped in the doorway, stared at the carnage, then at his daughter.

His expression twisted in pain before it smoothed out.

"Are we going to have fallout?" he asked Haley, as she turned to him.

Noble stared down at her, expecting her to leave him, to rush to her father, the man who stared at her now with such paternal love that for a moment, Noble wondered how the other man bore the cost of having ever let his daughter out of his sight.

Haley sighed. "Noble will catch me, Daddy," she said then, shocking Noble, as well as her father and brothers. "Don't worry. Noble will catch me."

Epilogue

Christmas with Haley was . . . different. For a breed who had never experienced Christmas, it was frankly terrifying. A terrified breed.

He did fine through all the visits, Christmas presents, cookie giving, and more food than he had seen in his entire life.

They went that morning to Sanctuary and delivered cookies. Other breeds smirked as he helped her hand them out. That didn't bother him. Breeds were always smirking. Until they mated.

They exchanged presents with Callan and Merinus, and Haley even gave Jonas a present. After all, she said, Jonas had ensured that plans to rebuild the library were moving quickly.

They visited the elderly, they visited a children's hospital. Not just he and Haley. He could have handled that. No, it was the whole damned McQuire clan, with her father glaring at him and her brothers dropping hints about wedding ceremonies and dates.

Even that damned sheriff got a present, and gave his own version of a warning.

As he had told all three McQuire males: date, time and location were her decision. She was his. No ceremony could make or break that claim. And then the older brother had arched his brow and asked about the engagement ring. Little things, the brother sneered, like asking a woman to marry him.

Hell, he'd heard of it. He just hadn't thought of it. And slipping away from her long enough to find a jewelry store had been hell. Mating a nonbreed was complicated, he decided. It had its perks. Of course, the perk part was being severely limited by family. Thank God the new hormonal treatments he had gotten for Haley were making it bearable for her. Bearable for him was another story.

But when she asked him—she didn't demand, she asked—that he attend church with her, he nearly backed out.

"I celebrate Christmas because of my beliefs," he remembered her saying. "I give gifts in remembrance."

This was her life. This was what made Haley Haley, and he wanted to know all of her. So he went. A breed, his hands stained by blood, his soul in question, and he stepped into a church and found a beauty he hadn't expected.

The entire McQuire clan celebrated. Christmas Eve and Christmas Day. They ate and laughed, visited and shed tears, and Haley's tiny mother bustled around everyone with a smile and drinks.

And on Christmas Day, they left. They were all glaring at him. The warnings were coming more often. Hell, he'd faced scarier sights than three red-haired Scottish soldiers in his life. They didn't scare him. Yet.

And finally, midnight came.

The tree was devoid of presents now, but it still twinkled merrily. The fire in the fireplace glowed cheerily, and Noble thought he might have had one too many shots of that homemade moonshine the McQuires had acquired.

There was a definite glow burning in him. And when he looked at Haley, curled on the couch watching him, that glow only heated.

And in her lap she held a small, gaily wrapped present. His present he knew.

In his hand, he held hers.

He swallowed tightly as he moved across the room, knelt in front of her, and handed her the little bag the jeweler had put the ring box in.

"You bought me a present?" Joy lit her eyes as she took the bag.

Noble swore he could feel nerves rising inside him, but breeds were taught never to be nervous. It couldn't be nerves.

"Open mine first." Her eyes were bright with excitement. "I want you to see it. I've been dying of anticipation."

He took her present. He'd watched her unwrap presents all day. She did it slowly, she savored it.

He unwrapped his present slowly and savored her excitement.

The long jeweler's box surprised him. When he lifted the lid, he had to blink back a surprising hint of moisture.

There were few things religious that he knew or understood. But this one, he knew. His trainer had, surprisingly, been a religious man. He'd told them once about St. Michael. That if they were honorable warriors, if they were good soldiers, then the saint would look upon them benevolently. No matter their lack of soul, he seemed to think.

Inside the box was a silver chain and medallion. St. Michael, the patron saint of warriors. To wear his medallion was to call upon his benevolence.

He licked his lips nervously as she lifted the chain from its bed of velvet and released the catch. He leaned into her and let her secure it around his neck before lifting it, turning it.

ALL MINE. LOVE, HALEY. His heart nearly burst at the words, his throat thickening as he stared back at her.

"Open yours," he whispered.

She opened the bag and froze. Her eyes lifted to his, and he saw the hope that filled them.

She drew the little box out, her hands shaking, and opened it slowly.

A single tear fell from her eye.

"Will you marry me, Haley?"

She covered her lips with her fingers as he drew the diamond solitaire from its place, lifted her left hand, and pushed it onto her finger. The fit was perfect. The diamond glowed with a rich cascade of color, just like her tree.

"Are you sure?" she finally whispered. "You want to marry me?"

"Haley, you're mine," he told her softly. "My heart, my soul. Your laughter, your tears, your sorrow and joy. And your beliefs. I want every tie I can put around us, so everyone knows that you're always mine."

She kissed him. A hard, tearful kiss before she jumped from the couch and ran to her room.

Noble blinked in surprise. He stood up and followed her, stepping into her bedroom and following to the open bathroom door.

She was digging through a little cardboard box. Tears were dampening her face, worrying him, until she evidently found exactly what she was looking for.

She turned and held them out to him.

Wedding bands. One thick gold band. The other smaller.

"My grandparents'." She looked back at him uncertainly. "Can we wear them?"

He touched the rings and stared back at her before sighing. "Haley, you could put a collar on me, and I'd wear the damned thing with pride. These? Baby, these I'll wear with joy."

She laid the rings carefully back into place, closed the box, and turned back to him.

"I love you."

And nothing had ever sounded sweeter.

He touched her cheek, lowered his lips to hers, and let himself feel her kiss, the love, the acceptance, the joy she found in him. The joy he found in her.

Haley parted her lips beneath his, licked at his, pressed until he gave her what she needed. What she craved. The mating heat was just a low simmer inside her, but his kiss, his taste was something she would always crave. The wild, hot taste of him fed her senses. His touch as he pulled her dress from her body fed her lust. His need for her fed her love.

She pushed his shirt from his shoulders, tore at his belt, at the buttons of his jeans until she released the weight of his cock into her hand.

It throbbed, fierce and proud, as she stroked it. The engorged head pulsed at her touch, and his groan fed her need for him.

"The bed," she whispered.

"Not moving." He nipped at her lips. "I've waited too fucking long now."

He turned her, and Haley found herself staring into the mirror, watching his face as he moved behind her. He bent her over the cabinet, holding her hips as he bent his knees and tucked the head of his fierce erection between her thighs.

He'd only pushed his jeans to his thighs, she felt the scrape of the fabric against the backs of her legs. She stared into the mirror, saw the gleam of the medallion she had given him against one of the dark spots across his chest.

Then her gaze lifted to his, and she was caught, snared, trapped within the heated black depths of his eyes. There, emotion swirled. Love, tenderness, sometimes confusion, and through it all was possessiveness.

Her back arched as he moved inside her. Slow, easy strokes, stretching her internal muscles, burning them, raking across tender nerve endings with exquisite pleasure.

His hands slid from her hips to her breasts, stroking them, playing with her nipples as they watched each other, loved each other.

Haley curled her arms behind her, held on to his neck and tilted her head, baring her shoulder. She knew what he needed when he looked at her like that. When the pleasure was growing between them like a ravening hunger, tearing at their senses, at their control.

"Haley." He groaned her name, his head dipping, his tongue stroking over the small mark at her shoulder. His tongue laved it, his lips caressed it.

His strokes inside her became harder, deeper, the slap of flesh, the earth moans that filled the bathroom gaining in volume until Haley felt herself come alive in his arms.

This wasn't a little death, as the French called it. It was life. It exploded within her. It lit her senses with a rainbow hue of colors to rival the brightest Christmas tree and filled her with an ecstasy that she knew she could no longer live without.

It completed her.

And when the barb locked him to her, and his release spilled into her, it finished that completion in a round of fireworks that she knew even the Fourth of July couldn't compare to.

When she could see again, when she could think again, it was to watch his head lift from her shoulder, to see his face relaxed and infused with pleasure.

"Merry Christmas, Noble," she whispered, touching his cheek, their gazes meeting in the mirror once more.

"Merry Christmas, Haley," he whispered back. "And thank you."

"For what?"

"For being the most precious present a breed could ever receive."